So Pretty It Hurts

So Pretty
It Hurts

A Bailey Weggins Mystery

Kate White

HARPER LUXE

An Imprint of HarperCollinsPublishers

To John Q. Holbrook, fabulous father-in-law

HarperCollins books may be purchased for educational, business, or sales promotional use. For information please write: Special Markets Department, HarperCollins Publishers, 10 East 53rd Street, New York, NY 10022.

FIRST HARPERLUXE EDITION

HarperLuxe™ is a trademark of HarperCollins Publishers

Library of Congress Cataloging-in-Publication Data is available upon request.

ISBN: 978-0-06-210716-9

12 13 14 ID/RRD 10 9 8 7 6 5 4 3 2 1

1

An old geezer of a reporter I used to work with once said that I had a rotten habit of biting off my nose to spite my face. An ex-boyfriend told me the same thing. And you know what? It's *true*. There've been more than a few times when I've tossed back a gift or stormed off in a huff, and on one occasion I jumped out of a car in the rain and walked home alone, ruining the hottest shoes I ever owned. But I've rarely regretted it. The satisfaction I've felt from making the big defiant gesture—and seeing the stupefied expression on the other person's face—has generally been worth the price.

Soaked shoes are one thing, though, and a corpse is something else entirely. During a frigid week in early December, I bit off my nose to spite my face because of something the new guy in my life, Beau Regan, did. And I ended up in a big fat mess that involved all sorts of nasty things: a suspicious death, requests for kinky sex, my ass on the line at work, and a showdown with a killer who wanted to make sure I couldn't tell what I knew. In the end I decided I'd have to behave more rationally when my knickers were in a twist. But I'm getting ahead of myself.

The trouble started the week after Thanksgiving. Beau and I had been dating exclusively for about two and a half months, seeing each other a few times a week. Over dinner that Friday night Beau announced—out of the blue—that he needed to leave the next day for Sedona, Arizona, and would spend the next eight or so days there, shooting extra footage for his new documentary film. Apparently some people who hadn't been available before were suddenly available now, or something or other.

But Beau's announcement had bugged me. It turned out that he'd known for over a week that he needed to go but had only shared the news at the last possible moment. Why? I'd wondered. To me Beau had always seemed slightly mysterious and elusive, and just when I'd convinced myself that this was simply a perception created by those dark Heathcliffian eyes and longish brown hair, he was telling me that he had to head off on some vague-sounding trip, suggesting it wasn't perception after all.

I didn't come right out and say I was annoyed, but he could tell, I'm sure, by my attitude. Of course, that wasn't the only reason I was testy as December rolled around. I'm a true crime writer, and in addition to my part-time gig covering celebrity crime for the Manhattan-based tabloid magazine *Buzz*, I'd been trying to hawk my recent book, a collection of articles I'd written called *Bad Men and Wicked Women*. The small publisher had put practically zilch into promotion and marketing, and my book was currently something like number 29,478 on Amazon—when I had the nerve to look. Failure always turns me into a grump.

Beau called me as soon as he arrived in Sedona, and then called or texted every day after that. Things were friendly but a little clunky. The week without him seemed to drag by, and I realized how much I had come to love his company—both in bed and out. Please, I thought. Don't tell me I've fallen for someone who doesn't want to jump in with both feet just at a point when *I* do.

On the Thursday morning before the Sunday Beau was due back, he sent me an unexpected text: "may finish early and b bk sat. will let u know."

The message should have warmed the cockles of my heart—and trust me, the thought of falling onto a mattress with him one night sooner than planned made my cheeks flush. And yet as I hurried toward the subway stop at Astor Place on my way to *Buzz*, I could feel my overall annoyance starting to swell. It was the last line that really bugged me. *will let u know.* So I should just hold open my Saturday night in case he made it back to town? Maybe I was wrong, but to me that sounded like a guy who didn't like to be pinned down himself, yet wanted to be sure *I* was.

I was still in a pissy mood when I arrived at *Buzz*. The place that morning seemed surprisingly quiet. Though the final closing day at *Buzz* is Monday, the phones tend to ring like mad on Thursday. That's the day the issue hits the newsstands, and Hollywood publicists love to call and scream in defense of any clients they feel we've maligned. Phones weren't ringing, and that wasn't a good sound. At *Buzz*, if you're not pissing off Hollywood publicists, you're not doing your job.

"Oh God, Bailey, are those the new Prada riding boots?" Leo asked me as I pulled out my desk chair in the large open bullpen area. Leo's a photo editor, but there isn't enough room for him in the overstuffed art department, so he was bumped to a workstation right behind me and my office bff, Jessie Pendergrass, a senior staff writer. Leo spends most of his day scanning through paparazzi photos on his computer for shots of celebs looking blubbery, blotto, badly dressed, or like they've suddenly got a bun in the oven.

"Yeah, in my dreams," I said.

"I thought maybe you got a big royalty check and splurged," Leo said, rubbing his hand over his shaved head.

"No check yet, but I'm sure one is due any day now," I replied. "Apparently I just got torpedoed by *Decorative Napkin Folding for Beginners* on Amazon."

"You seem grouchy," Jessie said. She'd just set down the phone and was scrutinizing me closely with her amber-colored eyes.

"Sorry—I'm just a little frazzled. Does anyone want coffee?"

They both declined, and I headed back to the kitchenette, where I filled up my mug. There were five or six people congregated there, arguing about the ending of a new movie; most I didn't even recognize. Not only was the staff at *Buzz* huge, but because of the pressure and late hours, it turned over faster than you could say "Jen's Latest Heartache."

When I arrived back at my desk, Jessie wheeled her chair over to me.

"Bailey, I've got a brilliant idea," she said, her eyes sparkling. "I know Beau is out of town till Sunday so I bet you don't have anything planned for the weekend.

How would you like to spend a weekend with me at a gorgeous house in the country?"

"You've definitely got my attention," I said, not bothering to point out that Beau might be coming back Saturday.

"Remember that record producer I told you I met a few weeks ago—Scott Cohen? He called yesterday and asked if I wanted to come to his weekend place—along with a friend if I wanted."

"Is it in the Hamptons?"

"No, it's north of the city someplace. We can hike if we want or just sit by the fire and drink hot toddies. There'll even be a masseuse on hand."

"Wow, that sounds so much better than treating all my boots with water repellent," I said. "But if this guy is after you, why would he want me tagging along?"

"He's invited a whole group of people—you know, a house party. It'll actually be less awkward for me if you come. Besides," she added, grinning, "we can take your Jeep."

"You sure about this?"

"Yeah, it'll be fun. Please say yes."

"God, I'd love to," I said. I meant it. It did sound fun. But as I smiled back at Jessie, I could sense the bite being taken out of my nose. I'd had the chance to possibly see Beau Saturday night and had chosen not to, partly to prove that I didn't have to just sit around waiting—and that I could have mysterious plans of my own.

I worked late that night, mostly chasing down quotes for two different items I was working on. *Buzz* is packed each week with stories on the hapless love lives, fashion faux pas, and generally futile weight battles of the stars, but when these same stars get into any kind of legal trouble, we cover that too, and that's where I come in. I report on any crimes they commit or are involved in on the East Coast, and I also consult on coverage we do in L.A. Many of the reporters on staff could certainly do as good a job, but I was hired because the editor in chief at the time believed having an experienced crime writer bylining those pieces would add cachet. I wasn't sure what good it had done in that department, but my new boss, Nash Nolan, seemed happy enough.

I finally headed home just after eight, shivering most of the way. It had been unseasonably warm the last two weeks of November, but winter had finally reared its head, and temperatures had plunged to the thirties.

My apartment—a nifty one-bedroom with a terrace on Ninth and Broadway that I'd kept after my divorce—was toasty warm at least, and after stripping off my work clothes, I made a gooey cheese omelet and began to pack for the weekend. The phrase "weekend house party" conjured up an image of people in tweeds and plaids, but based on the fact that Scott was in the music business, I decided I'd better opt for tarty over tartan. I'm five-six, fairly slender, and attractive in a kind of sporty way, so tarty is a stretch for me, but I like to give it my best shot when the moment calls for it.

The phone rang just as I was tossing the last stuff into my overnight bag. It was Beau, calling from Sedona.

"Good to hear your voice," he said.

"Ditto," I said. Bailey, keep it light and breezy, I told myself. "How's the weather? It's suddenly freezing here."

"It's been nice during the days—mostly in the seventies—but it gets pretty cool after dark."

"Any UFO sightings?" I asked, referencing the fact that over the years, more than a few people had claimed to see alien spaceships buzzing around the heavens above Sedona.

He laughed. "Not so far. But every time I look up at night, I half expect to see flashing lights."

Why are you out under a night sky anyway? I wondered, staring out at the skyline of Greenwich Village. Light, Bailey, I told myself. Keep it light.

"I guess I should be on the lookout if you start creating any weird sculptures when you get back," I told him.

"Speaking of that, did you get my text? I'm not positive yet, but I'm pretty sure I can hop on a flight early Saturday."

"Uh, I was actually just going to text you back," I said. "Don't rush back just on my account. I'm going away this weekend."

There was a pause, not interminable but long enough for me to know I'd caught him off guard.

"Where you headed?"

"Jessie asked me to tag along to some house party she was invited to—upstate. This guy who apparently has the hots for her owns a place up there. He told her she could invite a friend if she wanted, and she knew I was just hanging out this weekend. Plus it will be less awkward for her."

I was *sooo* over explaining myself. I could have retiled my bathroom in less time.

"So what's a house party anyway? I thought that's what real estate agents gave to court prospective buyers."

"Um, I think that's an *open* house," I said. "I guess this guy is just having a bunch of friends up—for hiking, that sort of thing."

Again there was a pause, this one longer.

"You still there?" I asked. What did you think, Bailey, I asked myself, that he'd been abducted by invaders from the planet Abdar?

"Yup."

"Is something the matter?"

"No. But I just can't help wondering if your weekend excursion is some kind of payback for my being away."

"*Payback*? That sounds pretty extreme."

"That would be my thought, too."

"Then what would possibly motivate me to do that?"

"You were ticked about my going to Arizona."

"I wasn't *ticked* about your going," I said, trying hard to keep my voice calm. "I was just surprised because it seemed to come out of nowhere. And honestly, there's no payback. This just seemed really fun."

Liar, I thought.

"Okay," he said. "Well, if you get back early enough, maybe we can get together Sunday night."

We muttered good-byes and hung up. I ignored the twinge of regret I was feeling over going away. It was clear that something needed to be addressed between Beau and me, but I didn't want to deal with it at the moment.

Jessie and I had vowed to leave the city before six the next night, but in the end it was closer to seven.

"So is this some big country estate we're headed to?" I asked after we'd finally made it through the frustrating snarl of Friday-night traffic just north of Manhattan.

"I'm not sure what the house is like, but it's gotta be pretty big—he told me we'd each have our own room."

"That's probably so he can sneak into yours at night."

"I really don't know what he's got in mind," Jessie said pensively. "We had this flirty lunch and then he asked me to dinner. But there were six other people out with us that night. I really *hope* he's interested—because I dig him—but a little part of me is worried that he asked me to come with a friend because he needed eye candy for other guests."

"Jeez, it's starting to sound like the Playboy mansion."

"No, Scott just likes having these old-fashioned kind of house parties."

"Who else is supposed to be there?"

"Well, you're not going to believe this. He told me late today that the main guest is Devon Barr."

"Devon Barr, the *model*?"

"Yup."

Devon Barr had been one of the most successful American models of the past two decades, and though at thirty-four or so, her career was starting to cool a little, she still was the face of several major fashion and cosmetic companies. Part of her mystique was due, some people said, to the fact that she never gave interviews.

"Wow, that should be interesting," I said. "Though the conversation may leave something to be desired. She looks like she has the IQ of a Louboutin shoe."

"I know, but she apparently has a killer voice and writes her own songs. Scott is producing her first album."

"*Really?*" I said. "That's fascinating. Anyone else of interest?"

"Scott says he usually likes to put together an eclectic mix, but Devon apparently insisted on bringing her own entourage. Her manager is coming, and one of her model friends. I'm just glad you could come. Beau didn't mind, did he?"

"He didn't sound overjoyed. But then . . . oh God, never mind."

"Tell me," she urged.

"I'm just feeling a little weird about his trip to Sedona."

"What do you mean? You don't think . . . ?"

"That he went down there to hook up with some retiree? No, I don't get any sense he's cheating. I just worry that he's not—I don't know, not ready to fully commit, I guess. I keep sensing that he talked himself into a relationship because he's attracted to me, and likes going to bed with me."

"Do *you* feel ready?"

"For a relationship, yeah. And maybe even more at some point. I'm not staring thirty-five in the face just yet so I'm okay being single. But I care more about Beau than anyone I've met up until now, and in the back of my head is the thought that if I *were* going to get married again, I'd like it to be him."

"This all sounds like David—remember him, the guy I told you about?" Jessie said ruefully. "He seemed to love me but then finally dumped me because he said he didn't want to make a long-term commitment to anyone. A year later he married someone else. You know how the porn industry has fluffers, women who keep the male stars hot before they perform? I felt like I'd been a *husband* fluffer with this guy."

I felt myself cringing as she spoke. Was that what I was for Beau—a husband fluffer?

We took the Taconic State Parkway north and after an hour and a half, exited onto rural roads. We stopped chatting while I focused on the GPS directions. Many of the scattered houses we passed had their doors and windows and even their roofs rimmed with Christmas lights. We found Scott's driveway and turned onto it. Suddenly we were engulfed in darkness.

"He told me the driveway's really more of a road," Jessie said, "a mile and a half long."

"Hold on," I said, as I hit the brakes. Five or six deer bounded across the road directly in front of the Jeep, their eyes unblinking in the headlights.

"Gosh, they scared the hell out of me," Jessie said. "Do you think there's a lot of other animals around here? Like wolves?"

"No," I said, laughing. "There aren't wolves in this area. Just jaguars and cougars."

"Very funny. Now you've really spooked me."

It *was* kind of spooky, and I was relieved when finally a few lights twinkled through the massive fir trees. And then a few seconds later there were more lights. The house looked huge, like a cruise ship steaming across a jet-black ocean.

"Wow," Jessie exclaimed. "Big."

"All of this could be yours," I said, "if you play your cards right."

As we drew closer, we saw that it wasn't a house at all, but rather a huge gray barn—or actually two large barns positioned parallel to each other. There was a scattering of small outbuildings just beyond.

"Not what I was expecting at all," said Jessie. "I hope we're not bunking down with a herd of cows."

As we stepped out of the Jeep into the crisp, clear night, a woman came up behind us, dressed in a dark barn jacket, khaki pants, and short gum-bottomed shoe boots, the kind you see in an L.L.Bean catalogue. She was fiftyish, with cropped blond-gray hair and a doughy face. She smiled at us, but there was no crinkling by the eyes. It was the kind of expression you offered when you were forced to make nice.

"Sorry we're so late," Jessie announced. "We got a late start from the city. I'm Jessie, by the way. And this is Bailey."

"Not a problem," the woman said, revealing a huge snaggletooth. "I'm Sandy, Mr. Cohen's housekeeper. Why don't I show you to your rooms first, and then you can join Scott. Have you eaten dinner?"

"Not unless you count a bag of tortilla chips," Jessie said.

"Well, there's plenty of pork ragout left over."

After we grabbed our duffel bags from the back of the Jeep, we followed Sandy in the direction of the smaller of the two barns, which she explained contained all the bedrooms—except Mr. Cohen's. Although we were only two hours north of the city, we might as well have been at an Adirondack logging camp. The place was ringed entirely by thick, dark woods. I glanced up. A bright white half-moon hung in the sky, surrounded by a zillion twinkling stars and the haunting film of the Milky Way.

The silence was suddenly cut by a howling from deep within the woods. Jessie nearly jumped into my arms.

"I thought you said there were no wolves around here," she whispered anxiously, grabbing my arm.

"That's not a wolf. It's a coyote. They're pretty common in these parts. But unless you're a chicken or a Pomeranian, you don't have any reason to worry."

"Yeah, I guess," she said, glancing all around us. "I grew up in Orange County, California, and I generally don't *do* woods. I didn't think it was going to be this creepy."

We were almost at the barn, lagging a bit behind Sandy. I could see now that the two structures were connected by a simple one-story passageway, made totally of glass. And suddenly a heavyset woman in jeans and bulky sweater came barreling down that passageway, her curly black hair bouncing with each stride and her face pinched in annoyance.

"Someone's in a hurry," Jessie whispered.

"Maybe she didn't like the ragout," I said.

Sandy had reached the door to the building and turned around, her expression slightly impatient, as if we were naughty schoolgirls who'd fallen out of line. We hurried and caught up with her. We entered a foyer with a large wooden bench and brightly colored kilim rug. The walls and floors were all made of old, pumpkin-colored barn wood. On the floor above I heard a door slam. I figured the noise came from the young woman we'd spotted barreling down the passageway.

"There are a few guest rooms down here, but you're both upstairs," Sandy said, nodding her head toward the stairs. "I think you'll find it nice and private."

What was *that* supposed to mean? I wondered. By the hushed way she said it, you would have thought we were here to negotiate something top-secret with Scott, like a Journey reunion album. Jessie flashed me a mock grimace.

Our rooms, side by side, were extremely spacious. Mine was filled with quirky old antiques, black-and-white-checked fabric and splashes of lemon yellow. Sandy explained that if we needed anything during our stay and she wasn't around, we should just dial extension seven on the landlines in our rooms. She added that when we were done freshening up, we should take the glass passageway to the main barn, where everyone was gathered.

I kicked off the shoes I'd been wearing in the car and tugged on a pair of gray suede boots over my jeans. I also swapped my top for a scoop-necked gray-blue sweater that matched my eyes. I'd been growing my blondish hair out for months, and it was long enough finally for me to put up on my head. I twisted it into a sloppy knot, adding a pair of dangling silver earrings. Tarty but not too tarty, I thought. Still, I felt a tiny twinge of guilt.

Jessie opened her door just as I was about to rap on it. She had changed too, into a tight, tight orange sweater that looked great with her eyes. After making our way along the glass passageway, we stepped into a warm, double-storied entrance space aglow in honey-colored light. There were old hayrack ladders and rusty farm tools mounted on the wall. Directly in front of us was a plank-wood staircase that rose to another level. Music, conversation, and the sound of clanging dishes all emanated from above.

Just as we headed over to mount the stairs, a man, dressed in black pants and a black V-neck sweater, came bounding down them. I knew it had to be Scott Cohen, and though there was a boyish quality to his face and he wore his dark hair longish, it was clear he was a good ten years older than Jessie—about forty, it looked.

"Hey, I'm so glad you finally made it," he exclaimed.

"Hi there," Jessie said, and accepted a kiss on the cheek. When she introduced me, Scott reached out and shook my hand, grasping it for an extra beat, like you'd expect from a politician or car salesman. His nearly coal black eyes held mine for an extra beat, too.

"You've got an amazing place," Jessie said. "What were these barns doing back in the woods?"

"I actually had them transported on flatbed trucks from Vermont."

"You didn't shoot that moose, did you?" Jessie asked, looking up toward a huge stuffed head hanging above the double front doors.

"Yeah, right," Scott said. "The only thing I've ever shot is a recording artist who didn't go platinum. Come up and meet everyone."

As we reached the top of the stairs, I got a better sense of the place. To the left of the landing was a great room—a combination kitchen, dining, and living area, with two couches, a bunch of chubby armchairs, a big round dining table, and another animal head mounted on the wall, this one an elk that had probably never set hoof east of the Rockies. Sandy was fussing with some things on the kitchen counter. Six other people were bunched directly behind her at a big wooden island, some standing, some sitting on barstools.

All conversation ceased as we stepped into the room. It felt as if we'd accidentally stumbled into a play mid-performance and caught the actors totally by surprise.

Scott dispelled the awkwardness by quickly introducing us to everyone present: Devon Barr's agent, Cap Darby, a square-jawed, superconfident Clive Owen type who appeared to be in his mid- to late forties; his blond wife, Whitney, who couldn't have been more than thirty and had a rock on her left hand the size of an iPod; Devon's booker, Christian Hayes, a slim African American with a shaved head and cropped, curly beard; a girl named Tory Hartwick with short, jet-black hair and striking hooded eyes, who clearly was Devon's model friend; and a tall, thin rocker type named Tommy Quinn, who had one of his bare, heavily tattooed arms draped over Tory. He must have been important, because I felt Jessie press her foot into mine when Scott introduced him.

And then there was Richard Parkin, whose name I recognized instantly. He was an award-winning journalist and author, hailing from the UK, who wrote profiles for magazines like *Vanity Fair* and *Track*, the music magazine that was part of the same media company as *Buzz*.

"So this is our house party," Scott said. "Devon isn't here at the moment. She went to her room after dinner, but she's coming back."

I caught Whitney shooting a look at her husband Cap, though I had no clue what it meant.

"And oh, Devon's assistant Jane is missing too," Scott added. "She slipped out to the deck to use the telescope."

Jane must have been the girl Jessie and I had spotted charging down the glass passageway like a bull through the streets of Pamplona. Based on the land speed at which she'd been moving and the ticked-off expression on her face, I doubted she was out there right now studying the moons of Jupiter.

"You didn't get lost, did you?" Christian asked us.

"I accidentally ended up in the town of Traugersville, population fourteen."

"I thought you didn't drive, Christian?" Whitney said, revealing a strong southern accent. With her long, flowing hair, translucent blue eyes, and curvy figure she was attractive enough, but it was a standard-issue look that made her indistinguishable from millions of other women with big blond hair and hard, fake tits.

"I don't—I used a car service," he explained. "The driver clearly hadn't been north of Westchester in his life, and he never took the car over fifty-nine miles an hour. I could have been in Montreal in less time."

"How about some wine?" Scott asked us, interrupting. We both accepted a glass of red.

"Scott has quite the cellar up here," Cap announced. "If you're a wine lover, you're in for a treat."

"You just have to keep putting your hand over your glass," Whitney said. "Or he'll top it off endlessly."

"Actually, I'm fine with you topping *mine* off," Richard said in his posh British accent. He reached out his empty glass. From the ruddiness of his face, it appeared he might have already enjoyed several. "It's absolutely splendid—saddlebags and a strong hint of black cherries, I'd say."

"I thought wine was always made from grapes," Tory said.

At first I thought she was kidding. But the look of befuddlement on her face said otherwise.

"You're not *serious*, are you?" Tommy asked her, feigning horror.

A door slammed downstairs at that moment, saving all of us from any explanation on Tory's part, and then we heard the sound of someone's long strides across the wooden planks.

"*There's* Devon," Cap said with a hint of relief. I wondered how he knew it was she and not Jane.

We all turned expectantly, listening to the *clop-clop* of her boots as she mounted the stairs.

She was wearing a black pea coat over her jeans, and her long, perfectly straight blond hair, parted in the middle, was fanned out around the collar. She was tall, though not quite as tall as Tory. But then she didn't need to be. Her *face* was her fortune, and it was as exquisite in person as in photos: big hazel eyes, shaped like almonds, a small, perfect nose, and a ripe mouth that was always slightly and sensuously parted, as if she were on the verge of telling someone softly that she'd like to fuck his brains out.

"Come meet our new arrivals," Scott suggested.

She glanced toward us without really taking us in. She looked bored, as if she had just arrived at a three-day conference on treasury bonds. In her right hand she was holding both a water bottle and a nearly flattened cigarette pack, and after setting down the bottle and stuffing the cigarettes into her pocket, she shrugged off her pea coat onto an armchair.

We all stared at her wide-eyed. On top of her skin-tight jeans she was wearing a filmy black top with a deep plunge. Each side had shifted, and her small but perfect breasts were totally exposed.

2

"You've had a slight wardrobe malfunction, darling," Christian announced.

Devon seemed to totally ignore him, but then, without a trace of self-consciousness, she slowly teased the fabric back over her breasts with long, slender fingers. I'd seen modeling shots of her almost totally nude before, and I wouldn't have expected her to feel awkward, but the languidness of her movement suggested something else: that it had all been intentional—for someone's benefit. Another thought shot through my brain. How thin she was. When Devon was first starting out, she was known for the heroin chic look, but she had filled out as she grew older, to something you could have described simply as "model thin." Her appearance tonight suggested a worrisome drop in pounds.

"There—better?" she asked blasély to no one in particular. And then, "I'd like some fresh water," before anyone could weigh in with an answer to the first question.

"Absolutely," Scott said, reaching inside the fridge for a bottle. "This is Jessie, by the way, and her friend Bailey."

"Hello," she said, without much enthusiasm, but she came forward and shook our hands. Her hand was slim and felt as fragile as a seashell. She held my gaze just a moment. For a split second I saw a flash of cunning in her eyes.

"Congratulations on your album," Jessie said. "It must be a very exciting time for you."

"Scott's the one who deserves the congratulations," she said. "He's the one who made it all happen."

"And Cap, of course," said Scott, a little forced. "He's the one who brought you to me to begin with."

"Have you been writing music long?" Jessie asked her.

"I wrote little songs, when I was young. Then I learned how to do it from watching Tommy."

She looked at him slyly, as if there was a secret between them.

"Scott tells us we're going to have a preview this weekend," Tommy said. "I can hardly wait."

Next to him, Tory formed her wide mouth into a pout, clearly not appreciating the way Tommy was taking in Devon—or maybe she was still pondering how you turned cherries into wine.

"Did you bump into Jane?" Cap asked Devon. "I sent her to look for you."

Devon shrugged as if she didn't remember and could care less where Jane had gone. "You know what I'm in the mood for?" she said. "Pool. Who wants to take me on?"

"I'd love a game, actually," Tommy said. "But you'll have to play fair and keep your clothes on."

The two of them walked across a large wooden plankway to the other side of the barn's upper level, where there was a billiard table and a small bar. Tory hesitated a moment and then followed after them, her strides as wide as an ostrich's. At the same time, Sandy announced that dinner for Jessie and me was ready. I glanced back at the island and discovered that she had set out two dinner plates heaped with the ragout and separate plates with a simple salad. There was also a basket overflowing with corn muffins.

"You don't mind eating here, do you?" Scott asked us. "We already spent two hours at the dining table, and I'm afraid if I sat down there again, I'd never get up."

"Not at all," Jessie said. "It looks wonderful."

"Whitney has given it her full blessing," Scott said.

"Do you like to cook?" Jessie asked.

"I've just finished a cookbook, actually," she said. "Texas food—but not the whole Tex-Mex or barbeque-and-chicken-fried-steak sort of thing. I'm focusing on the kind of *elegant* Texas food you're served in the best homes there."

"Oh, describe a few dishes to me, will you?" Christian demanded. "At First Models we're never allowed to talk about food during the day."

"Why not?" I asked, my fork poised.

"There are always models dropping by the agency, and they can't *bear* it if you mention food," he said, slowly sweeping his fingers back and forth along the collar of his shirt. "They're always hungry. They'd eat the blotter on the desk if you turned your back."

"I can't imagine how they resist indulging," Jessie said. "I'm too weak to say no to anything yummy."

"They use all these crazy ways to deal with it," Christian said. He glanced over toward the pool table, obviously making sure Devon was out of hearing range. "There's this girl we signed lately, and every day she buys one of those little bags of Wise potato chips, empties all the chips in the garbage, and then all day long she just sniffs the inside of the empty bag for a rush. You know how coke addicts have powder on their noses? She has potato-chip crumbs."

"Well, at least, as we learned tonight, some models appreciate good wine," Richard added sarcastically.

"But models weren't always as thin as they are today, were they?" Jessie asked.

"Good God, no," Christian said. "Just look at shots from the seventies. Christie Brinkley? I kid you not—at the height of her career, she was the size of a water buffalo."

"What happened?" I asked. "Why the pressure to be so thin these days?"

"Runway," he declared definitively, as if we would know exactly what he meant.

"I'm not following," Jessie said.

"Years ago, the supermodels never did fashion shows," Cap interjected. "There were two totally different types of models then: runway and photographic. The runway girls had to fit into the sample sizes and were supposed to be nothing more than hangers for the clothes. The photographic girls didn't have to be that small. When they put on a size four for a photo shoot and it didn't fit, you just slit it up the back and no one was any wiser. But then runway work started to really pay well, and the agencies pushed the photo girls to do it. Suddenly they needed to fit perfectly into the sample sizes, which by the way are even smaller today than they were ten years ago."

"So come on, Whitney," Christian said. "Tell us about your favorite dishes."

As she began to elaborate on a few of the so-called standouts in her upcoming cookbook, I enjoyed the pork ragout and only half listened to the descriptions of things like oyster soufflé and brownies with praline topping. I soon became aware that Richard had angled his body so that he'd boxed me out from the rest of the group and had me more or less to himself.

"So I finally get to meet Bailey Weggins," he said as the others chatted behind us. "Famous true crime writer." His eyes, I noticed, were heavily hooded but a nice, deep shade of blue. Whatever benefit they offered his face was unfortunately undercut by his rough, ruddy skin. He was the kind of guy you pegged for fifty but found out later was only thirty-six.

"I'm flattered you know of me," I said, genuinely.

"And not only as a writer. You figured out who killed the lovely Mona." He was referring to Mona Hodges, the she-devil editor in chief of *Buzz* who had been murdered this past summer.

"Am I to surmise that you knew Mona personally?"

"Just one encounter. After she went to *Buzz* and did the whole scorched-earth thing with the staff, she invited me to lunch at Michael's—said she wanted me to write for the magazine. I've churned out my fair share of celebrity profiles, but as I told her, I don't do gossip, and I certainly have no interest in issues like, 'Is It a Bump—or Just Belly Fat?' kinds of stories."

"I don't blame you," I said. "I'm sure it's *sooo* much more intellectually invigorating to profile celebrities for magazines like *Vanity Fair* and coax out their views on how to bring an end to world hunger or global warming."

"Touché," he said, tossing his head back in laughter. "I sounded like a pompous ass just then. What I was actually going to add is that I think what *you're* doing with the crime stuff is interesting. What led you to it?"

"I was a newspaper reporter for a few years, covering the police beat, and then moved to Manhattan to work in magazines. I never had any particular interest in celebrity crime, but this part-time gig at *Buzz* came up and I loved the idea of a regular income. You're totally freelance, right?"

"Yes, though I did my stint on Fleet Street in my twenties."

"I've read *your* books and thought they were terrific," I said. "Especially the one on Hollywood agents."

"Thank you. So how do you know Scott?"

"I don't, actually. I'm just a tag-along with Jessie this weekend. You?"

"I've known him a little over the years. Then I bumped into him lately and he lured me up here to meet Devon. He's angling for a *Vanity Fair* piece when her album hits."

"You're hogging Bailey, for God's sake, Richard," Scott called over to us, perhaps having overheard his name.

"She demanded I explain the thesis of my last book," he said. "I had to oblige."

Sandy cleared our plates and set down a wooden tray with coffee cups and a large cake iced thickly with white frosting. At the same time, the other three guests drifted back to our area.

"You *have* to have a slice of Sandy's red velvet cake," Scott announced to the group. "It's to die for."

Sandy pulled a large knife from a drawer and slid it silently into the cake. The four layers inside, separated by the creamy frosting, were as red as garnets. After lifting each piece onto a plate, Sandy passed them around the island. Everyone accepted a slice except Tory and Devon. Tory's sad, sullen "No, thank you" seemed to emanate from the lips of someone whose kitty had just been crushed by a car. Devon just shook her head as if she couldn't have cared less.

"You really wouldn't like a piece, Miss Barr?" Sandy asked her. "You didn't eat any dinner."

Devon's face formed into an expression of pure disdain. "If I wanted one, I'd say so."

"Thank you, Sandy," Scott said. "I can finish up here."

I didn't blame Scott for dismissing her. There had been something challenging about her comment to Devon. If Sandy was embarrassed about being banished, she didn't show it. She set the knife in the sink, wiped her hands on a dishrag, and quietly made her way down the stairs.

It took a moment or two to recover from the awkward lull, but then conversation started up again with Whitney describing the origins of red velvet cake. Cap and Devon went off to shoot pool, with Tommy and Tory watching. Christian and Richard—who'd refilled his wine glass twice since I'd been there—dragged out a backgammon board. Scott, Jessie, Whitney, and I continued to hang by the island, where we lobbed questions at our host about how he'd found the property and managed to haul two different barns here. I excused myself at one point to use the powder room on the ground floor, and when I emerged a couple of minutes later, Jessie was waiting in ambush for me.

"So what do you think?" she whispered devilishly.

"Interesting crowd," I said. "Should we plan on flashing our boobs tomorrow just to keep up?"

"What about Scott? What do you think of *him*?"

"Older than I'd pictured, but hunky—and very charming."

"Yeah, I know. Oh, by the way, you know who Tommy is, right?"

"A tattoo aficionado?"

"The lead guitarist for the band Tough Love."

"Oh, right, I thought the name was familiar, but I'm not much of a heavy metal fan."

"He's something else too—Devon's ex-lover. They broke up about four months ago."

She was about to elaborate, but Whitney suddenly descended the stairs, announcing she was heading to bed.

"My asthma acts up in cold weather," she said. "And I need to get plenty of sleep."

We returned upstairs. Cap, who was now absent-mindedly watching the backgammon game, yawned and announced he was going to take a quick walk around the premises and then turn in. Devon was the next to retire, offering only a desultory good-night. Richard staggered off about twenty minutes later, followed by Christian, Tommy, and Tory, and then it was just Jessie, Scott, and I standing at the island. I suddenly realized that I'd better beat it before Jessie strangled me. I made a point of glancing at my watch, yawning, and announcing my need to hit the sack.

"If you're interested, Sandy's husband Ralph is leading a couple of hikes tomorrow," Scott said as I slid off the stool. "There's one at eight thirty, and if that's too beastly an hour, there'll be another in the afternoon."

"I actually think I'll do the early one," I said.

"And if you're up for a massage at any point, there's a sign-up sheet by the door on the lower level of the guest barn. I have a local masseuse coming in for the day."

I wished them good night and scurried out of there. Jessie bit her lip and shot me an amused look, as if she wasn't sure what was in store, but she was game to see how it unfolded.

Before heading up to my room, I decided to pop outside for a blast of fresh air. Partly it was because I was feeling restless, but I also wanted a good look at the night sky, so far from the ambient light of Manhattan. My father, who died when I was twelve, had been a real naturalist and often took my brothers and me on walks through woods all over Massachusetts, teaching us about things like birds and turtles and where you could find the planets in the sky. Being out in the country always brought him close to mind.

The night seemed even more dazzling now than it had earlier, probably because most of the lights in the barns had been turned off. Once again my eyes were drawn toward the moon. It was still gleaming in the sky, higher than earlier, but now I noticed a filmy ring of ice crystals around it. Though some people assumed it was an old wives' tale, a ring like that really *was* a harbinger of rain—or if the weather was as cold as it was tonight, snow. When moisture gathers high in the atmosphere, you can see it reflecting the light of the moon.

Staring at the moon made me suddenly recall Scott's mention of a telescope on the deck. Wrapping my arms around myself for warmth, I made my way toward the rear of the barn. The coyotes were obviously sated; the only night sounds now were the snap of frozen twigs under my footfall.

But then there was another sound, a woman speaking—and it was coming from where the deck must be. Curious, I tried to step gently so I wouldn't be heard. As I neared the end of the barn wall, I spotted the edge of the deck. Cautiously I leaned forward and peered around the corner of the barn. Devon was standing there in her pea coat, talking to Cap. Though they weren't that near me, their voices carried clearly in the crisp night air.

"Devon, please," Cap said.

"You *have* to tell her," Devon declared petulantly. "You said you would, but you haven't."

I jerked back my upper body and, after quietly taking two steps in reverse, stopped in my tracks. It wasn't polite to eavesdrop, but as a reporter, my good-girl instincts had long since left the building.

"I *will* tell her," Cap said. "I promise. You know I always take care of things, and I will this time too."

"*When?*" Devon demanded.

"Very soon. But you know as well as I do that we need to handle this carefully, or it could all blow up."

Devon digested his comment, then spit out the word "*Fine,*" in a tone that implied that she expected results.

Were Devon and Cap having an *affair?* Wow, that could add some spice to this crazy little house party. I heard a scraping of shoes on the deck, as if they were about to move. I quickly retraced my steps around the big barn and made my way over to the smaller one.

Back in my room, I felt a sudden urge to call Beau. I wondered if he had decided to come back Saturday after all. But it was close to ten in Sedona, and if he *was* leaving tomorrow, he may have gone to bed by now. I would have to wait until tomorrow to talk to him. I sent a text that he'd find in the morning. Just a quick hello.

I pulled on my flannel jammies, slipped into bed, and pondered again what I'd just witnessed on the deck. The conversation had suggested something secretive and intimate. It didn't sync with the picture presented by Cap and Whitney earlier in the evening. They'd acted like the devoted couple—they'd even snuggled up to each other a couple of times, her arm snaked around his waist.

And if Devon was having an affair with Cap, how did that explain the sexual tension between her and Tommy? You could almost feel the heat when those two were within five feet of each other—and clearly Tory wasn't amused. Maybe Devon was flirting with her ex to make Cap jealous.

Wouldn't it be wild, I thought as I drifted off to sleep, if things came to a head this weekend?

I awoke the next morning just before eight. I checked my BlackBerry but there was no message yet from Beau. After dressing in a thick sweater, jeans, and hiking boots, I headed over to the big barn. Based on the bacon-y breakfast smells that greeted me when I stepped into the foyer, I expected to discover a handful of people upstairs, but it was only Richard, hunched over his iPad at the island, reading the *Times* from what I could see, and Sandy stirring something on the stove. She was wearing a huge tartan shirt that made her look as if she should be draped over the back of a car at a tailgate picnic.

Sandy offered the same perfunctory smile she'd flashed last night, the kind with just the mouth, not the eyes. Richard glanced up from his iPad. He looked bleary eyed, like someone in need of the hair of the dog that bit him rather than the gooey pile of French toast and syrup on his plate.

"Morning," I said. "Everyone else still snoozing?"

"Apparently," Richard said. "You slept well, I trust?"

"Very well, thank you. And you?"

"Yes—though I was roused several times by the pitter-patter of not so little feet outside my door."

Interesting. I wondered who it might have been.

"So I see there's WiFi here," I said to Richard.

"Yes, fortunately. I know we're only a few hours from the city, but it feels as if we're in the middle of Patagonia." He glanced over toward Sandy. "Is there even a town near here?" he asked her.

Before she could answer, we heard the sound of panting as someone mounted the stairs. It was a large woman with a mass of long, black, curly hair and stuffed into a pair of very tight jeans. She was in her mid- to late twenties. I realized it was Jane, the same woman I'd seen in the passageway last night.

"I hope you have green tea," she announced in a surly tone to Sandy. "That's what she wants."

"You know they do have certain customs up here in the north country, Jane," Richard said, his voice thick with mock charm. "One is that you greet people whenever you first step into a room."

"Good morning," she said, grumpily. I introduced myself, and she accepted my hand without enthusiasm.

"Now *please* tell me you have green tea," she said, turning back to Sandy. "Or both of us are going to be fucked."

By this point, Sandy had reached into the cupboard and taken down a small basket stuffed with individual bags of herbal teas. She set it on the island.

"I believe you'll find some in here," she told Jane evenly. Next she took out a white pot, a cup and saucer, and a small wooden tray to set them on.

"You don't have it *loose*?" Jane complained as she poked through the packet with her chubby fingers.

"I'm afraid not," Sandy responded, though she sounded almost pleased with the news. Jane let out a huge, annoyed sigh.

"Does your boss enjoy British customs?" Richard asked. "I don't know many Americans who prefer loose tea."

"I don't know why anyone would want tea to *begin* with," Jane said. "My *grandmother* drinks tea. And she's like a hundred."

We were spared more of her sour attitude by the arrival of a man I hadn't seen yet, zipped up to his leathery chin in a red parka that was limp and stained with age. Sandy nodded to him and told the rest of us that this was her husband Ralph. He looked close to sixty, about ten years older than she.

"Any takers for the first walk today?" he asked hoarsely, like someone fighting a cold.

"I'd love to go," I said.

"Count me in, too," Richard said. *That* was a surprise. Based on how wasted he looked, I wondered if there might be a need later to have him medevaced out of the woods.

"I'll meet you by the front door of the barn in ten minutes," Ralph said. "Just be sure to dress warm."

While I chugged the last of my coffee, Jane waited impatiently for Sandy to finish setting up the tea tray. Before lugging it away, she ripped open several tea bags and shook the loose leaves into the teapot.

"*Don't* say anything," she told us—as if we'd actually take pleasure in squealing to Devon that she was the victim of a major tea-leaf hoax.

"Would she like a muffin?" Sandy asked.

"Sure," Jane said snarkily. "If you can slice off one tiny crumb and feed it to her with tweezers."

Something was definitely going on with Devon's eating. I wondered if she might be suffering from anorexia and decided to pay close attention later at lunch. But for now, I needed to grab my coat. After retrieving it from my room, I knocked on Jessie's door just to see if she was up for the hike. There was no reply. I suspected she might have bunked down with Scott. I hurried downstairs, taking a few extra seconds to sign up for a late-morning massage on the clipboard by the door.

Ralph was waiting outside for us, a dusty old pair of binoculars dangling from his neck. Without chitchat, he led us single file along a trail that wasn't difficult but kicked up my pulse rate a little. Richard did his best to disguise the fact that he was huffing and puffing at times.

We stopped at just a few spots, once for Ralph to point out an owl pellet lying on the ground, the regurgitated indigestible bits and bones from the bird's last meal. A few minutes later he showed us a fox den just off the trail. A tuft of gray fur had been snagged by a branch just in front of the mouth of the den.

"Looks like Jane paid him a visit last night," Richard whispered in my ear.

"*Stop*," I said, pretending to elbow him.

We continued walking, and after a few minutes, we fell behind Ralph a bit on the trail. He was clearly giving us some breathing room.

"How are you enjoying our little house party so far?" I asked Richard.

"I'm having a marvelous time," he said sarcastically. "Though I must admit it's difficult keeping up intellectually. I'm guessing tonight we'll tackle Francis Fukuyama's latest thoughts on the consequences of the biotechnological revolution."

I laughed.

"It sounds like we'll be treated to a preview of Devon's album," I said. "Do you think she has a shot at making it as a singer?"

"Well, the same plan worked for Carla Bruni. And then some. It depends on how good her voice is and how well she's managed."

"Cap seems to be doing a good job guiding her so far."

"Yes, but he might be in a little over his head in this instance. Up until now his biggest achievements had been helping models snag parts in movies like *Scream IV* or become the spokesperson for something like the magic flab blaster. Music is a whole different arena."

"Do you think she might drop him?"

"A wonderfully sane, loyal, clear-thinking girl like Devon?" he said sarcastically. "Oh, I doubt it."

There was a sudden honking sound above us, and in unison we glanced up to see a V formation of what looked like thirty geese slicing their way across the sky. After they'd vanished, I continued to stare upward.

Clouds had muscled in during our hike, and the sky had a bruised, swollen look—the kind that at this time of year promised snow.

"Have you heard a weather forecast for the weekend?" I called up the trail to Ralph.

"Snow," he said. "Maybe six inches."

"Oh gosh, I hadn't heard that. Will that create any problems for us getting out of here?"

"It shouldn't. We've got our own plow here."

"Oh, come on, Bailey," Richard said. "Wouldn't it be fun to be snowbound together? Maybe Devon will throw her cell phone at Jane's head for not providing loose tea leaves and we'll have to make a citizen's arrest."

A few minutes later I could tell from the position of the sun that we had begun to circle back. At around ten thirty, we emerged from the woods just a little farther south than where we'd entered.

"That was wonderful, Ralph, thank you," I said. He accepted my thanks while coughing into an old bandana.

While Richard headed off, claiming to be in need of sustenance, I moseyed around, checking out the rest of the buildings on the property. In addition to the two large barns, there were three smaller structures, all made of barn wood. One was more of a cottage, a residence it appeared, and I assumed it was where Sandy and Ralph lived; another seemed to be mainly for storage, and the last served as a large garage. There were curtains in the windows on the second level, suggesting more living space.

I wondered if people were still sleeping because there wasn't a soul in sight. But just as I passed the garage, I was startled by the sound of someone clearly crying. I followed the sobs to behind the building. Several feet into the woods, by a giant pine tree, stood Devon in her jeans, black knee-high boots, and pea coat, smoking a cigarette and twisting her body back and forth.

"Are you all right?" I called to her.

"No, I'm *not* freaking all right," she said with equal parts anger and fear.

"What's the matter?" I asked. I wonder if she's broken a heel, I joked to myself.

"I'm not safe," she said, catching me by surprise. "I need to get the hell out of here."

3

"Why—what's happened?" I urged, edging my way through the dead, brittle brambles. A little alarm had started to go off in my head—clearly we were dealing with more than a broken heel here— and as I drew closer, I saw that Devon looked terrified. Her eyes, wet with tears, bounced around randomly, as if behind them she was thinking frantically, trying to hatch an escape plan.

"Devon, tell me," I said, since she hadn't answered. "What's going on?"

I couldn't help but wonder if her worried state related back somehow to the conversation I'd overheard between her and Cap last night.

"Can't you hear what I'm saying? It's not *safe*. Someone knows something."

"Knows what?"

For the first time she made direct eye contact with me, and from her look it appeared something had just clicked in her mind. I sensed she now regretted having been so candid. She quickly wiped away her tears and surveyed me coldly.

"I just shouldn't be here—in a *barn*," she said. "In the *woods*. I need to be back in the city as soon as possible." She made the proclamation almost defiantly, as if I had challenged her.

"But something's frightened you. Tell me what it is."

"I told you. I just don't want to be here."

I sighed. Apparently no amount of coaxing on my part was going to dig out the truth.

"Well, let me know if I can help in any way," I said. She climbed out of the brambles and brushed past me, looking irritated, as if I'd asked for an autograph while she was eating a meal in a fancy restaurant. Though, of course, it didn't seem like she ever *ate* a meal these days.

I received a much warmer response when I knocked again on Jessie's door a few minutes later. Wrapped in a white, terrycloth bathrobe, she was blotting her wet hair with a towel.

"There you are," she said, pulling me into her room. "I've been dying for you to get back."

"Did you just wake up?"

"Sort of."

"Meaning?"

"I stayed with Scott last night. In *his* room. It's on the ground floor of the big barn. I snuck back here a little while ago."

"Ahhh, so you weren't just eye candy after all. How'd it go?"

"It was pretty damn dreamy. And he's fun. Though the first thing I'll do when we get married is make him sell this place and buy a beach house instead."

It was almost time for my massage, and I told Jessie I'd catch up with her at lunch. I scurried downstairs and tapped lightly on the door next to the clipboard. A woman with an East European accent, who introduced herself as Nina, beckoned me inside.

Nina turned out to have awesome hands, strong enough to tear the head off a chicken. I'd just let myself go limp on the table when I heard what could have only been a shot from a gun. I let out a grunt of anxious surprise and jerked my head up. But Nina pressed lightly on my shoulder, indicating I should lie back down again.

"Don't vorry," she said, as another shot filled the air. "Eet's joost the skeet shooting."

I realized suddenly how jumpy I felt. It was due in part to our isolation but also to the encounter I'd just had with Devon. Her comment about not feeling safe had unsettled me. Of course, in the end Devon had tried to take it back and blame her tears on being stuck over a hundred miles from a Louis Vuitton store, but I was sure, from the look on her face, that she really *had* been frightened. Someone, she said, *knew* something. If Devon was having an affair with Cap, Whitney may have gotten wind of it. Had Whitney provided Devon with a reason to be afraid?

After my massage, I made my way over to the large barn. As I passed through the glass passageway, I saw that those swollen clouds I'd spotted earlier hadn't been kidding. Snow was falling. It wasn't coming down hard, but the flakes were the size of flapjacks.

I expected to find a few people already gathered in the great room, eager for lunch, but only Sandy was there, laying out a feast on the countertop of the island. There were all sorts of antipasti—cheeses, prosciutto and salami, white beans, olives, roasted peppers, onions and asparagus, and an arugula salad. Not wanting to be in her way, I found a spot on one of the couches on the other side of the room and opened the book I'd brought with me.

While I read, Sandy hummed quietly, clearly lost in her work. The woodsy scent from last night's candles still hung in the air, mixing in a good way with the deliciously garlicky smell of the food. From the windows in the barn I could see the snow gently falling outside. Despite my earlier worry, I finally let myself relax.

It only lasted twenty minutes, though—until Tommy and Tory came up the stairs, the sound of their boots as sharp as firecrackers. They waved perfunctorily at me and then turned their attention to the food on the island.

"Don't tell me we've missed breakfast," Tory said.

"I can fix you something if you like," Sandy said without even a morsel of enthusiasm.

"Christ, Tory, don't make her drag the breakfast back out for you," Tommy chided. "Just wad up some ham and cheese, stuff it in your mouth, and tell yourself you're eating an omelet."

"I don't *eat* cheese, you know that. Or ham either."

"Oh, that's right." He turned toward Sandy. "Maybe you could scramble up an egg white and smear it on a rice cake for her."

"Never mind," said Tory. "I'll just have juice."

"Suit yourself. As for me," Tommy said, turning now toward Sandy, "I'd like a little of everything. Just pile it all up on a plate, my lady—okay?"

Clearly he hadn't picked up on the serve-yourself-buffet concept. Even from where I sat, I could see how tight Sandy's jaw was set as she lifted one of the creamy white plates and began scooping food onto it for him.

I wondered if she *always* found Scott's houseguests to be irritating, or was it just this particular batch.

More clomping on the stairs, and then Devon appeared. She'd shed her pea coat somewhere along the way and was carrying a half-empty bottle of water. She ignored me and strode toward the island.

"Hi," she said to Tommy and Tory. "What's up?" Miraculously, she no longer appeared the least bit wigged out. And though she'd only said a few words, I detected impishness in her tone.

"So what are we supposed to *do* today?" Tory asked.

"You can hike," Devon said. "Or you can shoot. Or you can just stay in your room and fuck if you want." She'd said it playfully, with a naughty glint in her eye. Tory lowered her gaze, clearly uncomfortable, and Tommy just stared at Devon, obviously trying to assess what she was up to.

"Lunch is served, Miss Barr," Sandy announced from behind the island. She seemed to derive pleasure from challenging Devon about the food.

"I want more green tea," Devon said.

"Here it is," Sandy declared, reaching behind her for the basket of tea bags. Peering above my book, I saw that the edges of Sandy's mouth were turned up in a tiny smile.

"I want the *loose* kind, not the tea bags," Devon said.

"I'm sorry, we only have the *bags*," Sandy said, almost unable to contain how delighted she felt to be delivering the news.

"But—" Devon said. You could tell by the expression on her face that she'd just figured out what ploy Jane had played on her earlier.

"Never mind," she said, clearly pissed. She took a swig of water and set the water bottle down on a side table. "Where's Cap and Whitney?" she demanded of no one in particular.

"They're out shooting with Mr. Cohen," Sandy told her. "They probably won't be up for a bit."

Devon turned on her heels, strode toward the stairs, and headed down. A minute later, I tossed my book aside and sprang up from the couch, deciding to catch up with her.

She was still in the foyer when I reached the bottom of the stairs, her back to me. Her hand was stuffed in her brown hobo-style handbag, which was parked on a wooden bench. She spun around in surprise at the sound of my footsteps.

"Why are you creeping up behind me?" she demanded.

"I just wanted to make sure you were okay."

"I *told* you I was. Isn't that enough?" She stormed across the foyer and flung open the door to the passageway.

I trudged back upstairs and waited for Jessie. After she arrived we piled our plates high with food and carried them over to the table just as Tory and Tommy departed. Jessie was in a giddy mood over Scott, and kept glancing up in anticipation of seeing him again. He finally arrived, along with Cap, Whitney, and Christian. They joined us at the table and I couldn't help but note how lovey dovey Cap and Whitney appeared. Richard and Jane each stopped by for food at different points but took it away with them, Richard saying he was finishing up an article in his room, and Jane announcing sullenly that she was going to eat while she watched a movie in the media room downstairs. I wondered if she'd been chewed out about the tea.

Once lunch wound down, Scott said that he'd be leading a short hike himself before the snow got too deep. The others all volunteered to go, but since I'd had my hike earlier, I passed. Instead, I curled up on the couch once more with my book. I checked my BlackBerry again and found a text from Beau. He'd decided to return on Sunday, after all, and suggested we talk later. What did that mean? I wondered. Maybe he really *had* wanted to please me by coming back a day early, but since I wasn't going to be home, he'd decided there was no point.

At around five I finally headed back through the passageway to the small barn. I was stunned to see how much snow had fallen. It was the heavy, wet kind that sparkled in a million places and turned the woods into a wonderland. At this rate of accumulation, it was hard to imagine we were going to end up with only six inches.

Despite the sluggish feeling the afternoon had produced in me, I told myself that the evening was bound to be more entertaining. We'd all be together at that big dining table, and there'd be less of a fragmented feeling. At about seven fifteen, showered and dressed in tight black jeans and a sleeveless silver sweater, I knocked on Jessie's door. She was flashing major cleavage and had her brown hair half up in a totally fetching style.

"Let's go the outside route," she told me. "The area right outside is shoveled, and I want to see how pretty it is out tonight."

"We haven't got our coats on," I said.

"We'll run," she said, laughing.

No sooner were we out the door than Jessie promptly slipped on her butt. We both burst out laughing as she dusted off the smattering of snow from the seat of her pants.

The barn looked spectacular as we pushed the door open. There were dozens of votive lights flickering on surfaces. Sandy and two young female helpers were bustling about quietly in the kitchen area, and Scott,

Whitney, Cap, Richard, Christian, and Jane were already gathered on the couches around a huge platter of cheeses, talking animatedly. Everyone appeared to have dressed for dinner, particularly Whitney, who was decked out in a low-cut deep blue dress with sapphires to match on each ear. Snuggled in her deep cleavage was a tiny diamond-encrusted cross dangling from a chain. It seemed positively sacrilegious for it to be ensconced there.

Even Jane was gussied up—in a black spandex dress with her hair pulled back in a curly ponytail. I couldn't help but notice, though, that her fishnet stockings had a run as wide as a two-lane highway.

"I was just about to send out a sleigh for you two," Scott proclaimed.

"I insisted we come the outdoor route, and I fell flat on my ass," Jessie said.

"Well, come right over here and rest it," Scott said, scooting over to make room for us on the couch.

"You're not really injured, are you?" Whitney asked, oozing concern.

"No, just my pride," Jessie said, smiling.

"How about a glass of wine to take away the sting of humiliation?" Richard asked. His dark blue eyes seemed almost bright tonight and his skin even ruddier, suggesting he'd gotten an early start on the evening.

Jessie and I gave our drink orders and then settled into the group. The mood was relaxed, with Scott playing maestro.

Dinner wasn't served until close to nine because Devon, Tommy, and Tory were so late to arrive—and when they did, both Tommy and Tory looked stoned. Sandy had set out place cards at the table, and I discovered that I had Richard on one side—with Whitney to his left—and Cap on the other, with Tory to *his* right. Tory immediately grabbed Cap's attention, so I swiveled my head toward Whitney and Richard, who'd guzzled down two G and T's just since we'd been at cocktails.

"Were you born in Texas?" I asked Whitney, since Richard was studying the contents of his soup bowl with a blurry-eyed expression.

"Yes, Fort Worth. Born and raised. My mother passed ten years ago, but my daddy's still there— though he's not in the best of health."

"What made you decide to write a cookbook—do you have a food background?"

"I do, yes—but not in the restaurant business. I was in TV news in Dallas, and I specialized in health, nutrition, and food."

"How did you end up in New York?"

"I came up for a foodie event, and I met Cap while I was here through mutual friends. We spent an amazing week together—and I moved to Manhattan a month later."

"Do you miss Texas? I assume the answer is yes, since you're writing a book about the food there."

"I do—and the good news is that Cap and I are planning to buy a ranch near San Antonio so we can at least vacation there. He's going to like it as much as I do. People just connect better with each other in that part of the world. It's all about good, strong values."

Richard had begun to devour the squash soup with boozy concentration, but at the sound of the word *values*, he stopped, his spoon poised mid-air. He turned toward Whitney and eyed her, feigning perplexity.

"Don't you think values are highly overrated, though?" he asked. "I mean, where have they really gotten us?"

"Where have they *gotten* us?" Whitney exclaimed. "You just have to look around to see that what good there *is* in the world comes from the actions of people with values—fighting famine and poverty, eradicating disease. Protecting children."

"In the name of the Lord, you mean?" he asked.

"Sometimes. And with the Lord's guidance, too."

"I'll pose a question Christopher Hitchens asked. If Jesus could heal a blind person he happened to meet, then why not heal blindness?"

She smiled smugly.

"I don't pretend to know how God works," she said. "None of us can. We just have to vow to do the right thing."

"Ah, I see," he said. "But don't you find that the ones who jabber on the most about doing the right thing so often don't?"

"I'm not sure what you mean," she said, her back rigid.

"The Christian right. Just take a look at all these right-wing preachers and politicians. They're always pontificating about values, and yet half of them lie down with whores and the other half with young boys."

Whitney caught her breath in surprise, as if he'd just called *her* a hooker, but then she let it out slowly, clearly willing herself not to get steamed.

"How did you get *your* start, Richard?" I asked, hoping to chase him off the topic. Though he was clearly in the mood to be provocative, the temptation to talk about himself overrode it. Through a main course of roast chicken, new potatoes, and haricots vert, we heard about the Fleet Street years, the magazine years, and then coming to America. With each anecdote, his tongue loosened even more, until his words were slurred. Whitney listened and even asked a perfunctory question or two, but she could barely disguise her disgust for the man. He seemed to sense that and actually relish it.

At one point in the middle of all this I caught Jessie's eye, and she flashed me a mischievous look. It was obvious from Scott's body language that he had the hots for Jessie, who was seated next to him, but he did a decent job of including Jane, on the other side, in the conversation. Speaking of hots, you could almost see the smoke rising from below the table where Devon and Tommy were sitting side by side. She was smirking sexily at everything he said, and he was lapping it up. So did this mean she wasn't involved with Cap? Or was she flirting balls to the wall to make Cap jealous?

As Richard droned on, I tried to study Devon out of the corner of my eye. Though she often had a fork in her food, it became clear after a minute that she was just using it to rearrange things on her plate. I also realized after a moment that though Tory was pretending to listen to Cap, her eyes kept shooting over toward the pair of dirty flirters.

"I've got an idea," Scott announced suddenly, just as Sandy and one of the young helpers, a redheaded girl in her twenties, were clearing the plates. "Sandy's made us a fantastic apple pie, and I think we should indulge in it while listening to some awesome music by someone who's on the brink of becoming a major recording star."

"How could we argue with that?" Cap said.

Scott rose from his chair, took his iPhone from the pocket of his jacket, and docked it in a nearby iPod speaker. A few seconds later the room was filled with the haunting sound of a woman singing a song with the refrain, "You'll break my heart a second time." It was part ballad, part pop song, with a splash of country. I knew it was Devon Barr singing, but it was hard to reconcile the voice with the creature at the table. Everyone just sat there spellbound. When I glanced down a minute later and saw a wedge of apple pie, I realized I'd been so absorbed I hadn't noticed anyone slide it in front of me.

"That's absolutely sensational," Cap said when the track was over.

"Isn't it?" Scott said. "Devon Barr is going to be huge."

An awkward silence followed. I was about to ask the release date when Tommy tilted his chair back, a signal, it seemed, that he was about to make a pronouncement.

"Well, well," he declared. "You were holding out on me, Devon. I had no fucking clue you could sing like that."

She looked at him slyly.

"I—I thought you didn't like ballads," she said. Her words had sounded just a little slurred, which surprised me. I hadn't seen her drink anything but water before dinner, and her wineglass was nearly full.

"I believe I've just changed my mind. Of course, I do need to know who you wrote the song about."

Devon stared at him intensely. "You'll have to guess—like everyone else," she said teasingly. "But what a nice surprise you like it."

People shifted in their seats collectively, and I half expected someone at the table to shout, "Get a room!" I wondered what Tory was thinking. Turns out I didn't have to wait long to find out.

"Nice *surprise*?" Tory shouted, her voice shrill with sarcasm. She was just a few feet to my right, and her outburst startled me so much, I nearly jumped. "It's no fucking surprise at all. It's why you invited us, isn't it?"

The whole table just sat there in stunned silence. Devon didn't answer but stared at Tory, the famous mouth pursed and her eyes squinted, as if she had no idea what Tory could *possibly* mean.

"You wanted Scott to play your stupid ballad in front of me and Tommy," Tory said, "so I'd have to sit here watching him get a woody as he listened to it."

Ahhh, I'd *wondered* if things might come to a boil this weekend.

"I'm sure Tommy's just being complimentary," Scott said. "There's nothing to get excited about."

"It's none of your fat business," Tory snapped. "You want to fuck her, too, I bet."

"Oh, please, Tory, that's enough," Tommy shouted from across the table. "Stop being so freaking obsessed and eat your pie."

"Why don't you stick it in your pie*hole*," she said. She picked up the cobalt blue goblet in front of her and tossed the remains of her sparkling water at Tommy from across the table—though most of it ended up splashing on Whitney. As Richard watched the water trickle down Whitney's cleavage, Tory stormed off, digging the heels of her boots hard into the bare wood floor.

Sandy moved toward the table decisively, a large rag in hand, and simultaneously Scott passed Whitney his own napkin for her to dab the water off. Then he turned back to the rest of the table, where we all sat speechless.

"Well," he said, looking like a guy who'd seen far worse and wasn't going to be thrown off his game by a minor hissy fit, "who would like to join me for a few hands of poker?"

"I'm in," Richard said, his voice liquidy. Several other people volunteered as well.

"Not me," Devon said, pushing back her chair. "I'm—I'm going to bed." I realized suddenly that she was tipsy, and as she stood up at the table, she wobbled a bit. At her body weight, I guessed, even a couple of sips of wine could leave one blotto. "Jane, lez go."

"I'm not ready, actually," Jane announced bluntly. She looked self-satisfied, as if she'd been waiting all night for a moment to assert her independence.

"I don't care. You gotta come."

"Sorry, this is one mess you'll have to take care of yourself," Jane said.

Devon scowled halfheartedly and moved toward the stairs, swaying slightly with each step.

"Devon, let me help you," Cap called after her. He started to jump from the table.

"No," she called out over her shoulder. "Don't need you."

Whitney rested her hand on Cap's arm. "Honey, let her be. She clearly wants some time alone."

After a couple of awkward moments, people began to rise from the table and take positions around the room. For the next hour or so everyone played cards or pool—except Whitney, who sat tightly next to Cap and seemed to be lost in thought. Despite Scott's attempts to keep things jovial, the party never regained the festive mood from earlier. At about eleven Tommy threw down his cards and said he was calling it quits for the night. I couldn't help but wonder what might get tossed at *him* when he opened his bedroom door. Soon afterward, I said good night, not wanting to be the last to leave, and discreetly winked at Jessie.

Heading back through the passageway, I saw that the snow was coming down hard now—and that there was close to a foot on the ground already. I didn't like the look of it. Getting out to the main road tomorrow wasn't going to be easy even with the long driveway plowed.

As I dressed for bed, I couldn't help but think of Beau. If I hadn't let my annoyance get the better of me, I would have been snuggled up in bed with him in Manhattan right now, instead of being nearly snowbound in a barn with a bunch of totally wacky houseguests who liked to get sloshed or stoned, expose their boobs, and hurl drinks across the table.

Had I totally overreacted about the Sedona trip? I wondered. I knew part of the reason it bugged me so much was that it raised the ghost of the trip Beau had taken to Turkey last summer, not long after I first set eyes on him. I didn't like anything at all about *that* trip.

Beau and I had first met in the *Buzz* office building, on one of the corporate floors. I'd gone up there to talk to someone, and Beau was meeting with the head dude,

Tom Dicker, to discuss a documentary film project. When I spotted him across the reception room, it was like being hit by a lightning bolt, and not long after we were having this crazy fling.

He'd been very clear from the start. He was looking for fun, not a relationship—in part because he wasn't ready and in part because he was heading off to Turkey soon to make a documentary there. I was fine with the fling part for a while, but as I found myself falling hard, I told Beau I needed to break it off. To my surprise he said that he was pretty smitten and asked if I'd give him a chance to mull it over when he was in Turkey. He promised to stay in touch.

But then all I got was one lousy postcard. I gave up after a while, feeling more than sorry about the loss, and became involved with a young actor named Chris Wickersham. I never expected to see Beau again. But after he returned in September, he let me know that he'd fallen for me and wanted to make a full commitment. He sounded genuine, and things had overall been good with us since. Except that I couldn't unload my doubts. Like I'd told Jessie, I had the sense he'd talked himself into a commitment because he didn't want to give me up.

I grabbed my BlackBerry from my purse and checked to see if I'd missed a call or text from Beau.

I hadn't. I called his cell, knowing it was still early in Sedona. All I got was voice mail. I left a message telling him I was going to bed but would talk to him tomorrow after his flight landed. I wished him a good trip. There, I thought. I can be a big girl.

I fell asleep pretty easily, exhausted from the group psycho-dynamics of the evening. And then all of a sudden I was awake again and wasn't sure why. I squinted at my watch: 2:47. The wind was howling fiercely outside my bedroom window, and I guessed that the noise must have woken me. But as I lay quietly listening I heard a sound that wasn't the wind. Someone, somewhere was wailing.

Maybe it's just Tommy and Tory having makeup sex, I told myself, but a second later I heard it again—a cross between a wail and a moan, and it was louder now and desperate sounding. I took a deep breath, threw off the covers, and projected myself out of bed. Cautiously I opened the bedroom door a crack. I couldn't see anything but I heard someone—a woman, I thought—moan again off to the left. I opened the door wider and peered along the corridor.

A complete stranger, a female, was standing in front of the room across and down a bit from Jessie's. The door to the room was open, and the woman was leaning against the door frame, looking pale and disoriented.

She was dressed incongruously in a parka, a flannel nightgown, and a pair of snow boots. Just as I was about to ask where in the world she'd come from, I realized it was one of the two girls who'd assisted Sandy at dinner. Her long curly red hair, which had been pinned into a tight bun earlier, now flew in long strands from her head like wind socks. It occurred to me that she'd probably been marooned here because of the snow and had been given the room to stay in.

"What's the matter?" I asked, taking a few steps closer to her. "Are you sick?"

"She won't wake up," she said, shaking her head. "You've got to help me."

"Who?" I asked. "Who won't wake up?" It felt as if I was in some crazy dream sequence, and for a split second I wondered if she might be sleepwalking.

"Devon Barr," she said plaintively. "I keep trying to wake her, but she just lies there in bed. Her eyes are open but she won't say anything."

4

"But—what were you doing in her bedroom?" I stammered. I had no clue what was going on.

"Sh-she called extension seven and asked me to bring her some water. She said she didn't feel well and couldn't get it herself."

"Okay, okay," I said, hurrying toward her. "What's your name?"

"Laura. Laura Ash."

"Okay, Laura, calm down. Let me see what's going on."

There was a lamp burning on a bedside table, and when I stepped into the room I saw that Devon was lying on her back in bed, the duvet kicked to the floor. The top sheet was pulled up just to her waist, revealing her naked torso and small, delicate breasts. I moved closer, and when I saw her eyes, I nearly jumped out of my skin. Her eyes were wide open, totally blank, and slightly faded.

"Devon," I called. "Devon, talk to me."

Instinctively I grabbed Devon's shoulder to shake her, and when I touched her skin I found that it was a little bit cool, like a piece of porcelain. Frantically I fumbled for her wrist and took her pulse. Nothing. I felt a tremble through my whole body. Devon Barr was dead.

I spun around toward the door, where Laura was standing, peering into the room and looking helpless. "I'm confused," I told her. "When did Devon call you?"

"Why?"

"Just tell me, Laura." Based on the temperature of the body, it was impossible that Devon had just made a phone call.

Laura lowered her eyes, like a dog in trouble.

"About an hour and a half ago," she muttered.

"*What*? You mean at like one fifteen?"

"Yes."

"Where have you been all this time?"

"In one of the bedrooms above the garage. After she asked me to bring the water, I planned to, *really*, but I was already in bed and before I could get up, I—I fell back asleep."

"So you woke up about an hour and a half later and decided to just traipse up here?"

"No. Uh, she called again."

"You mean just before you came up here? That's impossible."

"Well, I *thought* it was her," she said, her voice quivering now. "The phone rang. By the time I answered, there was no one there. I just assumed it was her calling to see where I was, and I hurried up here. I didn't realize how much time had passed."

"Okay, I need you to go wake Scott. Tell him he has to come over here right away." By the look on her face, you would have thought I had told her that a spaceship full of Martians had just landed and we needed to start tearing ass through the woods. "Laura—" She was starting to work my last nerve.

"But I think he's with that girl. Your friend."

"That's okay. Just knock hard and tell him it's an emergency and he has to come to Devon's room."

"What should I tell Scott? That she passed out?"

"No, she's dead."

"Dead? Omigod."

"You've got to wake Scott, Laura. Just *please* hurry up, okay?"

I could have gone myself to fetch Scott, but I didn't want to leave Laura in charge of the scene—and to be honest, I wanted a chance to look around.

After Laura stumbled off, I glanced back down at Devon's body. Within hours the luminescent skin would turn waxy, her limbs would stiffen, and the face that had made a fortune would begin to sag. She had seemed like a bitch on wheels, totally self-absorbed, but I couldn't help but feel rocked and saddened by her death. She was so young, so beautiful—and, as it turned out, so talented, too.

How had she died, I wondered? The first word that flashed in my mind for some reason was *overdose*— maybe because she'd had a rocker boyfriend. I glanced toward the bedside table to the right of the bed. Besides the phone, there was an empty water bottle, an iPod, an iPhone, a tin of lip balm, a crushed pack of cigarettes, and a saucer piled with butts.

But just because there was no sign of drugs didn't mean she hadn't taken something or even shot it up, and she'd been wobbly when she'd left dinner. But suddenly a memory rushed my mind: Devon in the woods this morning, crying and saying she wasn't safe. I ran my eyes over her body. There were no visible bruises on her neck or torso—and no blood on the sheets.

What I did see as I stared at her naked torso was how thin she really was. Beneath her breasts, the outline of almost every rib was apparent. Several models had suffered heart attacks in recent years as a result of anorexia. Was *that* how Devon Barr had died? I wondered. Certainly being intoxicated tonight would have only complicated matters.

Until an autopsy was conducted, the police would treat her death as suspicious. Both a police crime scene unit and the local coroner would be brought in to check out the room. I had no right to snoop around, and I certainly wasn't going to do anything to muck up the scene, but there was no harm in letting my eyes continue to wander.

The bedroom was similar to mine—spacious, with a small separate sitting area at the far end—though decorated differently, in blues and greens. There were wads of clothes scattered on not only the chair and loveseat but also the floor.

As my eyes scanned the room, they finally reached the darkened doorway to the bathroom. I took a few careful steps in that direction. When I reached the door, I tugged the sleeve of my pajamas down over my hand and, after a couple of moments of fumbling, flipped on the light switch. If Devon had been doing drugs, there might be evidence in here.

The bathroom was a mess. There were black suede boots lying limply on the floor along with the cream-colored blouse she'd worn at dinner and two damp bath towels. Cosmetics littered the counter surrounding the sink, as if she'd simply upended her makeup bag. Mixed among them were used Q-tips and cotton balls, a tube of Elizabeth Arden Eight Hour Cream Skin Protectant, and different lotions and creams—plus another empty water bottle. Without moving my feet, I leaned forward and squinted at the bottles and tubes. No sign of drugs. But something else of interest. Standing among them was a small brown bottle of syrup of ipecac. I hadn't seen that stuff in years.

Syrup of ipecac, I knew, induced vomiting, something I learned when I was reporting an accidental poisoning story for the *Albany Times Union*. Parents were once encouraged to store it in their medicine cabinet in case their kid decided to chow down on some toxic household cleanser or a bottle of aspirin, but that strategy was no longer recommended by doctors. The problem was that vomiting could sometimes make a poisoning situation even worse. For instance, when you throw up lye, it just scorches your throat all over again.

But why would Devon be toting it around? I wondered. Searching my mind, I seemed to remember reading once that bulimics used ipecac to support their efforts. So perhaps Devon had suffered from bulimia, not anorexia.

Suddenly I picked up the sounds of people barreling down the corridor. I quickly flicked the bathroom light off and stepped back into the bedroom. Two seconds later Scott bolted through the door with Laura in tow.

"She's *dead*?" he blurted out. "What happened?" His jeans, which he had clearly thrown on in a hurry, were still unzipped and his shirt was unbuttoned, revealing his naked chest, covered lightly with greying hair.

"I'm not sure," I said. "She called Laura just after one o'clock for some water. Laura fell back asleep and finally brought it up a few minutes ago. It looks as if Devon has been dead for at least an hour."

"Christ, this is a total nightmare," he said, sweeping his hand through his hair. "What are we supposed to do?"

"You need to call nine-one-one. Do you know what shape the road is in—I mean, has Ralph started plowing it yet?"

"He's come down with a bad cold and he said he barely made a dent in it."

"Well, the cops will have a four-wheel drive, so hopefully they won't have much trouble. But an ambulance or morgue van might not be able to get through. When you speak to the nine-one-one operator, you better tell her about the road conditions here. And you might want to mention that this is a high-profile person."

He took a few steps closer, and I realized he was about to pick up the phone on the bedside table.

"Scott, I wouldn't use that phone," I said. "There's a chance foul play was involved. We shouldn't get our fingerprints on anything in the room."

"*Foul play*? You think someone *killed* her?"

"It doesn't *look* that way, but that's up to the police to rule out."

He sighed, shaking his head in discouragement.

"All right, I'll go grab my cell phone. Laura, you need to run down to the cabin and wake Sandy—and Ralph, if he's up to it."

She moaned, as if he'd just asked her to hike into town.

"Laura, go!" he barked, and she turned on her heels. He no longer seemed like the charming I-won't-even-mind-if-you-tell-another-guest-to-stick-it-in-his-piehole host from earlier in the evening. I guess finding a dead houseguest will do that to you.

"Where's Jane's room, by the way?" I asked as he hesitated in the doorway, looking discombobulated.

"She's next door on the right."

"Why don't I wake her while you're calling 911? She may have a number for Devon's parents. Once you're off the phone, I'd suggest you wake Cap."

"You're not planning to phone this in to the night desk at *Buzz* as soon as I leave, are you?" he asked, studying me intently. I couldn't tell from his tone whether he was being sarcastic or dead serious.

"The number-one priority right now is to get the police here," I told him. "But this is going to be a major story, and I will have to cover it—just like a zillion other reporters. You and Cap should work out a statement."

"I'm telling you right now, then. Everything I say from this point on is off the record."

"Understood," I said. "I promise to play fair with you on all of this."

I didn't like his testiness, but I could hardly blame him. After he left I surveyed the room one more time, closed Devon's door, and then hurried to Jane's room. It took about ten knocks to finally rouse her. When she swung open the door, it was like I'd woken a bear from hibernation. Her dark hair was a mass of frizz, and her mouth was twisted in a snarl.

"What now?" she demanded in a voice hoarse from sleep.

"I'm afraid I've got bad news, Jane. Devon is dead."

Her eyes widened, and I expected some bold exclamation to follow, but her face quickly relaxed and all she said was, "How?"

"We're not sure. She died in bed apparently, and it looks like she's been dead at least an hour. Do you have contact information for her family?"

"She's just got a mother—no father or brothers or sisters. I have a number for her someplace, but there's no guarantee she'll pick up. The woman's a total lush."

"Why don't you try, at least? Scott is calling nine-one-one. Is there anything else you can think of—someone who needs to be informed?"

"You mean, like a boyfriend? Not at the moment. I mean there was someone Wednesday night, but I don't believe she got his name."

Note to self, I thought: Do not assign Jane the task of writing my eulogy.

I told her that I was going back to meet with Scott and that we would probably wait in the big barn. She should look for us there and report on whether she connected with the mother. Backing away, I also warned her not to go into Devon's room and not to make any calls about Devon's death without consulting with Cap.

"I'm perfectly aware of the need to be sensitive about the media," she said. "That's my job twenty-four/seven—or at least it *was*."

As I headed back down the hall, Scott reached the top of the stairs. He'd managed to zip his jeans and button his shirt in the time he'd been away.

"The police are on their way," he reported, coming toward me, "but it's going to take a while because of the snow, they said. My guess—at least an hour."

We heard the downstairs door bang open. A moment later Sandy came storming up the stairs, wearing a puffy blue parka over her flannel pajamas, with Laura trailing behind her.

"She's really dead?" she asked anxiously of Scott.

"Yes," he said. "She's in her room—in bed. I've already called the police."

We were positioned just ahead of Devon's room. Sandy barged past us and started to reach for the doorknob.

"Please don't go in there," I told her firmly.

"I'm responsible for this place, and I'll go in there if I please," she snapped.

"That could be a crime scene, and the police won't be amused to learn that you've been in there just to satisfy your curiosity."

"Sandy, she's right," Scott said. "Don't go in the room. This is something the police have to handle. Where's Ralph?"

"I think he has bronchitis," she said, her expression sour from having been chided. "I don't think he can get out of bed."

To my surprise, the door to Jessie's room suddenly eased open and Jessie took a half step into the hall, squinting as her eyes adjusted to the light. She was all bundled up in the white terrycloth bathrobe.

"What's going on?" she asked. From the groggy expression on her face, it appeared she had just woken up. Hmmm, I thought. Why hadn't she been in Scott's room like the night before?

"Devon is dead," Scott and I both said in unison.

Jessie's hand flew to her mouth in shock.

"Look, this is going to be a long night," Scott announced to all of us. "Sandy, why don't you go over to the big barn and put on some coffee. We can all hang there. I'm going to wake up Cap—and Christian. They both need to know what's going on. As for the others, there seems no point in getting them up until later."

"I have to get dressed first," Jessie said. She flashed me a look that I couldn't read and retreated back into her room. Sandy and Laura headed toward the stairs.

I told Scott that I would get dressed too, and then meet him shortly.

"But before you go, Scott," I said, "I think it would be a good idea to lock the room."

He looked off, thinking for a second. "Okay, that's probably smart," he said. He called out to Sandy, who was just a couple of steps down the stairs, to throw him her house keys. Dutifully she drew a ring of keys from the pocket of her parka, but there was a begrudging expression on her face as she walked back and handed them to Scott. He locked the door and stuffed the keys in the pocket of his pants, where they created a jagged-looking bulge.

Back inside my room, I dug a pair of jeans out of my duffel bag and slipped them on with a turtleneck sweater. I was relieved to have a few minutes to myself.

Already people were popping out of doorways as if they were actors in a British farce, and things were only going to get crazier as the night wore on. I needed a few moments to process everything that had transpired.

According to Laura, Devon had called extension seven for water, saying she didn't feel well enough to get up. Whatever had killed her—whether it was a heart attack due to an eating disorder or some combination of drugs and alcohol—may have already begun to take hold. But I kept coming back to what I'd witnessed earlier: Devon freaking out in the forest. Devon feeling in danger.

What really mystified me was the second call Laura had received. Laura had assumed it was from Devon, but that wasn't possible. So why would someone else be phoning the help in the middle of the night?

No matter what had really occurred, this was going to be a huge story—and before long I would need to wake Nash Nolan, the editor in chief of *Buzz*, who would want to break the story online as soon as possible. But I had to talk to the police first. I'd landed in hot water earlier in the fall for filing a story *before* sharing key info with the cops, and I wasn't going to make that mistake again.

I also felt a huge urge to call Beau. I was feeling a bit shell-shocked over Devon's death, and it would be good to talk to him about what had happened. But it was one o'clock Arizona time, and he would surely be in bed by now.

A moment later, I knocked on Jessie's door. She'd thrown on a pair of cargo pants and a brown sweater.

"Thank God it's you," she exclaimed as she opened the door. "Tell me what happened. Did she OD or something?"

I shared the sequence of events and the guesses I'd made about cause of death.

"How horrible," she said. "There wasn't one single thing I liked about the woman, but that doesn't mean I'm happy she's dead."

"Can I be blunt here? What were you doing in your own room tonight?"

"Oh, God," she groaned. "You don't want to know."

"Lovers' quarrel?"

"I wish. I'm almost too embarrassed to say. It actually has something to do with *you*."

"*What*? Tell me."

"Well, everyone else had gone to bed, and we started making out on the couch. There I was, expecting another night like the previous one. And then—with my boob in his hand—he says . . . oh shit, I can hardly stand to say it. He said, 'Wouldn't it be fun if *Bailey* joined us.'"

"Oh, jeez." I groaned. "Was there any chance he was kidding?"

"Well, at first I thought it was just his idea of a joke—he'd had a fair amount to drink. But then he starts whispering about how he'd love to please both of us at the same time. I wanted to cry. No offense, of course. You know you're hot, Bailey, but I can't believe he had the gall to suggest a threesome. I just stood up and marched back to my room."

"Oh Jessie, I'm sorry. You must feel awful."

"Miserable. I really liked the guy—and what's worse, I *slept* with him. My number is already higher than I'd like, and now I've wasted a slot on a total asshole."

"Are you going to feel uncomfortable going up for coffee?"

"Yes—but it beats staying in my room knowing there's a dead body a few yards away. Speaking of which, what do we do about *Buzz*? Shouldn't we be phoning this in? Dead celeb sort of falls under your jurisdiction."

"I'm planning to call Nash, but I need to wait until the police have had a chance to talk to me. I was in the room, and it's my obligation to speak to them first."

The smell of freshly brewed coffee greeted us as we entered the living area. Sandy was bustling nervously at the kitchen counter while Scott, Jane, and

Cap huddled at the island. Laura Ash was sitting alone at the dining table, appearing glum as all get-out. And a solemn-looking Whitney was on one of the couches, working a pair of knitting needles and a fat ball of yarn.

"Is there anything I can do?" I asked, approaching the group by the island as Jessie slunk off toward a couch. Cap's face was pinched in despair. If he *had* been having an affair with Devon, this experience was a helluva lot worse than simply losing a longtime client.

"We're trying to put a statement together," Cap said. "We'd like a few minutes alone, if you don't mind."

Trying not to look thrown by the snub, I quickly poured a cup of coffee and joined Whitney and Jessie on the couch.

"This must be awful for Cap," I said softly to Whitney.

"For both of us," she said above the steady clicking of her silver needles. "Devon's been Cap's client for seven years. I just pray to God she didn't suffer."

"Did she have any health problems that you were aware of?"

"*Health* problems?" Whitney sniffed. "She was only thirty-four. What health problems could she possibly have had?"

"Anorexia. Or bulimia. Some kind of eating disorder."

"Devon *had* struggled with weight issues in the past, but she managed to put that behind her. Though I'm sure that will all be dragged out again in your magazine and places like that. This may sound horribly old-fashioned, but where I come from, we still believe that if you can't say anything nice about someone, don't say anything at all."

I wondered if she also believed in unicorns.

"As I told Scott, we're off the record here," I said. "This is a tough situation, and Jessie and I want to help in any way."

"There's just so much to do right now," Whitney said. "A statement to the press, funeral arrangements, a memorial service in New York possibly—and here we are, snowbound."

"Was Jane able to reach Devon's mother?" I asked.

"Yes, but she apparently wasn't sober, and Jane's not sure how much she actually digested. If I had my phone with me, I'd call her myself. I just dread going back to the room alone."

"Here, use my BlackBerry," I said, handing it to her in the hope she'd see that I wasn't the enemy.

"Thanks," she said, accepting it. She stared at it for a moment, then shook her head and handed it back.

"What am I thinking?" she said. "The number's on my phone. And it's probably best for Cap to make the call anyway."

Scott drifted over a moment later and announced that he had made an executive decision to wake the others and fill them in. Within the next fifteen minutes, Richard, Tommy, and Tory joined us in the great room. Everyone appeared stunned, but there weren't any tears. From the corner of my eye I watched Richard pour coffee and sink back with his cup into one of the leather armchairs. I was dying to know what was racing through his mind beneath the wild tufts of bed-head hair. He was a reporter too. Surely he was wondering who he should give the story to.

For the next hour and a half we waited, with people sometimes drifting in and out of the room. Finally, at around 5:00 a.m., we heard the sound of a gunned motor, a vehicle forcing its way through the snow on the driveway. Scott rose to go downstairs, and I followed him. He turned once in surprise but didn't question my presence.

Before anyone could knock, Scott flung open the double doors. Two plainclothes cops were standing in the cold, their coats dusted with snowflakes. They stepped inside and introduced themselves. Detective Ray was a short, beer-gutted guy of about fifty, with a silver skunk streak in his hair. Detective Collinson was tall, slim, and in his midthirties, I guessed. He was what my mother called black Irish—dark hair, charcoal black eyes, and very white skin, in his case almost Draculean. There was a swollen quality to his face, as if he were on steroids for some kind of health ailment. It was clear after a moment that Collinson, the younger one, was the man in charge.

Scott explained very quickly what had happened. He presented himself as open, eager to cooperate, but at the same time firmly in charge and not at all obsequious. I would have been impressed except I kept remembering that hours earlier he'd suggested to Jessie that he wanted to add me to his personal spank bank. When he finished talking, I briefly offered my portion of the story, describing how I'd been woken by Laura and had gone into Devon's room to investigate.

Natch, the cops wanted to see the body right away. We accompanied them to the small barn, and when we reached Devon's room, Scott unlocked the door. While the cops entered the room, Scott and I stood silently in the hall cooling our heels, not making eye contact. The police emerged about ten minutes later.

"Where is this Laura Ash now?" Collinson asked.

Scott informed them that she was back with the others, and Collinson said he would like to speak to her in private, and then to Scott and me in that order. The other guests could be interviewed randomly once the police were finished with us. Scott suggested using his study on the ground floor of the bigger barn. Devon's bedroom was relocked before we left.

Laura was questioned for about ten minutes, and when she came back upstairs, she appeared totally stricken, as if she'd just turned over critical info about a mob boss. I wondered if there was something Laura hadn't told me or whether she was being eaten up by guilt for not having delivered the water when Devon initially called her. Scott's interview lasted about twenty minutes, and then it was my turn.

"You've been up since before three," Collinson said to me, gesturing toward a chair. "You must be awfully tired by this point. I appreciate your cooperation."

I had dealt with more than a few local police over the years, and most seemed to overcompensate for their small jurisdictions by acting fairly gruff or bossy. This dude was different. His soft-spoken approach was a real departure. But I told myself to be careful. For all I knew, his easy style was simply a way to lower someone's guard.

"I'm on my fifth cup of coffee, so I'm awake enough," I said. "Before we start, it's only fair for me to point out that I'm a journalist. I cover celebrity crime for *Buzz* magazine—and this will definitely be something I'm expected to report on. But I haven't done anything yet. I want to first help in the investigation."

Collinson eyed me silently for a moment. Ray blinked and squeezed his eyes shut for a beat or two. It was a weird little tic he had.

"Thank you for your candor," Collinson said finally. "Now why don't you take us through what happened again, but this time step by step."

I did as he said, leaving nothing out—except of course Scott's request to take Jessie and me to pleasure heaven at the same time. Just in case Laura hadn't been a hundred percent forthcoming, I mentioned the time gap in Laura's response to the phone call from Devon as well as the mystery call—though from Collinson's blank expression, I had no way of telling whether this was new info or not. I also recounted my brief conversation at the edge of the woods with Devon Saturday morning. This, of course, *was* new, and he sat up straighter.

"That was all she said?" he asked. "Nothing specific?"

"No, nothing specific—and she seemed fine a short time later. But she definitely looked rattled in the woods."

"Was anyone using drugs here tonight?"

Aha. He might look mild-mannered, but he wasn't going to pull any punches with his questions.

"Not that I'm aware of," I said. I added, though, that Devon had appeared to be buzzed when she left for bed.

"Any theories then about what might have happened to Ms. Barr?"

"I thought of drugs, too, but I also wondered if she might have died as a result of complications from an eating disorder. She seemed very thin. And as you saw, there was the bottle of ipecac in the bathroom—the stuff used to induce vomiting."

Slowly Collinson turned his gaze toward Ray, who blinked hard and then shook his head.

"There was nothing like that in the bathroom," Ray said. "Nothing like that at all."

5

The first thought that flew through my mind—
and it wasn't a very nice one—was that maybe
Detective Ray had blinked too long and missed it. Then
I wondered if he might have mistaken the small bottle
for some kind of beauty potion.

"I'm positive it was there," I told the two men. "Do
you want me to show you?"

"Yes, please," Collinson said bluntly.

Back we went to the guest quarters. The sky was
faint with color now, as if someone were shining a
flashlight through a burlap sack. I could see that it was
still snowing. How would we all make it out of here
today? I wondered.

Collinson unlocked the door to Devon's room with
the keys Scott had obviously turned over to him and

motioned for me to enter. After leading me past the bed, he asked me to examine the bathroom, and without *touching* anything, point to where the ipecac had been.

"Someone's taken it," I said, shocked. "Someone managed to get into the room and remove it."

"Why do you think someone would do that?" Collinson asked evenly.

"I haven't any idea," I told him. "Maybe—I don't know, maybe to protect Devon's reputation? So it wouldn't come out that she was bulimic."

He ushered me back into the bedroom.

"The bathroom light was off when Detective Ray and I entered the room earlier. How then did you happen to see the bottle?"

My mind raced as I deliberated whether I should try to fudge my answer just to protect my butt—but I decided against it. I'd had my butt singed before from being less than forthcoming with cops.

"I looked in the bathroom when I found Devon's body," I said. "I thought it might be helpful to see if she'd taken any drugs."

"Helpful to you as a reporter?" he asked.

See, I'd been smart not to underestimate him.

"Yes, partly," I conceded. "But mainly I just wanted to know what was going on. At least we now know that someone with sticky fingers has been sneaking around."

"All right, Miss Weggins, you can go back with the others," Collinson said. "We will join you in a few minutes."

When I reached the great room, everyone looked up but no one said anything. I poured yet another cup of coffee in the kitchen area and motioned with a look for Jessie to join me at the island. As she made her way over, Detective Ray appeared at the top of the stairs and asked Scott to return to the study. I figured the cops wanted to chat with him about how someone had managed to slip into Devon's locked bedroom.

"You okay?" I whispered to Jessie when she reached me.

"Yeah, but this is so freaky," she said anxiously. "Am I going to be *interrogated*?"

"There's nothing to worry about. Just tell them what you know—and you and I will catch up later."

"This whole weekend has turned into a nightmare," she said. "The only good news is that Nash is going to kiss our asses for being at the scene. When are you going to call it in?"

"In just a bit. I want to keep my eye on what's going on here for a while."

As I sipped my coffee at the counter, I mulled over the missing ipecac. The person who had taken it would have needed a key, and Scott came immediately to mind—he had pocketed Sandy's keys after using them. At one point while we'd been waiting, he and Sandy had donned coats and gone across to the cabin to check on Ralph and then returned separately. That would have offered him the chance to stop by Devon's room. But why would it matter to him if the world learned she'd used something to make her puke after meals? He might have had a vested interest in protecting Devon's reputation when she was alive, but now that she was dead, the fact that she'd been bulimic probably wouldn't matter.

If it wasn't Scott who had done it, then who else could have had access to the room? Somewhere on the premises there had to be another set of keys.

As soon as Scott returned from his second round of questioning, Detective Ray called Jane's name and she trudged down the stairs. Scott walked over to the refrigerator, pulled out a carton of orange juice, and filled a glass.

"Can I talk to you privately?" I said after walking over to where he was standing.

"Okay," he said without enthusiasm. With me following, he edged over to a corner of the room.

"I assume the police asked you how someone might have gained access to Devon's locked bedroom," I said, when we were out of earshot of the others.

"How do you know *that*?" he asked.

"Because when I found the body, I saw something in the room that isn't there anymore—and I told them about it. It was a bottle of ipecac syrup."

"Ipe—*what*?"

"Ipecac. It's a liquid used to induce vomiting. Did you take it from her room?"

"I can't believe you're asking that. Of course not. I never went back in there."

"But someone did. How do you think they got in?"

"Shit," he said suddenly, and his eyes flashed with recognition. "I bet I know how they did it. I had Sandy's keys in my pocket, but they kept jabbing into my leg, so I took them out and laid them on the counter by the stove. I picked them back up when the cops arrived because I was going to have to let them into Devon's room. Someone must have swiped them for a while and then returned them to the counter."

I looked off, thinking. Though people had hung in the great room until the police arrived, mostly everyone had slipped out at some point for a few minutes. Jane had returned to her room for the phone numbers of people that had to be on the initial contact list Cap was putting together—and later I had overheard Christian say he was going back to *his* room for his cell phone in case he needed it. Whitney had set down her knitting needles about an hour into our wait and said she was going to take a shower. Cap had walked her back and returned. Tommy had announced the need for a cigarette and disappeared outside. Richard had made a point of saying he was heading downstairs to the loo, and he'd been gone for a good ten minutes. From what I could recall, Tory was the only one who had stayed put, falling asleep for a stretch on one of the sofas. Any one of the others could have snuck the keys into their pocket and let themselves into Devon's room.

"But look, maybe it's not that big a deal," Scott said. "Cap or Christian could have taken the ipecac just so the press would have less to trash Devon about."

"*Was* Devon bulimic?"

"I'm only going to talk to you if you guarantee that we are totally off the record."

"I told you we were. You have my word."

"It's pretty clear there was something fucked up about her eating this weekend."

"Was that a problem for you—the fact that she might have an eating disorder?"

"Look, I've had artists who were *heroin* addicts or alleged rapists. I'm not in the business of passing judgment."

"Let me shift direction for a second. Was there any reason that you know of for Devon to be frightened this weekend?"

"*Frightened?* What are you talking about?"

I described what Devon had said to me by the woods. Scott shook his head in disbelief, but he appeared agitated by the news.

"You're making it sound like *The Hound of the Baskervilles* up here, for God's sake. What could have possibly frightened her other than a few field mice running along the wall?"

"That's what I'm asking you. She said someone *knew* something."

He sighed and combed a hand through his hair.

"I haven't a clue what it could have been," he said. "As far as I know, she was just being a diva—making it up so someone would take her back to New York." He tugged at his ear and snickered. "Though if she'd gone back early, it might have foiled her brilliant little master plan."

"What master plan is that?"

"You saw the intense eye-fucking going on between Devon and Tommy. I'm pretty sure she wanted him back, and that was the main reason she invited him and Tory up here."

"What was her history with Tommy, anyway?"

"I don't know all the sordid details, but from what I've heard they were hot and heavy last winter, and then sometime this summer he dumped her. They apparently stayed on decent terms, though, and she was the one who set him up with Tory. I like a mix of guests on the weekends, and I was happy to invite some of Devon's entourage, but I had the last bedroom earmarked for a pal of mine. Until Devon insisted that I include Tory and Tommy."

"And you really think she was trying to steal Tommy back?"

"It seemed pretty obvious to me. She was trying to bewitch him—with the bare breasts and cocky attitude. But most of all by having him hear that voice of hers."

"Was Devon supposed to be pretty good friends with Tory?"

"I guess. Though how tight can you be with someone who thinks that the ozone is something you find yourself in right before you have an orgasm? Look, not that it isn't fabulous chatting with you, but I've got my hands full at the moment."

"Just one more question. What's the latest on the road? Are we going to be able to make it out of here today?" With every inch of snow that fell, the sinking feeling in my tummy was growing worse. I didn't want to get stuck indefinitely in the barns from hell.

"That's what I'm going to take care of now. Ralph is too ill to plow, and I need to find a guy who can."

As he wandered off, I pulled Jessie aside again.

"I'm going to call Nash now," I told her. "Keep an eye out here, okay? Something kind of weird is going on. I'll tell you more later."

Before I could leave, Jane came trudging up the stairs and made a beeline for the muffin basket. I put my plan momentarily on hold and moved toward the island myself, pretending to survey the food. Jane had clearly taken a few swipes at her hair with a brush since I'd last seen her, but she looked just as grumpy—and her face had an unappealing shine to it, which seemed incongruous on such a cold, snowy morning.

"Did you survive your talk with the cops?" I asked, trying to sound collegial but not overeager.

"There was nothing to survive," she said. "They asked some questions I didn't know the answers to, and I told them so. I have no idea in the world why Devon suddenly dropped dead."

She plucked a blueberry muffin from the basket and buttered it. It was clear I was going to have a tough time prying info from her, and I decided it might be smart to warm her up a little bit first.

"It must be tough for you today," I said, "having to deal with all this. . . ."

"Spare me the Dr. Phil routine, will you?" she said, her mouth still partially stuffed with muffin. "I'm not going to pretend to get all emo over Devon."

Okay, fake empathy wasn't working. Time to try a little trash talking.

"I take it working for Devon wasn't any picnic. How long have you been doing it?"

"Nine fabulous months."

"How did you end up being her assistant? It's not exactly the kind of job—"

"You'd expect a fatty to be doing?" she asked.

"No. The kind of job someone just stumbles into."

"A girl I know told me about it. The longest Devon had ever had an assistant was like six months. She didn't *hit* the help—like Naomi Campbell does—but she was a real uber bitch."

"How did you manage to survive so long?"

She snorted and took another bite of muffin. This time she waited until she swallowed before answering.

"It's simple," she said finally. "I stayed 'cause of the money. She paid combat wages. I made major overtime from driving her up here this weekend. And the reason she never fired me is because she liked having me around. She'd never had anyone in her life who she felt *this* superior to."

She set the muffin down and eyed the basket for another as if blueberries had lost their magic for her.

"Are we about done?" she asked, glancing back at me with almost a glare. "I'm not used to getting up at three, and I'm not really in the mood to talk."

I decided to try one more tack: Get straight to the point.

"Did you go into Devon's room tonight?"

"What are you talking about?"

"Just what I said. Did you go into Devon's room after you learned she was dead—and remove something?"

"You mean like the cash from her wallet? That's a pretty nervy thing to ask."

"No. A bottle of ipecac."

I could tell from the look in her eyes she knew exactly what that was, and I wasn't going to get any "Ipe-*what*?" line from her.

"Why would I do *that*?" she asked.

"So that no one would know she was bulimic."

"I couldn't care less what people think of Devon Barr."

"Did she have an eating disorder?"

"I assume this is going directly into *Buzz* magazine?"

"I would use it just as background."

"She might have," she said, shrugging. "A month or so ago I started noticing that she didn't seem to be eating very much. Unless you count green tea, bottled water, and the flecks at the bottom of the Special K box."

"Last night she called Laura, one of the girls who helped at dinner, and said she wasn't feeling well. Were you aware of that?"

"Why would I be aware of that? I assisted the woman. I didn't *sleep* with her."

"So you never checked in on her last night after you left here."

"No."

"Did you ever call extension seven during the night?"

"What? This is getting ridiculous. Do you mind if I eat my breakfast in peace?"

"I'm almost done. Devon told me she was frightened up here. Do you know why?"

Her brown eyes widened, curious.

"No," she said. "What was the reason?"

"She wouldn't tell me. After a minute she just clammed up."

Jane shrugged. "Maybe it was like a *Twilight Zone* episode," she said. "She took a look in the mirror one day and saw the real her. That would have been *really* frightening."

She plucked another muffin, this one corn, and after plopping it on a plate, headed over toward one of the sofas. There were other people I wanted to talk to, but it was time to get Nash on the phone and fill him in on what had happened.

I hurried back to my room, squinting in the passageway from the emerging daylight. To my surprise the snow had turned to a steady rain that streaked and fogged the windows. Hopefully it was warming up, and some of the snow on the road would melt away.

Back in my room, I called Nash's cell. Though he was used to being phoned at all hours—particularly with celeb DWIs—he answered groggily.

"Give yourself a minute to wake up," I told him. "Because I've got big news."

"Christ, that *is* big," he said after I'd taken him through everything. "How soon can you get me something?"

"I have my laptop with me, and it shouldn't take me more than thirty minutes to write something up and e-mail you. Then I'll file reports as things progress."

"Where are you exactly, anyway?"

"About two hours north of the city. The one fly in the ointment is that it's been snowing like crazy. On the one hand it's a good thing because I want to talk to people here—and they're stranded. But eventually Jessie and I need to find our way back to Manhattan. It's a little bit like *The Shining* up here."

He told me that he'd be pulling staff into the office to dig background for the story and begin producing the obligatory sidebars on the life and times of Devon Barr.

"See if you can find anything about her having an eating disorder," I said. "I think it could have played a role in her death."

I needed to start writing stat, but there was one thing I had to take care of first: let Cap know I was now filing the story. Plenty of reporters I knew at *Buzz* would just go ahead and deal later with any flak that resulted from all the people who'd been bruised in the process. But I never liked to play things that way. It's not that I'm such a goody-two-shoes, but in the long run people treat you better if you've been fair with them. I would need Cap as I pursued this story, and I wanted to alert him to the fact that within the next hour the *Buzz* Web site would be announcing the death of Devon Barr.

There turned out to be no need to go all the way back to the other barn. As I came down the stairs into the first-floor foyer, Cap was just emerging from the passageway.

"How are you doing?" I said. "This must be really devastating for you."

"Yes," he answered grimly. "It is."

"Do you have a few minutes? I'd like to talk to you."

"Actually I don't. I need to retrieve some papers from my room."

"How about later then?"

"I don't really think it would be very smart of me to talk to you."

"I'll be straight with you," I said. "I *do* have to file this story. It'll be live on the Web site before long, and it will most likely be the cover story of the magazine on Thursday. So wouldn't it be better for you to have control over the information that gets out there? Plus, I promise you, I won't sandbag you in any way. I'll keep you abreast of what I'm doing."

He shook his head in despair.

"Let me think about it," he said and moved off.

If Devon had been his lover, this had to be eating him up. Yet there was something else to consider. If the autopsy indicated foul play and he *had* been her lover, that would make him a prime suspect. I wondered if I should have told the police about the conversation I'd overheard between the two of them—Devon demanding that he would "have to tell her"—but I didn't like the idea of making trouble for him unnecessarily. If the death was ruled a homicide, I could always inform the cops later.

I reentered my room and headed for the small antique desk near the window. Stretching my arms out, I plopped down at the desk. My laptop was already set up there, since I'd planned to do a little research for upcoming articles. I started to open a file, and then I realized something was out of whack. My laptop wasn't in the same spot it had been in earlier. I like to rest my arms directly in front of it, so I generally leave about four or five inches between the computer and the edge of the desk But now my laptop was right up to the very edge of the desk—as if someone had pulled it closer.

I caught a breath and instinctively looked behind me. There was no one there, of course, but I knew that someone had been in my room. And it wasn't necessarily the person who had taken Scott's keys. Jessie and I hadn't been given keys, so my room had never been locked. Anyone could have gained entrance.

I jumped up from the desk and made a quick sweep of the room. Nothing was missing, and nothing else seemed disturbed. What could the person have wanted? And why check out my computer? To see what I was writing or whether I'd e-mailed *Buzz*?

I couldn't afford to dwell on it at the moment. I needed to write and file my story. I dashed out something fast, hitting all the high points. Devon Barr had died during the night at the weekend home of music mogul Scott Cohen. Cause of death still undetermined. The police were on the premises interviewing the houseguests. I listed who they were. I reread it twice and then e-mailed it to Nash and the deputy editor I generally reported to.

After I sent my story, I went on the Internet and did a quick search about eating disorders. I was surprised to see that they were fatal in up to 20 percent of cases. Most frequently in those cases the lack of vital nutrients caused heart arrhythmia, which led to a heart attack and death.

There was plenty more to read, but I wanted to return to the great room to see what was going on. I splashed cold water on my face just to revive myself, and then left my room. Just as I started toward the stairs, Jessie came bounding up them.

"I know I'm supposed to be standing guard, but I wanted to check in. Did you talk to Nash?"

"Yes, and I filed a story. You've had your interview with the cops?"

"Yup—and it was so freaky. I had to fight the urge to confess that I cheated once on an AP history test."

"What did they ask you?"

"Did I observe anything unusual with Devon this weekend? Did I hear anything during the night? And were people using drugs this weekend? I answered no, no, and no. I can't believe how *pale* the head cop is. I wonder if anyone's checked his platelet count lately."

"What's going on with all our guests at the moment?"

"Richard is drinking secret Bloody Marys—I caught him pouring a shot of vodka into his tomato juice. And after Tommy was done with his interview, he threatened to leave with Tory until someone convinced him that he'd never get four feet down the road in his Jag."

"I'm going back over there now, so if you need a break, go for it," I said.

"Thanks, I may take a short catnap and then I'll be back to help eavesdrop. You mentioned that something weird was going on. What did you mean?"

I told her about the missing ipecac and my suspicions about someone being in my room. As I'd anticipated, the last bit of news rattled her.

"Crap—there's a dead body across the hall from me, and someone's sneaking into people's bedrooms. You know those horror movies where you want to shout, 'Get out of the house!' at the screen? I'm starting to sense that *somewhere*, someone is shouting that at us."

"Don't worry," I said. "You can lock your door when you're in your room, and the cops have the keys now."

"And how long are we supposed to stick around here for?"

"Since I'm covering this, it'll be good to hang here for a while at least. And even if we wanted to leave, we might not be able to. For right now at least, the weather has us trapped."

As I began to descend the stairs, I heard a commotion on the floor below. I scurried down. A team of two men and two women—with water dripping in rivulets off their jackets—had just trudged into the foyer behind Detective Collinson. I figured they were either from the coroner's office or members of the crime scene unit or a combination of both. Each one of them eyed me curiously, and then proceeded up the stairs. I stood at the bottom of the stairs listening for a moment. Once they entered Devon's room, I couldn't hear what they were saying.

I returned to the great room, which turned out to be empty now. The group had obviously splintered after the police interviews, with people returning to their rooms. Unless I went knocking on doors, I wasn't going to be able to talk to anyone.

When I reentered the small barn, I found Scott and Sandy standing just outside the door of a small walk-in storage area in the foyer. The door of the closet was made of barn wood, and it was flush to the wall, so I hadn't even known it was there before. The expressions on their faces suggested that something wasn't right.

"What's up?" I asked.

"There's a set of keys missing," Scott announced. "The backup set to all the guest bedrooms."

"You're sure?" I asked Sandy.

"Absolutely," she said. "I saw them there last night when I was getting supplies. And there was no reason for me to touch them. I've got my own set."

"I'd assumed whoever went back into Devon's room used the set on the counter," Scott said. "But this is obviously how it was done."

I'd noticed the night before that there were no bolts on the inside of the bedroom doors, just buttons on the knobs. It also meant that whoever had the keys could gain access to our rooms when we were sleeping and the doors were locked.

6

"**Y**ou need to tell the police about this," I told Scott. "Something's not kosher here."

He sighed. "All right, I'll tell Collinson when we meet again." He headed off, with Sandy in tow. When I reached the top of the stairs a minute later, I saw that Devon's door was partially open and I could hear people moving around in there.

Back in my bedroom I checked out the *Buzz* Web site. My story was up. I also saw that the statement Scott and Cap had been working on had been released and incorporated.

I filed a brief update for *Buzz*, saying that Devon's body was being examined and police were going over her room—other than that, there wasn't much to say. I'd no sooner hit Send than one of the deputy editors called me on my cell to discuss coverage. She sounded more ornery than usual, probably from having been called into the office on Sunday.

"Why haven't you included quotes from any of the houseguests?" she demanded.

"I'm keeping it all off the record up here," I told her.

"*What?*" she barked.

"No one would give me a direct quote anyway," I said patiently. "And if I don't keep things off the record, people will stonewall me. This way I'm getting lots of info for background."

"But you—"

"I have to go," I said, cutting her off. For a woman whose greatest professional success up until now had been being called a whore by Snooki, she had a lot of nerve complaining about how I put a story together.

I checked my watch. I was dying to talk to Beau, and now would be a decent time to call him. I tried his cell, but there was no answer. I realized that he might be headed to the airport or already on the plane.

I kicked off my boots, collapsed into the armchair by the window, and propped my feet up on the ottoman. I needed a few moments to clear my head and just think. Devon's death, regardless of the cause, was unsettling, but that wasn't all that was bothering me. Like I'd told Jessie, there was something weird going on. Whoever had taken the keys and then pinched the ipecac from Devon's bathroom had decided that the truth shouldn't come out. *Why?*

And then there was the mystery call to extension seven. That continued to bug me.

After a while of trying to chill, I tugged my boots back on and made my way to the great room. There were certain people I was hoping to extract info from, and I figured the group might start to congregate again in anticipation of lunch. In the passageway I saw that the rain had morphed into a light drizzle. It was foggy out, almost steamy, obviously from the effect of the rain hitting the cold snow. I wondered what luck, if any, Scott was having locating a plowman. Or if the police were assisting in this mission.

The only person there turned out to be Richard. He was on the couch reading his iPad, a pair of tortoiseshell reading glasses perched midway down his nose. He'd clearly just showered because his hair was still damp around the edges, slicked back on both sides, and he smelled of talc. On the table in front of him was a large glass of tomato juice with a celery stalk sticking out of the top. Still into the Bloodies, it appeared.

"You certainly don't disappoint, Ms. Weggins," he announced cockily when he saw me.

"In what regard?" I asked, pouring a cup of coffee.

"Your story is already up on the *Buzz* Web site. You've beaten everyone to the punch."

"Cap and Scott knew it was being filed. I was straight with them."

"I'm sure you were. It's amazing, isn't it, though? You so often seem to be around when a dead body turns up."

"I guess I'm just a lucky girl," I said.

"Whatever the reason, I'd be a little careful if I were you."

"And why is that?" I asked, taking a seat in an armchair across from him. His provocative banter on the walk yesterday had been fun, but today it seemed slicked with meanness. I wondered if it reflected the number of Bloody Marys he'd consumed so far today.

"The police are always suspicious of too many coincidences," he said. "Coincidences, you see, have a nasty habit of calling *attention* to something."

"Ahh, good point," I said. "Do you think I might be a psychopathic killer and not even know it?"

"Or just a ruthless opportunist," he said, faking a smile.

I didn't like his tone one bit, but I wasn't going to get all pissy about it. I needed to be on his good side so he'd talk to me.

"Why not file a story yourself? Don't you have a blog on the *Huffington Post* or someplace like that?"

"I've decided to go the more traditional route on this one. I'll probably do a more in-depth story for *Vanity Fair.*"

"I look forward to reading it. How was your interview with the police, by the way?"

"Mercifully brief," he said. "There was really nothing for me to contribute. I did get the feeling, though, that the police are considering foul play. You saw the body—what do *you* think?"

"There was no sign of that, from what I could see. Off the record, I'm thinking that her death might be connected to an eating disorder. She wouldn't be the first model who died from one."

He stared at me for a moment, not saying anything.

"Well, let's face it," he said finally. "The only thing she ever did with her food was rearrange it on her plate. It was like watching someone play three-card monte. One minute the green beans are here, and the next minute they're over there."

So Richard had observed that, too. "It might have caught up with her this weekend," I said.

"Well, she never seemed ill, if that's what you mean. Bored, yes—unless Tommy was around to lock eyes with—and a tad tipsy last night."

That was possibly the best example in history of the pot calling the kettle black.

"Do you think there was anything going on between Devon and him?" I asked. "Or was it just for show?" I suddenly remembered something Richard had said at breakfast the day before. "I mean, you mentioned yesterday that you'd heard people scurrying around in the hallway during the night. Maybe they reconnected."

"Haven't a clue, since I never opened my door. She did seem to come and go a lot, always disappearing. She may have just been sneaking off for a ciggie all those times. You know how models love to smoke."

"Do they? I wouldn't know."

He shrugged his shoulders irritatedly, as if my cluelessness annoyed him. "You just have to look at the paparazzi shots. Kate Moss is always waving a cigarette."

He checked his watch suddenly, an obvious gesture of wanting to be done with our conversation. He stuck his reading glasses in the V of his sweater, flipped over the cover of his iPad, and rose to leave. Had I done something to make him so eager to exit?

"You'll excuse me, won't you, Bailey? I've got to go cancel my dinner plans for tonight."

"Do you have an update on the road?"

"Our lovely hostess Sandy informs me that a plow is headed this way. But I'd been planning to be back in the city by five, and there's no way that's going to happen."

"One question before you go. Did you, by any chance, call extension seven last night? Just before two thirty?" I was tipping my hand, but I needed to know if he was the caller.

He paused midmovement. By the expression in his red-rimmed eyes, I could tell that the question greatly intrigued him.

"Ahhh, is this an important clue you're giving me a hint to?"

"Not really a clue of any kind. As you may have heard, Devon called that girl Laura for water during the night. About an hour and a half later the phone rang again, but no one was there. Devon was dead by then."

"I'm afraid I can't help you. Now if you'll excuse me."

What next, I wondered? I needed more answers, but there wasn't a soul in sight. People were obviously in their rooms, catching up on sleep or praying for the plow to arrive.

When I reached the foyer downstairs, planning to return to my room yet again, I noticed that several rain ponchos had been hung on a row of pegs on the wall. Having viewed the weather only from windows over the past twelve hours, I decided to grab a poncho and head out to the deck.

It looked surreal outside, like a scene from a movie about a planet in a distant galaxy. Fog rose from the ground in patches all through the woods, as if there were smoldering brush fires. It had stopped raining, and the temperature seemed to have dropped again.

I took three steps out onto the deck and jerked in surprise when I spotted Tommy in the far right corner, the same spot where Cap and Devon had stood late Friday night. He was jacketless, a cigarette dangling from the corner of his mouth and a cell phone to his ear. It couldn't have been a private call because he didn't bother to lower his voice when he spotted me.

"Fuck it, man," I heard him say. "I'm not going to do that. So just fuck it."

The person on the other end must have offered a plea on his or her behalf, because Tommy listened for a bit, his face pinched.

"Like I said, fuck it," he said finally. "I'll talk to you later."

He flicked the cigarette over the rail of the deck and dropped the phone into the pocket of the oversize white shirt he wore above jeans so tight the only thing left to the imagination was genital skin tone.

"Hi," I said, walking toward him. "You want a poncho? There's a bunch of them inside."

"Why would I want a poncho? It stopped raining."

Okaaay.

"How you doing?" I said, trying again. "This must be pretty upsetting."

"Ya think?"

I wasn't sure what to try next. He seemed to be making it clear he didn't want to talk to me. But then he leaned back against the wet wooden rail of the deck and looked at me intently, as if we were two people who had things to say to each other.

"Devon was my lady for six freakin' months, you know," he said. "We weren't an item anymore, but we were—I don't know, connected still on some cosmic level."

"Why did you break up?"

He shrugged. "I got a little distracted on my summer tour, if you know what I mean. That didn't sit well with her at all. I couldn't stand the nagging, so I took a powder."

"And now you're with Tory?"

"Yeah. For now. My IQ is shrinking just being with that bitch."

"Any guesses about how Devon died?"

"Nope. She was as fit as a horse as far as I knew."

That was a stretch, considering she had probably weighed about ninety-five pounds sopping wet.

"I mean, she smoked, she drank," he added, "but she didn't do hard drugs, if that's what you're thinking."

"Was she anorexic or bulimic?"

"A lot of these model chicks are all fucked up about their eating. I brought out a can of Reddiwip once with Tory, just for a little fun, and she practically went insane. I think she thought the calories were gonna be absorbed through her nipples."

"But what about Devon?" I asked, trying not to let a picture form in my mind of Tory and Tommy in the sack with a bunch of sex props. "Was it more than just counting calories?"

"She never did anything on my watch. But from what I hear, it'd been a problem when she first started out. She was younger then—and she had a shitload of pressure on her. Everybody wanted her—she was the biggest model in the world."

"Do you know any reason Devon would have been scared this weekend?"

"*Scared*? What are you talking about?" He stepped closer, and in the harsh light I saw how deep the grooves ran in his skin and the pockmarks from adolescent acne. He had the kind of looks only groupies and models seemed to love.

"I caught her crying in the woods around mid-day yesterday," I explained. "She told me she was frightened—but she didn't say why."

He shrugged, wrestled a butane lighter and pack of Salems out of his jeans pocket, and fired up another cigarette.

"In case you didn't notice, Devon was a bit of a mind fucker," he said, after shooting a razor-thin stream of smoke out of the corner of his mouth. "Maybe she was just playing with you."

"It didn't seem that—"

"I can't help you, then. Like I said, there was still this connection between us, but it's not like we talked anymore."

"I had the feeling this weekend that she might want to restart the relationship—she seemed to be flirting with you."

He snorted, as if I had no clue what I was talking about.

"Didn't you hear me?" he said. "Devon was a master mind fucker. She liked playing with me, just like she liked playing with everyone else. Why're you so interested, anyway? Tory said you're a reporter for one of those tabloid magazines. Shouldn't you be trying to track down some story about a woman giving birth to wolves?"

"I work for a different type of rag than that."

"You good at what you do? You *look* like you'd be good at what you do." He ran his eyes up and down my body, letting them rest on my poncho. If I wasn't careful, he was going to suggest we hunt down a squeeze bottle of Hershey's syrup and spend the afternoon together.

I was thinking it might be just the right moment to take my leave, especially since it had begun to rain again—or make that sleet. Icy slivers of rain were suddenly bearing down on us, stinging my face. As I started to say good-bye, I heard a door nearby bang open. When I turned around, Tory was standing there, wearing only a pale yellow top and black leather leggings. She looked about as friendly as a fer-de-lance.

"You're standing out here, talking to *her*?" she screeched.

"I'm having a fucking cigarette," he snapped.

"But you said you were coming back in five minutes."

"Why don't you just chill, Tory."

"I need you to be with me right now," she said, her teeth chattering from the cold. "I'm going out of my mind in this place."

"You're gonna need Botox if you keep scrunching your face up that way. Why don't you go back to the room, and I'll be there in a minute."

"So you can be with *her*? You wanna fuck her like you wanted to fuck Devon?"

"How could I want anyone else when you're so freakin' brilliant in the sack?"

"I *hate* you," she screamed with a hard, fast shake of her head. In the minute she'd been standing outside, her hair had become coated with sleet, turning it into a shiny black helmet. I decided it was about time to extricate myself from this lover's skirmish, and besides, my feet were now soaked.

Before I could move, Tory turned and stormed back into the barn. Tommy watched the door slam and then moved closer to me, his body dripping wet.

"Why don't we finish this later," he said, though I wasn't sure what exactly we were supposed to finish.

Rather than trail behind them into the foyer and possibly end up in the midst of round two, I descended the short set of wooden steps on the side of the deck and made my way toward the small barn. I pulled the hood of my poncho tighter, since the sleet was practically coming down in sheets now. As I looked up I saw Scott emerge from the direction of the outbuildings. He didn't look like a happy camper.

"Anything up?" I called out.

"More problems with the damn road. I've got a guy out there now, and Ralph is feeling better, so he's gonna help. The problem is, it's starting to freeze again. We've got a layer of ice forming."

"That doesn't sound good."

"Nope. Sandy's putting out lunch now. It should be ready any minute."

He hurried off, and I fought my way through the sleet, headed back to my room. Detective Ray was holding guard outside Devon's door, sitting on the old straight-backed chair I'd seen at the desk in her room. The door was closed, and I assumed the crime scene personnel had departed.

"How's the work going?"

"It's going," was all he said.

"Is Detective Collinson still here?"

"He's returned to town with the coroner."

Before entering my room, I tapped on Jessie's door. She had creases on her left cheek that indicated she'd just finished napping.

"Where the heck have *you* been?" she asked. "You look like you've been out reporting on a hurricane."

"I was just checking out the scene outside." I relayed the bad news that Scott had told me about the road—and told her there was a chance that we might be spending another night on the property.

"Oh, great—though at least that keeps us at the center of the story. I'm on my way back to resume eavesdropping."

I told her that I'd be up shortly, but as she started to leave I reached out and touched her arm.

"One more thing, Jess," I said. I told her about the missing set of keys.

"That's rich," she said ruefully. "It's getting more like a horror movie every second."

Back in my room I checked the Internet to see how the word was spreading about Devon's death. CNN and *People* were running several quotes from Cap, which implied he'd been in touch with them directly. CNN and the *New York Post* also had some very general quotes from Collinson, who said the cause of death had not yet been determined and was under investigation. And TMZ had a mix of quotes from fashionista types paying tribute, and gossipmongers speculating about the cause of death. One theory was a drug overdose.

As I stood up, I felt suddenly overwhelmed with fatigue. I'd had only a couple of hours of sleep the night before and it was now catching up with me. I fell on the bed, telling myself I would grab just a short catnap.

When I woke, my head was throbbing and my mouth was gritty. Staggering toward the bathroom, I checked my watch and was surprised to see the time. 1:14. I'd been asleep for over an hour. I needed to hustle back to the great room and see what was going on.

I opened my door and peeked down the hall. Detective Ray was no longer standing guard, but I saw that Devon's door had been padlocked.

I couldn't believe my eyes as I passed through the passageway. In the gloomy afternoon light the trees glistened, their snow-covered branches now coated in a top layer of ice. Though it was absolutely enchanting out, it meant none of us was probably going anywhere anytime soon.

Jessie and Laura were the only ones around. Laura was clearing away dishes on the counter, and Jessie had her feet up on one of the sofas, reading a book.

"How are you holding up, Laura?" I asked, coming up to her.

"Okay, I guess." She didn't make eye contact with me.

"After we realized Devon was dead and you went to get Scott, you never went back into Devon's room, did you?" I asked.

"No, of course not," she said. "Are you accusing me of something?"

"Someone went back into Devon's room, and I'm anxious to know who it was."

"Well, it wasn't me."

"Okay, fine. Any more thoughts about who the second person to call extension seven was?

"What?" she asked defensively.

"You told me you got a second call on extension seven—at about two thirty."

"If I'd known who it was, I would have told you then."

My, my, she seemed awfully testy.

I picked a sandwich off a platter before Laura whisked it away, and then joined Jessie on the couch.

"Where the hell is everybody?" I whispered. "Are they all holed up in their rooms?"

"Whitney and Cap were up here earlier. They each had a glass of wine and a sandwich and barely said two words. He looks weird, all pinched and stuff. The second detective—the one who was guarding the door—came by for coffee and then left, saying they hope to be back later to pick up the body. Oh, and Scott was up here for a bit. I couldn't even look at him."

"Any word on the road?"

"Not good. It seems like we're all going to be bunking down here again tonight. By the way, at what point does a body begin to stink?"

"By tonight it's going to smell pretty ripe."

"Oh, fabulous."

"I still need to talk to Christian and Tory. I guess I'll wait around here for a while, and then I might have to start banging on a few doors."

"Laura mentioned that Sandy was going to be serving an early dinner—at around six. So people should start to surface then."

For the next few hours, Jessie and I hung in the great room, drinking coffee from an insulated carafe that Jessie had brought over to the coffee table. At around five, with darkness descended, we suddenly heard a burst of noise from the level below, as if three or four people were talking at once. It took me a minute to realize that it was the television in the media room. I went downstairs to check out who was there.

Christian was alone in the darkened room, staring at CNN on the screen.

"You okay?" I asked.

"About as well as can be expected," he said, not taking his eyes off the screen.

"I assume you've spoken to people at the modeling agency, right?"

"Of course. Everybody's in shock—total shock. But I don't know if I should be talking to *you*. You'll just feed it all to *Buzz*."

I gave him the off-the-record line I'd offered everyone else.

"Well, I don't have much to talk about anyway," he said, finally looking at me.

"This must be a blow to the agency."

"Absolutely. Devon was one of our top girls."

"Were you close to her?"

"Of course I was close to her," he said, flicking his hand back and forth over the collar of his tight beige crewneck. "I've been her booker since she was nineteen."

"I thought she started even younger than that."

"She did—she was with another agency the first couple of years, but I convinced her to come with us."

"Is that common, to make a switch?"

"It can be. Contracts in this business are never iron-clad. I mean, Devon was grateful to her old place. One of their scouts had spotted her in a bus station when she was sixteen. But they never saw her full potential. I don't believe in starting at the bottom and working your way up. I think you start at the top, and if it doesn't work, you keep going down a level and find out where it settles. From the very beginning I sent Devon out to the top photographers. They loved her. By the end of the year she'd made over a million dollars."

"When did Cap come into the picture?"

"A few years later. When you make that much money, you need someone like him. Especially if your momma's a drunk and you've got a no-good stepdaddy."

"Were Cap and Devon tight?"

"What do you mean by *that*?"

"Was it a good working relationship?"

"He absolutely doted on her. She was his prize client."

"Friday night, you were talking about how models are often screwed up about their eating. I take it Devon had an eating disorder of some kind."

"No, that was over and done with. A lot of girls in their teens suffer from that."

"But clearly Devon was experiencing a relapse lately."

"Oh, please, I knew you were going to do this. You're just looking for dirt. You won't attribute it to me, but it will still end up in that rag."

"I'm only interested in the truth. If she died due to an eating disorder, that's going to come out anyway."

"Like I told you, that wasn't an issue anymore."

"And she wasn't scared or worried about anything this weekend?"

"*Scared*? I have no clue what you're talking about. Devon wasn't scared of anything."

"Just one more question. Did you call extension seven during the night?"

"Extension seven? You mean to say I needed a *shirt* pressed or something? Hardly. What is this anyway? You're starting to sound like Miss Marple."

Suddenly the TV screen grabbed our attention. It flickered a few times, and then suddenly died. The room was now in total darkness.

Maybe, I thought, the freezing rain had knocked out the satellite dish. And then from a distance I heard Jessie yell, "Bailey, where are you?" and I glanced toward the hallway. There was no light coming from anywhere. The power had gone out. Great, just the hell what we needed.

7

"**O**h, brilliant," Christian exclaimed. "Just fucking brilliant."

"There are candles on the table upstairs," I said. "I'll go grab a couple. Why don't you call Scott and see where he is."

"Call him? *How*?"

"Here," I said, tossing him my BlackBerry. "His cell is in the address book." I'd programmed it in during my car ride with Jessie.

"*Bailey*?" Jessie called again from the great room. "Where are you?"

I yelled that I was coming and tried to maneuver my way out of the media room, though just before I reached the door I rammed my foot so hard into a piece of furniture, it felt as if I'd kicked a car. Finding and climbing the stairs was even trickier. The barn had become familiar to me over the past two days, but in the pitch-dark, I was clueless.

"Jess, you still near the couch?" I called out once I'd reached the top of the stairs.

"Yup. What made the freaking power go out? The snowstorm's been over for hours."

"It might be the ice," I said, inching my way toward her voice. "It's probably coated the power lines and made one of them snap. I'm gonna grab the two candlesticks on the dining table—can you start rooting around in the drawers and see if you can find one of those lighters Sandy was using last night?"

My eyes began to adjust to the darkness, and I could make out Jessie moving clumsily toward the island. I reached the table, snagged the two taper candles in antler holders, and then met Jessie by the island. She'd found the lighter, and we lit the two candles. With the tapers partially illuminating the room, we then located two chubby candles in hurricane lamps on a side table and lit those. I carried the antler holders downstairs.

"I couldn't reach Scott," Christian said, handing me back my phone.

"He should be here shortly," I said. "Here." I passed him a candle.

"This ought to be fun," he said. "A night in a house with no lights and a dead body."

I was tempted to add, *Oh, and let's not forget that the master key to all the bedrooms is missing.*

There was an explosion of voices suddenly. The power outage had clearly sent people scrambling in this direction, hoping to find candles or flashlights. I stepped into the foyer to see Cap, Whitney, Richard, and Jane emerge from the door to the passageway. They were followed thirty seconds later by Tory and Tommy, looking disheveled. It was hard to tell if they'd been in the middle of makeup sex or a slap fest. Everyone demanded to know what was going on. Before I had a chance to even offer an opinion, the front door opened and Ralph and Scott burst into the foyer, toting large flashlights and stomping hard to knock the icy snow off their boots.

"Tell me it's just a fuse," Cap said.

"Unfortunately not," Ralph said hoarsely. "The ice seems to have knocked out a power line. But we've got plenty of flashlights."

"What about heat?" Whitney asked.

"Unfortunately not," Scott said. "But the great room and guest bedrooms all have gas wood-burning stoves. Ralph will light them."

"But how are we going to get out of here?" Tory wailed. "I've got a job tomorrow, and it pays four thousand dollars. They're going to kill me if I don't show."

"We're all in the same boat, Tory, so why don't you just shut the hell up," Tommy snapped. Ignoring them, Scott directed the beam of his flashlight toward the candle I was holding. "There are more of those upstairs. Why don't we go up there?"

We all traipsed upstairs and huddled together in the center of the room. Using his torch to guide him, Scott opened a cabinet filled with votive lights, tapers, and pillar candles. By the time we were done lighting them all, the great room looked like something out of medieval times.

"Do you know what I think?" Scott asked the group. "I think we could all use a drink."

"You took the words right out of my mouth," Richard added.

"Why am I not surprised?" Whitney said, all the southern charm missing from her tone.

"Whitney, please," Cap pleaded. For the first time I realized just how truly frayed people's nerves were.

"*What*?" she said mockingly, her nearly transparent blue eyes sparkling in the candlelight. "Am I just supposed to sit around and act all sweet when he gets liquored up, slurs his words, and won't take his eyes off my breasts?"

"But Whitney, I assumed you liked it," Richard said. "Otherwise why make such a point of showing them off?"

"Shut your stupid mouth," Cap said, taking a step toward Richard with muscles tightened.

"You can stare at *my* tits if you want," Jane said. "I won't mind—and they're even real."

"Everyone, please cool it," Scott declared firmly. "The road isn't passable unless you've got a four-wheel drive, and the weather isn't fit to drive in anyway. That means we've got to spend the night here together whether we like it or not."

That was funny—whether we *like* it or not. I wondered who he thought belonged in the former group.

"Besides," he added, "I'm sure Devon wouldn't want us at each other's throats. Let's all be civil, okay?"

His suggestion lacked passion, but it did the trick at least. Cap's muscles relaxed and Richard slunk off into the shadows. Scott asked who would like wine, and after several people raised their hands in the dim light, he opened two bottles and began pouring glasses. We accepted our drinks and then gathered in various clusters on the couches and armchairs. No one said much of anything, though we had to listen to Tory wail on her cell phone to someone at her agency about the need to cancel her shoot tomorrow. I emailed Nash with an update.

At one point Jessie wandered over to the island, and I followed a minute later.

"Remember I said I felt like I was in a horror movie?" she said. "Well, I was kidding then. But I'm not now. I'm starting to feel spooked. What if Devon's death wasn't natural? What if someone's cut the power? What if we're all in danger?"

"I wouldn't worry too much," I told her. "I have no idea how Devon died, but I do know that we had exactly the kind of storm that knocks down power lines. I really don't think there's anything fishy going on with the lights."

I was doing my best to sound calm—and I really *didn't* think the power outage was intentional—but the situation was definitely creepy. Tomorrow morning couldn't come soon enough.

The somber mood of the room lifted a tiny bit when Sandy and Laura arrived and laid out the remains from the antipasto lunch we'd had the day before. Sandy apologized for the leftovers (without actually sounding sorry), and explained that she hadn't expected to serve dinner to everyone.

People pulled closer around the coffee table and began to make idle small talk—everyone except Tory. She had taken her plate over to the dining table and sat sulking in the dark shadows at the far end of the room.

At the risk of having a drink tossed in my face for supposedly flirting with her man on the deck earlier, I headed over there and pulled out a chair next to her.

"I hope you don't think I was actually making a play for Tommy earlier," I said quietly. "That's not my style."

"I'm not blaming you for anything," she said. "I just want to get *out* of here. This is like some freaking catalogue shoot that never, ever ends."

"This can't have been an easy weekend for you. That whole thing Devon pulled Saturday night—her coming on to Tommy in front of everyone."

She shrugged a shoulder. "It wasn't nice, but I don't want to say anything bad about her. I hear it's bad luck to say something nasty about a dead person."

Gosh, where did this girl get her information?

"I hear Devon actually introduced you to Tommy," I said.

"Yup."

"That's kind of interesting, isn't it? A lot of girls wouldn't feel comfortable seeing their ex-boyfriend with a friend."

"She said she didn't care. I mean, she was kind of upset when they broke up, but she said she got over it."

"What kind of time was she having this weekend? Whenever I saw her, she seemed to be a bit on edge."

"I dunno. I didn't actually talk to her all that much. Plus, it was hard sometimes to know what she was really thinking. She liked to keep things to herself."

"Did you notice how thin she was—and how little she ate?"

"That's our *job*—to be thin."

"But there's thin and there's thin. Do you think she was suffering from an eating disorder?"

Tory shook her head back and forth, lifting the shiny black layers of her hair.

"People always say stuff like that about models," she said after a moment. "I think most of the time they're just jealous."

"Did you happen to see a bottle of ipecac syrup in her bathroom? That's something people use to induce vomiting."

"I never went in Devon's room the entire weekend. I was too busy in mine—if you know what I mean."

She stood up, leaving her plate on the table, clearly done with the conversation.

For the next hour or so we all just sat around, bunched fairly close together as if we were on a lifeboat in the Atlantic. The lack of electricity meant no music and no coffee machine, though Sandy put out stuff for tea because the stove ran on gas. The two wood-burning stoves in the great room provided *some* heat, but the room could hardly have been described as toasty warm.

After a while Scott suggested poker, but only he, Tommy, and Richard played. Whitney pulled her yarn and knitting needles out of a bag and started clicking again. The rest of us leafed through books and magazines by candlelight and picked at the remains of our dinner. We ran through several bottles of wine, about 50 percent of which was consumed by Richard.

At around nine thirty, Ralph showed up with an update. The power was out all over the area, and it would probably be out through part of the next day. According to the most recent weather report, the temperature would rise again in the morning, and he was pretty sure he could have the road in shape sometime before noon. He and Sandy had rounded up more flashlights, and he distributed one to each of us and then deposited several on top of the big island.

"We've got plenty of candles, too," he said gruffly, "but we'd appreciate it if you rely mostly on the flashlights. The last thing we need right now is a fire."

I wasn't looking forward to heading back to my room, but after Ralph left, people started to drift away, the beams from their flashlights bobbing spookily as they descended the stairs. There seemed to be no point in hanging around. Jessie barely made eye contact with Scott when we said good night and then practically attached herself to my hip. I took a glass of wine with me.

"If it weren't for Mr. Kinky Pants, I would have stayed over there for hours," Jessie whispered as we reached our rooms. "I dread the idea of being back in my room alone."

I smiled woefully, in total sympathy with how she was feeling.

"I really don't believe anyone will try to get into our rooms tonight," I said, "but just to be on the safe side, why don't you pull a chair or table in front of your door? Or if you really want, you can bunk down with me."

"You don't know how close I am to saying yes to your offer. But if Scott found out tomorrow that we'd shared a room, he'd end up walking around with a boner until we left."

I smiled. "Just knock on my door if you get scared, okay?"

Once in my room, I took my own advice and dragged an end table over the floor and lodged it against the door. The gas fueled wood-burning stove had been lit and was giving off decent heat. Despite Ralph's warning, I lit the scented candle from the bathroom, placed it on the table by the armchair, and then collapsed, my legs tucked underneath me and BlackBerry in hand. I tried Beau again, with the little bit of power I still had in my phone. Never expecting a power outage, I hadn't bothered to charge it earlier. Once again, I reached only Beau's voice mail.

"Hey," I said. "Not sure when your plane is due. Call me, will you? Some crazy stuff has happened up here, and I would love to talk to you."

I started to press disconnect but instead gave him a brief description of Devon's death and how we'd been held hostage by the storm.

The flames from the candle and the wood-burning stove created phantomlike shadows that danced on the walls. I sipped my wine, trying to sort through everything that was jostling around in my brain. I was so immersed in my thoughts that I almost didn't hear the sound of someone knocking on my bedroom door. Jessie, I thought. She had obviously decided not to tough it out.

Holding the candle, I crossed the room and pulled the table away from the door. I opened it just a hair. Surprise, surprise. Jane was standing there, flashlight in hand. Her mass of dark hair was pinned to the top of her head and she was wearing a pink sweatshirt.

"Did I wake you?" she asked without sounding as if she cared.

"Nope."

"Mind if I come in? I want to talk to you."

"Sure," I said as she followed me into the room with a curious glance toward the table I'd used as a barricade.

"I'm sorry if I was rude earlier," she said. "This hasn't been a breeze for me, as you might imagine."

"Devon's death—or working for her?"

"Both."

She'd lowered the flashlight, and was illuminated only by the light of the candle. Her dark brown eyes were hollows in her large face.

"So what's on your mind?" I asked.

"I Googled you during the day, and I was pretty surprised by what I saw."

"How so?"

"You're a really respected crime reporter, aren't you? You don't write all that crap about who's screwing who or who gave the paparazzi a beaver shot while getting out of the car."

"No, I don't write that stuff," I said. What was she up to? I wondered. An ornery bear like Jane didn't start acting all nicey-nice without a damn good reason.

"You think Devon's death is going to be a big story?" she asked. "I mean, will it be all over the news for days and days?"

"That's going to depend a lot on what the autopsy reveals," I said. "If it turns out that Devon died from complications from an eating disorder, it will make the cover of all the tabloids this week and then there'll be some follow-up the next week about which rock stars showed at her funeral. And I assume the morning shows will all do segments on bulimia and anorexia. But then it will probably quiet down—except for maybe one long piece by someone like Richard in *Vanity Fair*. Why—are you worried about how the media circus will impact you?"

"Yeah—I mean, of course. But I don't understand why you think the story will die so quickly. Remember Anna Nicole Smith? Didn't her story go on and on for weeks?"

"Yeah, but that's because there were all those crazy layers—like who was the baby's father. When details keep unfolding each week, then the press stays on a story."

"I see what you mean."

"If Devon had been dating anyone hot right now, that would provide a little extra drama, but as you pointed out, she was single at the moment." I paused, watching Jane bite her chubby lower lip in the candle-light. "*Right?*"

"Ummm, I guess."

"If there's something you want to talk about and it's pressworthy, I promise not to attribute it to you in any way."

"There *is* something, actually," she said. She looked off in this exaggerated way, as if she was trying to make up her mind to tell me, but I sensed it was for show, that she'd come to my room for just this purpose. "I didn't say anything to the police about it—because it clearly doesn't have anything to do with Devon's death—but I feel I *should* tell someone. I mean, it just seems wrong not to. And since you're interested in the facts, and not just idle gossip—"

Spit it out! I wanted to shout, but I knew better than to pounce.

"I'm happy to listen," I said, "but only if you feel like sharing."

She turned her eyes back toward me.

"It's Cap," she said. "There was something going on between him and Devon."

I'd had my suspicions, of course, but the news gave me a little jolt. And it certainly shed fresh light on the words I'd overheard Cap say on the deck. Devon's "You'd better tell her" comment must have referred to Whitney after all.

"A little fling—or more like a full-blown affair?" I asked.

"I'm not sure, since I only realized this weekend that something was definitely up with them. I always *thought* there might be something, but I never had any evidence. Then yesterday, I spotted them kissing in the woods."

"Do you remember what time?" I asked. I wondered how this particular incident connected to the crying jag of Devon's that I'd witnessed near the outbuildings.

"Umm, not long after breakfast, I'd say. I didn't want to do the whole hiking thing, but Scott said there was a pretty stream down an easy path and I decided to go wander down there. I didn't even know Devon had left her room—the last I'd seen her, she was drinking her stupid green tea in bed. But there she was in this major lip lock with Cap. I didn't want them to see me, so I snuck out of there and hightailed it back to the barn."

So then what had Devon been crying about? Her tears hadn't seemed like the kind you shed when you are hopelessly in love with a man who might not leave his wife. She had said, "Someone knows something." Had she been afraid Whitney had learned the truth?

"I appreciate your telling me this," I said. "If there is any reason that it belongs in the story, and I decide to use it, I won't mention your name. Can I get your cell number, just in case I need to reach you?"

"Sure," she said. She dictated it as I typed it into my BlackBerry. "I appreciate your listening. There's something creepy about her manager becoming involved with her like that. Don't they have a name for that—a Svengali complex or something?"

"Something like that," I said.

"I better get going. I don't like being out of my room with all the lights out—and Devon's body lying down there."

I let her out and watched her tentatively make her way back down the corridor.

The wick of my candle was starting to sputter, in danger of being suffocated by a pool of hot melted wax. I quickly undressed, blew out the flame and crawled into bed. The room was pitch-black. As I lay on my back, praying for the sheets to warm, I mulled over Jane's revelation about Cap. If it turned out someone had actually killed Devon—though I had no clue how—that meant that both Cap and Whitney were suspects. Sexual jealousy was one of the biggest motivators of homicide. I felt particularly curious about why Jane had spilled the beans. Jane hadn't given a rat's ass about Devon, and it was hard to believe the "I feel I should tell someone" motive.

I could sense I wasn't going to fall asleep easily. I scooted back up in bed, and for the next hour or so, I read by the beam of the flashlight. Finally, with my eyes growing weary, I switched off the flashlight and wriggled down under the covers.

Earlier it had seemed so deadly quiet in my room, but now I began to pick up little noises: the fire crackling in the stove; the wind rattling the window; the ice snapping on the trees outside. Eventually, I felt my body sag into the mattress, and sleep overtook me.

And then something was stirring me. I had no clue what it was, but my heart had begun to beat faster. I raised myself up in bed and cocked my head, straining to hear. The noise was coming from the hallway. Footsteps. Was it Jessie? I wondered.

Then there was another noise: the sound of something scratching on wood farther down the hall. I leaned forward in bed as my heart gathered speed. The scratching sound happened again. It was to the left of my room, near the door to Jessie's room. What in the world was going on? I wondered. And then the scratching was happening right outside my room. Someone was running an object back and forth across my door. It sounded as if the thing was made of metal, like a coat hanger but thicker. With a gasp I realized it could be a knife.

"Who's there?" I called out. I grabbed the flashlight, fumbled for the switch, and then bounded out of bed toward the small entranceway. Instinctively I leaned hard against the table, making sure the person couldn't push open the door if he had a key. "Who's there?" I called again.

There was another rapid scratching noise—a couple of strokes, like Zorro making the sign of the Z. Next

I heard retreating footsteps and the sound of someone tripping down the stairs.

I ran back toward the phone to call extension seven but remembered the line was dead. I had absolutely no desire to bolt out into the hall, but I had to figure out what was going on—and to alert Scott. While I slid my feet hurriedly into a pair of ballet flats, I heard Jessie pound on the wall between our two rooms. After dragging the table away from the door, I peered outside. No one was there. I scurried down the hall and tapped on Jessie's door, announcing it was me. In the beam from the flashlight I saw four or five large scratch marks carved in the wood of her door. I aimed the flashlight back toward my own door. There were ugly scratch marks there, too.

"What the hell is happening?" Jessie asked as she opened the door. She looked terrified.

"I don't know. You've got Scott's cell phone number?"

"Yeah—why?"

"See if you can wake him. At the same time, I'll head over to his room."

"Be careful, okay?" she pleaded.

Hurrying toward the stairs, I trained the beam of my flashlight raggedly over every corner of the landing, making sure no one was hiding in the darkness. On the ground floor I could see scratch marks on two guest room doors. Richard, Christian, Cap and Whitney, and Tommy and Tory were all on this floor, but I had no idea whose room was which. Was one of them the culprit? Had the person already snuck back into his room?

I pivoted and made my way to the entrance of the glass passageway. Once inside, I saw that I almost didn't need my flashlight; the piles of snow outside partially illuminated the passage. Grabbing a breath, I picked up speed. Once I thought I heard someone behind me and spun around nervously. No one was there. The sound, I told myself, must have come from the glass being shaken by the wind.

I reached the other barn and pushed the door open. Just as I stepped inside, the freaking light of my flashlight died. I shook the torch a couple of times and the light came back on, but it seemed dimmer now.

I trained the stream of light toward Scott's door and made my way in that direction. I knocked several times, and when that produced no results, I banged and called out his name. Nothing. Where *was* he? I wondered anxiously.

Then I heard a noise to my right. I turned and aimed the feeble beam of my light there. The main door of the barn, the one that went outside, was shuddering a little from the wind, and I could see that it hadn't been shut tightly. It looked as if someone might have hurried outside and left it ajar.

Oh, fun, I thought. I'm gonna have to investigate out there. But, I realized, that might be exactly where Scott had gone—to check outside. I strode to the door, heart in mouth, and pulled it open.

Because of the snow I could see a little better outside than in, though that wasn't saying much. The surrounding woods seemed so big and ominous, ready to engulf the barn. But there were no humans in sight.

"Scott!" I called out several times. He might, I realized, have hightailed it down to Ralph's. There was no reply, just the sounds of trees crackling. I glanced down. There seemed to be fresh boot prints in the ice-crusted snow, but as far as I knew, they could have been made hours ago.

I stepped back inside and closed the door, wondering what I should do. The best course might be for me to head down to Ralph's cabin. A big knot of fear had started to form in my tummy. To make matters worse, my flashlight suddenly sputtered—and then died for good.

"Fuck," I said out loud.

I remembered that earlier Ralph had dumped extra flashlights on the island upstairs, and if I were in luck, one would still be there. Cautiously I made my way toward where I knew the stairs were and felt in the darkness for the wooden handrail. I found it after a few clumsy attempts and began the climb to the second level. Once upstairs, I took a moment to orient myself, trying to use my sense memory. I moved toward the area where I was sure the island was and finally bumped into it. I patted my hand over the entire surface, but there were no flashlights on top.

The smartest move at this point, I realized, was to return to Jessie's room, borrow her flashlight, and head for the cabin from the door of the smaller barn. I took cautious baby steps toward the landing. Just as I'd placed my foot on the stairs, I heard a sound and froze. Somewhere behind me in the blackness of the great room, something had just moved. Oh, man, I thought, please don't let this be happening.

"Who's there?" I called out, weakly. My legs felt as limp as shoelaces.

Suddenly I heard a whoosh of air as someone rushed up behind me. I caught a whiff of rancid sweat at the same moment that I heard a swishing sound, like the movement of fabric. And then, while passing me, the person shoved against the right side of my body, pitching me forward. Instinctively my hand flew out in search of the rail, but it was too late. I was being propelled down the stairs, headfirst.

8

With each roll of my body, the same thought kept shooting through my brain: Please don't let my neck snap in two. Though I tried to grab on to something, all I could reach was air or the edge of each stair step, and neither was any help. Suddenly my head thwacked hard against something—maybe the base of the banister—and my hand slammed into the ground floor. I stopped rolling. I lay on the ground, eyes closed. A million little lights pulsed in my brain.

I moaned. My head hurt and so did my butt and left wrist. And then there was a light nearly piercing my eyelids. I felt a rush of panic, thinking it must be the person who had knocked me down the stairs. But as I opened my eyes, squinting, I saw that it was Scott who was standing there, holding a flashlight.

"Are you okay?" he demanded.

"Uhhh, I'm not sure," I groaned.

"I don't want to touch you—in case something's broken. Can you just wiggle your fingers and toes and make sure you can move?"

"Yeah, just give me a second to catch my breath."

Though I knew I was probably bruised in places, it didn't feel as if anything was broken. One at a time, I lifted each arm and leg, making certain I could move them.

"I think I'm okay," I said after a minute. "Could you just give me a hand?"

Taking my arm, Scott eased me into a sitting position and then helped me stand. For a second I felt a wave of dizziness, but then it subsided.

"What happened, for God's sake?" Scott asked.

"Someone knocked me down the stairs. I'm not sure if they did it on purpose or were just trying to get around me. They were hiding in the dark up there."

"*What*? What do you mean, hiding in the dark?"

I described what had happened up until he'd found me sprawled at his feet.

"I thought I heard a knock," he said. "And my phone ringing. But it took me a minute or so to figure out if I was dreaming or not. Just as I reached the door, I heard someone tumbling down the stairs."

"And you didn't see anyone when you opened the door?"

"No, no one. My God, this is crazy."

He directed his flashlight around the ground floor of the barn. Lying in a small heap near the door was one of the dark green rain ponchos from the pegs.

"I think the person was wearing that," I said. "I felt something slick like it against my skin. Oh, and look there."

I pointed to a rusty branding iron, one of the old farm tools I'd seen displayed on the walls. It was lying a few feet away from the poncho.

"That must be what the person used to scratch on the doors," I said.

"What a fucking mess," Scott said. "Who in God's name would do something like that?"

"Good question."

"What about you?" Scott said. "Should we try to get you to a hospital?"

Wow, wouldn't it be sweet to see this place in the rearview mirror, but I didn't feel in dire need of medical attention—and I couldn't abandon Jessie.

"My wrist seems to be the only thing really hurting, but I think it's just a bruise. Why don't I just put ice on it for a while and see how it feels."

He scooted upstairs to the fridge, returning in a minute with ice wrapped in a dishrag, two ibuprofen, and a glass of water. He'd also managed to locate another flashlight. I winced as I touched the pack gingerly to my wrist.

"Let's get you back to your room," Scott said. "Plus I want to check it out over there."

He walked me back to the small barn, and we surveyed the damage to each door.

"I need to let the police know about this," he whispered. "But it's probably best to wait till morning. Otherwise we'll freak everyone out. Just to be on the safe side, I'll have Ralph sit on the ground floor of the barn and keep an eye out."

I asked him to leave me at Jessie's door, and as soon as she'd opened it, he took off. Jessie went bug-eyed at the sight of the ice pack. As I filled her in on what had happened, she began to tear up.

"What if something worse had happened to you?" she said, wiping at her eyes. "We've got to get out here."

"The road should be clear tomorrow morning. We just have to tough it out for a few more hours. Try to get some sleep, okay?"

The second she closed her door, I heard her drag the table back against the door. I stood for a few seconds in the hall, examining the scratch marks on her door with the flashlight, trying to determine if there might be message a there—a word or a symbol. But there wasn't. And none on my door either. They were just random scratch marks.

Back in my room I barricaded my own door and then, shivering, climbed into bed. As I lay there, taking a few long, deep breaths to try to relax, I heard male voices rising from the first floor. Scott had obviously brought Ralph, as promised.

Once the voices subsided, I replayed in my mind those few seconds at the top of the stairs. Come on, I urged myself. There had to be some kind of clue that would point to the night raider's identity. But the only thing I had to go on was that awful stench of sweat. It suggested a man, and yet a woman could sweat heavily too if she was racing around playing a nasty trick and then was forced to hide, fearful of being caught.

Scott had asked who in God's name would do something like that, and I honestly had no clue. It might be some kind of warning. One thing suddenly occurred to me. If Cap or Whitney or Tory or Tommy were the culprit, his or her partner had probably become aware of the sudden absence of the person sharing the bed.

Finally, at around four, I drifted off into a fractured sleep, fraught with vague, scary dreams.

When I opened my door the next morning at seven, bundled up in two sweaters, Scott was standing right there, his hand raised to knock.

"I'm getting everyone up," he announced. "The police are due shortly, and the morgue van won't be much later, since the road will be cleared within the next hour."

The power was still out, which meant no hot water. So I skipped a shower and just splashed cold water on my face and torso. There was enough light from the bathroom window for me to study my bruises. I had black and blue marks on my ass and legs and a small bump on my forehead. My wrist was sore, but it was clear nothing was broken. I popped two ibuprofen, dressed quickly, and picked up Jessie before heading to the big barn.

There were already a few people waiting when we arrived, including Sandy, who had set out bagels and muffins on the counter. The two stoves were working their butts off, but there was a chill to the room. As each new person came up the stairs, they demanded to know what was going on. All Scott would say was, "Grab a mug of tea. There's been a new development, but let's wait until everyone arrives." Once we were all seated, he broke the news—the vandalism of the doors, me being pushed down the stairs, and the fact that the cops would be back this morning. Every person sitting there glanced quickly around at the others, looking shocked. Clearly one person was faking it.

"I saw the marks when we were leaving the room just now," Cap said. "Are you saying one of the *guests* made them?"

"Yes," Scott said soberly. "I hardly think Sandy or Ralph came over here during the night and played a prank on us all."

"Now that you mention it, I thought I heard someone at my door last night," Tommy said, "but to be perfectly honest, I thought it was Bailey dropping by for a late-night interview. I was just too spent to answer."

Oh, yeah, just me and a can of Reddiwip.

"Well, I don't care if I have to hike out by foot and pick Devon's car up next spring, I'm getting the fuck out of here," Jane declared.

"Aren't there rescue workers who can help us?" Tory wailed. "We're trapped—like people in that Hurricane Katrina."

Tommy started to say something, and Scott raised his hand to quiet everyone. He explained that the road would be plowed by the time we were done speaking to the cops again, and then everyone would be free to leave.

"Shouldn't we be asking how poor *Bailey* is?" Richard said, though his tone didn't suggest much sympathy.

"Much better, thank you," I said.

The police arrived twenty minutes later, and my conversation with Detective Collinson went far less smoothly than the earlier ones. As I described my tumble down the stairs, an irritated look formed on his ghost-white face, as if I'd just announced I'd accidentally rear-ended one of the town's police cruisers.

"You've *no* idea who it might have been?" he asked impatiently.

"None," I told him. "Except of course that it had to be one of the houseguests. I doubt a stranger broke in and decided to go on a branding rampage."

He sighed. "And you thought it was a good idea to just follow this person in the dead of night?"

"I wasn't really in pursuit. In fact, I thought the person had probably gone back to his or her room. I was going to wake Scott, and when he didn't answer, I went upstairs to find another flashlight."

"Where do you think he was?"

"Probably crouched behind one of the couches in the great room."

"No, I mean Mr. Cohen."

Interesting question.

"He said he was in his bedroom but didn't wake up right away."

Collinson told me to call him if I learned anything new, and in turn I promised to be in contact with him as I followed the story. He seemed positively thrilled.

When I returned to the great room, people were buzzing about the fact that the road was finally navigable.

As soon as Jessie's interview with Collinson was over, we walked back to our rooms, packed up quickly, and prepared to leave.

"Can you take our bags out to the car?" I asked her. "There's one last thing I need to do."

Following Devon's death, I'd managed to talk to everyone but Sandy and Ralph. Now, with people in exit mode, it might be a chance to catch at least one of them alone.

I found Sandy wiping down the top of the island. Dressed in a camel turtleneck sweater and puffy sleeveless brown vest, she looked ragged, as if she'd gotten little sleep herself. Her short blondish gray hair was pressed flat against her scalp. Like me, she'd obviously decided to skip the cold shower.

"I just wanted to say thank you for everything you did this weekend," I told her.

"You're welcome," she replied crisply. "That's nice of you to say."

"This must have been a pretty harrowing couple of days for you."

"You could say that. But we get through—we always do."

She made it sound as if it wasn't all that unusual for one of the houseguests to leave the premises in a morgue van.

"You heard about last night, of course. Any ideas about who scratched the doors?"

"Why would I? I was fast asleep in my cabin."

"Well, you've probably got a sense of the houseguests by now. Does one of them seem crazy enough to do something like that?"

She finally stopped wiping and stared at me, her unblinking blue eyes telegraphing the fact that she thought we were *all* freaking crazy.

"Afraid not," she said.

"You didn't seem to like Devon very much," I said.

"I don't make it my business to like or not like the people who come here."

"She didn't eat anything you made. I had the feeling that annoyed you."

"Wouldn't it annoy *you*? Going to all the effort and having someone just stare at it in disgust—as if you've served them a slab of lard."

"I'm pretty sure she had an eating disorder. Her behavior may have seemed rude, but it wasn't anything personal. Devon wouldn't have eaten anything from anyone."

"If you ask me, she was just used to doing as she darn well pleased and having everyone at her beck and call. What do you call those women in New York? Divas?"

"Did she give you a hard time?"

"In every way you can think of. She didn't like her sheets, and we had to change those twice. We originally put Jane in one of the smaller bedrooms downstairs, but she wanted Jane next to her, come hell or high water, and so Mr. Parkin got stuck with the smaller room and Jane was moved upstairs. Even her water. She had told Scott to stock plenty of this Fiji water—can you imagine having to drink water all the way from there?—and then she complained about the taste. Ralph had to drive into town and buy another kind—Evian—and she complained about that too. I suggested she try our well water, which suits us just fine, and you would have thought I'd told her to run buck naked through the woods. Though she probably would have *liked* that."

Her face had turned red as she was speaking, not just a flush to her cheeks but a splotchy, angry red that exacerbated her dry, weathered skin. She pinched her lips, aware that she'd said more than she should have.

"I really do need to finish up here," she said. "Do you need help packing your car?"

I told her I didn't and made my way back downstairs. I pushed open the front door to see if Jessie was out by the car, and I found her saying an awkward good-bye to Scott. I tried to make my own good-bye as cordial as possible, since I knew I might need to be in touch with Scott. As I climbed into my Jeep, I noticed that several cars were already gone. People had wasted no time beating a retreat.

The drive toward the main highway was dicey, since there were still patches of ice on the road. My phone was totally out of battery, but Jessie still had a little power in hers. She called Nash to let him know we would be in the office in about two hours.

Next I tried Beau. He picked up his cell phone on the first ring.

"I've been really worried about you," he said and sounded it. "I keep trying your phone, and it won't even let me leave a message."

"We lost power in a storm, and I wasn't able to charge my phone. But thank God, we're on our way back now."

"What's the latest?"

"Things became a lot more complicated. But why don't I fill you in later—there's a lot of ice on the road, and I need to focus."

"I assume you'll have to work late tonight."

"Yup. But I'll keep you posted."

"Drive carefully, Bailey. I love you."

"Same here."

"Things back to normal?" Jessie asked after I signed off.

"Yeah. It's terrible to say, but Devon's death may have done my relationship some good."

Though Jessie and I felt grungy as hell, after deliberation we decided that the smartest course of action would be to dump my Jeep in a midtown parking lot and go directly to *Buzz*. We'd buy time that way, and it would mean I might be able to leave work earlier that night. It turned out it had rained rather than snowed in Manhattan, and we had to leap over huge puddles as we hurried up Broadway to the office.

The first thing I did, after putting off Leo's barrage of questions, was to head for Nash's office. Nash was handsome (if you like barrel-chested guys about forty-four with gray-tinged hair slicked back at the sides), fun, flirty, and occasionally moody. Rumor had it that he'd had flings with several different women in the office and his wife had apparently given him an ultimatum: Keep it in your pants or get kicked to the curb.

"I've got Devon slated for the cover," he told me, shoving his reading glasses from the middle of his nose to the top of his head, "unless something better happens in the next ten hours."

"What could be better?"

"Katie leaving Tom. Angie leaving Brad. Katie hooking up with Angie. So what's the deal? She o.d.?"

"No sign of that. Of course the tox report might turn up something. We won't know anything official for a couple of days."

"What's your hunch?"

"I keep coming back to the eating disorder angle. There's definitely a fatality rate connected with that. Your heart can give out from the strain."

"Keep me posted twenty-four/seven, okay? You'll write the main story. When the issue hits Thursday, I want you to do most of the TV for this. We could get you on sooner, but I want to sell as many copies as possible, and that means waiting for the right moment. The fact that you were at the scene is perfect. Everybody's going to be eating their hearts out."

I hoped so. From what I'd been hearing, sales had been sluggish this year, and it would be nice to see a boost.

As soon as I was back in my cube, I wrote an update for the Web site and then typed up a timeline of the weekend. Over the next few days it would just be too easy to lose track of the sequence of events. I met with the art department after that and reviewed the layout they were putting together for the story, and I also touched base with one of the writers working on the sidebar about Devon's life—just to make sure our stories didn't overlap in any way.

Next it was time to focus on writing my piece for the magazine. Back at Scott's, I'd e-mailed one of the interns and asked her to pull together everything *Buzz* had done on Devon in the past. A stack of magazines, with colored Post-its poking out from the pages, had been left on the floor by my desk.

As I thumbed through the past issues, I soon saw that about 80 percent of the coverage of Devon was devoted to her fashion acumen. *Buzz* is notorious for its weekly "Fashion Tragedies" spread, where celebs get slammed for the lame job they sometimes do getting dressed, but one person always gets singled out under the heading: "She Got It Right!" Not infrequently that person was Devon. She'd had a knack for putting together a totally hip look in a way that seemed completely effortless. Nothing was ever matchy-matchy, and though all the pieces appeared to have been plucked randomly from her closet, the final result was the embodiment of cool. She'd been a risk taker, too, and when major style trends were traced back, she was frequently at the epicenter. There was one shot of her from a while back in suspendered jean shorts and a black Amish-style hat. If *I'd* worn that outfit, people would have wondered if I was attempting to reprise the Harrison Ford role in *Witness*, but on Devon it was edgy and fab.

What was interesting to note was that though Devon had been model thin, there weren't any shots that suggested an eating disorder. The problem must have reared its ugly head again only recently.

As for actual articles on her, there wasn't much. Devon had kept a fairly low profile, and just as I'd known, she'd never agreed to interviews, so the press had little to play with. There was a flurry of stories a few years ago when she was arrested at Heathrow for carrying a small bag of pot. She'd ended up with a suspended sentence. And between February and August of this year there were about five or six photos of her and Tommy together— sucking face in the street, leaving clubs looking shit-faced. You know, the typical model-and-rocker-in-love shots.

But then a picture of Devon from an issue a year ago this past November suddenly snagged my attention. She was striding along the street in SoHo with her coat flopping open. Over her photo was a slug that asked, "Isn't that a bump?"

I had to admit she *did* look pregnant—but I'd worked long enough at *Buzz* to know that things in photos weren't always as they seemed. For instance, someone's breasts could appear enlarged or their nose slimmed, but it was due to the angle of the camera, not plastic surgery. I rolled my chair over to Leo.

"See this photo," I said, shoving the page in front of his face. "Can you get me other shots from that same day?"

"There are lots better shots for your story, you know. I mean, she was just shopping that day."

"I don't need it for the layout—I think it might be significant for another reason."

"Yeah, okay. Give me a few minutes."

While he searched, I left a message for one of the top eating disorder experts, whom I'd made a note of during my Internet search on Sunday. I also checked online for pieces that simply mentioned Devon. When she first burst on the scene eighteen years ago, she was referenced frequently, particularly in articles about pop culture. She was heralded for her haunting beauty but also criticized for propagating the heroin chic look. Initially she seemed just naturally scrawny, but about two years later, when she was eighteen, there were rumors of anorexia—and the photos seemed to back it up. But within a year or two, she seemed to have a handle on the problem.

"Here you go," Leo said about ten minutes later, handing me a batch of photos he'd printed out.

There weren't many shots from that day—apparently just one roving paparazzo had captured her during her SoHo shopping spree. But what was remarkable is that she looked pregnant in every single picture.

I wheeled my chair back over to Leo.

"Do me a favor, will you? Tell me if you think Devon Barr could possibly have been pregnant at this moment in time."

"I'm a gay man," Leo said. "I try not to think about anything that goes on *down there* in a woman."

"I'm not asking you to take a Lamaze class with me, for God's sake."

He sighed and flicked his eyes over the photos.

"Well, I don't think she looks so pregnant someone is going to get up and give her their seat on the subway—if Devon Barr ever even *took* a subway—but there does seem to be a noticeable protrusion there."

Jessie, who'd just hung up the phone, slid her chair over and asked what was going on. After I explained, she took one of the photos from me and studied it.

"Maybe it's just belly bloat—from PMS," she said. "Some women really get a paunch there."

"This is more than I can bear," Leo moaned. "I feel like I'm in a Midol commercial."

"You know who would know?" Jessie asked, raising an eyebrow.

"Yeah, I know."

She meant the team who worked on Juice Bar, the hardcore gossip section in *Buzz*. Under Mona Hodges, the section had been particularly venomous, often running unattributable quotes. Nash had toned it down just a hair, but it could still be cruel. The whole magazine was filled with gossip, but this was the ugly rumor stuff. Let me put it this way: If you ended up on their radar and they determined that your life was worth covering, you were almost better off going into the Federal Witness Protection Program.

I'd already made one enemy on the Juice Bar team, so I decided to target another member of the squad, an unctuous, preppie guy named Thornwell Pratt, who had chatted me up a couple of times lately. I was never sure if he was being flirtatious or just thought I might have info he could use.

After grabbing a cup of coffee I popped over to the Juice Bar area. It was toward the back of the floor, far away from the bullpen, as if the work they did required grade-nine security clearance or gave off a toxic odor that needed to be contained as best as possible. I would have expected to find Thornwell with two phones to his ears, but he was just sitting at his desk staring off into space, with his elbows on the table and his too-small chin in his hands. I imagined a caption above his head: "The Day the Rumors Stopped."

"Hi there," I said as charmingly as possible, hoping to detract attention from the fact that with my matted, unwashed hair, I looked about as good as a yak.

"Well, don't *we* have a big story this week," Thornwell said, leaning way back in his chair. He had the prep thing going today—blue-and-white-striped shirt, sleeves rolled; khaki pants.

"Yeah, pretty incredible story, isn't it? You never covered Devon much, right?"

"Not *really*. She was actually a bore for someone so self-absorbed. She never talked to the press, and she tended to date B-level people. There was that one little drug bust at Heathrow a few years back, but that blew over pretty quickly."

"I was checking out some pictures of her from last November, and I noticed she looked pregnant in one. We even implied it might be a baby bump. Anything to that? I mean, *could* she have been pregnant at the time?"

He studied me with an amused, superior air and then shook his head slightly, as if my approach had involved a blunder of judgment on my part. I suddenly flashed on the scene in *Silence of the Lambs* in which Hannibal Lecter scolds Clarice for becoming too eager in the interview after doing so nicely at the start.

"What?" I asked.

"I *might* have some information. But we're not real generous back here, Bailey. When we offer anything up, it's always quid pro quo."

"I'm not opposed to a barter arrangement," I said. I was tempted to add, "As long as it doesn't involve you and me in a bar together."

"Scott Cohen."

"What about him?" I asked, more than curious but trying hard not to show it.

"I've been holding back on running a blind item on him until I score a tad more information. You just spent the weekend at his house. What can you tell me about him?"

"What kind of item?"

"Now, *now*—I asked first. But I will tell you that it has nothing to do with how he runs his record label. It's of a more *personal* nature. So what was it like to be his houseguest?"

I wondered if it had anything to do with Scott's fondness for threesomes, but I certainly wasn't going to spill anything.

"Nothing leaps to my mind, but let me mull it over. I'm sure when the dust settles about Devon's death, something may come to me."

He looked at me without answering for a minute, his pointer finger pressed against his mouth. I was about to invoke Nash's name, but finally Thornwell leaned forward in his chair, a signal, I thought, that he was ready to talk.

"How long is this so-called mulling-over going to take?"

"Come on, Thornwell," I said. "I said I'd try to think of something, and I will—after I get my story out of the way."

"And what was your question again?"

"Devon Barr. Do you think she might have been pregnant last year?"

He smiled malevolently.

"I don't think," he said. "I *know*. Devon was as preggers as the day is long."

9

Despite the fact that I had seen the photos with my own eyes, the answer still caught me by surprise. For one, Devon hadn't seemed at all like the motherly type; plus, and more importantly, she clearly hadn't *had* a baby. Just a few months after these photos were taken, she was photographed in various spots with Tommy, her tummy flat as a board.

"How do you know for sure?" I asked. "As you pointed out, she wasn't a blabber."

"Well, I didn't exactly get a note from her doctor," Thornwell said, "but for starters she confided to someone in her inner circle last year that she wanted a baby and she wasn't going to wait around for the right man to make it happen."

"That's not proof that she actually went ahead."

"There was a report, which we couldn't confirm, that she'd been seen leaving a fertility clinic. Right after that, she reportedly canceled several big modeling assignments. But here's the real proof: no drinking or smoking. Devon never stepped out in the evening without enjoying five or six chardonnays and a pack of Marlboro Lights. Suddenly she gives up booze and stops smoking, except for the occasional drag on someone else's cigarette."

"If you were so sure, why didn't you run an item?"

"It was pretty clear she'd had a miscarriage."

I did a quick calculation. A miscarriage must have occurred between November and February, when the shots of Tommy and Devon hobnobbing together began to surface.

"So when does a little human tragedy get in the way of a *Buzz* exclusive?" I asked.

"We're not *monsters*, you know, Bailey," he said. "Want to hear what *really* annoys me? People fuck up their lives, we report it, and yet for some reason, we're the ones that end up being despised."

"So in this case you decided to be real nice and keep the info all to yourselves."

"It was—if you can believe this—actually Mona who decided we shouldn't run it. Someone told me Mona once had a miscarriage herself and didn't want to go there. I think she thought it would jinx her somehow."

"Any idea who the father was?"

"Nope. And my guess is that *Devon* didn't either."

"Are you saying she had a one-night stand?"

"Possibly. She wasn't dating anyone that we know of at the time. But I'm thinking more along the lines of artificial insemination. All the best girls are doing it these days. And would explain why she was seen at a clinic."

"Any idea *why* she'd want a baby? She didn't seem like the type." I was still having a hard time wrapping my arms around the idea of Devon raising a kid.

"Haven't a clue," Thornwell said. "Maybe someone told her it was the new fashion accessory. You know— hotter than a Birkin bag."

"But—"

"Bailey, I've already been *far* too generous," he said, scooting his chair closer to the desk. "And plus I have work to do. Someone very, *very* big is about to get the boot from her scumbag boyfriend."

I wandered back to my cubicle, through the cacophony of closing day at *Buzz*, mulling over Thornwell's revelation. It was a surprising tidbit to have learned— but in the scheme of things, what did it really mean? The pregnancy had occurred months ago. It hadn't been successful. And it didn't appear as if Devon had been all that grief-stricken. Based on her smoking and drinking at Scott's, it also seemed clear that she'd had no immediate plans for restarting her baby-making efforts.

Of course, the experience may have stressed her out and even eventually contributed to the relapse of her eating disorder. But if someone *had* murdered Devon, it was hard to imagine that her pregnancy had played a role.

Plopping down at my desk, I saw that the message light on my phone was on; it turned out to be the eating disorder expert I'd left a message for earlier. I quickly called her back, praying not to end up with her voice mail again. Luckily an assistant picked up and put me right through to her.

"Isn't *Buzz* one of those celebrity magazines?" she said coolly. "How could I possibly help you?"

"I'm doing a story on the model Devon Barr—who died early Sunday morning. There hasn't been an autopsy yet, but she'd lost weight lately and she appeared to be avoiding food. There's even evidence that she may have been taking syrup of ipecac."

"Oh, dear, how tragic. I'd heard she died, but that the cause was still under investigation."

"I know you wouldn't be able to make a diagnosis from a description, but does the fact that she was avoiding food and using ipecac suggest she was suffering from an eating disorder?"

"You're right—it *would* be unprofessional of me to diagnose someone like that. But speaking *generally*, those *are* indications of an eating disorder."

"Bulimia?"

"No, anorexia nervosa," she said.

"I always thought it was bulimics who vomited."

"You said she was avoiding food. Individuals with bulimia will eat a huge amount of food and then throw up to keep from gaining weight. Anorexics, on the other hand, starve themselves by eating very little. But because they are morbidly fearful of gaining weight, they may also exercise compulsively, take laxatives or diet pills, or purge. Ipecac is an emetic. It stimulates the central nervous system and the stomach, causing the person to vomit."

"If Devon Barr *did* have an eating disorder, she could have died from it, correct?"

"Again, speaking generally, you most certainly can die from an eating disorder. Anorexia has one of the highest mortality rates of any psychotic condition—a significant number of people eventually die from it."

"From heart failure?"

"That's one possibility. People who are anorexic frequently have a disturbed electrolyte imbalance—they're not ingesting enough potassium, for instance—and that can lead to arrhythmia and cardiac arrest. Heart failure is even more likely in those who use drugs to stimulate vomiting or bowel movements. I can't believe they still *sell* ipecac. It's certainly not recommended anymore by pediatricians for poisoning emergencies."

"This is kind of a crazy question. Is there a particular reason why someone would try one method over another to reduce their weight—vomiting versus laxatives, for instance, or diuretics?"

She didn't answer right away, and until I heard her clear her throat quietly, I wondered if she was still on the line.

"You can't use this in your article, all right? It will only give people ideas. But someone can actually become addicted to throwing up their food. Dopamine is secreted in the brain when you vomit, which creates a feeling of euphoria. A girl tries it once, and then can't stop."

Wow. That hadn't turned up in any of the articles I'd read online.

"Suddenly there are two demons at work," she continued. "There's not only the need to lose weight but also the desire to repeat the rush vomiting creates."

"You've been very generous with your time," I said. "Just one more question. If someone suffered from an eating disorder years ago but had appeared to recover, why might it suddenly be triggered again?"

"There's a high recidivism rate with anorexia. Stress can trigger it again. Or feelings of low self-esteem."

I wondered what had been going on in Devon's life that could have helped restart her eating disorder. Heartache over her breakup with Tommy? Trouble with Cap? Disappointment about not getting pregnant again? I flashed again on the scene of Devon crying by the woods. Had something been scaring her for a while?

After signing off, I phoned Beau, explained that I'd be burning the midnight oil and would call him tomorrow. Then I put the pedal to the metal. I checked with art once more on the final layout, reviewed a bunch of Web sites to make sure there were no updates on Devon, and finally pounded out my article.

Once I'd forwarded the piece to the deputy editor, I stretched my legs and then read the e-mail from the PR department, explaining what they had in store for me on Thursday. I would be doing the *Today* show and a ton of other media.

Nash asked for a couple of tweaks with the story, and I didn't end up leaving the office until 2:00 a.m. Though Jessie could have bailed earlier, she hung around, partly out of solidarity. When we were finally out in the nearly deserted street, standing in front of the town car she was taking home courtesy of *Buzz,* we hugged each other tightly. Further south, the lights of Times Square still gyrated.

At that hour of the morning the drive from midtown to the Village took practically no time. After heaving my duffel bag into the living room, I yanked off my boots and jeans and crawled into bed with my sweater still on.

I woke around nine the next morning, with my head aching slightly and my wrist still sore from my tumble. Gingerly I swung my legs out of bed and pulled on pajama bottoms. As I waited for coffee to brew, I plopped down in my home office—a former walk-in closet—and checked out a few Web sites just to make certain I wasn't out of the loop on anything. The press had scrounged around everywhere for quotes on Devon—there was even a comment from the waxer who'd allegedly done her monthly Brazilian—but they'd turned up nothing of real interest.

I was now really in a waiting game. The autopsy had either been performed last night or was scheduled for this morning. And though a full toxicology screen would take days, even weeks, the police would surely issue some kind of preliminary report by the end of the day. Unless the results were totally ambiguous, I might at last know whether Devon had died from natural causes—or if she'd been the victim of foul play.

With coffee mug in hand, I located my phone to call Beau. I was yearning for a real conversation with him—and for the chance to see him. Since we'd started dating exclusively a few months ago, the most we'd ever been apart was three days, so this had been a real stretch. Though I'd only spoken to him for a couple of minutes yesterday, I'd sensed, as I'd indicated to Jessie, that our Sedona tiff was behind us. And that was a total relief. Earlier in the fall, I'd had to make a big romantic choice—between Beau and an actor named Chris Wickersham—and I'd never for a second regretted my decision. I felt enchanted by Beau—by his passion and creativity and slight air of mystery. But I was getting in deep, and I needed to be sure he was really committed.

"So you're up," he said, sounding really happy to hear my voice. "I was dying to call you but didn't want to wake you."

"I'm a little frayed around the edges, but the adrenaline rush is helping."

"I checked out your Web story. Pretty incredible."

"Maybe even more incredible is some of the stuff I *didn't* put up there. I can't wait to fill you in."

"How about doing it at dinner tonight? I was thinking since you'd had such a rough weekend, I'd pamper you and cook dinner."

"That sounds fantastic," I said. "Unless something huge related to the case breaks, I should be able to leave *Buzz* at a decent time tonight."

"Great. Just give me a heads-up when you know for sure."

I felt like letting out a big sigh when I disconnected. Everything seemed back to normal.

I'd expected that my day would be busy, but in some ways it just sputtered along. I showered and then knocked on the door of my sixty-something next-door neighbor Landon, hoping to catch up, but there was no answer. Throughout the morning I made several calls to Detective Collinson's office but didn't reach him until noon, at which point he told me the autopsy wasn't being performed until the afternoon and there would be no statement until tomorrow. Midafternoon, I dropped by the office, but discovered the typical anti-climactic day-after-closing scene. It was like walking into a party at midnight and finding nothing but empty plastic cups, wet potato chips plastered to the table, and a few people passed out on the couch.

I called Beau shortly afterward and let him know that there was no reason I couldn't be at his place by seven.

"Great. You could probably stand to go to bed early tonight."

"Yes, I could," I said, laughing. I felt my cheeks begin to burn, just thinking about slipping between the sheets with him. I hit the gym on the way home from *Buzz,* showered again at home, and later grabbed a cab to head over to Chelsea.

Even though we'd only been apart a week or so, when Beau opened the door to his apartment, it felt as if it'd been much longer. His face was slightly tanned from the Arizona sun, and his hair, which he had been wearing longer now, seemed to have grown an inch in the time he was gone. I felt the jolt of surprise I'd experienced when I first saw him in September after he'd been in Turkey for weeks and weeks.

"Hey there," he said in greeting. He gave me a long, sexy kiss and then wrapped one arm around me in a protective gesture. "You look pretty amazing for someone who has been snowbound with a dead body."

Beau looked awfully good himself. He was wearing tight jeans, loafers, and a blue-and-white checked shirt, with the top two buttons undone. He smelled good too—that dusky, exotic scent that he always wore.

"I'm still a little shell-shocked, but just being back in Manhattan has helped."

"Well, come in and let me pamper you. You can sit by the fire with a glass of wine while I finish dinner."

"*Fire?*" I said.

I looked past him into the living room, and my eyes widened in surprise. There was indeed a fire burning in the fireplace. I'd been in Beau's apartment a few dozen times through the fall, but it had never occurred to me that the fireplace worked. Up until my last visit, there'd been a large straw basket in there.

"You didn't think I'd let you sit here on a cold winter night without a fire, did you?"

The glass of wine was already poured, and I did as instructed—sat on the sleek black sofa, sipping the French red. My eyes roamed the walls, to the photographs Beau had taken in far-off places like Istanbul and Hanoi, but they kept straying back to the freaking fire. A small knot started to form in my stomach. I guess in the back of my mind I'd assumed that like so many fireplaces in the city, it could no longer burn wood, though in truth I hadn't ever really thought about it. Was it a symbol of something at the core of our relationship? That despite the fact that we'd dated exclusively for two and a half months, I didn't really *know* Beau? Stop it, Bailey, I wanted to scream. You're starting in again.

Dinner was lamb chops, roasted potatoes, and asparagus, served on the round table he used as a desk in a room off the living room. He'd set it with cloth napkins and candles. I *am* being pampered, I thought—

seriously pampered. As we ate, I relayed all the gory details about the weekend. I also shared the gossipy tidbits—such as Cap's reported lip lock with Devon—though I left out the part about Scott wanting three-way action with Jessie and me. Beau listened intently, leaning back in his chair at points, and sometimes shaking his head in disbelief.

"Wow, that—that sounds like a damn movie," he said.

I had this momentary feeling that he'd been about to say, "Wow—that will teach you to go off to a house party for the weekend without me" and changed his mind, vowing like me to just leave the snippiness behind us.

"I know—lots of tension," I said. "I won't know until the police report, though, whether all that tension somehow led to Devon's death."

"And this person who knocked you down the stairs. If you had to make a guess, who do you think it was?"

"I don't have a clue. The only sense I have is that it was a man—because there was a really heavy odor of sweat. Of course, anyone would be sweating after racing around the halls, but still the smell was *so* pronounced—"

"I've read a few pieces by Richard Parkin. He sounds like a pompous ass. Could he have been your sweat hog?"

"Maybe. Based on the amount of alcohol he'd had during the course of the day, it's hard to picture him playing Zorro, but who knows? He certainly managed to keep up during a hike we took in the woods one morning."

"Have you got any residual aches? I mean, maybe you should even see a doctor."

"I think I'm okay—just a few minor bruises. And this fantastic dinner has totally taken my mind off it."

He cleared the plates and returned a few minutes later with two full coffee mugs. But rather than sit back down himself, he came up behind me and laid his hands on either side of my neck.

"Would a head rub make it better or worse?" he asked from behind me. Though I couldn't see him, I sensed him raising just one eyebrow in that intriguing way of his.

"Umm, better, I think," I said, smiling.

He started with my neck and then moved up to my scalp, his slender but strong hands rubbing gently at first and then more firmly when it was clear I could handle it. Just having those hands on me again, and thinking of all the things they would certainly do later, made my breathing grow more shallow. I also felt a flush begin to creep up my chest.

The massage lasted a good ten minutes. I alternated between languidly relishing how nice it was to have my low-grade headache begin to subside and enjoying the wave of lust that was beginning to wash over me.

"Better?" Beau asked finally.

"*Sooo* much better."

His fingers dropped from my head to my shoulders and then he slowly slid them down my chest, slipping them under my top and my bra until he had cupped both my breasts. His palms felt cold against my skin but exhilarating. I let out a moan as he began to knead my breasts, sometimes gently pinching my nipples between his fingers.

"Now that's definitely taking the pain away," I whispered.

With one stroke he grasped the bottom edge of my top in his hands and tugged it over my head. He reached down behind me, unhooked my bra, and pulled that over my head as well. Leaning forward, he kissed the side of my neck.

"Why don't we go out into the living room?" he asked. "I don't believe I've had the pleasure of ever seeing you naked by firelight, have I?"

He laid two more logs on the fire, flicked off the lights in the living room, and brought a blanket from the bedroom to lay on the floor. I unbuttoned his shirt, slid it off, and let it drop to the floor. When I started to reach for his jeans zipper, he pulled me toward him and began to kiss me, slipping his tongue in my mouth.

"I was almost useless at work today," he said, pulling back. His skin glowed in the firelight. "I just kept thinking about all the things I wanted to do to you."

He kissed me again, fiercely this time. I felt nearly ravenous for him. I reached for his zipper again, but he pushed my hand away and laid me on the blanket. Crouching, he tugged off my jeans and my thong, and then stepped out of his own jeans and underwear. The only sounds in the room were the crackle of the logs and our ragged breaths. I felt in an altered state as he began to kiss his way down my body and then parted my legs with his hands.

Sex had been good with us from the start, and it hadn't yet lost its newness. At one point Beau dragged three throw pillows from the sofa and stacked them under my butt. It felt intoxicating to be so oddly elevated and free as he plunged deeply into me.

I slept straight through the night, completely exhausted. We woke at about eight and headed over to a little café in his neighborhood for a quick breakfast of coffee and croissants. Beau had a full day of editing ahead, followed by a business dinner, and he wanted to get an early start. Figuring Collinson wasn't going to call me with the news, I wanted to begin hounding him as early as possible. It was just below freezing out, and Beau and I felt a shock of electricity as we kissed good-bye in front of the café.

"Keep me posted, okay?" Beau said.

"Absolutely."

Though the walk home from Beau's place to mine would take a half hour, I decided to go for it, snaking east and south through Chelsea and the western part of Greenwich Village. As I crossed Fifth Avenue, I checked my watch. Ten of nine. I dug for my BlackBerry and tried Collinson. To my surprise he not only answered but also sounded vaguely receptive to my call.

"We're releasing a statement in just a short while," he said. "But there's no reason I can't tell you now. Devon Barr died of heart failure."

So my initial instinct had been right after all.

"Was it connected to an eating disorder?"

"It appears to be. There's evidence she was purging. And her body weight was lower than normal."

"What did she weigh exactly?"

"I don't think there's any reason you need to know the exact figure. But it seems she was suffering from an electrolyte imbalance."

"I assume the autopsy also showed evidence of a pregnancy," I stated calmly.

"Why do you ask that?" he said, clearly surprised.

"I hear she lost a baby last winter. I have a couple of sources."

He took a moment to respond.

"I'm not really at liberty to say."

But I knew from his hesitation that I'd been right.

"If that's all, I need to be going," he said.

"Just a couple more questions, please. You've been so helpful, and I really appreciate it. Do you have any idea yet who scratched all the doors—and why?"

"No, our investigation into that is ongoing."

I wondered how ongoing it could be with all the players back in Manhattan.

"What about the missing ipecac? Do you think someone removed it in order to cover up the fact Devon was taking it?"

"That might be the case. There were traces of ipecac in her system, so yes, it appears she had it in her possession."

Appears? Was the guy ever going to accept the fact that I had actually seen the bottle?

As I started to form another question, I heard Collinson clear his throat. Something else was on his mind.

"Ipecac wasn't the only thing she'd been ingesting," he said. "She'd been taking a diuretic, too."

"You found traces in her system of that, too?"

"Yes, a drug called Lasix—the generic name is furosemide. And, off the record, we found traces of it in the water bottle on her nightstand."

"Is it something you mix with water?" I asked.

"No, it's in pill form. But she obviously crushed it and mixed it with the water."

"I wonder why she would have done that."

"Maybe she didn't like taking pills. Or didn't like the taste."

"But it would still taste funny in the wa—"

And then suddenly I heard Sandy's words echoing in my mind: Devon had told her that the bottled water had tasted funny. Even when they'd bought her a different brand.

The realization nearly made my eyes bug out. Maybe someone other than Devon had put the diuretic in her water.

10

I blurted out what I'd learned from Sandy, nearly tripping over my words.

Collinson didn't comment right away, and I could
almost hear his thoughts racing over the phone.

"So you're suggesting *what*?" he said finally.

"That someone else, not Devon, put the diuretic
into the water."

"But just because she said the water tasted funny
is no reason to think someone else added the diuretic.
Ms. Barr was apparently a very demanding woman.
She may have decided she disliked the taste before she
even added anything to the bottle. And it all fits with
the pattern. Taking a diuretic is not uncommon for
someone with an eating disorder."

"Did you *find* any Lasix among her things?"

"I'm not at liberty to say."

If he *had* found it, I thought, he would have told me, because that bolstered his position.

"But don't you think something odd is going on?" I asked. "What about the bottle of ipecac disappearing?"

"I'm not saying there was no Lasix among her possessions, but if someone got rid of the ipecac to protect Ms. Barr's reputation, don't you think they might have done the same with the Lasix?"

"Well . . ."

"And *ipecac* is hardly something someone could slip into her food or drinks. She would have had to take that voluntarily. We know she was taking that, so it makes sense she was also ingesting a diuretic."

"It just seems odd to me—her complaining about the water. I hope you'll look into it more."

As soon as the words were out of my mouth, I regretted them. They sounded uppity, like I knew more than he did.

"I assure you that we will be examining every angle. Good day."

I phoned an update into the *Buzz* Web site and told them to flesh it out with the official statement the police had released online. Then I scurried across the street, ducked into a coffee shop, and ordered a cappuccino. I needed more caffeine to help me think.

Though I'd known foul play was a possibility, the info from Collinson was still pretty stunning. I thought back to the weekend and the several occasions I'd seen Devon with a bottle of water. When she wasn't taking a slug from one, she'd set it down nearby. It probably would have been possible for any of the houseguests to drop something into one of the water bottles without being noticed. And what a vicious cycle that would have created. The diuretic would have made Devon thirsty, leading her to drink more water, which would have meant more of the diuretic in her system and then more thirst. With each sip, she was adding greater pressure to her system—already taxed by her low weight and vomiting.

I didn't buy Collinson's theory that Devon had dissolved the Lasix in water because she didn't like the taste of the pills. She drank bottled water all day, so why would she want to muck up the taste of *that*? Taking a pill would have amounted to only a brief unpleasantness. Besides, the girl had swallowed ipecac, and that surely tasted like hell.

If someone *had* added the diuretic, they did so knowing that Devon was struggling with an eating disorder and this would help push her over the edge. They may have even known that Devon was on ipecac. Is that why the ipecac had been removed? To decrease overall suspicion?

Two names popped into mind right away as possible suspects. The first was Cap. He was supposedly having an affair with Devon. And Devon might have been putting pressure on him to fess up to Whitney. Once again I replayed the words she'd spoken to him on the deck Friday night: "You *have* to tell her. You said you would, but you haven't." And though he'd promised he *would* "tell her," when a man drags his heels, it's generally a sign that he's not fully committed to the plan at hand. Maybe all Cap had wanted was a fling with his supermodel client and he had never intended to ditch Whitney—and all those plates of pralines. Fearful of losing Whitney if she learned the truth, he'd decided to remove Devon from the picture.

Maybe he'd even convinced himself that he wasn't actually murdering Devon. He was just hurrying along the inevitable.

Of course, the other possibility was that Whitney herself had done it. Perhaps she'd gotten wind of the affair and decided to eliminate her rival. That might explain Devon's meltdown in the woods and her concern for her own safety. She could have sensed that Whitney was onto her and Cap, and truly feared for her life. I wondered if I should now tell Collinson what I'd learned about the affair.

After finishing my cappuccino, I hurried home and went immediately online, where I looked up Lasix.

It was what was called a loop diuretic, which prevented the body from absorbing too much salt. It was used in the treatment of hypertension and congestive heart failure—and to prevent thoroughbred racehorses from bleeding through the nose during races. But there was a downside. By forcing all that salt out through the urine, it could lead to a depletion of potassium—and an electrolyte imbalance. One of the first symptoms of a potassium deficiency was dizziness—which would explain why Devon seemed tipsy that night. She hadn't been drunk at the table. She'd been in danger.

The bottom line: giving Lasix to someone with anorexia—who was already low on potassium—was comparable to giving a person on the edge of a cliff a hard shove.

And it wouldn't be all that difficult for someone to lay his or her hands on it. Maybe the killer suffered from high blood pressure or knew someone who did.

From my desk drawer I dug out a clean composition book and bent it open to the first page. I'm pretty much wedded to my laptop, but I find that while I'm working on a story, making notes and asking questions with a number-two pencil in a notebook kick-starts my brain nicely.

I jotted down the names of all the houseguests and considered them one by one. Besides Cap and Whitney, Tory grabbed my interest. After all, she'd morphed into a cross between a bitch and a banshee over the dirty flirting taking place between Devon and Tommy. There was also a chance she'd known what Devon was up to with the ipecac—that stuff was probably common knowledge in the world of modeling. But she'd appeared to be on good terms with Devon when the weekend *began*, so why would she have come armed with a diuretic? Unless she had it in her own stay-skinny arsenal.

There were other possibilities. Jane clearly hated Devon. And she knew she might have an eating disorder. I couldn't dismiss Tommy either. Devon had toyed with him. He'd made that comment to me about her being a tease. Maybe she'd jerked him around one too many times.

As for the others present that weekend, none seemed to have any obvious motive for pushing Devon over the edge, but that didn't mean that they lacked one. For the moment, though, I was going to concentrate on Cap and Whitney—because that's where the most likely motives lay.

I thought suddenly of Devon's pregnancy. She'd conceived a little over a year ago. I wondered if the supposed affair between Devon and Cap had been going on for at least that long—and if the baby was his. "You've got to tell her" might have actually referred to the pregnancy. Devon may have been urging Cap to come clean about their situation for months and had finally reached the point of being seriously pissed off with her lazy-butt lover.

After finding a number for Cap's agency through 411, I called his office. The girl who answered exuded the kind of confidence you can only possess if you are twenty-two, wear designer shoes, and have never paid for a drink in your entire life. I gave my name and asked if Cap was free to speak to me.

"Mr. Darby isn't available," she said, suggesting with her tone of utter disinterest that as far as I was concerned, he would never *ever* be available.

"Just put me through to his voice mail then," I said.

"He doesn't use voice mail," she replied. She said it with distaste and disbelief at my suggestion, as if I'd just urged her to check out the new winter shoe shipment at Payless.

"Then please tell him to call me," I said. "It involves Devon Barr and is extremely important." I'd added some haughtiness to my tone, thinking that might catch her interest.

Now it was time for a little background research on Cap and Whitney. An Internet search was hardly going to tell me if either of them had the potential to be a devious murderer, but certain details about their pasts might hint at character, temperament, and needs.

I started with Cap. I couldn't find a whole lot, but his name turned up in a few places and I found one short profile of him in a trade magazine. He had practiced law for a few years and then worked his way into managing talent. His clients included some actors but mostly models. Devon, as Richard had suggested, seemed to be the biggest star he managed, and her death would certainly be a blow to his income. If he was the one who had murdered her, he would have known he'd be killing the goose that laid the golden egg.

There wasn't much about his personal life, but I learned that his marriage to Whitney was his second. He'd met her just over four years ago, two years after divorcing, and married her within a year. He had no children from either this marriage or the first.

When it came time to check out Whitney, I started with her own Web site. Scott had introduced her as Whitney Darby, but over the weekend I'd learned that professionally at least she used her maiden name—Lee. The bio on the site described Whitney Lee as a motivational speaker, cookbook author (though the book *Elegant Texas Food* wasn't slated to be released until next fall), and a media star, which seemed a stretch considering she hadn't had a regular job in TV since she left the Dallas/Fort Worth market. Her three-year stint at the television station—where she'd

covered food and health and won two local Emmys—
was described in the kind of glowing terms you'd
reserve for someone like Diane Sawyer or Barbara
Walters.

Now it was time to dig for info that hadn't been
sugarcoated by Whitney herself. But there wasn't a ton
to be found. Not surprisingly, the station's Web site had
nothing on her anymore, and there were no recent profiles of her. What I did find were pictures. She and Cap
apparently relished being seen at major social events,
and she liked to dress up, showing off her jewels and,
as Richard had suggested, that proud bosom of hers.
She'd been shot a fair amount by society photographers
like Patrick McMullan.

I found the number for her former TV station on
their Web site, and after calling it, asked for the PR
department. I told the person who answered that I was
a writer doing a profile of Cap Darby and his lovely
wife Whitney Lee and just wanted to verify a few facts.
It was *sort* of true. And it wasn't like I was going around
impersonating Johnny Depp's personal assistant just so
I could snare a better table at a restaurant.

The woman who answered drew a complete blank at
the mention of Whitney's name.

"But that doesn't mean anything," she explained
in a thick Texas accent. "I've only been here nine

months. Let me connect you to my associate, Skyler McKenzie. She should know. She's been here six or seven years."

"Which magazine?" Skyler asked after I'd done my spiel again.

"*Gloss*," I lied. It was actually a double lie because not only did I no longer work there but they'd never have done a piece on a hope-to-be-famous-if-my-book-ever-sells type like Whitney.

"Whitney was a reporter here for several years. If you want the exact dates, you'll have to speak to our HR department instead."

You *never* wanted to be banished to HR when you were writing a story. They were the Gobi Desert of information because, fearful of lawsuits, they refused to cough up a freaking thing.

"Oh, I have the dates, so that won't be necessary," I said. "I'd just love to include a few highlights of her career, and I thought your office would be best for that. I know she covered mostly food and health. Is that correct?"

I didn't really give a rat's ass about the highlights of Whitney's career, but I wanted to work my way into a conversation about the woman, hoping to score a few juicy details. I heard the rhythmic clicking sound of Skyler's nails on computer keys as she pulled up info, but I had sensed from her tone that she might have known Whitney personally.

"Yes, that's right. Food, entertainment. And health stories during her last year."

"Any examples? It would be great to have a few for my story."

"Lots of restaurant openings. A segment on which area church served the best flapjacks at their Sunday breakfast. As for health, well, let's see. There were stories on back pain . . . Botox injections—and a two-parter on allergies."

She'd listed everything in a fairly deadpan tone, but there was a soupçon of sarcasm when she added the title of the allergy series: *The Mite That Roared.* I had the feeling Skyler hadn't been a fan of Whitney's.

"I know that Whitney won two Emmys. Can you tell me what those were for?"

"Those would be *local* Emmys, you realize?"

Eww, she really *hadn't* liked Whitney, had she?

"Of course. But I'd still like to know what they were for."

There was a pause as, I assumed, she was scrolling down her computer screen.

"One was for the series on allergies," she said. "And the other? Umm, okay here it is. She did a two-part series on eating disorders."

My jaw fell open in total surprise. I couldn't even find words to respond.

"You know, like anorexia—and bulimia," she said, as if I might be confused about what she was referring to.

"Yes, sorry. I was just considering what you said. Do you know if that was a topic of special interest to her?"

"I'm afraid I wouldn't know." I heard papers rustle on her desk—she was growing itchy to end the call.

"Would you be able to send me a link to the eating disorder series?" I asked.

"That's going to involve some effort," she said.

"I'm sorry to put you to so much trouble, but it will help me add a nice splash of color to the story." Jeez, I was sounding like Martha Stewart.

After sighing audibly, Skyler promised to email me the link when she could.

I tried Cap's office again, and this time I matched his assistant snip for snip. "I really need to speak with Mr. Darby," I told her. "Tell him that critical information about Devon's death has come into my possession."

That, I thought, ought to inspire a response. And it did. Ten minutes later Cap returned the call.

"If you're calling to tell me about how Devon died, I already know. I've been in touch with the police today."

"No, it's something else. Something very important— and very private."

"Shoot," he said.

"I'd prefer not to discuss it on the phone. Can you meet me in person?"

"Why so cloak-and-dagger? What's going on?"

"I'll explain when I see you."

"I'm meeting an associate for lunch on West Fifty- fifth Street. I'll arrive early—at noon—and you can meet me there." He gave me the name of the restau- rant, not bothering with good-bye.

Worried about being late, I ended up at the restau- rant ten minutes before Cap was slated to show. It was a small Italian place with mango-colored walls, just below street level. It was the kind of restaurant you saw in old movies about Manhattan. I wondered if he'd picked it for his lunch because he'd be under the radar with his guest compared to places like Michael's and The Four Seasons.

Rather than sit at one of the tables, I slid onto a stool at the small bar and ordered a sparkling water. There weren't any diners yet, and waiters moved silently about the room, needlessly adjusting fan-shaped mango- colored napkins and shrugging their shoulders at no one in particular.

Cap arrived just a few minutes later. He slipped off his camel-colored cashmere coat and turned it over to the coat-check girl. After spotting me at the bar, he made his way over.

"A pinot grigio," he said to the bartender, lifting himself onto the stool next to me. He was wearing a perfectly fitted navy suit and crisp blue shirt, no tie. Though I'd been aware of his confident, powerful aura all weekend, the suit turned it up several notches.

"I appreciate you meeting me on such short notice," I said. "And by the way, everything's off the record."

"I don't have time for small talk, so please get right to the point," he said. "What's going on?"

"Okay, fine," I said. "I don't have a super good feeling about this past weekend. I'm wondering if someone who knew about Devon's eating disorder found a way to push her over the edge."

"You mean egged her *on*?" he said sharply. "Encouraged her to be even thinner?"

I cocked my head. "Maybe," I said. I hadn't considered that idea, but regardless, I decided not to spell out my own theory in detail; it would give too much away.

"Why would someone do something horrible like that?"

"Because they wanted Devon out of the picture."

"And something tells me you've got a theory about who did the pushing."

"Actually, I don't have a *specific* person in mind. But I do have a specific concern—and it involves you."

His strong jaw clenched visibly.

"I know your magazine specializes in the preposterous," he said after a moment, "but you seemed too smart to engage in that sort of thing. I hope to God you're not implying that I had anything to do with Devon's death. Besides my personal feelings toward her, she was my most successful client."

"People often lose sight of one advantage when something more important is at stake."

"You've totally lost me. What in God's name are you talking about?"

"You were having an affair with Devon, weren't you?"

He pulled his whole body back in surprise and his full, soft mouth dropped open. I couldn't tell if it was genuine or just for show.

"You can't be *serious*," he exclaimed. "What on earth gave you that ridiculous idea?"

"I saw the two of you together—out on the deck on Friday night."

"*So?* She was my client. I often had to speak to her privately."

"It didn't sound like a business discussion."

"Were you *spying* on us?" He took a distracted sip of his wine and shook his head in disgust.

"I headed out to the deck that first night, not knowing you were there, and I heard a few snippets. It sounded as if she was pressuring you to talk to Whitney."

He scrunched up his face as if trying to recall something.

"You said, 'I *will* tell her, but the timing has got to be right,' " I said, prodding him.

His eyes shot back toward me.

"I did agree to tell someone something, but it wasn't Whitney we were talking about. It was Barbara Dern, the head of Devon's modeling agency. There were a few issues with the agency, and Devon wanted me to approach her about them. I was worried about the timing of doing it immediately before the album came out. I thought it could blow up in her face."

"Okay, but that's not the only evidence I have. You were seen kissing Devon in the woods."

"What? That's *preposterous*." That was the second time Cap had used the word. "Who's telling you this garbage?" There was nearly smoke coming out of the guy's ears, and a few waiters were shooting looks in our direction.

"One of the other guests saw you talking to Devon in the woods on Saturday. You leaned down and kissed her. Later I saw her crying nearby, and she told me she was frightened."

"I admit I talked to Devon privately in the woods that Saturday. I went looking for her to follow up on our conversation from the night before. But I certainly didn't kiss her. I can't believe someone is telling you these lies. Are you actually suggesting that I was having an affair with Devon, and when things weren't going right, I decided to kill her by exacerbating her eating disorder?"

"That's one possibility. The other is that *Whitney* did it. She may have discovered the affair. Did you know that when she was a television reporter, she did a story on anorexia? That means she's familiar with the physical and psychological aspects of an eating disorder."

"She also did a story on Middle Eastern food, but that doesn't make her a damn terrorist. You better not be planning to print these total distortions. In my job I know an awful lot about libel and slander, and you'd be stepping on dangerous ground."

"I'm not planning on reporting any of this at the moment," I said, trying to keep my voice calm. I had tried not to become flustered during the conversation, but it was tough, considering how agitated Cap was. "Like I said earlier, I had some concerns and I wanted to discuss them with you. If Devon was murdered, I want to know about it."

"Who said I was kissing Devon in the woods? I want the name."

"I was told in confidence."

"You ought to know that you're dealing with a complete and utter liar."

"Were you privy to the fact that Devon was pregnant last year?"

His eyes registered awareness. But he jerked his head, a little surprised, it appeared, that *I* was privy to that fact.

"Yes, we knew. In fact, part of what I was doing in the woods was comforting Devon about that. She wanted a baby, and the miscarriage had been hard on her. But Whitney had talked to the doctor recently, and he was certain that there was every chance Devon could conceive again. I told Devon that. And don't ask me who the father was. That's private information."

I didn't say anything, just met his eyes and didn't let go.

"Good God, you're not thinking *I'm* the father, are you?" he said "If you start making ridiculous accusations in print about me, you'll regret it."

"You keep calling everything I saw preposterous, but it's not hard to imagine you having an affair with Devon. Two attractive, successful people whose lives are entwined . . ."

He turned completely around and looked toward the door, obviously making sure his guest hadn't arrived yet.

"There's just one very important detail you're *not* privy to," he said, his voice tight with anger.

"And what would that be?" I asked.

"This is totally off the record?"

"Yes."

"We couldn't have been having an affair. I'm not capable of having sex with anyone."

11

Cap's comment flabbergasted me. The guy radiated virility. And he was married to a younger woman who seemed like she'd demand her fair share in the sack.

"Oh," I said awkwardly. I mean, what was I *supposed* to do—ask him point blank what was up (or not up) with his package?

"You don't believe me?" he asked.

"No, that's not true. I'm just trying to process the information."

"Wait here," he said unexpectedly and slid off his stool. Oh, boy, I thought, he's not going to drop trou and show me what's the matter? But instead he strode toward the door of the still-empty restaurant and pulled his cell phone from his pocket. He was calling someone. I hoped it wasn't a libel lawyer.

While he spoke to the person on the other end, several red-nosed customers hurried in, looking happy to have escaped the cold. What in the world was he doing? I wondered. Cap's guest would surely be here any second, and we wouldn't have any more time to talk.

"All right," he said after returning to the bar. "I made arrangements for you to speak to Whitney—right now."

He grabbed a cocktail napkin from a stack toward the back edge of the bar and scrawled down his address with a chubby Montblanc pen.

"Whitney?"

"Yes, she's waiting at our apartment—and she can explain everything."

"Why are you going to so much trouble? One minute you're threatening to sue my ass off, and the next minute you're sending me up to your apartment."

"Because I can't allow you to go down this ridiculous road. Whitney will tell you what's going on and why it would have been impossible for me and Devon to be having an affair."

A few minutes later I was in an overheated cab, headed toward the West 60s. I couldn't believe this latest turn of events—but I certainly wasn't going to pass it up. The apartment turned out to be in a supermodern condo building near Lincoln Center, the kind with a huge, gleaming brass and marble lobby. My ears popped a little as the elevator hurled me toward the forty-third floor.

I didn't really have time to envision what the apartment would look like, but if I had, I probably would have guessed it'd be a nice, pretty spacious two-bedroom, purchased in this kind of building because you get more for your money here than in a fancier address on Park or Fifth Avenue. I would have been wrong. As soon as Whitney opened the door, I could see enough from the gallery-style entranceway to know that I was in a jaw-dropping apartment that took up most of the floor. The air was fragrant with the smell of something sweet baking somewhere on the premises.

"Come into the living room," Whitney said curtly and turned abruptly, suggesting I should follow. She was wearing brown tweed slacks, short-heeled leather boots, and a satiny off-white blouse with so much sheen I could almost see my pores in it. Her blond hair was pulled back with a brown suede headband. More Westchester County than Texas today.

The room she led me to was huge, large enough to include several seating areas, and was decorated in cream, ginger, and minty green tones. The walls were covered with faux Impressionist landscape paintings, and the coffee and end tables were loaded up with expensive-looking accessories—silver bowls, alabaster balls, and books about Tuscany and the Aegean Sea.

But none of that really mattered anyway because the best thing to gaze at was the view. There were floor-to-ceiling windows on three sides of the open living/ dining area. It felt almost as if we were in the cockpit of a plane.

"I'm only doing this, you realize, because Cap asked me to," Whitney said, taking a seat.

"Well, I'm very curious to hear what Cap wanted you to share with me," I said. I took a seat, too, though as Whitney's eyes followed my movements, I sensed she was worried I might stain the fabric.

"Cap is horrified about what you're suggesting— that either one of us had anything to do with Devon's death," she said. "Admittedly, Devon could be difficult, but she'd been Cap's client for many years, and he was very fond of her. And though I wouldn't have called Devon and me—what's the expression everyone uses today, bff's?—we had a good rapport. In fact, we went to a spa together several weekends ago."

"Nothing kills a good rapport like sexual jealousy, though?"

"Cap was *not* having an affair with Devon."

"Because he had some kind of sexual problem?"

SO PRETTY IT HURTS · 215

"First and foremost because we're very much in love. But, besides the point, is the fact that he couldn't physically anyway. It's horribly embarrassing for us to have to talk to you about this but if we don't, you'll print ugly speculations in that dreadful magazine of yours."

I could see her cheeks coloring up as she spoke. She pressed one of her hands to her chest.

"Are you okay?"

"I have asthma. And it can flare up when things become unpleasant."

"I'm sorry if I've upset you," I said. "But I'm really just interested in the truth, not idle speculation. I want to get to the bottom of things."

She cast her eyes downward as the tip of her small pink tongue slipped out and touched her top lip. Finally she glanced back up at me.

"Cap has lupus. He's been suffering from it for over a year. We are very hopeful that with God's help and the best doctors in New York, his condition will improve. And right now all the signs are pointing to a full recovery."

"I'm happy to hear that."

"But until that recovery is complete, Cap can't fully function as he once did—because of a combination of the disease and the medication. There's no way Cap could have been having an affair with Devon. It's not physically possible."

I flashed on a phrase I'd once read in *Gloss*: emotional adultery. Or what you could call head sex. You form an intense bond with someone who isn't your partner, and though it may not involve a physical relationship, you share your deepest feelings and secrets with that person and eventually hope to take it to the next level.

"Isn't it possible for two people to be smitten with each other without necessarily consummating it?" I asked. "Some of the great love stories in history would fit into that category."

She made a sound that was something between a laugh and a snicker.

"That wouldn't be Cap," she said. "He's a very sexual man."

"I appreciate your candor," I told her. "Like I said, I'm just trying to figure out what really happened. Certain aspects of the weekend just seem disturbing to me."

"What do you mean by *disturbing*?"

"Well, for one, someone ran around scratching our bedroom doors with a branding iron during the middle of the night."

"I have no idea who played that awful prank," Whitney said. "Maybe someone with a mean sense of humor—like Richard Parkin."

"That's not all that worries me. As I told Cap, I'm concerned about how Devon's anorexia seemed to spiral downward so quickly."

Whitney pinched her lips together for a moment before speaking.

"You asked about a possible eating disorder this weekend," she said. "For obvious reasons I couldn't be candid at the time. But now that it's out in the open, there's no need for me to beat around the bush. Devon's anorexia had actually been rearing its head again for several months now, and Cap and I were doing our best to try to deal with it. The main reason I took her to the spa was to encourage her to eat. I thought if she knew the food was nutritional and low-fat, she'd be less resistant."

"As a reporter, you did a story on anorexia, right?"

Her eyes widened slightly—in surprise, it seemed. Cap obviously hadn't mentioned on the phone that I was aware of this.

"Actually, yes. And I knew from doing my story that many girls relapse. Cap and I were just hoping that we could nip it in the bud."

"Why do you think it reared its head again?"

She sighed and leaned slightly back into a small herd of throw pillows behind her.

"They say stress triggers it," she said, her clear blue eyes holding mine. "And Devon *was* stressed lately.

She was . . . well, worried about what the future held for her."

"What if I told you someone might have helped her anorexia along?"

"Helped it *along*?" Whitney said, irritably. "What are you talking about? How could someone help it along?"

"You did the story on the disease. You know as well as I do that certain things can exacerbate the problem."

"The only thing exacerbating the problem was Devon herself. Like I told you, she was anxious about her career. She may have looked all nonchalant about things, but she *wasn't*. With her modeling career winding down, she needed that album to be a success."

"If she only had a few years left in her modeling career, why get pregnant?" I asked.

I saw her pull back ever so slightly, like Cap, clearly surprised I knew.

"Devon was impetuous," Whitney said sharply. "She did what seemed right for her at the moment, without thinking about the consequences . . ."

Her voice trailed off, but I waited, hoping my silence would encourage her to continue. She looked away, gathering her thoughts, and then returned those nearly translucent eyes to me.

"And one day," she added, "she decided a baby was what she wanted. To be honest, I think it had to do with her dog dying. She'd had this little Pomeranian for years, and she was crushed when it passed early last year. But rather than buy another dog, she developed a ferocious case of baby fever. She wanted a baby simply to have something love her unconditionally."

"Do you think she would have tried again?"

She looked off again, as if thinking. "Possibly," she replied.

"Of course, conceiving would have been tough with her eating disorder," I said.

"I'd really prefer not to speculate," Whitney said.

"What can you tell me about the other houseguests?" I said. "Do you think Devon had an issue with any of them?"

"Issues? They were her friends. That's why she'd invited them."

"But what about Christian? Cap said there were some problems with the modeling agency."

"Nothing that couldn't be addressed. You know what it seems like to me? That you're tryin' to get blood from a stone. Is that how you've made your mark as a so-called journalist?" She clenched her hands in her lap, and I could tell that the irritation she'd been mostly attempting to suppress was starting to shoot up to the surface. Time to cut my losses.

"No, like I said, I'm just hoping to learn the truth. Why don't I say goodbye now? I appreciate how helpful you've been."

She led me back through the apartment to the entrance gallery. She seemed distracted suddenly, rather than simply anxious for my departure. Was she jumping ahead mentally to the next thing she needed to whip up for her cookbook? Was she thinking about Cap and filling him in? I couldn't tell what was tugging her attention away.

"Will there be a funeral for Devon?" I asked as we reached the door.

"Yes, on Saturday. It's going to be very private—in that sad little town she grew up in out in Pennsylvania."

"Did her mother plan it?"

"Yes. Sherrie supposedly sobered up just long enough to make a few decisions. Of course, there will be a big memorial service here sometime in the next couple of weeks. A chance for all her New York friends to honor her memory."

"Speaking of her New York friends, do you have a number for Tory?" If Cap *hadn't* been having an affair with Devon, I needed to focus on the other houseguests, and I had no direct way of reaching Tory.

"Why Tory?"

"I just want to follow up on a conversation I had with her this weekend."

She sighed.

"Wait here. I do have a number for her, since she was pressuring Cap this weekend to represent her."

She disappeared somewhere in the apartment. While she was gone, I glanced around, studying the place in a way I hadn't been able to when we'd been talking. On the hall table were almost a dozen silver-framed photographs of Cap and Whitney—the two of them lounging on a boat deck, laughing at various black-tie events, sitting with a group of friends at a café.

There was no mistaking their connection. *Buzz* constantly analyzed celebrity body language, and though it occasionally seemed like a stretch, much of it made sense on a gut level. Anyone looking at those photos would attest to how tight Whitney and Cap's bond seemed to be. They backed up Whitney's insistence that Cap had been faithful to her. I was going to have to have another talk with Jane. She may have lied to me about Cap and Devon, and I needed to know why.

With Tory's number in hand, I flagged a cab and headed for *Buzz*. I lay my head against the back seat and tried to wrestle my thoughts to the ground. If Cap and Whitney were telling the truth, it meant Cap hadn't murdered Devon in a crime of passion and Whitney hadn't done so out of sexual jealousy. But either one of them could have had *another* motive. Perhaps Cap had been embezzling money from Devon and was freaked he was about to be found out.

With Cap and Whitney off the hit list for now, though, there were others I needed to focus on. Tory, for one. It was interesting what Whitney had said about Tory wanting Cap as her manager. I wondered how much it bugged her that she hadn't reached supermodel status the way Devon had. If she'd been the one who added the Lasix to Devon's water, the reason actually may have been twofold: envy over Devon's career and jealousy over Tommy's renewed interest in her.

And speaking of Tommy, how much had Devon's game-playing disturbed him? Maybe he'd made a move on Devon during the weekend, only to discover that Devon didn't truly want him back—she'd just been playing with his head. That could make a man with a short fuse mad.

But once again I considered the wrinkle in the idea of Tommy as a killer, or Tory either. Whoever had put diuretic pills in Devon's water must have devised the plan beforehand and brought Lasix with them. Unless, of course, they had it in their possession for medical reasons or had discovered it on the premises. I wondered if Ralph had high blood pressure.

There was also Jane to think about. If Jane had lied about Cap and Devon, then why? What was her reason for wanting to cast suspicion on Cap? Because she was the guilty one?

I also needed to explore Devon's problem with her modeling agency. Did it involve Christian? Had Devon threatened to make trouble for him?

The *Buzz* office was quiet when I arrived. Jessie was out on a story, and Leo was staring at a screen full of shots of Suri Cruise.

"Anything going on here?" I asked.

"Not that *I'm* in the loop on. I'm too busy working on photos for a chart on Suri's shoe obsession. From what I can tell so far, she has about seven thousand pairs."

After dumping my bag and popping my head in Nash's door to say I was around if he needed me, I checked my voice mail and found to my surprise that Richard Parkin had left a message. I hadn't expected him to stay in touch. Of course, since he was going to write his own story for *Vanity Fair*, he was probably sniffing around to see what I knew.

As I punched in Richard's phone number, a thought flitted across my mind. Richard looked like a poster boy for hypertension. Could he have a prescription for Lasix? He didn't have a motive—at least that I knew of—but someone could have pinched it from his room. After all, there'd been no way for guests to lock their rooms when they left them.

"Thank you for calling back," he said, all British charm and surprisingly sober sounding for this deep into the day. "I just wondered how you were surviving. I've been following your Web postings—nice job."

"Thank you. It's been a little crazy the last day or two."

"Still aching?"

"Pardon me?"

"You took that very nasty spill."

"All better," I said, deciding to spare him a description of the yellow-and-purple mark that had now spread over most of the left cheek of my ass. "How are things on *your* end? Did you decide to tackle this story, too?"

He paused a beat.

"Actually, I may not do it after all," he confessed.

"*Really.* How come?"

"I've got a pretty full plate right now. And frankly, as I poked around, I've found Devon's life about as exciting as a boiled ham sandwich—without the honey mustard. Oh, she was a supermodel with a dirt-poor past and that's got a Dickensian ring to it, but there's nothing particularly fresh about her version."

"I take it you've seen what the police released about her death."

"Yes. Her ticker stopped ticking. Won't the world be a sad place without her?"

Gee, he hadn't been a fan, had he?

"What if someone really wasn't so sad to see her gone?" I asked.

Another pause.

"What are you saying?" he asked.

"What if her death wasn't really accidental?"

"Have you dug up something you're not telling me, Ms. Weggins?"

"No, just thinking out loud," I said.

"Oh, come now, Bailey. I can tell you've got something. Aren't you going to be nice and share, one journalist to another?"

"There just seemed to be a lot of tension this weekend. And I was shoved down the stairs. Stuff like that always arouses my curiosity."

"I see. Well, let me know if you want to brainstorm. I'd be happy to assist."

As soon as I hung up, I tried the number Whitney had given me for Tory. She answered, though I could barely hear her thanks to the pounding music in the background.

"It's Bailey Weggins," I said loudly. "I need to talk to you. I have some very important information I think you'd want to hear."

"About what?" she shouted over the music.

"I'd prefer to tell you in person, and I know you'll be interested. It's about Devon."

"I'm on a job right now. I can't talk."

"What time do you finish? I could meet you."

Even with the music I heard her sigh.

"All right," she said wearily. "You can meet me at six." She quickly rattled off the name and address of the studio—it was in the Meatpacking District—and then cut off without a good-bye.

After leaving messages for Jane on her cell phone and Christian at First Models, I researched Devon Barr's "sad" little hometown—which turned out to be Pine Grove, Pennsylvania—because more than likely Nash would want me to check out the scene at the funeral service on Saturday. And finally I reviewed tomorrow's TV and radio plan with one of the PR people. In addition to the *Today* show, they'd secured a lot of other media. Mentally I tried to place the one wool suit I owned.

Just after five Jessie blew in, her cheeks red from the cold and her eyes wide with excitement.

"You're not going to believe the info I have," she whispered, grabbing my arm. "We need to talk in private."

I followed her to a conference room toward the back of the floor.

"What's going on?" I asked as she quickly shut the door.

"Guess what our ornery friend Jane has been up to. She's apparently planning to write a tell-all book on

Devon and has been secretly peddling the proposal for weeks."

"How'd you find that out?"

"From a contact I have in the book biz. I was trying to wangle some info from her on a whole different subject, and it came up because she'd read I was one of the infamous houseguests last weekend. Though her company saw the proposal, they passed on it."

"But wouldn't Jane have signed some kind of confidentiality agreement when she went to work for Devon?"

"You'd think. But this editor told me that because Devon had such trouble keeping assistants, in the end she didn't make Jane sign one."

"Did anyone end up buying the book?"

"The chick told me she's not sure. She said she'd heard Jane was having a hard time placing it."

"Because?"

"According to this girl, there wasn't much there. I mean, Jane had only been with Devon for nine months, so it's not as if there were a ton of secrets she had first-hand knowledge of. Plus, let's face it—Devon was kind of a bore. She liked to bitch out her assistants and date skinny rockers, but hey, what else is new?"

I stared off, my mind racing.

"*What?*" Jessie asked. "You've got that Bailey-Weggins-has-a-dangerous-idea look on your face."

"Maybe Devon's life was kind of a bore when she was alive, but now that she's dead, it's a bit more interesting, right? A publisher might be suddenly eager for a book on Devon that they could rush to press."

I quickly filled Jessie in on what I'd learned this morning from Detective Collinson and how it fit with what Sandy had shared about the funny taste of the water.

"Omigod," Jessie muttered. "Are you saying that Jane killed Devon so that she'd have a better chance of selling her book?"

"It's just a thought. A crazy one, but *someone* in that house had a motive. I'm almost sure of it."

She started to lob more questions at me, but glancing at my watch, I saw that I needed to hightail it out of there for my meeting with Tory. I told her I'd catch up with her later.

"Just one more thing," Jessie said. "Everything still good with Beau?"

I smiled. "Yeah, all good."

Because of how cold it was outside, there was tons of snarky cab competition, and it took me fifteen minutes to flag one down. Then I was stuck in traffic. I used the time to check voicemail. I discovered that while I'd been with Jessie, Beau had left a message saying he'd be tied up for dinner until about ten but he'd love to see me afterward.

I made it downtown just in time. The photo studio turned out to be in an old brick building that had once probably contained small factories but had since been gutted to create large, loftlike spaces. I took the elevator to the fifth floor and found myself in a huge lobby with at least four photo studios spilling off from it. There were leather-backed chairs and a small bar in the waiting area, with an old-fashioned popcorn maker on the counter and a cluster of guys in jeans and hoodies talking aimlessly. Several messengers moved around on the periphery, lugging stuffed black garment bags. All of sudden a huge dog—a mastiff, I thought—trotted by itself out of one of the studios and headed down a hallway.

"May I help you?" the receptionist asked. I noticed she had last week's *Buzz* opened in front of her.

"Studio Two?"

"Are they expecting you?"

"Yes, I'm here to see Tory Hartwick."

She pointed to a studio just across from me. Thankfully there was still music emanating from the open doorway, so the shoot obviously hadn't ended yet.

As I crossed the pockmarked cement floor, my BlackBerry rang. Thinking it might be one of the other houseguests I'd left a message for, I dug it quickly out of my bag. Nash's name showed on the screen. Something big must have happened.

"Hey, what's up?" I asked.

"Where are you?" he asked brusquely. Nash could be moody, but I'd never heard him speak to me in such an abrupt tone.

"Downtown, about to do an interview for the Devon Barr story. Why?"

"You need to come back here. Right now."

"You sound pissed. Is anything the matter?"

"Yeah, something's the matter. Your job is in serious jeopardy."

12

"What?" I said. My legs suddenly seemed to liquefy. "Tell me what's going on."

"I don't want to get into it on the phone. How soon can you get here?"

"Uh, depending on traffic, a half hour to forty-five minutes," I said.

"All right," was his only response. No good-bye. Not even a "See you then."

To my chagrin, my hand was trembling slightly as I slipped the BlackBerry back into my bag. I had stepped in doo-doo somehow, but I couldn't imagine how. I'd been working hard on the Devon story, investigating every angle possible, so it was tough to figure what he might see as a shortcoming in my efforts. Had another magazine or Web site—like TMZ, which broke heaps of celebrity news every week—scooped us on some detail about Devon's death? If that was the case, Nash might be annoyed or frazzled, but he wouldn't have sounded like a cougar that hadn't eaten in days.

I needed to get back to the *Buzz* offices and find out what was going on, but I also didn't want to blow my chance to pump Tory. I'd told Nash I might be as long as forty-five minutes, but I was pretty sure I could make it uptown in thirty. I decided to use the next fifteen minutes to try to elicit what I could from Tory—though it was going to be hard as hell to concentrate.

With my stomach grinding, I walked through the open door of Studio Two, and found myself immediately in a small seating area. Ahead of me to my right was a partitioned-off area where the actual shoot was happening, with a backdrop of seamless paper that created the illusion of the space going on forever, like a piece of white sky. The photographer was snapping away at a girl, using phrases I'd thought they only tossed out in movie scenes about photo shoots—like "That's perfect, hold it just there," and "Okay, give me the smile again. Chin up." Next to him an assistant watched the photos flash instantaneously on a computer screen.

To the left was an open makeup and dressing area, with a huge mirror lined with lights. Several people in black were standing near the window, talking. At the counter one model was having her hair wrapped in jumbo Velcro rollers, and another was rifling through a python-printed tote bag. It took me a second to realize it was Tory.

As I was deliberating about the best way to grab her attention, she glanced up and spotted me. I saw her shoulders sag in annoyance. She said a few words to the people by the window and then made her way over to me. She was wearing tight, tight black jeans, black boots that went above her knees, and a red turtleneck sweater that looked really striking with her cropped black hair. I figured those were her own clothes, not something for the shoot, because the other model on the set was in a sheer, flowy outfit that had next spring written all over it.

"This is really uncool, you know—you coming to my job," Tory said after she'd walked over to me.

I was about to point out that she was the one who'd invited me but decided it was probably best not to aggravate her anymore.

"Are you done?" I asked. "Can we talk now?"

"I'm done for the day. But I don't want to talk here."

She moved past me, leading the way on her giraffe legs out of the studio, past the sounds of "That's right, very nice," and "Perfect, perfect." As I followed her into the hallway I stole a glance at my watch. I had about twelve minutes now, and I was going to have to make the most of them. Just thinking about my time restrictions made Nash's words echo in my head, hard as a car horn—"Your job is in serious jeopardy." It took everything to shut them out.

"I suppose you've heard the news about Devon's death," I said as we positioned ourselves in a corner of the lobby.

"You mean, that she had some kind of heart problem."

"Yes. She died of a heart attack."

"That's so freaky. My grandfather had a heart attack, but he was like eighty."

"Actually, heart attacks aren't all that uncommon in people who have eating disorders," I said. "I know you told me last weekend that you weren't aware of any problems with Devon regarding her eating, but the autopsy found differently. The bottom line is that she was anorexic."

"Why are you so freaking interested?" Tory demanded. "You didn't even *know* her."

"You're right. I didn't know her. But there are some aspects of her death that confuse me. I want to find out exactly what happened to Devon."

"But you said you *did* know," Tory whined. "That she died of a heart attack."

"True, but I'm curious about why her anorexia flared up again. From what I understand from Cap and

Whitney"—invoking their names seemed like a good way to gain some cred with her—"Devon had suffered from anorexia years ago but had overcome it. Why do you think it cropped up again now—when she had so much going for her."

"Maybe she was nervous about her album," Tory said without much conviction. "Or about being without a guy. Devon didn't like being on her own."

"So *had* you noticed her eating issues?" I asked. "I appreciate you covering for Devon earlier out of respect for her privacy, but the truth is out now—so there's no need to."

"I didn't know for *sure*," she said. "I mean, I noticed she was skinnier. And then I heard her puking in the bathroom of a club one night a couple of weeks ago. I mean it didn't even really sound like puking. It was more like this dry heaving—like after you've puked all night and don't have anything left."

Yummy, I thought.

"About two weeks ago, you say?" I asked.

"Maybe. Yeah, I guess."

"Anything else going on then?"

"No. I mean, I guess, as you could see, she was probably more upset about being dumped by Tommy than she let on. She wanted him back. And she brought me to Scott's to be some kind of—what do you call it? Scapegoat?"

Gosh, the girl made an olive seem smart.

"Did Devon seem scared at all to you lately?"

"No. What would she be scared about?"

It was becoming clear that what had freaked her on the day she died—"Someone knows something"— might have surfaced this past weekend. Somehow I was going to have to figure out what it was.

"There's something else I'm curious about, Tory. Have you ever heard of Lasix?"

She twisted one side of her mouth as if she were concentrating.

"Is that the surgery for your eyes?" she said. "Where you don't have to wear glasses anymore?"

I couldn't totally fault her for that one—they *did* sound the same.

"No, Lasix is a diuretic. Had you ever heard of Devon using it?"

She shook her head. "No, never heard of it," she said.

I'd been watching her closely, and nothing in her face suggested that this information was making her uncomfortable. It could be because she truly had no idea what I was talking about—*or* because the dull, slack expression she usually wore was incapable of betraying what was really crossing her mind.

I decided to go down another road and see where that took me.

"How've *you* been doing in light of all this? It must be hard to have that kind of weekend and then go right back to work."

She shrugged. "It's okay," she said. "I mean, what are you gonna do?"

"Speaking of work, I hear you may start using Cap—to help manage your career."

"Who told you *that*?" she demanded. There was a flash of anger in her deep, hooded eyes, and I was glad she wasn't holding a drink.

"I forget—someone this weekend," I said. "But that's good, right? He did so much for Devon's career."

She began rooting through her python bag—to avoid eye contact, I suspected.

"I'm not sure what I'm doing," she muttered. "I wanna keep my options open for now."

"What about Tommy? Is he still in the picture?"

She jerked her head up.

"That guy is such an asshole," she declared. "I can't believe I ever looked twice at him. He goes around as if he's the rock king of the world, and his last album sold about seventy-five thousand copies. I dropped him off Sunday night—he's got a suspended license, so *I* had to drive his Jag—and told him to not even think of calling me."

"Do you believe Tommy and Devon were up to more than flirting this past weekend?"

"Who the fuck cares?" she said. She shook her head back and forth. "Maybe. *You* saw how they were acting, right? Plus," she added after a second's pause, "he disappeared later Saturday night—for about an hour."

I felt the hairs on the back of my neck jump to attention.

"What time was that?"

"Around one. He's *such* a turd."

"And you think he went to Devon's room?"

"When he came back, he said he'd been in the big barn the whole time—having a cigarette and a brandy. He said that he couldn't sleep. But what the asshole didn't know was that I went up there looking for him, and he wasn't there. I was tempted to knock on Devon's door, but I'm not going to stoop to that kind of thing. He comes back an hour later and tells me I must have showed up at the moment he went to the head."

"Did you know that Devon was pregnant last winter?"

"*Pregnant? By Tommy?*" The idea seemed to freak her out.

"No, it was around this time last year—before she met him."

"But where's the baby?" she asked. Good question. Maybe I hadn't given the girl enough credit.

"She apparently miscarried at around four or five months. You didn't know about it?"

"I didn't know her last winter. We got to be friends this past summer."

But of course. Devon and Tory lived in that world of instant friendships that then ended up lasting about four seconds.

I shot another quick look at my watch. I needed to haul butt. I told Tory I had another appointment but might touch base with her later, which seemed to really thrill her. Then I asked for Tommy's cell number.

"I've got a few questions for him, too," I said, in case she thought I might be making a play for the guy.

"You know what would be funny," she said, writing it down. "You should publish his number in your magazine—so he gets a billion calls."

"I'll run that by the editor. I have just one last question for you. Was Devon having any problems with her modeling agency?"

"We have different agencies, so I didn't really know what went on at hers. But I'll tell you one thing: she and Christian practically never talked last weekend. Every time he was on one side of the room, she went to the other."

Not having known the players and their relationships, I hadn't picked up on that, but as I flashed back through the weekend, I realized I'd never seen them interacting.

"Why invite him then?"

"I don't think she did. Scott must have." But Scott had told me Devon had dictated the guest list.

I said a quick good-bye and flew out of there. Knowing that finding a cab would be a bitch, I opted for the subway instead. As the train shot through the tunnel, with me squashed in a mound of parkas and wool coats, I tried to ignore the knot in my stomach and turned over what I'd learned from Tory. Tommy had left his room Saturday night and had probably popped into Devon's. But that raised plenty of questions. Devon had seemed unsteady when she went back to her room after dinner, and in hindsight it was clear she was already in a precarious situation physically. And around one thirty she had called Laura, complaining of feeling ill. So it was hard to imagine her being up for any fireworks in the sack. Why had Tommy hung around, then? Had he tried to help her? And if so, why hadn't he said anything about it? Perhaps he'd been more forthcoming with the police, but I doubted it. He didn't seem like the type of guy who made nice with cops.

Up on the street, I yanked my BlackBerry from my purse and called Jessie. Please, please pick up, I begged, and sighed in relief when she did.

"Look, I'm apparently in some kind of trouble with Nash," I told her. "Have you heard anything?"

"No, nothing," she said, lowering her voice. "What kind of trouble could you possibly be in? Our Web site is getting a zillion hits thanks to your story. He should be giving you a fucking raise."

"And you haven't seen anything weird or tense going on there? I'm wondering if someone scooped me on some part of the Devon Barr story."

"No, nothing weird . . . Oh, God, wait a minute. One of the lawyers was down here earlier—the scary one with the long chin who makes your bowels loosen the minute you see him. He was in Nash's office with the door closed for about fifteen minutes. I figured some celebrity was threatening to sue our ass off."

"When was this?"

"About an hour ago."

"I'm almost there now, so I'll see you in a few."

I knew it might not be connected, but considering the lawyer had been in Nash's office immediately before I'd received the call, there was a good chance they were related. Lawyers paying house calls to editorial floors often meant a threat of either libel or invasion of privacy. I racked my brain, trying to think of anything I'd included in Web site stories that might have set off a stink, but I couldn't come up with a thing.

I spilled out of the elevator onto the floor just five minutes later. I dropped my coat and bag on my chair, accepted Jessie's look of support with a grim smile, and headed for Nash's office.

"Come in and close the door," was all he said when I popped my head in.

"What's going on?" I asked as I took a seat. He wore a stern, almost stricken expression I'd never witnessed on him before, even after the worst tussle with a Hollywood publicist. I did my best to keep my panic under wraps.

"I think you know what's going on."

"What's going on from my end is that I'm spending every waking moment reporting my story," I said, failing, of course, to deduct the hour and a half I'd been spread-eagled nude in front of a roaring fire last night. "But clearly something else is up, or you wouldn't have called me in here. I honestly have no idea what you're talking about."

"I'm talking about your conversations with Sherrie Barr."

"You mean *Devon* Barr, don't you?"

"No, Sherrie. Devon's mother."

"But I've never spoken to Devon's mother."

"She says differently," he snapped.

"What?" I said. "Like I just said, I've had no contact at all with her mother—I was told that the reporter doing the sidebar on Devon had tried to reach her but hadn't had any luck. And even if I *had* talked to her, what's the big deal?"

Nash massaged his right hand hard with the other, as if there was a kink in it, and stared questioningly at me.

"Here's the deal," he said bluntly. "Her mother called my office, saying you got in touch with her right after Devon's death and claimed that you had embarrassing information about Devon—but that you'd be willing to keep it under wraps if she paid you ten thousand dollars."

I snorted, a weird honking sound that reflected not only my assessment of his revelation but also how freaking awkward I was feeling. What Nash was saying was absurd, but the tight, white look of his lips suggested he *believed* it. I was aware suddenly that people outside his glass-walled office all seemed to be staring at us, as if we'd both stripped down to our undies.

"I have no idea why she would tell anyone that," I said, trying not to let my voice catch. "From what I hear, she's an alcoholic. Maybe she's also a total whack job. Or maybe she's just trying to get back at me for filing the reports about Devon's death. She may even have me confused with someone else. Some other reporter might have actually tried to shake her down for money, but in her drunken stupor she couldn't recall the name so she finds my story online and decides it must have been me."

"If you've never called her, how is it that she has your cell phone number? That's certainly not listed on the *Buzz* Web site."

"I—are you sure it was even Sherrie Barr that called? What if it was simply someone posing as her?"

"We've checked that all out, of course. It's definitely her."

"I don't know what's going on, then." My mind was racing, but not getting anywhere. "It sounds like someone with access to my number gave it to her. Maybe *that* person wanted to make trouble for me."

"But why would Sherrie Barr choose to cooperate?" he asked.

"I have no idea," I said, shaking my head. I desperately wished I could come up with something—*anything*—because being without a theory seemed to suggest I was guilty. But I honestly didn't have a clue why someone would be pulling a stunt like this. "I—I have to think about it. The bottom line, though, is that I didn't do it. Nash, we haven't worked together all that long, but I hope it's been long enough for you to have a sense of who I am. I would never try to extort money from someone. I honestly can't believe that you'd think that of me."

His face softened, and he leaned back on his desk, scooching his butt up onto the surface.

"Look, Bailey, to be perfectly honest, I *don't* believe it. You know how I feel about you. But the woman called me up with this story—and she called our legal department too—and it's hard to figure out why she'd just make it up. What's in it for *her*? I had no choice but to put it to you this way. I needed to see how you'd respond."

"And so you believe me now?" I said. From the first time since he'd begun talking, I relaxed just a little. It no longer felt as if someone was running over my stomach with a power lawn mower.

"Yes. But it's not just me who's in the mix. The lawyers are involved now, of course—and so is Tom Dicker." He was referring to that nasty little man who ran the company.

"You'll vouch for me, right?"

"Yes, but that's not going to be enough. They're going to have to investigate."

"What does that mean?" The brief relief I'd felt with Nash's words of support had shriveled, and my heart was beating like the wings of a bird trapped in my chest.

"They'll look into it. Check this woman out. Probably check your phone logs. Unfortunately, until they finish, you're off the story."

"*What?* I'm right in the middle of the story," I exclaimed. "And I'm supposed to do all this press tomorrow."

"Someone else is going to have to take care of that. And we'll keep other reporters on the story."

"You can't be serious. Nash, I've done nothing wrong. You can't punish me this way."

"It's not up to me, Bailey. The company could end up in real trouble if it turns out you're guilty of extortion."

"But you said you believed me."

"I do—but the company has to check it all out. I'm sure it won't take more than a day or two."

I've never come close to crying at work, but at that very moment I felt a prick of tears in each eye, and I did everything in my power to fight it off. Not only was my gig at *Buzz* on the line, but also my reputation as a reporter. The situation couldn't be worse. Wrong. One second later I learned that it could be.

"I think it's best if you keep a low profile too," Nash said. "You need to steer clear of this place until everything's resolved."

"Am I being paid during this time?"

"I need to check with the lawyer."

"I—" I started to take one more stab at defending myself but it seemed utterly pointless. Even if Nash believed me—and I wasn't a hundred percent sure he did—it was clearly beyond his control. I muttered a good-bye and slunk out of the office. Almost everyone in the bullpen was checking me out as I walked back to my cubby. They'd seen the tension between Nash and me through the glass.

"What the hell is going on?" Jessie whispered as soon as I returned to my desk.

"It's bad," I said. "But I'll have to call you. I'm supposed to clear out of here."

"Omigod."

"Say something funny to me, will you? So people will think everything's normal."

She scrunched up her mouth as she thought.

"You know that girl in production with the Rapunzel hair?" she said. "She told someone she's dating a guy who can only get off if he pinches her butt so hard she screams."

I forced out a "Ha-ha," but my heart was sinking rapidly. Though I was anxious now to leave, I didn't rush. If I refused to flee as if the place was in flames, maybe people would assume I'd simply been given a tongue-lashing for being scooped by TMZ. I downloaded something from my computer, left a quiet message for Beau saying I desperately needed to talk to him, and discreetly stuffed my most important files into my tote bag.

But as I finally made it through the bullpen toward reception, I realized how pointless my little exercise had been. Surrounding me were dozens of reporters who were onto every boob job and blow job performed in L.A. If they didn't know the details of my situation already, they would know soon enough. Plus my cheeks were a dead giveaway. I could tell they were flaming red, as if they'd been scorched from standing too close to a rocket launch.

As I stepped into the elevator, a terrible thought flashed through my brain. What if today had been my very last day ever as a reporter for *Buzz*?

13

It actually felt good to be outside because the cold air was like a compress against my red-hot cheeks. As I hurried toward the subway, Beau returned my call. I blurted out the story to him.

"Bailey, this is all going to work out," he said reassuringly. "They can't possibly end up buying this story."

"But right now it's my word against Devon's mother's, and they seem to have no confidence in *my* word."

"Can you think of anything you said to this woman that she might have misconstrued?"

"But that's the point, I never *spoke* to her. She's making the whole thing up."

"Look, I want to see you as soon as possible, but I've got six people showing up at my studio any minute. What if we meet at my place at about ten?"

"That would be great. I guess I'll just go home first and try not to throw myself off my terrace."

"I've got an idea," he said after a pause. "Do you have my key with you? You can go straight to my place. There's food in the fridge, and you can make yourself dinner."

"Uhh, sure. I'd love that. Thanks."

"You know where the wine is. Just open a bottle. I'll call you right before I leave."

For some reason just talking to Beau had eased my misery a little. Plus, I felt a quick giddy rush from his suggestion that I let myself into his place. A few weeks ago we had agreed to exchange keys to each other's apartments just in case one of us arrived before the other, but as of yet there had never been a time when it was necessary. Encouraging me to go to his pad alone tonight seemed to nudge our relationship forward a little.

As I hurried to the subway, I called Jessie and filled her in on what I hadn't been able to share in the office.

"I can't effing believe this," she whispered. "What are you gonna do?"

"Try to get to the bottom of it. I don't want to put you in the middle or jeopardize your situation, but will you keep me posted if you hear anything?"

"Of course."

"And use your cell to call me, not your office line. You don't want them to know you've been talking to me."

Twenty-five minutes later, I was turning the key in the lock on Beau's front door. It felt positively weird to be entering his place by myself. As I opened the door, I caught traces of the exotic, musky fragrance Beau wore and the lingering scent of wood smoke from the fire the night before. I flipped on a light, pulled off my coat and boots, and took a couple of deep breaths, trying to chase away the feeling of doom.

In the kitchen I rummaged through the fridge and turned up a few ingredients for a salad. I threw them into a bowl, made a vinaigrette dressing, and then opened a bottle of wine. It was simple fare, but I didn't need to think too hard. I brought my plate and wineglass into the living room, set them on the coffee table, and after grabbing my composition notebook and a pencil, plopped onto the floor with my legs spread along the length of the table.

My mind had been racing since I left Nash's office, trying to grasp what was going on, but my thoughts had all been a terrible jumble. Now, in the warm solitude of Beau's tenth-floor apartment, with the city sounds so muffled I could hardly hear them, I finally had the chance to try to sort out the mess.

From my vantage point, there were a couple of reasons that Sherrie Barr might tell people I'd been trying to extort money from her. One, she was hoping *she'd* pocket some dough from it. Perhaps in a drunken stupor she'd convinced herself that if she claimed someone on the *Buzz* staff was harassing her, management would turn over cash to shut her up. But that didn't explain how she had my phone number.

I decided the more likely scenario was that someone had convinced Sherrie to do it in order to create trouble for me. It would have to be someone who had sway over Sherrie and/or was offering her big bucks to do it.

If so, *why?* Because I was digging deeper into Devon's death and looking aggressively for answers?

I set down my fork and reached for my pencil to make a few notes. Just then Beau's landline rang from his office, making me jump. I wondered if I ought to pick up in case it was Beau, but I realized that he would have called my cell phone. After four rings the machine picked up, and seconds later, I heard a deep, slightly imperious-sounding voice that I recognized instantly as Beau's mother. I'd met her only once, at lunch, but it was a voice you couldn't forget.

"Sweetheart, give me a call later, will you? I'm trying to nail down our Christmas plans. I told your brother and sister we'd discussed the Caribbean, and they're both game. Your father doesn't care where we go, as long as it's warm. But do let me know for sure. It's going to be hard to find a flight as it is."

Funny, *my* name hadn't been raised at all. If Beau's family hightailed it to some posh Caribbean resort for the holidays, would I be asked to join them? Highly doubtful, it seemed. I should have known. Beau's mother had been perfectly pleasant to me over lunch, but hardly embracing. I had the feeling she didn't like the idea of Beau with *any* girl, but something about me particularly set her off. I figured she considered that my job reporting celebrity crime was just a few notches above doing lap dances at Scores.

What would *I* do for the holidays if Beau took off for a hot spot like St. Kitts or Jamaica? My mother had called two weeks ago and announced that she'd been invited to spend Christmas week in Mexico—in San Miguel de Allende—with a retired professor she'd once taught with. Figuring I might want to be with Beau, she'd asked if I'd mind. I'd given her my blessing, assuming I *would* be hanging with my new boyfriend.

I took a swig of wine and returned my gaze to my notebook, trying to concentrate on Sherrie Barr. Damn, I thought. Why did I have to overhear that call?

Two minutes later the phone rang again. Great, I thought. Maybe it was his mother again, calling back to remind him to take his Flintstone vitamins or floss his teeth. But it was a different female voice: flirty and fun—and with a British accent.

"Hello, Beau, it's Abigail," she said. "I've been back from Turkey for about a month, and it's taken me this long to clean the grime from under my nails. My thesis is done, and I'm coming to New York for some holiday shopping. I'd love to see you. Can you give me a call?"

My heart was in my throat as she rattled off a UK number.

"Oh, André sends his best, by the way," she added. "I bumped into him in London recently. You remember him, right? He was the German student who stayed in the room next to ours."

Room next to *ours*? If my legs had felt liquidy during my phone call from Nash, my entire *body* now seemed like a big floppy cloth doll. I flung my head back onto the rug and just lay there, unable to even move. In fact, I was barely able to breathe.

I could not freakin' believe it. When Beau had headed for Turkey, I'd imagined the worse—namely a gorgeous archaeology student, brown as a nut from the sun, totally falling for him. But later, after we reconnected, he shared stories about Aphrodisius, and it had seemed as if the experience there had been almost monastic. Far more dust than lust—and all supervised by an elderly German. He'd even talked about lying in bed a few nights wondering what in hell he was going to do about us. I guess he'd forgotten to point out that while his brain tossed around thoughts of me, there was a chick named Abigail lying butt naked in the crook of his arm.

Summoning every ounce of energy I could find, I propelled myself onto my feet. I carried the dishes into the kitchen, resisting the urge to hurl them at the wall. After pulling on my coat and boots, I departed, slamming the door so hard that one of the pictures hanging in the corridor bounced a couple of times.

As I hunted down a cab, I called my next-door neighbor Landon, and to my relief he was home.

"I'm in one of the worst jams of my life," I said. "Please tell me you don't have an apartment full of dinner guests."

"I have a miserable cold, but I'd love to be of assistance. Come now. Just wear a mask."

I stopped at my apartment first, dropped off my stuff, and grabbed a bottle of brandy from the cabinet where I kept my paltry liquor supply.

"Don't hug me, don't even come close," Landon croaked after he'd opened the door. He was wearing the kind of comfort clothes people fall back on when they're sick—saggy-bottomed jeans, an old cream-colored zip-up cardigan. "This thing is nasty."

"Are you sure you're up for a visit? You sound awful."

"Yes, the distraction will do me good. Plus, you sounded horrible yourself. What's going on?"

He ushered me into his lovely living room and took a seat across from me. Even under the weather, Landon, at nearly seventy, looked great, with his short-cropped silver hair and small trim body. He dabbed a crisp white handkerchief to his nose and then urged me to tell him everything.

I described the weekend at Scott's, giving him the major highlights, then relayed the troubles with Nash, and ended with the nightmare at Beau's tonight. Landon dabbed at his nose a few times and cleared his throat.

"Bailey, I think you need an attorney," he announced.

"An attorney?" I exclaimed. "What am I supposed to do? Sue Beau for alienation of affection?"

"No—an attorney to deal with the situation at *Buzz*."

"I don't have the money to pay some high-priced Manhattan lawyer—they're like seven hundred dollars an hour. Plus, I might make things worse if I bring in legal counsel at this point. The main thing I need to do is find out why this woman is saying this shit. I think someone put her up to it."

"Any ideas who?"

"It's got to be one of the people who was at Scott's last weekend. The person knows I'm digging around about Devon's death, and they want me to stop. And they must want to stifle me because there's something to find, something they want kept under wraps. I'm not certain what that is, but I suspect it's the fact that this person wanted Devon dead and put the diuretic in her water bottles."

"But that means this person is dangerous. You've got to be careful."

"Don't worry, I will."

Landon let out a little moan. "But you've said before that you were going to be careful, and then the next thing I know you've got some wild Russian chasing you through a basement with a knife."

I managed a smile. "In this instance I have no choice but to proceed on my tippy toes. That's the only way to smoke out the killer, and besides, I can't let Nash find out I'm poking around after he told me not to."

I untucked my legs from under me and strolled over to the antique cabinet where I'd set the brandy bottle.

"I'm having another splash—are you sure you don't want one?" I asked. "Or should I make you a hot toddy?"

"Maybe just a thumb full, thanks," he said. "Tell me more about Beau? Where do you go from here?"

"Where do we *go*? I don't know. Maybe nowhere."

"But let me play devil's advocate for a second," he said. "When Beau left for Turkey, didn't he tell you that he wasn't sure if he could make a commitment? It wasn't till he returned that he said he was ready."

"That's right."

"So technically he did nothing wrong. It's not like he was cheating on you. And at the time *you* were involved with that strapping actor, Chris whatever-his-name was. Going to bed with a guy as good-looking as Chris wouldn't be considered mere infidelity by most people. It's more along the lines of *treason*."

"But I'd been dumped."

"Like I said—you and Beau were both free agents really."

"Agreed—technically Beau did nothing wrong. But the whole thing just doesn't *feel* right to me. He goes to Turkey and he's conflicted about what he wants in regards to me, so the way he deals with it is to shag the dig-site slut? It just comes down to the fact that I don't feel I really *know* Beau. He's Beau Regan, International Man of Mystery."

"Bailey, dear, I wish I could help, but I think you're just going to have to figure this one out for yourself," Landon said. "Personally I'd kill for a man of mystery right now. I'd even take a man of *misery*. We all have to figure out what we can and cannot tolerate."

I couldn't blame Landon for not having all the answers, but somehow I'd hoped he would. I slunk back to my apartment feeling absolutely morose. There was a concerned message from Beau on my cell wondering where in the world I was, since he'd found traces of me in the apartment but no explanation as to where I'd disappeared to. Then there was another message, clearly after he'd played his answering machine and realized what I'd heard, saying we needed to talk as soon as possible. I felt no urge to talk it out at the moment, mainly because I didn't know where I stood in my own mind. Instead I pulled out the desk chair in my tiny home office and began to make a game plan about how I was going to save my ass at work.

One possibility would be to confront Sherrie Barr directly. A search of the white pages online turned up no phone number, but property records indicated she owned a home on Brackton Street in Pine Grove. And yet it was hard to imagine that if I confronted her, she'd spit out the truth. Better to keep focusing on the houseguests; obviously one of them was involved.

I picked up my cell phone and tried Jane again. This time she answered.

"I was hoping we could meet first thing tomorrow," I said. "I've stumbled across some important information that I thought would interest you."

I figured that bait would entice her regardless of whether she was the killer because she was anxious for dish she could load her book with.

"Can you give me a hint at least?" she said in her typical crabby tone. "You make it sound so clandestine."

"I think it's best to do it in person."

"I have to be at Devon's apartment all morning tomorrow—I guess you could come by there."

"What's going on there?"

"I told her mother I'd take care of some stuff."

So Jane was in contact with Sherrie. Interesting tidbit. I agreed to meet her at ten and took down the address on Spring Street in SoHo. After I signed off, I left a message on the cell number Tory had given me for Tommy. I tried to sound kind of flirty—which I thought might help guarantee a response. As for Christian, I decided since he also hadn't returned my call from earlier, I would just show up at his office tomorrow for a chat. I remembered from my Google search that First Models was also in SoHo, so I could combine a trip to Devon's apartment with a pop-in at the modeling agency.

I changed for bed and crawled under the covers, hoping that being wrung out with fatigue would guarantee I'd fall asleep almost instantly, but I ended up flopping around on the bed like a sturgeon hauled onto the deck of a fishing boat. I'd been dogged by insomnia for nearly two years after my divorce, and I dreaded a recurrence of the problem. But there was no fighting it tonight. My anxiety over my job situation,

Beau's Turkish delight, and the murder of Devon Barr formed a perfect storm that kept sleep at bay for hours.

The next day I apparently looked as bad as I felt, because when Jane opened the door to Devon's place, her eyes widened.

"Are you *okay*?" she asked, her voice tinged with morbid curiosity rather than concern. "You've got, like, huge circles under your eyes."

"I'm just a little under the weather," I said. "I was with a friend who had a cold and I might have caught it."

"Well, don't give it to me," she snapped.

Interestingly, Jane looked better than when I'd last seen her. The snarly expression was gone, her hair appeared to have been tamed with a flatiron, and she had a spring to her step as she led me from the entrance hallway. Devon's death seemed to be agreeing with her.

"I read your story," she said as we walked. "The one online. How come you didn't write up the stuff I told you about Cap and Devon? You sure seemed juiced up when I mentioned it."

"To be perfectly honest, I haven't been able to verify it. Cap vehemently denies it."

"Well, of course he would," she said defensively. "He's hardly going to cop to it."

"And you're sure you saw it? Could they have just been talking?"

"I saw what I saw," she said crossly, but there was hardly a ring of truth to her tone.

We were in the middle of the living area now, a huge, open loft space with honey-colored wood floors, white pillars, and an exposed sprinkler system on the ceiling. At the near end was a seating area with an L-shaped sofa, and at the far end, an ultra-modern, spare-looking kitchen featuring all stainless steel appliances. Between the two areas was a sleek metal dining table and eight chairs that looked like they might never have been used. A huge abstract painting took up one wall. And that was about it. The place looked barely inhabited.

"How long had Devon lived here?" I asked.

"About two years. I know—not very homey, is it? But she traveled all the time, so I guess that was her excuse. She has a place in London, and I hear that's nicer. Not that she ever invited me."

"So her mother called and asked you to take care of a few things?" I said.

"She says she wants to be sure all the *valuables* are protected. Yeah, *right*. She just wants to guarantee that no one else gets their dirty little paws on them. Plus, I've got household bills to go through. Cap asked me to stay on the payroll and take care of stuff for a while."

"So you're dealing mainly with Cap, not Christian?"

"Well, Cap *was* her manager," she said, as if I'd failed the Supermodels 101 course in college.

"I just wondered. I figured there'd be loose ends to tie up with the modeling agency."

"Cap will take care of that. Devon probably wouldn't want me talking to Christian anyway."

"Why's that?" I asked.

"I think she'd gone off him lately."

So Jane was clued into the situation, too. "How do you know?"

Jane shrugged. "She ignored him all weekend."

"And you have no idea why?"

"Nope. And it doesn't matter now, anyway."

"Tell me about Devon's mother," I said. "What's she like, anyway?" I asked it evenly, not taking my eyes off Jane's face.

"TP type. You know, real trailer park. I don't know if she actually *lives* in one—I only met the woman once, when she came to New York—but she had single-wide written all over her. Chain-smoker face like a dried prune."

"I hear the funeral's private—are you going?"

"I would soooo *love* to get out of it, but I have to show. It's back in her hometown in Pennsylvania. I guess it's about a two- or three-hour drive from here."

Of course, you're going to go, I thought. You'll be able to gather more grist for your tell-all. I was dying to ask if she knew where the service would be, but I didn't want her to know I was giving any thought to possibly going out there myself.

"Look," she said. "Can we hurry this along? I thought you had some top-secret news you wanted to share."

"There *are* a couple of things I need to discuss with you."

"All right, why don't you come back here?" she said, cocking her head toward the back of the apartment. "We can talk while I keep working."

I followed Jane, walking past an all-white master bedroom with clothes flung over nearly every inch of the bed and furniture. It was the only part of the apartment that seemed lived-in.

"In here," Jane said, indicating what appeared to be a second bedroom that had been turned into a fairly basic office. There was a simple desk with a flat-screen computer, several filing cabinets, and cardboard boxes haphazardly strewn near the walls. A small window offered a view of the rooftops of SoHo, studded with shingled water tanks and soot-covered chimneys. Jane plopped down into the chair at the desk and motioned that I should help myself to a white folding chair.

"*Soooo?*" Jane said impatiently as she tore open a piece of mail.

"I don't know if you've heard the news yet. Devon died of heart failure due to her anorexia."

"I guess us fatties don't have it so bad after all. So is *that* why you came here? To tell me something I already knew?"

"No, but before I share, I wanted to pick your brain. I'm wondering if something might have exacerbated Devon's condition."

"Like what?" Jane said. "She saw outtakes from a photo shoot and decided she needed to crash-diet?"

"No, not exactly. Certain drugs can make the condition worse. Remember we talked about the ipecac? Well, diuretics can create problems, too. Did you ever know Devon to take any?"

"Nope."

"And you never saw anything like that in her bathroom?"

"There were two places that were off-limits to me. Her purse and her bathroom. So if she was stockpiling anything like that, I wouldn't know."

"There's no harm in taking a look in her bathroom now, is there?" I asked.

"Shouldn't the *police* be the ones checking it out?"

"Well, they're over two hours away. And if we find anything, we can turn it over to them. It will help in their investigation."

"Sure," Jane said after a moment. She seemed curious suddenly, and I wondered if she was thinking that a discovery could help her book pitch. "Why not? The master bath is off her bedroom."

I followed her back down the hallway and into the bedroom. While I stepped gingerly around some of the clothes on the floor, Jane kicked stuff away with her feet as if it was trash.

"The cleaning lady comes in later today," she said. "Sometimes I think Devon liked to leave her as big a mess as possible."

The bathroom was huge, white, and spa-like, and the entire area behind the sink was wall-to-wall mirror. Just as in the bathroom Devon had used at Scott's place, there were upended beauty products scattered on the countertop. I glanced down at them, searching for any kind of prescription drugs, but there were only cosmetics, skin care products, and an ashtray full of cigarette butts.

"What about in the medicine chest?" I asked, cocking my head toward it. Jane yanked open the door. It was crowded with more beauty products, but the middle shelf was devoted only to drugs. There was Ambien and Zantac and a couple of bottles of over-the-counter painkillers. No sign of any diuretic. A large white bottle was behind the front row, and delicately I reached behind and plucked it out. Prenatal vitamins, prescribed by a Dr. David Stein on Park

Avenue. Date: October of last year. As I glanced toward Jane to check out her reaction, I saw her dark eyes widen in surprise.

"What the hell?" she asked, gawking at the label. I noticed that her face now had a sheen of sweat, as if the space was making her feel overheated. "Oh, wait, don't some chicks take these to make their hair glossy?"

"Actually Devon was apparently pregnant last year, and then miscarried," I explained. "I take it you didn't know."

"What? No, no, I—I didn't know," she sputtered. I could almost see her brain churning.

This might be the moment, I realized, to go for a blunt approach and see what Jane coughed up.

"That tidbit should be of real interest to you, right?" I said. "I mean, it's a nice little element to add to your book."

She'd still been staring at the label, but now she spun her head toward me in surprise, her nostrils flared.

"I hope you're not going to deny it, Jane," I said. "You've been busy for weeks trying to sell a book about Devon."

She smirked and shrugged a shoulder.

"So what?" she said. "It's a free world and I can write what I feel like writing—just like you can." Her tone was a mix of defensiveness and defiance, like a shoplifter who's convinced she deserved the stolen clothes as much as the rich girl who would have paid for them.

"Except that I'm not making stuff up so that it comes across as more salacious," I said quietly.

"What are you talking about?" she demanded. I could tell she was getting agitated. The sheen of sweat on her face seemed to be glistening even more now.

"You invented the stuff about Cap and Devon. Probably to make Devon's life seem juicier."

"Oh, please," she said. "You're just jealous 'cause I beat you to the punch with the book."

I shifted my position slightly, feeling less than comfortable with her in the contained space of the bathroom. And then I noticed something—the ripe, sour smell of sweat. It was the exact same odor that had been thrown off like a stink bomb by the person who sent me tumbling down the stairs.

14

Rank sweat was rank sweat, and it might be hard to tell one person's from another, but a little voice in my head was screaming that it was Jane I'd smelled Sunday night.

Any satisfaction I felt from my eureka moment was trounced by the fact that I was currently alone in a bathroom with her. If she'd purposely shoved me down the stairs, she might not think anything of harming me now, and I could feel my heart starting to pump harder, urging me to hightail it the hell out of the apartment.

"I guess the bottom line is that we've all got to do what works for us," I said as casually as I could manage. I began to ease my way toward the door, hoping she wouldn't sense my sudden panic. "From one writer to another, though, I'd be careful. People sometimes sue if you make them mad enough about what you've written."

"Thanks for the tip," she said sarcastically. Please, I thought, as I took a step out of the bathroom, don't let her tear out the shower rod and try to crack my skull with it—or go for my jugular with the cuticle nippers. Thankfully, she didn't seem to be reading my mind.

"Look," she said. "Like I said, I've got work to do. . . ."

"Understood," I said. She led me back to the front door, and as soon as I stepped into the hall, she slammed the door hard behind me.

I felt a rush of relief. I jabbed at the elevator button several times, knowing I wouldn't feel totally safe until I was out on the street.

On my way to the apartment I'd noticed a small French café just up the street, and now I hurried over there. I found a table, ordered a cappuccino, and took out my composition book. I jotted down my conversation with Jane as word for word as I could remember.

The more I thought about it, the more sense it made that Jane was the one who'd scratched the barn doors. The vandalism had occurred roughly an hour after Jane left my room, an hour after I'd told her that Devon's saga lacked the kind of layers a story needs to go big-time. Jane probably decided a scary, middle-of-the-night swashbuckler during the weekend Devon died would help make the story more enticing to potential publishers. Hell, it might even help get the whole thing optioned for a movie.

What I didn't have any sense of was whether Jane had slipped the Lasix into Devon's water. Interestingly her sweat attack in the apartment had occurred when I'd brought up the diuretic, but on the other hand, some things didn't add up. If Jane *had* killed Devon by doctoring her water, it would have been smart to lie low afterward, *not* create any more drama—and let everyone assume that Devon had died naturally. By tearing through the halls at night and trying to terrify people, Jane had fostered the idea that something sinister was going on at the barn. Which meant to me that she might have been Zorro, but not the murderer.

And yet, if she was nutty enough to run around in the dead of night in a poncho with a rusty farm tool, she might not be rational at *all*.

I'd been staring off as I mulled all of this over, and for the first time my eyes snagged on something across the room: a guy with longish brown hair, drinking an espresso at one of the small wooden tables. He looked a little like Beau, and suddenly the events from last night, which I'd temporarily sandbagged from entering my brain, all came flooding back. I'd been avoiding Beau, but sooner or later I was going to have to return his calls. He'd made it clear that he wanted to talk things over. I just didn't know where talking was going to get us. After Devon's death, I'd brushed away my worries about his trip to Arizona—because it felt so good to share with him all the awful stuff about the weekend— but the problem hadn't really gone away. The bottom line was that no matter how much time I spent with Beau, he continued to seem elusive and mysterious to me. He was even planning on spending the holidays with his family rather than me. That didn't seem like a man who was fully committed.

I checked my watch. As I'd determined earlier, it was just a short walk to First Models, and this seemed like as good a time as any to ambush Christian with a visit. But before I headed over there, I decided to phone Beau. I just couldn't bear going any longer without confronting the situation.

No one was sitting close to me in the café, so I took out my BlackBerry and made the call. I didn't hear any background noise when he answered, which suggested he was still at home rather than at his studio.

"Hi, it's me," I said, not knowing how else to begin.

"Where are you, anyway?"

"SoHo."

"So you're not home, after all."

"What do you mean?"

"I dropped by your place about fifteen minutes ago. The doorman said you'd gone out, but I thought you might have bribed him into saying that if I came by. I suspected you were really up in your apartment stewing."

"*Stewing*? That expression kind of implies I'm doing a slow boil over something unnecessarily."

"No. I was just acknowledging that you're obviously pissed. But to just go incommunicado makes me think you're making a lot more of this than you should be."

"You're kidding, right?"

"Look, Bailey, I can totally understand why it would tick you off royally to hear a phone message like that. But that girl means nothing to me. It's not an issue for us."

"But she meant something once, didn't she?"

"*What?*" He'd sounded annoyed when he blurted out the word, but then his voice softened. "We need to talk face-to-face, Bailey. This isn't something we should be dealing with over the phone."

"Okay." I said. "When?"

"How about tonight then? At around eight?"

"That should be fine. If for any reason I'm going to be late, I'll let you know."

"What's happening with your work situation? Did you find out who's trying to sabotage you?"

"Nothing yet. But I'm turning over every stone."

"Okay, well, we can talk more about it when I see you," Beau said.

We signed off, polite toward each other, but hardly gushing.

And yet it seemed, I realized, as if Beau truly wanted to work things out. I felt a momentary easing of my anxiety, like the relief you feel when you run a hand you've just burned under a stream of cold water. Good for the moment but most of the time it doesn't last.

I paid the check, took a deep breath, and headed for First Models. The agency turned out to be in a sleek ten-story building that also housed an ad agency and some other random businesses. When I boarded the elevator, an insanely tall platinum-blond girl, who had to be a model, followed me inside. She was carrying a huge silver tote bag and in her right hand an itty-bitty Chihuahua puppy. She cooed at it a couple of times, and in response the dog flicked his tongue at her lips. It made me think of what Whitney had said about Devon. She'd wanted a baby for the same reason she'd wanted a dog: for the unconditional love it guaranteed.

The blond disembarked with me on four, where the elevator opened directly onto a small reception area. A receptionist sat at a desk, leafing through a copy of *W* magazine. To the left of the desk was a conference room with the door open. A woman was snapping pictures with a small camera of a gangly, red-haired girl who looked like she'd come directly from the Port Authority after a twenty-four-hour bus ride from the Midwest.

The blond model nodded at the receptionist, walked toward the door at the far side of the room, and swung it open. Before she closed it, I caught a glimpse of the nerve center of the agency: a large, loftlike room with several separate sections of workstations, about twenty desks altogether. One entire wall was papered with headshots. There were a bunch of people working in there, but I didn't see Christian.

"May I help you?" the receptionist asked. She ran her eyes down my five-foot-six frame with a look that seemed to say, "Wait, you don't think you could be a *model*, do you?"

"I'm here to see Christian," I told her. "My name's Bailey Weggins." I glanced off to the right then, as if I was done talking and there was no reason for her to inquire, "Is he expecting you?" It was a trick I'd learned from an old reporter I'd worked with: when you don't want someone to ask a question, indicate by your body language that you've said everything necessary.

It worked.

"Just a minute," she told me and punched in a number on her phone. She announced my presence to

Christian and then listened, scrunching her mouth up. After a moment she said, "Okay," and set the phone back in its cradle.

"He said that unfortunately he's working out a campaign for one of his girls right now, and he can't meet with you," she said. "But he's got your number, and he'll give you a call later."

"Actually, I can wait," I said, walking toward a cowhide-covered bench. "I have plenty of time."

As I took a seat, she flashed me a look that was part annoyance, part uncertainty, as if she'd just stepped in gum and wasn't sure how to get it off her shoe.

"That's not such a good idea," she said finally. "It's open call day. There's gonna be lot of girls here."

"I'll stay out of the way, I promise," I said.

This time I was granted a big sigh. She stood up from her desk and, after opening the door to the main room just wide enough for her to enter, slipped inside. While I hung in the reception area, the redhead was escorted to the elevator by the woman who'd taken her pictures. It appeared she hadn't received much encouragement because as she waited for the elevator in her stained cropped jacket, her lower lip was trembling and she looked close to tears.

Two minutes later the receptionist reemerged from the nerve center with Christian right behind her.

He was dressed in black jeans and a black, supertight V-neck sweater, which revealed a chest that seemed as smooth and polished as candle wax. He glanced at me and then toward the now-empty conference room.

"Why don't we go in there," he said curtly and led the way.

Once we were inside, I noticed another door to the big room, this one partly open, and I had the chance to take a better peek. The people inside, mostly model bookers I assumed, tapped at their computers or spoke quietly into their phone headsets. I'd been expecting a place that looked and sounded as crazy as an office of Wall Street bond traders, with bookers shouting out the orders they'd just taken—like "I've got Becca on the twenty-eighth for CoverGirl. Shooting in Cabo"—but it was far more subdued than that. Christian quickly closed the doors to both the reception area and the booking room and then strode back to the table.

"I can't believe you just came barging into where I work," he said, all pissy.

"I did try to make contact by phone," I told him. "But I never heard back from you."

"Has it ever occurred to you that some people may not want to be included in one of your gruesome *Buzz* magazine stories? We're not *all* media whores, you know."

"It's really not a *media* thing I'm pursuing at the moment. I'm concerned about Devon's death, and I'm looking for answers."

"Oh, are you all up in arms because I told you she didn't have an eating disorder? I'll be perfectly honest with you. I didn't know she was having trouble again. I mean, she looked a little thinner to me, but I thought she'd just been working too hard—doing the album."

"No, that's not where I'm going. I think someone was trying to make her situation worse."

He stared at me for a moment with his deep brown eyes.

"Oh, *I* see," he said after a moment, arching his back and tapping his long slim fingers on his chest. "This is the part where you try to accuse the modeling agency of pressuring her to keep her weight down. We're such evil people, aren't we? I've got news for you. Though women *say* they want to look at real women in ads, they're total liars."

"No," I said. "That's not where I'm going either. Devon's situation was probably aggravated by certain factors. One of them was ipecac. I saw a bottle of it in her bathroom the night she died, but someone removed it before the police arrived. Do you know anything about that?"

"I certainly know what it *is*. We've had girls who used it. But I had no idea Devon was one of them."

"What about diuretics?"

"Are you asking if I know what *those* are, sweetheart?"

"I want to know if she was taking them. Do you know if she ever had a prescription for one called Lasix?"

"Not to my knowledge, no."

"Did you ever see her crushing any kind of pills in her water bottle?"

"Good God, no. I can't imagine Devon wanting anything to interfere with her precious water. She should have been entitled to stock in the company that produces Fiji water."

"She was drinking a lot of bottled water last weekend and leaving half open bottles around. Did you ever see anyone go near one of them?"

His eyes widened.

"Oh, *my*. It sounds like you're suggesting someone tampered with the water."

"Possibly."

"No. I never saw anyone else holding a water bottle. Other than Jane, of course. As Devon's sherpa, she was always taking things to her master, including water bottles." He paused and held a hand to his chest. "You don't think *Jane* tampered with the water, do you?"

"I don't know. What do *you* think?"

"Jane resented the hell out of Devon. Devon was everything Jane wasn't. I kept telling Devon to get rid of that girl, but she felt lucky that Jane hadn't quit like everyone else. She held the world record at about nine months."

"Speaking of nine months, you knew, of course, that Devon was pregnant last year."

"Who told you that?" he asked, his tone indicating that it was the truth but that he was surprised I knew.

"I saw pictures of her last November. But if she'd carried to term, wouldn't it have hurt her modeling career?"

"To some degree, yes, and I wasn't *overjoyed* when she told me she was trying," he said. "But I'm sure she would have rebounded quickly. Girls like Devon gain about a pound and a half during their pregnancies and look normal again in two weeks. And besides, there would have been no way to talk her out of it. Devon wanted a baby."

"*Why*, do you think?"

He did a little pose before speaking, lifting a shoulder and pursing his lips. "She was lonely. Being a super-model looks like oodles of fun, but it can be a solitary existence when you're not actually working. You travel all the time, and you never know who your real friends are. And Devon had never had much luck with men. She picked bad boys who liked to take machetes to their hotel rooms and eventually cheat on her. You know that expression, don't you? 'Show me a beautiful woman, and I'll show you a man who's tired of fucking her'? That seemed to fit Devon to a T."

"If she wanted a baby so badly, why not try again?"

"She probably didn't want to go through it all again. It was just too much work."

"Did she have morning sickness or something?"

"No, I mean before that. All the—" He caught himself and clamped his mouth shut.

"Wait, are you saying Devon had fertility issues?" I urged. Thornwell had mentioned a clinic but I'd assumed Devon had used one for artificial insemination.

"I really shouldn't say. I've said too much all ready."

"Look, Christian, I don't have any prurient interest here. I'm not a gossip columnist. I'm just trying to figure out if someone murdered Devon."

"*Murdered?* You can't be serious."

"It's a possibility. And though I don't think her pregnancy is connected, I want to investigate every angle. Help me out here."

He let out an exaggerated sigh.

"Yes, she had some fertility issues," he admitted. "To quote *Gone with the Wind*, 'I don't know nothin' about birthin' babies,' but something wasn't working perfectly *down there*. She got some kind of special treatment, and after a few months, voilà. I don't know what the treatment involved, but there was one month where she was too bloated to work. She ballooned to a size six or something."

Sounded like she might have gone through in vitro. The drugs, I'd heard, could cause lots of swelling.

"Thank you," I said. "That information may prove useful."

"Speaking of useful, I really do have work to do. Do you mind letting me get back to it?"

"Of course. How are things going here, by the way? Devon's death must be a blow to the agency."

"It is," he said. "But we have *lots* of fabulous girls."

"I heard, by the way, that Devon had some issues with the agency lately—that she wanted Cap to take them up with Barbara Dern."

I'd dropped it like a bomb in his lap, and I saw a breath catch in his chest.

"That is *sooo* not true."

"But isn't that why Devon was avoiding you last weekend? That she was miffed about something to do with the agency."

He let out a little shriek. "I knew I should never have spoken to you," he exclaimed. "Please leave *now*."

He swiveled his body around dramatically in the chair and marched out of the room into the reception area, expecting me to follow. Not taking any chances, he punched the elevator for me, and before long I was out on my ass, just like all the girls who'd been deemed too thick in the thighs or chubby in the cheeks for First Models.

Now what? I thought as I left the building. I'd gleaned a few insights from talking to Jane and Christian, but I hadn't come any closer to learning what I needed to know. I placed another call to Tommy and also left a message for Scott at his office. It was time to touch base with him again.

Back home, I cracked open my composition book once more. I scribbled down notes from my conversation with Christian and then reviewed the other notes I'd taken so far. Then I summed up what I had so far:

- Cap was suffering from lupus, which supposedly meant he couldn't get it up and thus wasn't able to have an affair with Devon. Since he wasn't a spurned, angry, or jealous lover, it supposedly took away his motive. And Whitney's too. But Cap might have another motive.

- Jane had most likely pushed me down the stairs—accidentally or not. But did that make her the murderer? Jane was also writing a tell-all book about Devon. It seemed like she might have lied about seeing Devon and Cap kissing to add more sizzle to the story. But would the need for sizzle make her want to kill Devon?

- According to Tory, Tommy had gone missing in action the night Devon had died. Had he dropped by Devon's room? If so, why not summon help for her?

- Tory was hankering to work with Cap. Had she decided to eliminate Devon so he'd need to add another client?

- And then there was Christian. Despite his assurances that everything was peachy keen between Devon and him, she gave him the cold shoulder last weekend. Was Devon about to make trouble for Christian at the agency?

Regardless of the information I'd gathered, I still had no clue who had doctored Devon's water. Maybe, I realized, I should work backward and focus instead on who had persuaded Devon's mother to lie about me.

If I learned that, I would probably know who the murderer was.

I picked up my phone and called Jessie.

"I was two seconds away from calling you," Jessie said. "You doing okay?"

"I've been better. Anything up?"

"I've tried to hang near Nash's office as much as possible, but I haven't picked up anything. I did find out, though, where the funeral is." She gave me the name of a church in Pine Grove and said it was scheduled for one o'clock on Saturday.

"Thanks for the info," I said. "I bet by now the whole office has heard about my sorry little plight."

"Yeah—you know what it's like here. People know when you have a rash on your ass. But you'll be happy to learn most people are greeting it with plenty of skepticism. They just don't see you doing something like that."

"Unfortunately they don't have any clout in the matter."

We chatted for a couple of more minutes, and then signed off, with Jessie promising to call if she learned anything else of value.

For the next hour I researched the houseguests I hadn't yet Googled, hoping that some little detail would pop up and point to a motive. I found nothing online at all about Jane and only a couple of tiny, meaningless references to Tory. There turned out to be plenty of stuff on Tommy—photos of him flipping the bird at paparazzi, mug shots from his two DWIs, etc.—but nothing that shed light on the case.

Though Richard certainly didn't appear to have motive, I needed to check him out regardless. There was a ton of stuff online *by* him and *about* him. I skimmed the most recent material for now, but didn't find anything noteworthy.

I also searched for Scott. The comment my *Buzz* coworker Thornwell had made—about wanting to confirm a naughty piece of gossip about the music mogul—had been nagging at me. Maybe the guy had a real dark side. Perhaps Devon had stumbled onto ugly secrets about him while they were recording her album, and he knew it. He could have built the house party around her just to have an opportunity to kill her. If he *did* have a hidden life and weird sexual predilections, no one had squealed on him up until this point. All the press on him focused on what a genius he was in the music business.

I leaned back in the desk chair of my office and replayed Devon's words to Cap: "You've got to tell her." Cap had insisted that the woman Devon was referring to was Barbara Dern, head of First Models. It would be good to know exactly what the head of the modeling agency might need to know, especially about a booker. What could a booker do that would make a model fit to be tied? For a second I considered calling my old boss at *Gloss*, Cat Jones, but she didn't deal with models directly.

Then another thought wormed its way into my mind. Chris Wickersham. He was the actor I'd had an on-again, off-again fling with before starting a steady relationship with Beau. He'd worked as a model before his big break in TV. Talking to him could shed light on the subject.

It could also create trouble for me with Beau. But at the moment I didn't give a damn.

15

It had been three months since I'd seen Chris in person, and in that time things had exploded for him—in the sweetest of ways. *Morgue*, the show he was costarring in, had premiered in late September and been a major hit in the ratings, turning him into the kind of guy who was designated as a hunk of the month in magazines like *Cosmo*. There had been several red-carpet shots of Chris in *Buzz* recently, and Leo had showed me a spread of him in *Details*, wearing a three-thousand-dollar Gucci leather jacket.

We'd met almost two years ago, when he was bartending at a wedding I'd attended, something he'd done back then to supplement his income as a model and struggling actor. We had a flirtation over a number of months, and then finally fell into bed together this past September when he was shooting his show in New York. Our attraction had been intensified then because we'd shared a passion—finding the person who had killed his friend Tom Fain. But when Beau arrived back from Turkey, I'd been forced to make a torturous choice. In the end I'd picked Beau over Chris—not only because of my fierce attraction to Beau but also because of the inherent drawbacks of a relationship with Chris. For starters, he was ten years younger than me. And he was the new "It" boy, the kind of guy women everywhere would be trying to poach—right out from under my nose. I didn't feel up to dealing with that on a daily basis.

I wondered if Chris would return my call if I left a message for him now—he had been pretty miffed when I'd told him about Beau. I wondered, in fact, if he even had the same cell phone number. The way his career was going, he'd probably already had to change it two or three times to keep the riffraff at bay.

So I was kind of shocked when, after I punched in the number I had for him, his voice announced, "It's Chris, leave a message."

"Hi, this is Bailey," I said. "You're probably less than thrilled to hear from me, but there's something you could help me with, and I'm hoping you'll return my call. Thanks."

I left my number, too, just in case he'd angrily purged it from his phone.

Another shocker: he called back just fifteen minutes later, while I was brewing a cup of coffee in the kitchen.

"You're probably the last person I was expecting to hear from today," he said. "What's up?"

"Thanks for calling back. I wasn't sure if you would—you know, considering everything that happened."

"Come on, Bailey. I can't begin to repay you for what you did after Tom died. I wasn't happy when I last saw you—but I still owe you."

"I love your show, by the way. And you're really terrific in it."

"The hours are generally brutal, but needless to say, we're stoked it's a hit. So what exactly do you need my help on?"

He was being perfectly pleasant, but he was also making it clear he wasn't interested in chitchatting with me.

"I'm working on the Devon Barr story—I'm sure you heard about her death. I desperately need information about the modeling business. I wouldn't have bothered you but I'm in some serious hot water at work, and it could get worse."

"If you don't get the story, you mean?" he said. There was a trace of cynicism in his tone. Chris had never loved the fact that I worked for *Buzz*.

"I wish. But that's not it at all. Devon Barr's mother has accused me of trying to extort money from her. I'm trying to figure out why she's saying that."

There was a pause. Was he weighing my words? I wondered.

"I'm in the middle of something this afternoon, but I have to be uptown later for dinner with a producer," he said. "It's about a movie I could end up doing during our hiatus. I'll have about thirty minutes before then; I could meet you somewhere. Are you at your office?"

"No, I'm at home. I'm persona non grata at *Buzz* for the moment. Can you meet me at the coffee shop in my building?" It didn't seem smart to ask him to come to my apartment. He might take it the wrong way.

"Sure," he said. He promised to be there at seven fifteen. That would give me time to reach Beau's place by eight.

I felt even more keyed up when I disconnected. On top of everything else that was going on, the idea of seeing Chris again tightened the big fat knot in my tummy. He was funny and caring and absolutely gorgeous, and despite how crazy I was about Beau, I still felt a weird connection to Chris. When I watched his show, particularly the episode in which he'd kissed a murder victim's grieving sister, it had been hard not to reminisce. I'd thought about his amazing body. And what it had been like to have that body next to me in bed.

Deep down, I wondered, did I have some ulterior motive for wanting to see him? I immediately chased that thought away. Chris was more familiar with the modeling business than anyone I knew.

At around five, as the sky was darkening, I phoned Nash, figuring it would be a good time to find him in his office. His assistant Lee, probably the oldest person at *Buzz* by about fifteen years, answered and asked me to hold. Though she was polite when I announced myself, I detected a trace of pity in her voice. There was no pity in Nash's voice, however, when he finally came on.

"What's up?" he asked, almost curtly. Not a good sign.

"I was just checking in, seeing if you'd learned anything."

"About?"

"About why Devon's mother made up that story about me."

"It's still being investigated," he said.

"But how? Wouldn't you want to see my cell phone records to prove I never called her? I can provide them."

"I can't go into specifics, Bailey. You must know that."

As I hung up, I realized the cold, hard truth. He didn't have faith in me. I'd busted my butt for him for over six months, breaking stories, generating buzz about *Buzz*, but he didn't feel he really knew me or was sure he could trust me. My whole body suddenly felt like a big tub of Jell-O.

I tried to distract myself by jotting down a few questions to ask Chris. While I scribbled, trying to fight off a new groundswell of anxiety, Scott finally returned my call.

He started with the same curt "What's up?" that Nash had snapped at me. Obviously a call from me these days was about as welcome as a rat sandwich.

"I'd love to grab a few minutes of your time," I said. "Some details have emerged regarding the weekend that I think you ought to know about."

"Such as?"

"Can we do it in person?" I said. "I could swing by and see you tomorrow?"

"Oh, I guess you *Buzz* reporters have to be concerned that your phones might be hacked by other tabloids," he said sarcastically. Then a sigh. "All right. But I don't want to meet at my office." He suggested a place called Café Euro on Fifty-seventh and Seventh at eight the next morning.

I still had an hour to kill before Chris arrived, so I poured a glass of wine and took a steaming hot bath. Rather than helping, the mix of heat and alcohol only made me lightheaded and kick-started a headache that had been threatening all day. It also churned my thoughts up even more. What a big fat ugly awful mess I was in, I realized as I lay with my head back, staring at the flickering flame of the candle I'd lit. I began to wonder if Landon was right, that for the professional part of my problems, I needed a lawyer. But hiring a high-priced Manhattan attorney would seriously leach my savings.

No, I was going to have to clear my name with detective work, and that meant heading out to Pine Grove on Saturday. Certainly I wasn't going to learn anything by confronting Sherrie Barr. She'd clam up fast, and if Nash found out I'd approached her, my ass would really be grass. Instead I'd have to play the spy and hopefully discover who Sherrie seemed closest to.

Of course, even when I proved I wasn't guilty—and I *would* prove it—the revelation wouldn't erase the fact that Nash had failed to trust me or lend me his support.

Though I'd promised myself I wouldn't make any special effort for Chris's visit, once I'd heaved myself out of the bath, it only made sense to change for the night—I'd be heading over to Beau's place after Chris left, anyway. I threw on clean jeans, a navy blue V-neck cashmere sweater, and my riding boots. Nothing special, nothing that suggested I was harboring impure thoughts. Though I felt a twinge of guilt as I headed down to the coffee shop on the ground floor of my building.

Chris arrived right on time, and after a moment's hesitation, I stood up halfway and we kissed each other on the cheek. His appearance caught me by surprise. On one level he looked the same: green eyes, thick brown hair, that beguiling cleft in his chin, great body. But there was a difference. He exuded a whole new level of confidence than when I'd last seen him. Not that Chris had ever been tentative, but he held the space around him now as if there was nothing that could undermine his self-assurance. So this is what happens to you, I thought, when you become an overnight sensation playing an investigator with the New York City medical examiner's office, and every girl you meet wants to jump your bones.

"Do you want anything to eat?" I asked.

"No, I'd better just do coffee," he said. "I really need to be out of here by about seven forty-five." He shrugged off his brown leather jacket—not unlike the one he'd worn in *Details*—and laid it next to him.

After we ordered, I cut to the chase. I quickly described the weekend at Scott's, my theory about Devon's death, and how my career was now in jeopardy.

"It kills me to think of you in such a jam, Bailey, but what could I possibly do to help?"

"One of the guests last weekend was Devon's booker, and it's possible Devon was upset about something he was doing," I said. "From what you know, is there anything a model booker could do that might tick off one of his clients?"

He leaned back into his chair, thinking. Because of the worried look on his face, I couldn't help but flash back on the night in mid-September when he'd stood in my living room, experiencing the full impact of the news about the death of his close friend Tom. We'd hugged each other in consolation, and moments later we were tearing each other's clothes off.

"Well, the thing that makes you angriest with a booker is when he—*or* she—doesn't seem to be working hard enough for you," he said finally. "Bookers always concentrate the most on their major stars, and it's easy to get short shrift if you're not in that league. Of course, bookers would like to make money off *everybody*, but they only have so much time and energy, so they tend to focus on the models with the clearest potential. Devon was a superstar and a real priority for the agency. But she wasn't getting any younger, and her booker's attention may have been slipping a little as he concentrated on upcoming girls—the ones who would make big money tomorrow."

"I wondered about that. Anything else? Anything not aboveboard?"

"Most of the bookers I worked with—and remember, I was never some supermodel—were great to deal with. But I do remember there was one guy in my agency who was there one minute and gone the next. The rumor was that he'd gotten caught skimming money from the agency somehow, and he was booted out on his ass."

"Any idea how he was doing it?"

"No. I actually probed a little because I was curious, but no one knew anything. Most of the guys I worked with weren't exactly rocket scientists."

"Do you remember his name?"

"Jason something. I'd call the agency for you, but they'd probably clam up and deny the whole thing to me."

We spent the next minutes catching up—Chris answering my questions about *Morgue*, me answering his questions about my book. Finally he checked the time on his iPhone.

"I probably should split now," Chris said. "I'm sorry I couldn't be more helpful. I think the bottom line is that there must be opportunity for some hanky-panky, because at least one booker tried it."

"Thanks," I said. "You've given me something to think about."

There was an awkward moment as I wrestled with my coat. One of the sleeves was partially inside out, and as I tried to punch my arm through it, I realized I looked like someone writhing in a straitjacket. Not a sight, I realized, Chris would ever be treated to on dates with hot young starlets styled flawlessly by Rachel Zoe. Because by now, those were surely the girls he was dating.

As we made our way to the front of the coffee shop, a female customer, clearly recognizing Chris, went bug-eyed at the sight of him.

"I guess you get that a lot now," I whispered.

"Yeah," he said. "People sometimes insist we met at a party when they don't realize they actually know me from the tube. It's not a pain yet or too intrusive. But all it would take is one date with someone like Blake Lively or Jessica Biel—and my life as I know it would be over."

"Or one of the Kardashians," I said, smiling.

"Excuse me for not inquiring about *your* love life," he said after a few moments, "but I'll spare myself the torture." We were outside now, on the sidewalk in front of my building.

"Chris, you could have anyone in the world you wanted."

"Yeah, maybe," he said, smiling ruefully. "But you're the one who knocked my socks off, Bailey." He leaned down and kissed me on the cheek again, but more tenderly this time, placing one hand on my shoulder as he did.

"If I think of anything, I'll call you, okay?" he said.

With that he sprinted toward Broadway. I watched as he flagged down a cab and slid in effortlessly.

And then I heard my name called. Startled, I spun around. To my utter shock, Beau was standing behind me.

"Wh—what are you doing here?" I stammered. He was wearing a long camel-colored overcoat and a brown scarf wrapped around his neck.

"It's almost eight o'clock," he said with frustration. "We agreed to meet now."

"But I thought I was coming to your place," I told him. I realized suddenly that we had never really nailed down the details.

"Whatever," he said dismissively. He seemed pissed, and it wasn't hard to figure out why. "That guy there. Isn't that the actor you were seeing?"

"Um—yeah, it was," I said, faltering a little. "I needed his help—with my story on Devon. And finding out who's been trying to sabotage me."

"His *help*? Let me guess—did he and Devon know each other as members of the Big Hair, Small Brains Association of America?"

I almost laughed—at the absurdity of the comment and Beau's obvious distaste for Chris—but I didn't, which was a good thing. That would *not* have helped matters. And I could see that help was what I needed.

"Well, you're partially right," I said, trying to sound cooperative. "Chris used to work as a model, and I need information about modeling agencies."

"And you had to have him up to your apartment to discuss it?"

"No, we were in the *coffee shop*. And he just dropped by for a minute, Beau—on his way someplace else. It's no big deal."

"No big deal. Is that right?"

"That's really funny," I said, starting to feel a swell of anger. "I'm not supposed to mind when a girl you used to screw in Turkey calls and suggests you meet up, and yet you seem irritated by the fact that I spent thirty minutes with someone who could help save my job and my reputation."

I had a head of steam going now, like I was Joan of Arc trying to make my case on horseback to a legion of French soldiers. To my embarrassment, I sensed that Bob, the evening doorman of my building, was watching us out of the corner of his eye.

"Isn't it really just more payback, Bailey?" Beau demanded. I'd never seen him look so annoyed. "Like your taking off for the weekend just because I had to be out of town."

"That's absurd."

"Something absurd is going on here. But I'm not the one responsible."

With that he turned on his heels and strode off angrily, the back panels of his coat flapping in the cold night air. I just stood there, not knowing what the hell to do. For a brief moment I felt a temptation to take off after him, but I then overrode the urge. I didn't like how Beau had managed to turn the tables so that our spat tonight had been about some totally innocent activity on my part—excluding my flashback to the night I ripped Chris's clothes off—rather than his fling with Abigail, the dig-site slut.

As I slunk into the lobby of my building, Bob offered a rueful smile. I wondered if he sometimes went home and yammered to his wife about me over a cold Bud. "There's this girl in the building who seems nice enough, but no sooner does she get into a relationship with some guy than she's picking a fight with him on the curb."

In desperation I thought of pounding on Landon's door, but it wasn't fair, considering his head cold, to subject him to more pathos about my love life. I thawed a chicken cutlet in my microwave and cooked it halfheartedly to within an inch of its life. A few times I felt an overwhelming urge to call Beau, but I fought it off. Why should *I* be the one trying to make things right?

At eleven I considered hitting the sack, but I knew it would be pointless. I could already envision the horrible bout of insomnia that lay ahead of me tonight. A thought suddenly snagged my brain. This might be a good time to reach Tommy. He hadn't answered or returned my calls, but at this hour I might catch him off guard. From what I remembered from the weekend, he was nice and loose as midnight rolled around.

I was right. He answered hello with the deafening sounds of live music and bar yell behind him. And, surprisingly, he didn't seem to mind hearing from me now; *that* was a nice change of pace.

"I've been wondering how you were doing," I half shouted.

"Well, ain't that sweet of you to be concerned," he shouted back.

"I'd love to get together and talk—I have some information I'd like to share with you."

"Is that right?" The music had subsided and been replaced by the sound of a car zooming by. Wherever he was, he'd managed to step out onto the street, away from the epicenter of noise.

"It's about Devon. I think you'll want to hear what I've learned."

"No time like the present."

"Pardon me?"

"I *said* there's no time like the present. I'm at the Living Room. A dude I know is performing here. Why don't you mosey that cute little butt of yours down here?"

I knew the Living Room. It was a bar on the Lower East Side, known for showcasing emerging bands in the back room. I'd been there a few times over the years, but not lately. The Lower East Side, once a ghetto for European immigrants in the 1800s, was now a hip area filled with wine bars, boutiques, and trendy restaurants, and it tended to attract mostly twenty-somethings. At my age I now felt like I needed to obtain special clearance to go down there. But that didn't matter tonight. I was anxious to see Tommy and promised to be there within thirty minutes.

I left on the jeans and V-neck sweater but added a black leather jacket. I also swiped on black eyeliner, mascara, and lip gloss, hoping it would assist in the extraction of info.

I figured it would take a while to find Tommy in the dense crowd of the bar, but when my cab pulled up, he was standing out in front with the smokers, dressed in just a T-shirt and black jeans, sucking on the last of a cigarette. From the look on his face, he appeared to have a nice buzz going.

"That was fast," he said. "You must be just dying to see me." He flicked his butt into the street. "Why don't we go inside, and you can buy me a drink?"

"You've got it," I said. I loved the idea that the drinks would be on *my* tab. Maybe Tory was right— the last album *had* really tanked.

The place was packed and smelled of beer, sweat, and dampish wool coats. Somehow we managed to find a space to stand at the end of the bar. The band was obviously on a break, though I could see lots of people milling around in the back room.

Tommy asked for a Maker's on the rocks, and I ordered a beer for myself. He gripped his drink with long, slim fingers that must have served him well on the guitar. Though we'd had a couple of brief conversations at Scott's, this was the closest I'd ever been to him. He was way too bony and inked for my liking, but his gray eyes were compelling. Maybe that's what had hooked Devon and Tory.

I flashed him a friendly smile but tried not to seem too flirty, knowing that if I gave off the wrong vibe, he'd start talking about turning me into a human hot fudge sundae.

"How do you know the band?" I asked over the din.

"What?" he asked.

"The *band*. How do you know them?"

"The drummer is the brother of a buddy of mine. They fuckin' stink—but I promised to show tonight."

"That's nice. I mean, it must still be pretty hard for you right now—with Devon's death and all. As you told me, Devon was your lady for a while."

"Yeah, I'm a big hero, aren't I?"

"I suppose you've heard the news," I said. "That it was definitely Devon's eating disorder that led to her death."

"That's what they tell me. But like I said to you last weekend, she never pulled any of that stuff on my watch."

"The night she died, she was obviously suffering the side effects of losing vital nutrients—like potassium. It's that loss of nutrients that leads to a heart failure."

"I wouldn't know," he said. "I'm not an M.D." I almost laughed out loud. That had to be the understatement of the year.

"When you lose potassium, it also affects your muscles," I explained. "That was probably why she seemed dizzy before she went back to her room. And by one o'clock she would have been feeling pretty awful."

He drew his upper body back, as if I'd just spattered something on the bar.

"I can tell you've got a point to make," he said, the friendliness dissipating. "Why don't you just come right out and make it."

"Okay. Devon was flirting with you last weekend, and she may have even invited you and Tory up there just so she could try to win you back. I think you went to her room Saturday night."

He smirked and shook his head.

"Who told you that—*Tory*?"

"Tory said you were missing in action for over an hour."

"Yeah, I was missing in action. I was sick of her bony-ass whining."

"So you went to Devon's room. Why didn't you notice how ill she was? Surely you must have seen it."

"Because I didn't go to Devon's room. I hooked up with that little redhead waitress who helped at dinner. She was giving me the eye the whole night."

"*Laura?*" I exclaimed, not able to contain my surprise.

"Was that the chick's name? I didn't ask. Anyway, I'd overheard her say something to that other woman— the one with the tooth you could carve up a cow with— about staying in the garage apartment rather than driving home. I decided to pay her a little visit."

"Was it around one fifteen?"

"Yeah, maybe. I don't keep a log on my sex life."

My mind raced, reviewing the details Laura had shared with me that night as well as the guilty aura she'd displayed. I'd assumed at the time that she'd felt troubled about having fallen back to sleep after Devon called, but that's not what was nudging her conscience. She'd promised to bring water to Devon, but when the visiting Rock Star had showed up—probably moments later—she decided to attend to his randy needs instead.

"Did you call Laura's room later—after you got back to yours?" I still had no clue who had made that second call.

"*Call* her?" he said, snickering. "You mean, like, Hey, that was special, let's do it again sometime? I don't *think* so. Why all the fascination with some townie? I've got better stories to share than that one if you want a little fun."

"Why my fascination? I'm just a little surprised—I could have sworn things were starting to heat up with you and Devon again," I said, refocusing. "I heard she'd been pretty upset when you two broke up, and it looked like she was hatching a plan to get back together again."

"I guess she was bummed. But I wasn't interested in having a ball and chain wrapped around my dick."

"You met last February?"

"That's when we hooked up. But we'd actually met a few months before at some party." He shrugged. "She told me later that it was like being hit by a thunderbolt when she met me. We got into a serious make-out session, but she was a little coy about going any farther. Then she secretly hatched this big plan to meet again, like, two and a half months later—she got friends to bring her backstage after a concert."

"Do *you* think she wanted to restart things last weekend?"

"Like I told you before, Devon was a real mind fucker. Who knows what she was thinking?"

"Did that make you mad?"

"*Mad*? What's that supposed to mean?"

"Well, she was kind of toying with you. That couldn't have been much fun."

"Maybe I wasn't clear enough with you. I had plenty of action last weekend."

"By the way, did you know Devon had a miscarriage around the end of last year?"

He narrowed his eyes, clearly taken aback.

"Well it wasn't mine. Like I said, we didn't get down and dirty until February. Besides, I don't *do* kids. Can't stand the little bastards. . . . Look, I thought you wanted to have a nice friendly conversation. You're starting to sound like a cop or something."

Suddenly there was the discordant sound of electric guitars being tuned in the back. Tommy craned his neck in that direction.

"I'm sorry if I'm tossing lots of questions at you," I said, attempting not to lose his interest. "But there's a reason for it. I think someone might have caused Devon's death—by aggravating the symptoms of her anorexia."

That had his attention. He spun back in my direction.

"Is that what the cops are saying?"

"No. It's just a theory *I* have. Any ideas?"

"Read my lips," he said. "I don't know anything about eating disorders or any shit like that. As far as I'm concerned, I'm never hooking up with another model. I want a chick with some meat on her bones. That redhead didn't have a clue what to do in the sack, but at least there was something to hold on to."

"Okay, so you don't know anything about eating disorders, but Tory might. Do you think she wanted Devon dead? Because Devon was after you again?"

He started to do the shoulder shrug again, but I saw the idea snag in his brain. He took a long swallow of his drink, staring into the glass.

"You're gonna have to ask Tory that," he said. "But keep it short so she can understand what you're saying."

"I—"

"I gotta get back there. I'd ask you to stay, but you don't seem like the type who can just chill and listen to music."

"One more thing," I said, as he slid off his stool. "Do you know Sherrie Barr?"

"Devon's old lady? Yeah, I had the unfortunate experience of meeting her once—and I'm really not looking forward to watching her slur her words on Saturday. Look, I *really* need to get back there."

He started off and then unexpectedly turned back to me, his gray eyes boring into me. "Be careful getting home," he said. "It gets a little sketchy down here late at night."

Oh, thanks, I thought. Mr. Chivalry. I snaked my way through the crowd and stepped outside into the cold night air.

Though the bar had been mobbed, the street outside was deserted and most of the lights in the converted tenement buildings were off now. With no traffic at the moment and none of the usual hip crowd spilling out into the street, it wasn't hard to imagine the pushcarts and carriages that had once rumbled along here.

What I needed at the moment, though, was a cab, not a pushcart, and I could sense right away that it was going to be tricky to find one. I gave it a minute, though, hoping there might be some canvassing the area even at this hour, but no such luck. Stupidly, thinking I'd be out for only a short time, I hadn't even bothered to wear gloves, and my fingers would soon be freezing.

Just as I was about to bag the location for another, a gypsy cab pulled up, the kind that patrolled late at night when there was a scarcity of regular taxis. Gypsy cabs were unlicensed car services, but because they fulfilled a need, there was a live-and-let-live attitude toward them. I'd taken them on several occasions when I was desperate, but I didn't feel *that* desperate at the moment. The driver made eye contact and raised his chin, as if asking if I needed a ride. I shook my head, stuffed my hands in my pockets, and started to walk, headed north.

The first intersection I passed was Rivington, and there was no sign of a cab there. I walked another block north to Stanton. It was a relief to see a few more people in the area, but they seemed to be looking for cabs too. I had no choice but to head another block north to East Houston. I already had that sinking sense you get when a little voice in your head tells you that at least as far as tonight goes, there's no way in hell you will find a taxi.

There was a ton of traffic on Houston, but it was all just regular cars barreling along. Ten minutes passed with my hand in the air and me flicking my head left and right, searching futilely with my eyes.

I stuck my hand back in my pockets just to warm my fingers. I could hoof it home, I realized. It would take about a half hour. But I'd be freezing cold by the time I arrived. And I didn't feel comfortable being alone at this hour on the deserted downtown streets. I also didn't feel like hopping on the subway this late.

Suddenly I heard a car come up slowly behind me on Ludlow, and instinctively I spun around. It was another gypsy cab. Or, rather, the same gypsy cab I'd seen outside the Living Room. The driver was obviously having the same amount of luck as I was. He made eye contact again and cocked his head. I nodded my head in response. This time I felt desperate enough to hop in.

"Ninth and Broadway," I told the driver once I was in the back seat. The car, to my disgust, reeked of cigarette smoke.

"Twelve dollars," he told me, not bothering to turn around. Gypsy cabs didn't have meters.

"How about ten?" I said. Twelve seemed outrageous.

He nodded, again without looking back, and put the car in drive. I leaned my head back, exhausted. I'd barely slept last night, and my insomnia was catching up with me now. I closed my eyes, just resting them. I heard Beau's words from earlier echo in my head suddenly: "Something absurd is going on here. But I'm not the one responsible." Was he going to end our relationship? I wondered.

I opened my eyes again, feeling miserable. I was too churned up right now, and I couldn't think any more about it. When I gazed out in the darkened Manhattan street, I realized something wasn't right. We were back on Houston Street, headed east, not north. The driver was going the wrong way.

16

"W ait," I yelled, jerking my body forward. "I said Ninth and Broadway."

For one brief moment I actually thought the driver had misheard me or had arrived in America six days ago and had no freaking clue where he was going. But he never turned around, just gunned the motor so that the car sped even faster. I realized that after I'd closed my eyes in the backseat, he must have circled back to Houston. It was suddenly clear: he was abducting me! My heart hurled itself against the front of my chest, like it was trying to leap off a cliff.

"What do you want?" I called out. My voice was squeaky from panic. "Do you want money?" But the driver ignored me.

I glanced toward the door. The lock was still up at least. I had no choice—the only escape was for me to leap out onto the road. Yet the car was moving so fast, I couldn't imagine how I'd pull it off.

I reached for my handbag and searched frantically until I found my BlackBerry. My hands were shaking as I punched in 911.

"A cabdriver kidnapped me," I yelled to the operator. "Uh—a gypsy cab. We're going down Houston Street. East."

"Miss, what is your name?" the woman asked.

"Bailey Weggins. Please, you've got to help me."

With one swift movement the driver reached his right arm into the backseat and tried to slap the BlackBerry from my hand. I jerked away, pressing my body against the door.

"What is the license plate of the car?" the operator asked.

"I have no idea," I exclaimed. "I didn't see it."

"What's the car look like? What's the make?"

"Uh—I don't know. It's dark. A four-door." I peered into the front seat toward the glove compartment. I couldn't see anything.

I prayed the guy would head onto a side street, where he'd be forced to slow down. But he turned south onto the FDR Drive, which ran between the East River and the eastern edge of Manhattan. My fear ballooned. There was only a small amount of traffic, and the driver now had the car up to at least fifty miles per hour. If I jumped out, I'd kill myself.

"We're on the FDR now," I yelled to the operator. "South."

I grabbed the window handle and rolled it down. Cold air gushed into the back of the cab.

"Help me," I screamed to the stream of cars to my right, but my voice was crushed by the wind. Finally a woman in the backseat of one of the cars seemed to notice me. She leaned forward, said something to the couple in the front seat, and then glanced back at me, her face scrunched in worry. But the car pulled off at the next exit.

I felt nearly dizzy with dread. Where was he taking me? I wondered desperately. Did he want to rob me or rape me, or both? He nearly careened off the South Street exit, and then to my horror swung onto the entrance to the Manhattan Bridge. He was taking me to Brooklyn, where it would be easy to find a deserted spot. He was forced to slow down just a little on the bridge, but there was too much traffic for me to even think of jumping out. On my right a subway car hurtled by alongside us. Inside passengers dozed or stared listlessly. I tried to motion to them, but no one noticed.

From my hand I could hear the operator calling out to me. I pressed my Blackberry to my ear.

"Miss, please, give me your location now," she said.

"We're on the bridge now," I told her. "Manhattan Bridge."

"Can you signal to anyone near you?"

"I'm trying, but they don't see me."

"We are alerting the police in Brooklyn to your location."

Get control, I told myself. I had to think of a plan. When we left the bridge, the driver would *have* to slow down. That would be my chance to leap from the car. I pressed myself against the door and gripped the handle tightly.

Finally we came off the bridge, rolling into a dark, deserted part of Brooklyn. I could tell the driver was trying his best not to lose speed, but he had no choice but to ease off the gas. The traffic light ahead had just turned from yellow to red and he zoomed right through it. I'd never have a chance to jump if he refused to ever stop the freaking car.

There were only stop signs at the next two intersections and the driver just barreled through. He was about to do the same with the next one, but miraculously a delivery van came lumbering through the intersection. The driver touched the brake, slowing the car. I jerked the handle down. At the same moment the driver shot his right arm into the backseat and tried to grab hold of my jacket, but I was faster than he was. I shoved open the door, propelled myself out, and rolled onto the sidewalk.

I scrambled to my feet, veered right, and started to run. I was on a dark and empty street, lined with old warehouses and storefronts with their metal gates pulled down. Behind me I heard tires squeal as the driver jerked the wheel. Oh God, I thought. He was going to come after me, even though he'd be headed the wrong way down a one-way street.

"I'm out now," I yelled into the BlackBerry. "On, uh—I can't see."

I couldn't take the time to see. I just had to move. Running as fast as I could, I screamed for help a couple of times, but there wasn't a soul in sight, just darkened or boarded-up windows everywhere I could see. In a minute I could hear the car coming up behind me. I propelled myself even faster, trying not to trip in my damn riding boots. My lungs seemed ready to explode.

I heard the driver gun the engine. He was almost parallel to me, just off to my left. I didn't look over, just kept my eyes straight ahead, focusing on a point in the distance. About two blocks ahead I could see a big halo of light at an intersection, as if there were businesses and traffic there. *Go!* I screamed to myself. I only had to make it two long blocks. I yelled for help a few more times, just to let the guy know it would be a bitch to stop the car and try to get me inside again without a fuss.

We were coming to a stretch of the street where there weren't even any parked cars along the sidewalk, and I wondered, horrified, if the driver might try to jump the car up onto the sidewalk and mow me down. And then it was like he'd read my mind. I heard the thud as he yanked the car up over the curb. Without even processing what I was about to do, I dropped my phone into my pocket and grabbed a garbage can near a doorway. I spun around and hurled it right at the hood of the car.

It didn't do any damage, but it stayed on the hood. As I started running again, my lungs nearly screaming, I heard the driver curse through an open window and put the car in reverse, making the can roll off the hood. Within seconds, though, he was in pursuit again.

But it was too late. I was close to the intersection now, and I could see that it was filled with traffic, and there were even a few people up there too, a cluster of hipsters hanging by a bar. And on the far side, there was something that filled me with joy. A police cruiser.

I burst into the intersection and started waving my arms frantically. Behind me I heard the gypsy cab screech to a halt and then do a U-turn, the driver jerking the car forward and backward a few times. I slowed my speed a little, and looked back. The car was totally turned around, ready to take off in the opposite direction. In the dark I could make out only the first part of the license plate—L3. The driver suddenly thrust his head out the window and looked back at me. He screamed something in my direction. It sounded like "Stop. Be a body." And then he took off like the proverbial banshee down the street.

Relief poured through my body, warm, almost intoxicating. I turned back to the intersection, waited for the light, and started to jog across to the police cruiser. As I moved, fighting a stitch in my side, I dug into my pocket and found my BlackBerry. The 911 operator was still connected.

"I'm okay," I told her, trying to catch my breath. "I see a cop car."

"Good. Please let me speak to one of the officers."

As soon as I approached, the cop in the driver's seat rolled his window down. He looked like he was twelve years old and might be wearing Spiderman underpants.

"What can we do for you, young lady?" he asked. The cop next to him set down the disposable aluminum dish he was eating from and leaned his head in my direction.

I blurted out that I'd been abducted and then handed him my BlackBerry. He listened intently, signed off, and then handed the BlackBerry back to me.

"Are you okay?" he asked, climbing out of the car. When I assured him I was, he asked for the best description of the car and driver I could give and then called it in on his radio.

I suddenly noticed that despite the cold, the sweater inside my jacket was wet with sweat. I also noticed a weird crashing sensation beginning to build in me, maybe from all the adrenaline that had been briefly pumped through my system and was now in retreat.

"We should cruise around and see if we can find this guy," the cop told me when he was finished talking on his walkie-talkie. "But we don't have much to go on. And we also need to make sure you get home somehow."

Out of the corner of my eye I saw a yellow taxi head through the intersection, and the light was on.

"Why don't I grab this taxi," I told the cop. I shot out my arm and waved. The car screeched to a halt. "Thanks so much for your help."

"You'll need to file a police report tomorrow, okay?"

I promised I would and darted toward the cab. I spent the ride home fighting tears. I felt badly shaken.

By the time I let myself into my apartment, I was trembling, as if the fear was now really catching up with me. I stripped off my boots, jeans, and sweater and took a long shower. It felt so good to have the hot water course over me, as if I was washing the terror away too. My leap from the gypsy cab had left another ugly bruise on my left butt cheek but fortunatly that was the only damage. I thought of how reassuring it would be to talk to Beau, but even if things were fine between us, I would have resisted the urge to wake him so late.

When I finally slipped into bed, I felt a little bit better. I knew I wasn't going to fall asleep anyway, so I tried to go back over everything in my mind. I was positive that the driver who picked me up was the same one I'd seen earlier in front of the Living Room. Obviously he'd been trolling for someone to rob or rape. I decided to let the bar know tomorrow so the management could keep an eye out for the guy.

I still had no sense of where he had been taking me or why. One thing seemed odd. If he were going to rob me or rape me, why not just pull over on one of those deserted streets when we first came off the bridge into Brooklyn? Maybe he had wanted to find an even more secluded spot. I was also still baffled by the words he'd hurled at me: *Stop. Be a body.* He'd had a faint accent, one that I couldn't place, but I was pretty sure I'd heard him right. Had it been some kind of a sexual threat? I had no clue.

I eventually fell asleep around four and woke at eight the next morning. I felt like shit, but I had my breakfast meeting with Scott and I had no intention of taking a pass on it. I did my best to look presentable—Scott, after all, was a player, and I sensed I'd extract more if I catered to that part of him. I wore my black suede boots, a tight black pencil skirt, and a plum-colored silk blouse. But the circles under my eyes had darkened badly. By the time I was done with my makeup, you could have taken an elevation level on the amount of concealer I'd been forced to apply.

I was the first to arrive at the café-style restaurant, and I grabbed a private table at the back of the room. I asked for coffee but then instantly changed my order to tea. I still felt completely on edge from the night before, and I was afraid anything with too much caffeine might make me jump out of my skin.

Scott was nearly twenty minutes late—and I almost didn't recognize him. His hair was slicked back and he was wearing a long black cashmere coat. Not the kind of look that went with skeet shooting.

He slid into the chair, shook off his coat, and with a flick of his chin, summoned the waitress to our table pronto. He smelled of expensive, manly cologne.

"Sorry I'm late," he said. "What would you like to eat?"

"Uh, I guess I'll try the asparagus and goat cheese omelet," I said.

And then I felt dumb because all he ordered was coffee, black.

"How are you doing anyway?" I asked once the waitress was gone. There was something supertense going on in his jawline that made even his face look different today. It was tough to accept that this was the same Scott who had bounded down the stairs to greet Jessie and me with a big, boyish grin on his face.

"Well," he said, cocking his head to the left, "my hot new recording artist died at my house, and for the next two days most of the world assumed I'd loaded her up with cocaine—but other than that I'm just fine."

"I appreciate your taking the time to meet in the middle of all this," I said.

"I'm a little surprised *you* could make the time," he said. There was a tiny edge to his voice as he spoke. "I figured things must be crazy for you at work. Though I'm a little confused. I turned on the *Today* show yesterday morning, and there's some guy on there from *Buzz* talking about Devon Barr as if the story was *his* exclusive. Don't tell me your boss doesn't think you're mediagenic enough to chat with Matt Lauer."

Scott never took his nearly black eyes off me as he said it, and I could feel a rush of blood headed for my cheeks, like a mob of paparazzi that has just spotted Lady Gaga coming out of a building wearing only a couple of Band-Aids. He'd either somehow heard that I was in the doghouse or he just had brilliant intuition.

"I do media appearances occasionally," I said, fumbling a little as I spoke. "But if I'm still in the middle of a story, I might hand the press part off to somebody else." Lame, I knew, but it would put me at a disadvantage to admit the truth to Scott Cohen.

"Oh, is that it?" he said, disbelievingly. "Well, who am I to know how your wonderful brand of journalism works?"

So that might explain why he was goading me. He obviously felt burned from all the coverage over the past few days, and saw me as entrenched in the enemy camp.

"What I'd really like to concentrate on for the moment is Devon and this past weekend," I said, rushing off the subject. "I have a few big concerns."

"As long as we're still off the record, I'm willing to talk with you," Scott said. "Because I've got a vested interest in knowing as much as I can. That incident with the doors still bugs the hell out of me. Why would someone pull a fucking stunt like that?"

"That's one of the things I wanted to discuss. Have you any idea yet who might have done it?"

"The cops checked for fingerprints on the branding iron and apparently didn't find any. Of course, what good would it do? They don't have any of the houseguests' prints to compare anything to."

"And you didn't turn up any clues yourself?"

"Just a small one courtesy of Cap on Sunday. His bedroom was at the base of the stairs in the guest barn, and not long after the time you took your spill, he woke to the sound of someone bounding up the stairs."

That seemed to be another clue pointing to Jane. Because she was the only one on the top floor besides me, Jessie, and Devon—and Devon sure as hell hadn't done it. Scott eyed me questioningly, as if he suspected I knew something. But I wasn't going to out Jane to him.

"Let me think about that," I told him. "Anything else that emerged later? Anything that Ralph or Sandy might have noticed?"

"About the night raider?"

"Or about Devon. Her death. Things leading up to it."

"What do you mean? What are you suggesting, exactly?"

"Frankly, I've been wondering if Devon might have been murdered. Like I mentioned to you on Sunday, she told me she was afraid that someone *knew* something. And then suddenly she was dead."

He shook his head, borderline exasperated. "I know you were hot on some theory like that last weekend, and I admit I had moments of concern—the stuff pinched from her bathroom, the missing keys. But the police were very clear. She died due to her eating disorder."

"But what if someone pushed it along a little? She kept complaining that the bottled water tasted funny?"

Scott snorted. "Wait, are you suggesting someone doctored the water? Yeah, Devon complained about the water, but she also said the sheets were itchy and the sink in the bathroom didn't drain fast enough. And besides, who would want her dead? She was making a load of money for most of us."

"Do you think there's any chance Cap and Devon were having an affair?" I asked.

"No way," he said emphatically. "Skinny rocker was more her type. Though I sure as hell hope she appreciated all Cap had done for her. When he first took her on, I bet he thought her career would evolve into something beyond modeling—movies, or even reality TV, à la Heidi Klum. From what I hear, though, she was a total dud in front of a video camera. But then he found out she could sing, and he really pushed her. I believe her career as a performer could have been big. I'm not talking Rihanna or Katy Perry big, but still, a major success."

"You said you *hope* she appreciated Cap. Why wouldn't she?"

"Devon was fickle. She changed her mind easily. I don't think there was any immediate danger of her dumping Cap, but I could see he was very careful with her—bending over backwards to please her. When she said itchy sheets, he made damn sure they got changed."

"And what about her relationship with Christian? Could that have been strained?"

"*Strained?* I hardly think so. She asked me to include him."

"But Tory told me Devon gave him the cold shoulder all weekend."

"Maybe she was—"

He'd been gesturing as he spoke, and when he paused, his hand did too, midair above his coffee cup.

"What?" I prodded.

He made a noise, halfway between a laugh and a snort.

"There may have been something up, now that I think about it," he said. "I'd arranged the place cards on the table for dinner and Sandy told me that at around seven o'clock, Devon came in and switched a few of the cards around. I figured it was so she could sit next to Tommy and fondle his groin with her foot. But originally she'd been seated next to Christian. Maybe the real story was that she didn't want to sit next to him."

He drained the last of his coffee cup, and I knew he was going to want to be on the move soon. I started poking with a fork at my untouched omelet in the hopes of encouraging him to hang around. But it didn't work. He pulled his wallet from the pocket of his pants.

"Look, I know you have to split," I said, "but I'd love a phone number for Sandy—and one for Laura too. I want to double-check with them that nothing seemed amiss."

"I already talked to them before I left," he said.

"But something may have occurred to them since then. If we want to get to the bottom of this, I think it's essential to talk to them."

"All right," he said, reluctantly. "But I don't want them harassed in any way." He tugged an iPhone out of his coat pocket, asked for my cell number, and then texted me numbers for both women. "And this is a two-way street, remember?" he said. "If you learn anything important, I want to know."

"Sure," I lied.

I tried to pick up the check, but he insisted and tossed down a tip that was almost as much as the bill. Out on the street, he buttoned his coat with one hand and then pulled the collar up against the cold.

"Are you going to the funeral service?" I asked as people rushed by us on their way to midtown offices.

"Of course. I assume you'll be covering it?"

"Probably not," I said, fighting the urge to look away. "I've got other things to do on the story."

"*Really*?" he said. "I would have thought that the funeral would be one of the plums of covering Devon Barr's death."

There was that goading thing again. A thought flashed in my mind: Could I have annoyed Scott so much that he'd tried to derail my career with Sherrie's help?

I didn't say anything, just studied his face. He didn't give anything away.

"Well, I'm sure I'll see our friend Richard out there," he said. "I bet he's all over this"

"Actually, he told me he probably wasn't going to do a story on Devon, after all."

"Don't kid yourself. He was probably trying to throw you off the scent. He's more than interested in Devon Barr. In fact, he nearly begged me to let him come last weekend. Since it meant a possible story in *Vanity Fair*, I was hardly going to turn the man down."

"But—," I said, flipping through my memory. "I thought you'd *invited* him—because you wanted him to do a story."

"Nope," he said. "I ran into him at a party, and somehow the weekend came up. He nearly foamed at the mouth when I told him Devon was going to be there. He all but guaranteed me the story if I let him freeload."

I knew I wasn't remembering incorrectly. Richard had made a point of saying that Scott had pressed him into coming. Why had he lied to me? I wondered.

Scott glanced toward Seventh Avenue, obviously checking out the cab situation.

"By the way, have you met Devon's mother before?" I asked hurriedly.

"No," he said, bluntly. "The music business isn't like college basketball, where you have to meet the players' mommies before you sign them. Look, I really have to go."

"Sure," I said. "Thanks again for your time."

He stepped off the curb and shot up his hand for a cab. Not surprisingly for a guy with his power aura, one jerked to a stop ten seconds later. Unexpectedly, he turned back to me.

"Since you and Jessie are such good buddies," he said slyly, "my guess is that she shared the details of our little misunderstanding Saturday night."

"More or less," I said lightly. I didn't want to offend the dude in case I needed him later. "But I'm not judgmental. One person's idea of fun can sometimes be way too kinky for someone else."

"What if it wasn't kinky I was interested in? What if I said I just hadn't been able to take my eyes off you from the moment we met?"

Oh, please, I thought, who was this guy trying to kid? And I'd want a date with him about as much as I'd like to be hurtling down his stairs again. At a loss for words, I smiled weakly at him.

"Maybe when this is all behind us, I can prove it to you over dinner," he said.

"Actually, I'm seeing someone," I said. "But thanks for the offer."

He didn't look so happy as he slid into the cab.

Of course it took *me* ten minutes to find a taxi. I should have opted for the subway, but I was too antsy. There were a couple of things I needed to do, stat.

I tore off my coat the minute I stepped through the door of my apartment and didn't bother to hang it up. The first thing I did was call the number Scott had sent me for Laura. Though I'd requested Sandy and Laura's numbers, I'd been creating a bit of a smokescreen; it was only Laura who interested me at the moment, and I wanted to reach her before Scott had a chance to warn her I might be making contact.

She answered with pop music playing in the background. I had the sense she was at home, maybe still in her jammies. When I identified myself, she sounded less than pleased.

"I thought I'd just check in and see how you were doing," I said.

"How did you get this number?" she asked warily. "Who gave it to you?"

"Scott did. He knows I'm calling you."

"I'm really busy right now. It's not a good time to talk."

"I understand," I said. "But it's very important for me to clarify a few details with you. Some of the information you gave me doesn't gel with what else I've learned."

"What are you talking about?"

"Tommy Quinn told me he went to your room just after one on Saturday night and had sex with you. That would have been good to know, because it explains why you didn't go to Devon's room right away."

"What?" she exclaimed, faking shock. "That's a lie."

"You know, Laura, it's against the rules to lie to the press. It's not as serious as perjury, but you can still get in trouble." She seemed naive enough to fall for it.

"Are you going to *print* this?" she asked. She suddenly sounded distraught.

"No, I'm playing nice, and if you're straight with me, I won't print what Tommy said. I just want to know what really happened."

"Because if my mother finds out . . ." She was nearly wailing now.

"You have my word," I said.

"Okay, yes. He came to my room. Right after Devon called. I was afraid if I went up there to bring her the stupid water, she'd come up with something else for me to do, and he would just get tired of waiting."

"And when he left, you finally went up there."

"Yes. That's when I saw you."

"What about what you said about the other phone call? Was there really another call?"

"Yes. I swear that part is true. But I have no clue who it was."

I grilled her for another minute, just making sure there was nothing she was leaving out. I was pretty sure she was being truthful this time, terrified of being busted by the journalism police I'd conjured up in her mind.

As soon as I hung up, I hurried to my home office and went online. I was more than curious as to why Richard had misled me about his reason for going to

Scott's. Though I'd done a search through some of the articles by and about Richard Parkin, it had been only cursory and I hadn't gone very far back. Time for a closer look.

There was a ton of stuff to wade through around the time each of Richard's books had been published, and then there were large gaps in between with just a smattering of press on him, usually related to a pro- vocative, or even incendiary, comment he'd lobbed on the Charlie Rose or Bill O'Reilly shows. He believed that religion was indeed the root of all evil, considered Gen Y the most vile generation in history, and thought there should be a fat tax, requiring overweight people to pay more than the rest of us. Nothing at all sug- gested he had a reason to hate Devon Barr. At *her* weight, she certainly hadn't put a strain on govern- ment resources.

When I'd gone back a decade, I was tempted to stop. It seemed pointless to search any further. But there wasn't much left—just a few UK stories—and I was curious enough to continue. Richard had come to America twelve years ago after stints at various Fleet Street papers, where he'd built a reputation for not only breaking news but also writing brilliantly.

I found a profile from fourteen years ago and opened it. There were pictures, too, including one of Richard walking in front of a stone wall on a cobbled street, looking slim, handsome, and grim. Farther back there was a cluster of people, their jaws slack. I glanced down at the caption and caught my breath.

"Journalist Richard Parkin leaving the funeral of his half sister, runway model Fiona Campbell."

17

I reread the caption twice, totally shocked. There was no story accompanying the picture, so I Googled Fiona Campbell. I found only one tiny reference to her, in an article published the year before her death. It was about the party and drug scene in London. I wondered if drugs were behind her tragically early death.

I knew what I'd found had to be significant. Doing the math, I realized that Fiona was probably working as a model at the same time Devon's career was exploding. And someone—yes, it was Jane—had told me that Devon kept a place in London, that she felt at home there. Maybe that's where she had worked early in her career. And if that was the case, there was a good chance she would have known Fiona.

I smiled to myself as a memory fought its way into my conscious brain. Richard and I, sitting in the great room the morning after Devon's death. I'd asked for his impressions of Devon that weekend. And he'd made the comment about how models liked to smoke. I'd been surprised, wondering how he would know that. Almost immediately afterward, he'd left the room.

So *had* the two girls actually known each other? And was that why Richard had maneuvered to be in Devon's presence on the weekend? Perhaps he'd never had any particular interest in tracking Devon down, but when he'd heard that she was going to be at Scott's, he decided that it would be a chance to talk to her about his sister, to learn what he could. But I'd never seen Richard interacting with Devon for even a second. He'd just watched her, sometimes out of the corner of his eye.

Quickly another thought charged across my brain. Richard may have had an ulterior motive when he secured the invitation for the weekend. What if Devon and Fiona had been into drugs together, and that's how Fiona had died? What if Devon had actually encouraged Fiona's drug use? Richard might have held her responsible and then jumped at the chance to confront her.

And that could be the reason Devon had looked so frightened that day in the woods—Richard may have just ambushed her. After our walk, while I'd idly checked out the buildings on the property, he had headed toward the large barn, but he could have bumped into Devon on the way and initiated a showdown with her. It was, after all, only ten minutes or so after the hike that I had found Devon sobbing. And maybe a verbal bitch-slapping wasn't all Richard had arranged for the weekend.

I was going to have another little chat with the cagey Richard Parkin. But first I needed to learn more about his sister. For the second time in a couple of days, Cat Jones's name popped into my mind. Before she'd taken over *Gloss* magazine, she'd been the editor in chief of a hip downtown magazine called *Get*, where I'd worked as well, and there was a chance she knew Richard, or at least was friendly with people who did.

I phoned her office, and of course her assistant picked up. Cat hadn't answered her own phone since the 1990s. I wasn't surprised when I was handed the "Unfortunately, Cat is in a meeting right now—may I have her call you back?" line, but I *was* surprised when the assistant suddenly asked me to hold, as if someone had gestured to her. When she released the hold button, she offered an update. "Cat says she will call you back in twenty minutes. What number can she reach you at?"

So I had piqued Ms. Jones's curiosity. She probably thought I was calling with hot industry gossip, which Cat absolutely thrived on. When it came to herself, she of course favored only flattering chatter and tidbits, especially press items accompanied by fetching photos of her with captions like "*Purrrfect* Comeback" or "Puss in Boots," but as for anyone else in the media world, she preferred the mean and salacious, even if it was all mere speculation.

While I waited for Cat to return the call, I phoned a rental agency for a car to drive out to Pine Grove the next day. There was no way I could drive my Jeep. Last weekend all the houseguests at Scott's would have had the opportunity to see it, and I couldn't take the chance of being spotted in Pennsylvania.

"Well, well," Cat said when she called back exactly twenty minutes later. "Are you still on your book tour?"

"No," I said, snorting. "My publisher doesn't believe in them. But they set me up on a wonderful blog tour. I've stayed at some of the best Web sites."

"I enjoyed your book party, by the way," Cat said, disingenuously. "Lots of interesting people there." She had stayed all of fifteen minutes, two of which were spent air kissing and the rest eyeing the *Buzz* reporters I'd invited, as if she had come face-to-face with the last leper colony on earth.

"I was glad you could make it," I said.

"Though I would have liked more of a chance to talk to you. I honestly didn't think I'd be seeing so little of you when you went to *Buzz*."

That was funny. She was making it sound as if *I'd* bolted. And yet she was the one who'd given *me* the boot, when she'd decided to jettison the human interest and crime stories in *Gloss* to make room for pieces like "78 Ways to Apply Body Butter" and "Green Tea: It Does *Anything* You Could Possibly Think Of." I'd been pissed at first, but in the end I couldn't blame her—if she didn't boost circulation fast, her job and her ever-present herd of town cars would be at risk. I'd figured in time we'd manage to restart our weird kind of friendship, but so far it hadn't happened.

"I'm sure you're crazed right now, but maybe we could do a dinner after the holidays," I said.

"I take it that's not why you're calling today, though."

"No, you're right," I said, smiling at her little zinger. Cat was the master of those. "I need a favor—or rather a piece of information. I'm in a bit of a jam, the details of which I won't bore you with, but I desperately have to get my hands on some facts about Richard Parkin. Do you know—"

"What kind of jam?"

"I promise to tell you when I see you next time, but it would take too long now—and I need to move quickly."

There was a pause, and I could sense her plum-colored lips forming into a pout and a finger brushing a strand of long blond hair away from her face.

"Well, I never *fucked* him," she said after a few seconds. "But I've certainly met him. I've even sat at the same dinner table with him on several occasions."

"He had a half sister who died about fourteen years ago. She was a model in the UK. Have you ever heard anything about that?"

"God, no. And that surprises me. It's not like him to forgo an opportunity to milk some human tragedy."

I sighed, feeling nearly defeated.

"Can you think of any way for me to dig up this info?" I asked, nearly pleading. "It would help if I could talk to someone who knew him during his Fleet Street days."

"Well, though *I* never fucked him, I know someone who did. Claire Trent. She's a friend of mine in London. She used to write, but she married a rich banker and now sits around all day eating the proverbial bonbons. Would you like her number?"

"Absolutely," I said. "Do you want to get in touch with her first and let her know I'll be phoning?"

"Not necessary. I'll put my assistant back on, and she'll give you the number. Just tell Claire I suggested you call. She's looking for diversions these days."

"Thanks, Cat. I'll talk to you after Christmas."

"Right," she said, as if only seeing would be believing.

When I phoned Claire Trent a minute later, a house-keeper answered, her British accent so thick I could barely make out what she was saying. It sounded as if Mrs. Trent was out but would be returning within the hour. I told her I'd prefer not to leave a message because it was a surprise.

After I hung up, I made coffee and paced around my living room. I was tempted to call Richard right then and confront him, but I knew if I did it without all the facts in hand, I might not be able to elicit anything valuable.

As obsessed as I was about the case, Beau kept intruding on my thoughts. I'd thought I might hear from him this morning, and yet so far nothing. Up until last night, he'd been the one on the offensive, bad-gering me for contact. Now things were flipped. Once Beau had spotted me with Chris, he'd cast me in the role of bad girl. Did this mean that if I didn't reach out, I'd never, ever hear from him again?

To distract myself, I checked my email. And lo and behold, the lovely Skyler had finally sent me links to several of Whitney's stories. I watched each of them, which was about as much fun as cleaning out my wal-let. Whitney, it turned out, had been no Diane Sawyer.

She was gushy on camera and hyper concerned looking, as if she were reporting live each time from Darfur
and she couldn't help but let her emotions get in the
way. I soon found the story on anorexia. According to
Whitney's intro, an "explosion" of cases in Fort Worth
had many local parents "worried sick." The piece was
light on science, heavy on emo.

One thing became clear as I watched the rest of the
stories, Whitney had definitely been trying to branch
out of food stories and into the health arena. In addition
to the anorexia piece, there were stories on excessive
sweating, skin cancer, women conceiving with donor
eggs, and the brilliant Emmy Award–winning series
the publicist had mentioned, *The Mite That Roared.*
Nothing set off any alarms.

Though an hour wasn't quite up, I phoned London
again. I was still struggling to translate what the house-
keeper had just told me when a new voice came on,
announcing, "This is Claire." She was eating as she
spoke—perhaps the proverbial bonbons that Cat had
mentioned.

I relayed how I'd secured her number and explained
the purpose of my call.

"It's been an absolute eternity since I've heard
Fiona's name mentioned," Claire said. "I would have
assumed she was long forgotten."

"Did you know her personally?"

"I met her just once, at a party with Richard. She was at least a good ten years younger than he was, but he adored her and was very protective of her. She was quite pretty, though hardly what you'd call dazzling. The London fashion shows had started to take off, and I believe she worked regularly in them, but I don't think she had much luck with photographic work. I suppose that's where the problems began."

"What problems?" I asked, feeling my muscles tense.

"She was anorexic. She apparently convinced herself that being even thinner would help secure more jobs."

"Omigod," I said.

"I know," she replied, not knowing, of course, the real reason for my shock. "She died a horrible death. The family had put her in hospital by that point, and she was all hooked up to feeding tubes and the like—but it was too late."

"I assume Richard was very upset by her death."

"Oh, yes. He was devastated. We were no longer dating at that point, but we were still friends, and I did my best to comfort him."

"There's just one more thing I need to know. Was Fiona friends with Devon Barr? Or do you know of any connection between the two?"

"Ah, Devon Barr. Everyone here is buzzing about her death. And how ironic that she ended up dying the same way Fiona did. Though not so ironic, I guess, when you think of that world. But I digress. Yes, they *were* friends at one point. But there must have been some kind of falling-out, because I remember that Richard didn't want Devon at the funeral service—and in the end she didn't come."

"Do you have a clue what the falling-out was over?"

"I didn't at the time—Richard never said anything—but in hindsight I suspect it was a competitive thing. Devon's career was already on fire. Everyone wanted her for their campaigns. Fiona, like I said, was probably never destined to be a star."

"I appreciate your help," I said.

"Tell Cat I send my best. I'd love to see her—though not when I have my husband with me. Cat has that funny habit of yearning for what other women have and then trying to steal it for herself."

I signed off with my heart thumping. Did Richard blame Devon for his sister's death? Perhaps, feeling less successful than Devon, Fiona had begun starving herself. I shook my head at how stupid I'd been. Over the past few days, I'd dredged up what I could on everyone except Richard, dismissing him as someone with no real connection to Devon. But he'd known her and possibly resented the hell out of her. Had he also wished her dead?

I wanted some face-to-face time with Richard, and I needed a decent excuse. I thought for a few moments and dialed his number.

"Well, if it isn't the plucky Bailey Weggins," he said, sounding relatively sober when he picked up. "To what do I owe this honor?"

"Oh, just checking in. It's been a couple of days since we spoke."

"Oh, please, Bailey. You've never just *checked* in with anyone," he proclaimed. "I'm quite certain you've spent your entire life with an agenda."

I laughed, pretending to be amused.

"Okay, you've caught me. I *do* have an agenda. I know you're having second thoughts about doing a story for *Vanity Fair*, but I've stumbled on information that I thought was worth sharing. It's relevant to both of us."

"Do tell."

"Could we meet? I'd like to talk in person."

I sensed him glancing at his watch.

"I don't want to pass up a chance for a chat with the infamous Bailey Weggins, but I'm a bit jammed at the moment. Tell you what. I'm meeting a few pals at Hanratty's for dinner tonight at seven, but right before then I'm going to try to squeeze in a walk in the park. You're welcome to join me on my walk if you wish."

"Sure," I said. "Where and when?"

"I like to stroll about in the Central Park Conservatory. The entrance is on 105th and Fifth. Why don't I see you there at six thirty?"

"Got it," I said. That part of the city was like a million miles away from the Village, but if I took the 4 or 5 on the Lex to Eighty-sixth and then the local to Ninety-sixth, it wouldn't take forever to get there.

"I'll be meandering around in there. You should see me when you come down the stairs."

After I signed off, I finally called the precinct in Brooklyn and reported the incident with the gypsy cab driver. Just talking about the experience made my stomach tighten so hard it hurt. Later, I fixed a late lunch, puttered, and thought miserably of Beau.

Finally it was time to meet up with Richard. I made it to Ninety-sixth Street in thirty minutes, bundled up in a down jacket, scarf, and old cloche hat. After ascending the subway station steps, I hurried west on 96th, my hands stuffed in my pockets as I fought a mean, dry wind that blew west from Central Park toward the East River. The street was crowded with grocery shoppers and people hurrying home from work. I passed three different places on the street selling Christmas trees, makeshift wood structures hung with colored

Christmas lights. At one a woman about my age stood waiting as her tree was bound with mesh. Her little boy looked on in pure delight.

After crossing Fifth Avenue, I turned north, walking along the cracked sidewalk that bordered Central Park. The wind was less brutal there because the trees formed a barricade. It was less crowded there, too, though periodically someone entered or exited the park, mostly dog walkers with their pets in stupid little coats. Though I'd heard about the Central Park Conservatory, I'd never been up there and didn't know what to expect. After passing the statue of some New Yorker long forgotten, I saw a large black gate on my left. A sign indicated that I was standing in front of the conservatory.

It appeared to be a park within a park, though instead of grassy spaces it was all gardens, or what would be gardens come spring again. There were several dog walkers and an elderly couple out for a frigid stroll. I spotted Richard immediately, just as he'd predicted. He had his back to me, but I knew it was him. I'd stared at that shaggy head of hair for two hours on a trek through the woods.

The wind was up again, overriding the sound of my booted footsteps, but Richard turned suddenly, as if I'd just opened the door to a quiet room he was standing in.

"Is this place one of your secret pleasures?" I asked, approaching him.

He was wearing an extra-long gray overcoat with a tattered Burberry scarf that had either come from the first batch the company had ever made or been run over years ago by a lorry on the streets of London. His face was already red from the cold, and his eyes were watering.

"Actually, yes," he said over the wind. "I come here all the time. You know how we Brits love a good shrub or a cluster of foxgloves."

"Not many foxgloves at *this* time of year."

"No, but after a day at my desk, I find a walk around the grounds gets my blood pumping. But enough about me. You said you had something to talk about."

"Yes, a few details have emerged as I've been researching Devon's story, and there's one I'd like to discuss with you. I know you're not pursuing the story yourself, but—"

"Excuse me for mixing negatives, but I never said for sure that I wasn't pursuing it," Richard said. "I haven't decided yet. I'm still keeping a toe in the water. In fact, I'm thinking of going to the funeral tomorrow."

That was interesting. What was he up to now? I wondered.

"Okay, fair enough," I said.

"Aren't you going too?" he asked, beginning to stroll. I moved along with him.

"I'm not doing a profile of Devon. I'm interested in how she *died*. Attending her funeral isn't going to advance my story at all."

"Oh, come, come, Bailey. Don't be a tease. You've probably got your little roadster all fired up."

"Since *you're* going, why don't I just call you later for the details?"

"Happy to oblige."

Casually I glanced around the area just to see how many people were still around. The elderly couple was still strolling, gloved hand in gloved hand, but one of the dog walkers was now beating a retreat, trying to urge a resistant poodle up the steps.

"I thought the funeral was private," I said. "Just for family and close friends."

"I won't be in the church. I'll be outside, as an observer with all the hoi polloi."

"Of course. You didn't really know Devon, did you? You told me you'd never met her before last weekend."

Even through his long, heavy coat, I could see his body tense.

"That's right," he said stiffly. "As I mentioned before, Scott was hoping for an article. I had no idea if I could sell it—or even wanted to—but I was hardly going to pass up a weekend with a man whose wine cellar is as legendary as Scott Cohen's."

We rounded the end of a section of the conservatory and moved into the next, this one with small pocket gardens. A man with a bulldog was walking the perimeter. Please don't leave, I silently pleaded. I was ready to go for broke, and I didn't want to be alone in the dark with Richard when I did it.

"*Really?*" I said, letting the disingenuousness seep through. "You see, I thought maybe you *had* known Devon—from your London days."

"My London days?" he asked, turning and looking hard at me. He sensed I was up to something—and he didn't like it.

"I thought you might have crossed paths with Devon in London. She used to live there. I figured she knew your sister."

He stopped, his body completely rigid now.

"My, my, aren't you the dogged little researcher," he said meanly. "I hope they're paying you the big bucks at *Buzz*."

"This isn't about money," I said. "I want to know the truth."

"The truth?" he said. "About what exactly?"

"About Devon's death. I think she was murdered."

I let my eyes wander, as if I was processing a thought, but it was really to survey my surroundings. The dog walker was tugging the bulldog, anxious to leave. I would soon be alone in the gardens with Richard Parkin.

"Well, if you're so damn interested, I'll share one piece of the truth with you—off the record," he said fiercely. "My *sister* is the one who was murdered. And Devon Barr killed her."

18

I shivered—from both the cold and the words I'd just
heard.

"Murdered?" I asked. "But how? I was told Fiona
died from anorexia."

"To understand how Devon murdered my sister, you
first have to understand their relationship," he said.
"Devon befriended Fiona—in part, I believe, because
she knew Fiona could never come close to her in terms
of success. Devon derived her strength from having
more of something than anyone in her immediate uni-
verse. It was almost like a game for her, watching her
own star rise while Fiona's simply stalled."

"Did they become estranged for some reason?"

"No, no. The games simply intensified. Devon
enticed my sister into a partnership of starvation."

"I don't understand," I said.

"They became anorexia buddies, enabling and empowering each other not to eat. Fiona died of malnutrition, and Devon survived. Proof once again that Devon always came out on top."

For a moment I felt too stunned to talk. I had never heard of such a thing.

"Why did none of this ever come out in the press? Was there a cover-up?"

"No cover-up," he said. "The official story that my mother perpetuated was that Fiona died from dehydration, following a long illness. My mother and stepfather were horrified and ashamed about what had happened and wanted it all kept hush-hush. The press didn't bother looking into it—Fiona wasn't on anyone's radar, really. And though there was some buzz about Devon's weight then, there wasn't any link to Fiona. My sister just wasn't famous enough."

"Fascinatingly," he added, his voice tight with bitterness, "Devon began to recover from her anorexia shortly after Fiona's death."

"I'm terribly sorry," I said. "How old was Fiona when she died?"

"Nineteen. My mother was never the same after that."

It sounded as if Richard Parkin had never been quite the same either. So had he spent the last fourteen years biding his time, waiting for the chance to pay Devon Barr back? It was the English, after all, who had coined the phrase, "Revenge is a dish best served cold."

"So what was the real reason you went to Scott's?" I asked quietly.

"Morbid curiosity," he said. "As soon as Scott mentioned that he was having Devon up for the weekend, I started angling for an invitation, claiming I might be open to doing a profile of her. Once I'd procured it, my better judgment nearly convinced me to back out, but in the end I couldn't resist. I'd not laid eyes on Devon since weeks before my sister's death—she never came to the funeral, never got in touch. Oh, I've been forced to look at her bloody face a hundred million times like the rest of us, but our paths never crossed. I wondered what she would be like, wondered if she would even put two and two together when she saw me."

"Fiona had a different last name than you, of course."

"Yes, and I was just a reporter when she died—well known in certain circles but hardly in the ones Devon Barr had begun traveling in."

"Are you sure she didn't pick up on who you were? I found her crying in the woods Saturday morning, and she told me she was afraid."

"Absolutely not. She looked right through me the entire weekend, and it was very clear she had no bloody idea."

"I appreciate you being straight with me," I said, after taking a few moments to digest what he'd shared. "Why are you so concerned, anyway? From all I can tell Devon was a vile human being, and her only real contribution to humanity may have been teaching us how to pair the right boots with a bustier."

We rounded the back corner of the gardens, and the wind tore through the trees. We were headed back to the front of the conservatory, and the street was in view farther up ahead.

"Like I said, I think she was murdered. I'd like to know who did it."

He snickered and shook his head.

"Oh, someone *forced* her not to eat?" he said. " 'Take a bite of that red velvet cake or you'll never sit in the front row of a Marc Jacobs show again'?"

Because Richard was a dogged reporter, I was sure he probably had checked out the full police report and knew about the Lasix.

"Not that way, no," I said. "You may be aware that Devon was taking diuretics. That's a very bad thing for someone with anorexia to do. I'm wondering if one of the houseguests was slipping them to her—putting them into her water perhaps."

He snickered again but leveled his gaze at me now.

"My, my," he said. "Quite an accusation. Any ideas who?" In the glow from the lamppost light I saw him narrow his hooded blue eyes even more, and then widen them in surprise. "I hope you're not suggesting it was Mr. Parkin . . . in the barn . . . with a diuretic?"

I swallowed, glancing out of the corner of my eye toward the far-off street.

"You tell *me*, Richard," I said.

He suddenly yanked his hands from his pockets, and I drew my upper body back involuntarily. It took him a second to realize what had happened—that he had startled me—and he chuckled in amusement.

"Trust me, Bailey, I have no intention of offing you in the middle of the Central Park Conservatory. I come from a long line of people who took great care of their gardens."

He rubbed his ungloved hands briskly back and forth. I couldn't tell if it was to generate warmth or from pure glee at having made me flinch.

"I've told you what you wanted to know," he added. "And now I'm off to Hanratty's to warm my bones."

Hands stuffed back in his coat pockets, he mounted the stairs without looking back at me and turned south on Fifth Avenue. Despite the droll tone he'd just used, I could tell I'd rattled him by having learned about his sister. Was it simply because I'd drudged up painful memories that he ordinarily didn't share with anyone? Or was it because I was getting closer to the *deeper* truth—that he'd concocted a fitting scheme to kill the person who'd helped ruin his family?

I jogged up the steps and headed down Fifth Avenue myself. I could see Richard up ahead of me, though before long he crossed over from the park side of the street and headed east from there. I stayed on Fifth, retracing the route I'd taken from the subway. Along the way I kept replaying our conversation, hoping my gut would answer a question for me. Richard had clearly hated Devon. But had he hated her enough to kill her?

Closer to the subway, I passed the Christmas tree stands again, and this time I stopped in front of one of them and breathed in the intoxicating scent of spruce and pine. Christmas was just weeks away, and the only present I'd bought so far was a little cap and scarf for my brother Cameron's new baby. And even worse, I had no plans for the holidays. My brothers would be with their wives. My mother would be in Mexico. Beau would be in the Caribbean and/or out of my life for good. And I'd be all alone in my apartment. What was I supposed to serve myself? A trifle layered with cat food and old newspapers?

And what was I supposed to do about Beau? I wondered, despondently. We were clearly at a stalemate. If I were going to talk to him, I'd have to be the one to make the first move.

Back home, I nuked a package of frozen mac and cheese and jotted down the conversation with Richard in my composition book. It was ironic. Yesterday he hadn't been on my radar at all as a suspect, but today he was the one person with a firm motive. Tommy or Cap *might* have been angry at Devon; Whitney or Tory *might* have been insanely jealous; Christian—or even Scott—*might* have been panicky over something Devon had stumbled on. But there was no *might* have been with Richard. He held Devon responsible for Fiona's death.

Curious about the dynamic between Devon and Fiona, I went online and searched eating disorder partnerships. There were several articles, including a first-person account. When two women took on the challenge of staying superthin together, they empowered each other. It was as if they were part of a special club with a secret code only they communicated in. One woman wrote poignantly about having gone through this horrible dance with a friend. In the end, she had survived but the friend had died.

After I finished eating, I decided to check in on my mother. It had been over a week since I'd spoken to her, and several weeks since we'd discussed her Christmas trip to Mexico. Part of me was hoping that her plans had fallen through and she now felt desperate to roast me a Christmas turkey.

"How's the weather there?" she asked. "It's absolutely freezing here."

"Yeah, pretty cold."

"Is your apartment warm enough?"

"Yes, yes. Believe it or not, I upgraded a couple of years ago to a heated one."

"And your job is good? What are you working on?"

"Not too much." I'd learned years ago that the best time to tell my mother about any dangers related to my work was after everything was over. "The usual celebrity-train-wreck stuff. How about you, Mom? What's happening on your end?"

"Things are good. I've decided to teach a course next term after all. I won't be able to travel as much, but it will be nice to be back on campus again."

"Speaking of travel, are you still planning on going to San Miguel?"

I found myself holding my breath before she answered, which seemed so damn pathetic.

"Oh, yes, everything's lined up. They have a pool, and I don't have a suit yet, but I suppose I could wear that black one I wore on the Cape this past summer. Was it too dreadful? I kept expecting people to yell 'Orca!' every time I emerged from the water."

"No, you looked quite smashing in it," I said as jovially as possible, though my heart was sinking. What the hell was I going to do for the holidays?

"I do feel weird being away from you kids this year," she said. "But you'll all have fun. And the less Cameron has on his plate right now, the better."

"Is he just overwhelmed with the baby?" For a brief moment I couldn't even remember my new nephew's name.

"Yes. But your sister-in-law seems even *more* so, and he's got that to contend with, too. She has this perpetual whine going these days. I feel awful complaining, but it's becoming tiresome."

"What's she whining about, anyway?"

"How her life is out of her hands now. She says she has no time to do anything for herself. I do feel a little bit sorry for her. Babies change your life so much. Nothing is ever the same after that. How's Beau, by the way?"

Yikes, she'd ricocheted from babies to Beau in one second. Was she subconsciously linking the two in her mind? Through no real fault of my mother's, the conversation was starting to depress the hell out of me. I felt suddenly desperate to end it.

"Oh God, Mom, my dishwasher is making a weird noise," I blurted out. "Like it's going to blow up or something. Can I call you back later?"

"Shouldn't you call the super?"

"Yeah, yeah. I better call him. I'll try you later—or sometime tomorrow."

I rested my head in my hands for a few seconds and then stood up and began pacing the living room. A weird feeling had suddenly snuck up on me, and I couldn't define it. Yes, there was a twinge of guilt over the dishwasher hoax, and the melancholy from knowing I'd be on my own for Christmas, but something about the conversation I'd just had was nudging me slightly, like a breeze you see rustling the leaves of a tree far across the yard but don't feel yourself.

I knew I had to distract myself, because only then would it come to me. So I trudged to my desk and looked online at the route I needed to take to Pine Grove the next day. After familiarizing myself, I laid out the disguise I planned to wear—baseball cap, an old black ski parka, and hiking boots.

And then I took a deep breath and called Beau. It was torturing me not to talk to him, to not *know* what was going to happen with us. He picked up right away, sounding as if he was on foot someplace on the streets of Manhattan.

"Hi," I said. "I was hoping we could talk."

"Sounds like a good idea," he said. A part of me relaxed a little. I'd been fearful of hearing a comment like "I don't think we have anything to discuss, Bailey."

"I can tell you're out, so probably right now isn't good. I'm going to Pennsylvania tomorrow—to Devon's funeral—but I should be back late in the day."

"Actually," he said after a moment's hesitation, "I'm not far from you at the moment. Just off Washington Square Park. Want me to come by?"

"Sure," I said. "I'll see you in a few minutes then."

I hadn't glanced in a mirror since my return from seeing Richard, and when I did, I discovered that I looked like hell. I had a wicked case of hat hair from the wool cloche I'd worn, and my makeup had vanished, exposing the dark circles under my eyes. Quickly I brushed my hair back into a ponytail, applied concealer, lipstick, and mascara. The buzzer rang just as I was tugging on a fresh sweater.

When I swung open the door and set eyes on Beau, with those deep brown eyes of his and his hair tucked sexily back behind his ears, the jitteriness I'd felt in anticipation of his arrival ballooned into something bigger: fear about where our discussion would lead. And then came a heart-squeezing sadness over the fact that our relationship might be doomed. Beau shrugged off his coat, letting it drop on a chair; I was surprised to see he was wearing a jacket and tie.

"Do you want a beer?" I asked.

"Yeah, thanks."

When I returned with two bottles, Beau was sitting on the couch. He cocked his head toward my composition book and a pile of folders on the dining table.

"Have you figured anything out yet?"

"No, not yet. But I'm not giving up."

"How's the situation at *Buzz*, by the way? Have they accepted your version of things?"

"Not even close," I said. "That's why I'm going to the funeral. I need to figure out who's tight enough with Devon's mother to have put her up to this."

"But the person wouldn't be stupid enough to tip his hand in front of you."

I offered a grim smile.

"I'm not going to let anyone know I'm there," I said. "I'm going to spy, watch everything from a distance."

"And if you don't learn anything tomorrow?"

"I have no clue what I'll do next. I like to think that the cops will determine Devon was murdered, and it will become clear that the killer wanted to sully my reputation. But the cops upstate don't seem to buy my theory. So if I can't prove to Nash that I'm innocent, I'll be out of a job. And it might affect me getting work elsewhere."

Beau shook his head in concern and tugged the knot of his tie away from his neck, loosening it.

"You're all dressed up," I said. "What were you doing tonight?"

I didn't mean it as any kind of accusation—it was curiosity plain and simple—but when the words emerged from my mouth, there was a definite edge to them.

"Jeez, Bailey. I can't make a move, it seems, without you wondering if I've been up to something totally clandestine and sinister. What is it? Do you think I'm really 007? Or just your garden-variety cheater?"

"I wasn't wondering *anything* just now," I said. "You said you were in my neighborhood, and I was simply curious about what you'd been doing."

He sighed.

"Okay, maybe this time it was innocent enough," he said. "But we've got a problem. You don't trust me, and when you fester enough about it, you feel you have to pay me back somehow. Is this always going to be our pattern? I end up needing to go out of town or don't tell you every detail about my past, and then you feel obligated to pour your heart out to some actor who plays a mortician on TV?"

"As I *explained* to you," I said, "he was helping me with the Devon Barr case and nothing more."

I was tempted to add, "And for your information, he plays a forensic detective with the medical examiner's office, not a freakin' *mortician*," but I had the surprising good sense not to.

"You're missing the point, Bailey," Beau said. "It's going to be *some* kind of payback. You feel a need for it because you don't trust me."

I'd perched on the edge of an armchair, directly across from Beau, but I rose now, crossed my arms against my chest, and paced a few feet in one direction and then a few feet in the other.

"On the one hand it seems I—I should trust you," I said. "You say all the right things. And believe it or not, I'm not one of those maniacal women who rummage through a guy's drawers or hack into his computer. But sometimes you just seem oddly vague about your actions. Take Sedona, for instance. You suddenly announce you have to see this guy, and yet you don't want to give away much in the way of details about him. Like—God, I don't know . . ."

"Like I was just making him up?"

"You said it, not me."

"I'll give you his cell phone number, and you can call him. The bottom line is that you should know me well enough by now to realize that I'm not a fan of the unessential. I needed to include the guy in the film, but frankly he's too boring to get into a discussion about."

"What about that British girl in Turkey? Was *that* really unessential information?"

"You and I weren't in a relationship at that time."

"But when you came back to the States, you implied to me that Turkey was a bore socially—it was just you and the dust and a lot of ancient stones."

"It *was* a bore. If you really want the truth, yes, Abigail and I were having sex, lots of sex, but it was not a particularly satisfying experience for me. I was beginning to realize that I really wanted to be with you—and only you. When I got back I made a commitment to you, so what good would it have been to share the gory details?"

Try as I could, I was unable to chase away an image of Beau and Abigail naked in the sack. Abigail was bouncing up and down on him, the spitting image of Pippa Middleton.

I felt suddenly tongue-tied.

"Look, I'm sorry for being so blunt," Beau said. "But I am at my wits' end here."

"No, I appreciate the truth. As you say, we hadn't made any commitment before you went to Turkey. And I see now that there was nothing to be concerned about in Sedona. But—" I halted a moment, trying to pull my thoughts together. "I think deep down what's really bothering me is that your vagueness when you tell me something shows a kind of hesitation on your part. I worry that I've pushed you into making a commitment, and you're really not ready for it."

Ouch. I couldn't believe I'd said it. Beau set down his beer bottle on the coffee table and tapped his finger gently on his lips a few times. I could tell by his eyes that he was deciding exactly how to respond. Finally he let out a big sigh.

"Bailey, I know there are guys out there who don't know their own minds, but I've never considered myself to be one of them. I said I was ready, and I am. But it seems more and more to me that *you're* the one who has the problem making a commitment. I feel you look for excuses to push me away—and then you blame *me*. Pardon me for playing shrink, but I honestly feel as if you're trying to transfer your own fear of being in a relationship to me."

I absolutely cringed at his words—not only because they stung but because I'd heard them before. I struggled to find some way to respond, but nothing came out.

"Okay," he said, tossing his hand up. "You have lots of other stuff to contend with right now, and I don't want to put extra pressure on you. But the ball's in your court, Bailey. You've got to decide what you want—or we both need to move on."

He rose from the couch, crossed the room, and reached for his coat. That was enough to jump-start my vocal ability. "I—I really want to think about what you said, Beau," I told him, walking toward him. "Will you give me a couple of days?"

"Of course," he said quietly. He leaned down and kissed me lightly on the lips. As he slipped out the door, I had the sinking sense that things between us were now totally tenuous.

I paced the living room for a few minutes, beer bottle in hand. My stomach was churning big-time. Did the problem *really* lie with me? I asked myself. Jack Herlihy, the psych professor I'd broken up with last winter, had said I had a problem committing, and Chris Wickersham had suggested the same. Was it all part of a life pattern with me, the result of having a father who'd died when I was twelve and an ex-husband who lied again and again to cover up monstrous gambling debts? I winced, just thinking about how clichéd it all sounded. If they made a Lifetime movie of my life, I realized, it would have to be played by some triple-named actress like Jennifer Love Hewitt or Tiffani-Amber Thiessen.

My cell phone rang from inside my purse just as I drained the last of my beer. It was Jessie.

"I just wanted to check on how you were doing," she said.

"Thanks, Jess. I'm trying not to wallow in my misery, but it's tough."

"Did you definitely decide to go to the funeral tomorrow? If you did, there are a couple additional details I wanted to share."

"Yep, I'm headed out there—but incognito."

"Okay, from what I could find out, Thornwell is going, and so is that girl Stacy, the senior editor who just started. And there'll be a bunch of freelance paparazzi. Some of them might recognize you if they saw you."

"Good to know. I'm going to have to do my best not to let anyone spot me. If Nash finds out, it will make matters even worse."

"I can barely look at the guy without puking. Have you found out anything more?"

I told her about my investigation so far, the revelations I'd dug up, including the info about Richard's sister. Also, because she was my friend and not simply a work pal, I told her about my harrowing experience with the gypsy cab driver. Just talking about it made my pulse start to pound.

"That's horrible," Jessie exclaimed. "Did you tell the police?"

"Yeah, but they weren't very helpful. To be honest, I'm *more* upset about what's happening to me with *Buzz*. Do you think that Nash is really trying to clear me?"

Jessie sighed.

"He may be," she said, "but from my vantage point out on the floor, it looks like he's just going about his business. I thought something was up this morning. He was in a pissy mood, and later he was talking to a bunch of guys in his office, but someone told me those were dudes from the circulation department. Our newsstand numbers are down, like all the other tabloids. That seems to be his main focus, from what people are saying."

"I wonder if he turned the investigation over to the legal department."

"I don't know. I arranged to have lunch on Monday with one of the younger lawyers I know on the corporate floor. I'm going to see what I can find out from her."

"Jessie, I so appreciate your help. Just don't make trouble for yourself by snooping around."

"Don't worry. This chick is a real busybody. She gossips an awful lot for a lawyer."

"Wait," I said. My heart had just done a weird lurch. "What did you say?"

"She likes to gossip."

"No, before that.

"She's a busybody."

"Um, okay," I said, distractedly. I had to fight for a second to catch a breath. "Look, I better sign off and get ready for tomorrow. I'll call you when I'm back and let you know how it went."

I tossed my BlackBerry in my purse and collapsed on the couch. My heart was beating hard now. Because I finally knew what the gypsy cab driver had yelled to me from his window. Not "Stop. Be a body." He'd said, *"Stop being a busy body."*

It was a threat. As if he knew exactly who I was and what I'd been up to.

19

It was after one before I finally fell into bed. After the call with Jessie, I helped myself to another beer, hoping it would take the edge off, but as I sat on the couch drinking it, with the winter wind rattling the glass door to my terrace, I started to feel even more alarmed. It seemed as if someone must have paid the gypsy cab driver to scare the bejesus out of me, possibly even hurt me. I'd thought he'd been waiting outside the bar for potential customers, but he'd been waiting specifically for *me*.

Had *Tommy* set the whole thing up? I wondered. He was the only one who knew I was headed to the Living Room that night. Unless someone had followed me from my apartment.

Tomorrow I was going to have to share this new development with Collinson. Maybe it would help him see that there really *was* someone out there who was terrified of the truth coming to light. And I knew that I would have to be extremely careful tomorrow. I couldn't let my guard down out in Pine Grove.

I thought that going to bed on the late side would help me avoid insomnia, but no sooner had I crawled under my comforter than it came roaring into the bedroom like the Terminator, intent on its mission. I tossed and turned for a few hours. It wasn't just the trip to Pine Grove that was weighing on me. I couldn't stop replaying the words I now knew the cabdriver had hurled at me. *Stop being a busybody.* And when that wasn't sounding in my head, I was playing the tape of what Beau had said. Gee, I thought, my life kind of sucks at the moment, doesn't it? Finally, when the digits on the bedside clock had flipped past 3:30, I felt myself drifting off.

My alarm beeped obnoxiously at 6:00 a.m., and I awoke feeling groggy and achy. Since my disguise called for looking as grungy as possible, there seemed to be no major reason for a shower, shampoo, and blow out, so I splashed cold water on my face and slipped into my outfit. I filled an old thermos with steaming hot coffee and packed a small cooler with a sandwich and fruit. Chances were that I'd be stuck in the car for hours, and I didn't want to traipse around town looking for lunch.

The rental car turned out to be a Toyota Corolla. Not as sturdy as my Jeep, but the weather forecast called for clear skies, so at least I wouldn't be fighting a blizzard in it. And it came with GPS.

After pulling the car out of the garage of the car rental place, I double-parked on the street just long enough to organize all the gear I'd lugged with me. I placed the cooler and thermos in the front seat next to me, along with my binoculars. While I had the chance, I checked my BlackBerry for messages. I wasn't expecting anything this early, but a tiny part of me was hoping there might be a message from Beau, wishing me luck today.

There was nothing from him, but there *was* a text message from a number not in my system. And my heart jerked as I read it.

I have info about Devon Barr you must know. Meet me outside of Pine Grove today. 4:00. In front of gray barn on rte. 22. Just before turn onto Sunday Rd.

It had been sent at 4:46 a.m.

Crap, I thought. Who was it from? I'd told no one other than Beau and Jessie that I was definitely planning to drive to Pine Grove, but all the houseguests knew there was a possibility I'd be there to check out the funeral. Most of them, in fact, still thought I was covering Devon Barr's death for *Buzz*. And because I had phoned each of them at some point, they all had my cell phone number. The big question, though, was whether the message sender was someone who really wanted to help me solve the murder—or the killer, wanting another crack at me, since the one with the gypsy cab had failed.

"Let's meet in town," I texted back. "It'll be easier." And safer for me. I waited a couple of minutes, but there was no return message. It was time to move. I tossed the BlackBerry on the seat next to me and fired up the engine.

As I maneuvered my way out of Manhattan, with the sun rising behind me, I tried to put the message out of my mind for now and concentrate on driving. The traffic was relatively light, but still steady. Headed west on Route 78, I passed mile after mile of dense New Jersey sprawl, and then suddenly, almost magically, there were hills and fields and farms with silos that glistened in the morning sun. A Fox News van zipped past me suddenly, and though I still had two more hours of driving ahead, I wondered if they were headed to the same place I was. I was glad Jessie had given me the heads-up about Thornwell being at the funeral today. I'd be able to keep a look out for him. And knowing Thornwell, he'd have his eye out for me, watchful for wigs, weird hats, and sunglasses, and doing a double take at anyone who looked vaguely like me.

I planned to keep my distance, hanging back at the outer fringes of the crowd. Besides, observing the funeral doings wasn't the main reason I'd signed on for a road trip today. What I really needed to do was stake out Devon's mother's house and see who she was tight with. If someone were in cahoots with her, trying to cripple my career, there was a chance that person would be paying her a visit in private.

I stopped once for a bathroom break and to check my BlackBerry. Another text was waiting. And I didn't like it.

No. The wrong person might see us. I have vital information.

Nothing about the language gave even a hint about who had written it. It was clear that if I wanted to learn who the sender was and whether he really wanted to help me, I was going to have to stop by the barn on Route 22. I decided not to respond, though. Better to keep the sender a little bit on his toes.

At around ten thirty, two and a half hours after my departure, I exited Route 78, and after short stretches on a couple of two-lane highways, I pulled in to Pine Grove.

The town was one of those blink-and-you-miss-it models—with a general store and two churches, one with a few TV vans already parked outside. I drove through the center without stopping, but slow enough to check out the scene. I spotted a bunch of paparazzi, zipped into tired-looking parkas and puffing on cigarettes. Let the games begin, I thought.

I found a parking spot along the curb about two blocks away from the church, and killed the motor. I needed a minute to think. Though I'd planned initially to go straight to Devon's mother's house, I had changed my mind. I needed to check out the barn first and make sure I wouldn't be led into a trap later. I also wanted to see if there was another text.

To my dismay, I discovered that my BlackBerry wasn't picking up a signal. I was in a dead zone. I cursed, thinking of the problem this now posed. If I came across info today that I needed to pursue further—and quickly—there'd be no freaking way to get hold of anyone. It also meant I couldn't give anyone a heads-up about my rendezvous at four.

After programming the GPS, I headed toward the mystery barn—and found it easily, right where the message sender had said it would be. Route 22 was a quiet rural road not far from town, and the weathered, slightly dilapidated gray barn sat just off the shoulder on the edge of what appeared to be a cow field—though there wasn't a cow in sight. I parked the car right in front and looked around. On the opposite side of the road, set far back and on a rise, was a 1970s-style split-level. Surely the barn couldn't be part of that property. Straining my body around, I glanced out the rear window. A half mile back along the road was an old farm, and I guessed that the barn belonged to the farmer—maybe it was an extra place for storing equipment.

I didn't like how deserted the road was. And I didn't like that I'd be meeting someone all alone out here. I decided that the best strategy would be to arrive at least thirty minutes early. That way I'd see the person drive up and could make a decision on how to proceed, based on who was in the car.

And that person, I guessed—whether he or she was someone I knew from the infamous house party weekend or maybe even an acquaintance of Sherrie's reaching out to me—was probably planning to attend the funeral. The timing suggested as much. The four o'clock appointment left plenty of time for the person to go to the service and then head out here.

Now it was time to check out Sherrie Barr's happy little home back in Pine Grove. Once again I programmed the GPS. The street turned out to be on the outskirts of town, like an afterthought. Sherrie's place was a shabby white house, with a sunken porch and bald yard. If Devon had been helping her mother out financially, sending money home after each major ad campaign, there sure was no sign of it. Perhaps Devon had refused to turn over money until Sherrie sobered up, because otherwise she'd only burn through it in drunken stupors. Or maybe Devon had just hated to share. That sounded more like it.

I parked several houses away on the opposite side of the street, close enough to observe the goings-on, but not so near that I would attract attention. There were cars parked all along the front of Sherrie's house, but I had no way of knowing which belonged to neighbors and which to mourners. Then my eye found a vehicle that looked familiar—a black Beemer. Cap and Whitney had driven a black BMW to Scott's, though I didn't remember the license plate and couldn't be sure this was theirs.

Only time was going to tell. I opened the thermos and poured coffee, and then helped myself to an apple. I'd once joined a police stakeout when I was on the crime beat in Albany, and I knew how mind-numbingly boring it could be. But at least I had an end point today. The service started at two, and everyone would have to be at the church—or at the funeral home if that's where they were meeting—by at least one thirty.

In the end it didn't take long for me to see a little action. A black town car suddenly began nosing its way down the street in my direction, the gray-haired driver craning his neck as he looked for house numbers. He pulled up right in front of Sherrie's. I thought it might be a car from the funeral home, but a minute later Christian stepped out of the house and hurried down the saggy stairs toward the car, holding his black leather coat closed with one hand. The expression of disgust on his face suggested he was contemplating getting deloused as soon as he returned to Manhattan. I slunk down slightly in my seat, but he was situating himself in the backseat of the town car and never glanced in my direction. It made sense that he would have stopped by to offer his condolences. But what else had been discussed? I wondered.

Ten minutes later Cap emerged from the house, looking dapper as usual in his camel topcoat. I slunk back down again and raised the binos to my eyes. He looked distracted. Just like Christian, he had a legitimate reason to be visiting Sherrie, but was there a second agenda? He surveyed the street and then unlocked his car door. While he had his back to me, I slid all the way down in the seat, not wanting him to catch even a glimpse of a person in the car. As I heard his BMW cruise by, I wondered where Whitney was. I couldn't imagine her not attending the service with Cap. Maybe she was coming separately—or she might even be inside with Sherrie.

The next two hours dragged. It was like sitting in an airport after they've announced your plane needs a new part before it can take off. At around twelve thirty there was a flurry of activity. A couple of local types arrived, carrying platters covered with aluminum foil, probably the standard death-in-the-family cold cuts and tuna casserole. They reemerged from the house ten minutes later.

I ate my sandwich but avoided more coffee, knowing I'd only have to pee. There were no more comings and goings. I glanced at my watch. One twenty. Probably the only action I was going to see now was Sherrie coming out for the funeral, and sure enough, a minute later another black town car pulled up, this one so shiny it had to be from the funeral home. The driver, neatly dressed, rapped on the door and was ushered inside.

But then another car moseyed down the street and came to an abrupt stop, a dusty white VW Passat that seemed incongruous among the pickup trucks and old Fords on the block. And goodness gracious, guess who slowly hauled himself out of it? None other than Richard Parkin. Was he coming to tell Sherrie just what a piece of shit her daughter was? Or explain that he'd let bygones be bygones? Or to pay Sherrie off for lying about me?

I let a story play out in my mind. Richard had killed Devon, convinced that her death would be blamed on her own self-destructiveness. But then I started poking around, raising other theories. He quickly hatched a plot to undermine me. And who better than another journalist to realize how disastrous Sherrie's call to my boss would be to my career? But how could he have formed an association with Sherrie? Maybe he had decided he could stomach it long enough to obtain what he needed.

I started to breathe harder, churned up by this latest development. If Richard were guilty, how in the world would I possibly prove it? Despite his propensity for booze, he was clever and wily, someone it would be tough to outsmart. Maybe Detective Collinson would at least be interested in hearing Richard's history with Devon.

Richard was in the house just a few minutes—long enough, though, to hand over cash. The solemn expression on his face when he exited revealed absolutely nothing. By the time he drove off, I'd made sure I'd slunk down all the way in my seat again.

At 1:40 Sherrie Barr finally emerged, following the limo driver and propped up by two women. She was fifty-five, tops, and her physical form bore a striking resemblance to Devon's, but even in my binoculars I could see that she was haggard looking, blotchy, and unsteady. I wondered how much of that was due to grief and how much to booze.

I waited for the limo to pull out before I started my car and followed at a distance behind it. I parked in the same spot I'd found before, two blocks away from the church, and made my way on foot to the outskirts of the crowd that had gathered. There were about two hundred people outside—local residents who'd come to rubberneck, and at least seventy-five press, a combo of photographers, print people, and TV crews, most of whom were doing a shuffle with their feet to stay warm. Usually with a crowd of onlookers and press this size, the noise level can get pretty high, but there was a funeral pall cast over this one. The only sound was the murmur of whispers and the hum from the TV vans. Scanning the crowd, I failed to spot Thornwell, but I did see, the *Buzz* staffer, Stacy, whom Jess had mentioned. I was pretty sure that in my getup, I wasn't going to nab her attention.

I was just in time to see Sherrie stagger into church, and then the doors were closed behind her. It was clear that I'd missed all the arrivals—and the casket—while I was on my stakeout. I'd have to wait until the end to see who had showed. I held my position on the fringe of the crowd. Temperature-wise, it was only in the midthirties, and the wind had started to kick up, whipping around everyone's hair. Even though I'd worn hiking boots and several pairs of socks, it wasn't long before I was doing the foot shuffle myself.

The service lasted only about thirty minutes, and as soon as the doors were flung open, the crowd sounds swelled. Cameras began to click and TV commentators droned into their mikes. As you'd expect, Sherrie was one of the first to exit, along with her prop-her-uppers, followed by a cluster of people who were obviously friends and relatives. Scott emerged next, along with Christian, Cap, and Whitney, clutching Cap's arm. So she was in town after all. She'd opted for a black mink for the occasion and her blond hair was brushed back, held in place by what seemed to be a matching mink headband.

And then, to a crescendo of murmurs from the crowd, came Tommy and Tory, holding hands. It looked as if Tory hadn't let the fact that she thought Tommy was a loser and an asshole get in the way of some red-carpet-style shots that would be seen around the world. He was in tight black jeans and a black suit jacket, no overcoat. His ego clearly generated enough heat to keep his body warm in near-freezing conditions. Tory was wearing skinny, skinny black pants with some sort of tabs on the calves, black stilettos, and a black coat that seemed to be made of a techno fabric. While she descended the stairs, she flipped the hood up, revealing the thick black fur that lined the coat. Tommy might not care about the weather, but Tory was going for a downtown–meets–Doctor Zhivago effect.

Jane was one of the last to appear, followed by a spurt of people who looked like area residents.

No Richard, interestingly. And no casket either, I suddenly realized. That actually should have been the first thing out the door. Just as I was contemplating what was going on, I overheard a TV sound guy explain to someone that there was going to be no burial. It seemed as if Devon was going to be cremated. Maybe her ashes were going to be dropped from a plane over Seventh Avenue.

And then all of a sudden, I was staring right at Thornwell. He'd been tucked away in a throng of reporters but was visible now as the crowd had begun to disperse. I could have sworn he stared right at me. Had I been tagged? I wondered anxiously. But then he jerked his head to the left to say something casually to the man next to him and didn't glance back in my direction. I exhaled in relief. Thornwell had definitely looked right at me, but clearly hadn't realized who it was in the baseball cap, sunglasses, and butt-ugly parka.

Since there'd be no mad dash to the cemetery, I headed back to Sherrie's. There were more cars lined along the street now, probably visitors at her house, and I ended up parking farther away than last time. But it didn't matter. In the next half hour, no one of note came in or out of the house. There was no Passat in sight and no Beemer.

At three twenty I took off. I had promised myself I'd arrive at the barn a half hour early as a precaution. One thing I knew for sure. If a Passat pulled up, I was going to beat a hasty retreat. The fact that Richard had not attended the funeral indicated he'd come to Pine Grove not to mourn Devon but to discuss something with Sherrie. And if he were the person behind Devon's death and Sherrie's incrimination of me, I certainly didn't want to be chatting with him at dusk on a deserted country road.

I found the barn again easily. Parking my car along the side of the road was going to be a hazard to anyone driving by this late; I realized that my only alternative was to pull into the short drive that led up to the double doors of the barn. I backed in so that it would be easy for me to peel out if necessary.

I stepped out of the car and surveyed the area. There was an outdoor security light shining already from the house on the rise, but no lights on yet at the farmhouse down the road. The sun hung low in the sky, shining dispiritedly. I glanced down at the ground. It was frozen hard, but there was one small area where I could make out the edge of a tire print. Had the person who'd texted me parked here earlier, checking out the location?

Back in the car, I took two unenthusiastic bites of the sandwich I hadn't finished earlier and tried to stay calm. I had to hope that the person coming really wanted to help me. Regardless of who drove up, I wasn't going to emerge from my car. I'd insist that we talk from our windows, and I'd keep the motor running. I just couldn't let my guard down for a second when he—or she—arrived.

At ten to four, a car headed down the road from the south, the direction I'd come from, and my heart skipped. But the driver kept on without even glancing my way. The next ten minutes passed torturously slow. And then ten more minutes went by. And ten more. Someone, it seemed, had decided to play a nasty little game with me.

I stepped out of the car again and scanned my surroundings. There was absolutely no one in sight. Maybe the person I was supposed to rendezvous with had sent an updated message to me, not realizing that I had no service here.

I glanced back at the barn and noticed for the first time that one of the double doors was slightly ajar.

The wooden bolt that was used to fasten it closed had been slipped over into its sling. I leaned into the car, grabbed the flashlight I'd brought with me, and walked up to the barn. After glancing instinctively behind me, I grabbed the wooden bolt. As I slowly pulled the door open, it let out a long, sad creak. The last rays of daylight reached a foot or two into the barn, but most of the interior was pitch-black. I swept the beam of the flashlight over the insides. Stacks and stacks of hay filled the back half of the barn. And that was it.

Was I meant to find a message in here? I stepped a couple of feet inside and trained my light over every surface. Nothing. Pulling my BlackBerry from my jacket pocket, I reread the message. It had clearly stated that the person would meet me here. It was time to get the hell out of Pine Grove.

And then I thought I heard something. Toward the back of the barn. I froze for a second. No, now the sound was coming from along the side of the barn, *outside*. I spun around, a wave of fear crashing over me. As I faced the door, I saw it slam shut with a wallop.

"Hey," I yelled. Except for the light from my flashlight, I was in total darkness. "Who's there?"

There was no reply. Just the sound of the wooden bolt being slid into place.

20

I dashed to the door, guided by the flashlight, and yanked. Nothing gave.

"Hey," I yelled again.

For a split second I thought that the farmer had locked the door, making his rounds before dark. But that stupid idea morphed almost instantly into the truth: I had been tricked—and trapped on purpose. My heart began to pound so hard I could feel it in my ears.

I peered through a crack in the barn door, but all I could spot was a sliver of my rental car. Where had the person *come* from? If there'd been a car, I would have heard it. If he had arrived by foot along the road or the field, surely I would have seen him—I had only been inside for a few seconds.

Then suddenly there were footsteps, scurrying along the north side of the barn. I hurried over and peered through a crack in the planks. I saw a flash of dark coat, so close I could have almost touched it. The person continued, running along the edge of the barn toward the back, but the endless stacks of hay blocked my view down there. The footsteps receded. Whoever had done this *had* come by foot apparently—at least part of the way—and had now taken off.

I stuffed my hand in my coat pocket to grab my BlackBerry and then remembered, panic-stricken, that it got no service here. I checked the screen anyway, just to be sure I hadn't managed to pick up a signal somehow, but it was dead.

I tried the door again, yanking as hard as I could, but I could see there was no way to open it. Remembering all the old farm tools on the walls of Scott's barn upstate, I trained the beam of the flashlight over these walls; there was nothing like that, only a rusted oil can sitting on a small shelf. I checked for another entrance. Nothing.

I leaned closer to the door, pressed my mouth against one of the gaps in the wood, and yelled, "Help!" seven or eight times, hoping the person who lived in the house on the hill might hear. I saw through the crack that it was almost dark. I realized the chance of someone being out now was next to nil.

I was starting to feel nearly freaked with fear. No one who cared about me knew that I'd come to the barn, and even if Beau became concerned by late tonight and reported my disappearance to the police here, they'd be looking for my Jeep, not a rented Toyota. I would have to count on the fact that the homeowner up the hill or the farmer who owned the barn would begin to wonder what the hell my car was doing out in front and investigate.

But what if they *didn't*? I paced a small section of the barn, the beam of my flashlight twitching crazily. I willed myself to be calm. I had to figure a way out of this.

I did a few jumping jacks, just to keep the cold at bay, and then perched on a haystack. The straw pricked through my jeans uncomfortably, but still, sitting down seemed to relax me a little. The good news, I realized, was that I probably wouldn't freeze to death. It was going to be below freezing tonight, but there was tons of hay for me to snuggle into. Wasn't that how little calves and lambs stayed warm? I had a candy bar in my pocket, too, and that would stave off any serious hunger pains.

Though I was desperate to find a way out, I also wanted to know who had done this to me. I tried to hash through everything in my mind. Though I had driven out to the barn a half hour early as a safeguard, the person who had lured me here had probably come out even earlier and hidden nearby, lying in wait. He or she must have left the barn door open, banking on the fact that when I decided I'd been stood up, curiosity would have compelled me to take a quick look inside before leaving. As soon as he saw me enter the barn, he must have sprung forward and slammed the door shut.

So who was it? Richard? He could have easily guessed I'd be coming to Pine Grove and laid the trap.

But there were others I'd recently provoked as well: Jane, by revealing that I knew of her book deal and that she had probably lied about Cap and Devon; Christian, by implying there might be trouble with the modeling agency.

As my mind danced around the houseguests, a troubling thought began to surface. What if the person came back? What if the idea wasn't simply to leave me here to freeze my ass off, but to return and attack me under cover of darkness? I had to get out.

I thrust my hand in my pocket and grabbed my BlackBerry again. Last winter, during a trip to West Virginia for a freelance article, I'd ended up in a similar situation with my cell service, but during the night I must have picked up a faint signal because a few e-mails had come through. Just in case this same phenomenon happened here, I typed an SOS to Beau with copies to

Jessie and Landon, explaining my dilemma and giving not only my location but also a description of the rental car. Though Landon only checked his e-mail about once a day, Beau looked at his frequently and Jessie was good for every minute and a half.

Once again I trained the beam of my flashlight over the barn walls. I was looking for either a loose piece of wood I could use as a crowbar or a way out. But I didn't see a thing. I squeezed my forehead with one hand, trying to make my brain work better. *Barns.* What did I know about them? When I was a little girl, my father took my brothers and me to a working farm for a weekend, where we fed newborn calves with bottles and attempted to milk the cows. I remembered grimy windows in the barn there—not like in Scott's big barn, where most of the windows had all been added after the fact, but one or two cut in a wall to let light stream in as the farmer worked. This barn didn't seem to have any. Maybe because it had always been for storage. Or for animals to sleep in.

There might, however, be a window at the far end, blocked by the hay. Or even a back door. The killer might have assumed I would never guess it was there with all the hay. But if it was, I needed to find it.

I bounced the light over the bales of hay. They took up almost the entire rear half of the barn. I realized that the only way to reach the back would be to shift the bales, one by freaking one.

The bales weren't exactly light, but I could tell right away that moving them would be doable. I wedged the flashlight into some hay, so that it was pointed toward the back, and quickly chucked a few of the top bales out of the way. Before too long, I'd worked my way toward the back. I grabbed the flashlight again and ran it over the top of the wall. As I did, I heard something scurry off on tiny feet. Great. Nothing like a few rodents to up the terror factor.

But there *was* no way out, from what I could see. My heart sank. How, I wondered frantically, could there not be a door in the back? If the barn had once been used for cows, there would have had to be an exit to the field. The word *pigs* suddenly flashed in my mind. There had been pigs, too, at the farm we'd visited with my father, a separate barn for them. As I pictured them in my mind—huge and pink with their funny snouts and woeful eyes—I remembered something. The pig door. It was the hatch they used to move the animals from the barn to the outdoor pen. Maybe this barn had one at the bottom of the back wall.

I started to work again, heaving bales of hay from the back row out of the way. Underneath my jacket I could feel my body growing sweaty from exertion.

And then, as I worked, I heard another sound. I froze. It wasn't scurrying this time but someone moving outside in the dark, to my right, along the north edge of the barn again. Shit, I realized. The person was still out there. Was he planning to come inside now?

The sound stopped, but I could sense where the person was—about halfway down. His body was like a force field I could feel. What was he doing? I wondered desperately. Then there was a noise again, the sound of a coat shifting, and then something thick and liquidy being splashed on the barn. Some of it, I could tell, spattered inside. Omigod, I thought, what was going on?

A second later I knew. A wisp of smoke snaked into the barn, and my nostrils were filled with the pungent smell of wood burning. The freaking barn was on fire! The breath froze in my chest, and my eyes pricked with tears.

I swung around and frantically hurled another bale out of the way, and then another. My hands were trembling now, but I kept going. Over the thunder of my heart, I heard barn wood begin to crackle. Please, please, I thought, don't let this happen to me.

Outside the back of the barn, an engine suddenly roared to life. A car. For a second I thought the driver was going to ram right though the back wall of the building, but a second later I realized the person was rounding the barn, heading back to the road.

I glanced back to where the fire was. Flames were now licking the walls. They weren't huge, but the smoke was another story. It was starting to fill the barn, like a fog rolling in from the sea. I turned back and desperately kept working, reaching down and grabbing bale after bale. Finally I'd managed to create a corridor along the back wall. I grabbed the flashlight and jumped down. I bounced the flashlight over the wall. And there it was. The pig door. About three feet by three feet, with a wooden bolt on one side. I nearly sobbed in gratitude. I knelt down on the cold floor of the barn and, after undoing the bolt, slid the door over.

A blast of cold air hit me. I dove through the opening and scrambled up to my feet. I was shaking—in both fear and relief. I'd made it out, maybe with only seconds to spare before the smoke overwhelmed me. In the western sky, there were still smudges of light, enough to see that there was no one around. I raced to the front of the barn.

The lower north side was now engulfed in flames. Smoke was circling upward, and big flames flicked along the old, dry wood, making loud crackling sounds. Instinctively I glanced up to the house on the hill.

There were lights on inside, practically in every room, and I thought I could make out the shape of someone standing just outside the front door. I jumped in the car and drove it down the road twenty yards or so.

I was shaking hard by then, and I wasn't sure exactly what to do. Should I go up to the house and make sure they'd called 911? But then, from far off, I heard the wail of a siren. I decided to sit in my car on the road and wait for help to arrive.

Two minutes later, a fire truck came roaring up the country road. It pulled up in front of the barn, and five or six guys in big boots, helmets, and slickers sprang from inside it. By now the flames were shooting up the whole side of the barn. It took the firefighters a minute or two to unload the hose, and then they were shooting a hard stream of water at the barn. Even from inside my car I could hear the flames begin to hiss into submission. About ten minutes later, the flames were gone, and there were just curls of dark smoke ascending toward the night sky.

I knew that the firefighters had more work to do, but I didn't want to wait any longer. I opened the car door and propelled myself toward the fire truck.

Before I'd made it just a few feet, the fireman nearest me caught my movement out of the corner of his eye and spun around. He put a hand up, motioning for me to stop. He was about thirty, hefty, with a big strong jaw.

"You're going to need to step back, ma'am," he said. "We can't have spectators getting this close."

"But I'm not really a spectator," I said.

"Do you own the barn?"

"No, but I was in the barn when someone set the fire. They locked me in. They were trying to kill me."

His jaw fell in surprise. He turned around and called for one of the other guys to come over—an older man, who'd taken his helmet off and was wiping sweat from his brow with a handkerchief. I figured he might be the dude in charge.

I went through my story quickly with them, trying not to sound like a lunatic because I knew how far-fetched the whole damn thing sounded. They exchanged a couple of looks as I spoke, especially when I touched on the Devon Barr connection, but I couldn't really read them. I got the feeling the young guy thought something funny was up, especially when I described escaping by the pig door, but the older man, the chief, seemed to buy what I was saying. Behind us the rest of the crew kept dealing with the fire. A few of them had gone in the barn and were looking around with big torches.

When I'd finished my story, the chief stepped back to the fire engine, grabbed a clipboard from inside, and returned.

"I want you to write down your name, address, and phone number, okay?" he said. "The arson investigator is going to want to talk to you. And then I need you to stop by the state trooper's office and report this."

I nodded in agreement.

"Are you sure you don't need medical treatment?" he asked. "How much smoke did you inhale?"

"Very little," I said. "I got out before it filled the barn."

I said good-bye and trudged back to my car. I used the GPS to find the state trooper office, which turned out to be about fifteen minutes away. At least it was in the same direction as the highway toward New York, because I was completely frayed around the edges by now. When I stepped inside the squat cinder-block headquarters, there were a couple of troopers huddled by the front desk, and they glanced at me almost expectantly. I realized after a second that the fire chief had called ahead.

A detective named Joe Olden took my statement. His face looked like it'd last cracked a smile in 1997. He seemed pretty curious initially, but the more details I offered—the weekend at Scott's, the Lasix in the water, the gypsy cab experience—the more skeptical he appeared. It was like I'd started off reporting a minor traffic accident, but was now describing how I'd discovered alien spacecraft when I stepped out of the car to inspect the damage.

Finally, I gave him Collinson's info and begged him to call the man. Just as I was wrapping up, the fire marshal arrived and asked me a series of questions as well.

Later, as I nearly staggered out to the parking lot, I called Collinson myself, reaching his voice mail. I told him I had important news and desperately needed to speak to him.

It was an utter relief to be back in my car and headed for Manhattan, but even with the heater cranked up and Maria Callas arias playing, I couldn't keep my body from trembling. It was partly from the exertion of hurling all those bales of hay, but also from the sheer terror I still felt. I knew that if there hadn't been a pig door in the barn, I probably would have died tonight.

I hadn't traveled far on the highway when my BlackBerry rang. I had service again. I realized that I had never deleted my SOS e-mails to Landon, Jessie, and Beau, and they'd all gone through. When I answered my phone, a frantic Beau was on the other end.

"Are you okay?" he demanded anxiously. "Are you still in the barn?"

"No, I'm out and I'm fine. But I was nearly killed." I felt myself tearing, and I shook the drops away. I blurted out what had happened since I'd sent the message.

"God, Bailey, I can't believe this," he said, his voice laced with worry. "Is there any chance this person could be following you?"

"No, I bet they beat it out of Pine Grove once the fire started. . . ."

"Do you want me to come meet you someplace?"

"I'm okay. But—it would be great if you could be there when I get home. I'm still pretty shaken up." Without warning, a sob caught in my throat. "It was just so scary when the smoke filled the barn."

"Why don't you call me when you're about twenty minutes away. I'll just hop in a cab."

"You've got to do me one other favor. Will you get in touch with both Jessie and Landon and tell them I'm fine? I want to concentrate on the road."

As soon as I signed off, I checked the rearview mirror instinctively. I was positive I wasn't being tailed. There'd been stretches on the trip so far when no one had been behind me. But that didn't mean I was safe. Once the fire starter learned that his efforts had been thwarted, some other deadly plan would surely be hatched.

I'd have to be as careful as I possibly could. My trouble in Pine Grove had sprung in part from not watching my back well enough. I'd thought I was being such a smarty-pants by arriving at the barn early, but my assailant had come even earlier, and must have been parked out in back the whole time. And lucky for them, my BlackBerry hadn't worked.

Suddenly my stomach flipped over. *Had* it just been luck? I wondered. Or had the killer *known* I had no service in that part of Pennsylvania? And then, one after another, my thoughts fell into place, like a key tripping a lock. Yes, the killer *had* known, I realized. I now had an idea who the fire starter might be. The problem was, there were two possibilities. I was going to have to figure out which one was the culprit.

I made better time than I'd planned, driving eighty miles an hour in my desperation to put as much distance as possible between Pine Grove and my sorry ass. I dropped off the rental, and once I found a cab, I called Beau, telling him I was on my way to my apartment. I felt almost weak from hunger and asked him to pick up food, anything. Plus, having a few more minutes to myself would give me a chance to pop by Landon's and reassure him.

It turned out to be a good plan because Landon was nearly bug-eyed with worry when he opened his door.

"I can't tell you what a fright your e-mail gave me," he said after we'd hugged. "I was about to call not only the police but also Homeland Security. Thank God Beau called me a few minutes later."

I took him through the story quickly, knowing Beau would be arriving any minute.

"Who's *doing* this to you?" Landon asked.

"I'm not a hundred percent sure, but I have a few ideas."

"And you're going to fill the upstate police in, right?"

"Yes. The detective in charge up there didn't seem to buy my idea that Devon might have been murdered, but this may change his mind. The problem is that he doesn't have any jurisdiction down here, and that's going to limit what he does. Hopefully he can involve the state police."

"Please don't give me the usual Bailey Weggins punch line—that you'll have to take matters into your own hands. It terrifies me when you say that."

"I don't really have a choice."

"Oy."

"But I'll be careful. I made a mistake at the barn—I let down my guard. I just can't do that again."

After giving him another squeeze, I scampered back to my place. Jessie called just while I was letting myself in, and I reassured her, too. And then moments later the doorman was buzzing to tell me that Beau was on the way up. He arrived carrying not only a deep-dish pizza but also a bottle of wine. As soon as he set the stuff down, we hugged each other fiercely.

"I'm just so relieved you're all right," he said, pulling back enough to study my face. "In those two minutes between when I read your e-mail and talked to you on the phone, I felt totally frantic."

"Thanks for being there for me tonight."

"What do you need first? Pizza? Wine? A shoulder to cry on?"

"Everything at the same time," I said.

I practically inhaled the pizza, though I also managed to fill in the blanks of the story for Beau. When I'd polished off three slices, I leaned back into one of the chairs at my dining table and took a slug of wine. Beau sat across from me, his back to the window. Behind him was my enchanting Manhattan view, at this hour just the dark outline of a dozen apartment buildings dabbed with lights and topped with old wooden water tanks. It always seemed wonderfully fake to me, like the backdrop for a Broadway show.

What a relief to be here, I thought—not just safe in my apartment, but with Beau.

"I've never seen you devour food that way," Beau said, laughing. "There were a couple of times where I thought I might have to administer the Heimlich maneuver."

"I think it's because I'm so hyped up. Being trapped in that barn and then smelling the smoke and not knowing if I'd get out. I guess feeling lucky to be alive has made me ravenous. I want to consume everything in sight."

"Should I take that as a promise or a warning?" Beau said, smiling.

I laughed. We had once again shoved our troubles aside because of Devon Barr, but that was okay.

Beau's expression turned suddenly sober. He pushed his chair back and crossed one leg over the other.

"So the person who did this was surely one of the houseguests. And they were all out in Pennsylvania, right?"

"Yes, they were all there," I said. "And I'm pretty sure that whoever locked me in the barn is also the one who put Sherrie up to calling Nash. It's all part of a plan to shut me down."

"And obviously the reason for their actions is that they're afraid you could expose them."

"Exactly. The person must be the one who put the Lasix in Devon's water."

"So who has your vote at the moment?"

"It's someone pretty clever," I said. "They found a desolate location, waited for me to arrive, and had the accelerant ready. The only person I'd automatically eliminate would be Tory—she doesn't seem smart enough to know how fires even *start*."

"But they weren't all that clever, were they? You could have called 911 and been rescued fairly quickly. It was fortunate for them that you had no service."

"No," I said. "That's what I thought initially, but on the drive back I realized it wasn't at all a matter of them being lucky."

Beau squinted his deep brown eyes at me.

"What do you mean?" he asked. "I'm not tracking."

"I'm pretty sure the person *knew* I didn't have service in Pine Grove. They knew that even if I had my phone with me in the barn, it wouldn't work."

"So somehow they knew what carrier you used?"

"Yes. And I know who it is. Or rather who *they* are. Last weekend two of Scott's houseguests used my BlackBerry. And I think one of them must be the killer."

21

"Who?" Beau exclaimed.

I stared into my wineglass for a moment, gathering my thoughts before speaking.

"Whitney, for one," I said. "I loaned her my BlackBerry briefly after Devon died. I know she's been to Pine Grove before—because she made a comment about the town being some sad little place. And that's no surprise. Cap was Devon's manager, and he'd probably driven out there at times and taken Whitney with him."

"So do you think that Cap really *was* having an affair with Devon—and Whitney found out about it?"

I shook my head slowly back and forth.

"I just don't have a good read on that right now," I said. "Whitney is so adamant that there was nothing going on between Cap and Devon, and she and Cap seem fiercely devoted to each other these days. I'm wondering if something may have been going on *earlier*, and Whitney just discovered it. Maybe she also found out that Devon had been pregnant with Cap's baby, which would make the news even harder to stomach."

"So the whole thing about Cap being unable to have sex could just be bullshit?"

"Well, perhaps he can't now but could last fall. And here's a wacky detail to consider. According to Christian, Devon conceived through some kind of fertility treatments. I assumed when he told me that it was in vitro. But what if the fertility issues had involved Cap, not Devon? Devon may have wanted to conceive by him, and he agreed, but he has lupus, and that can affect a man's ability to have an erection. So perhaps they arranged for Cap's sperm to be extracted and artificially inseminated."

"Sounds awfully far-fetched."

"I know. But there's something odd about Devon's whole pregnancy, and I keep wondering if it fits into her murder somehow. One second she's pregnant, and then all of a sudden the baby's gone and she's happily dating Tommy, like the whole thing was barely a blip in her life. Of course, maybe she considered losing the baby a lucky break because she'd just developed the hots for Tommy, and as he told me the other night, he doesn't—"

I paused in shock. An incredible thought had just flung itself into my brain.

"He doesn't *what*?" Beau asked.

"He doesn't 'do babies,' " I said quietly. "He basically loathes kids. Devon met Tommy in November of last year, when she was a few months pregnant, but probably capable of disguising it with the right outfit. What if she learned about Tommy's aversion to rug rats—she probably fished for his thoughts on the subject because of her condition—and realized that, unlike Brad Pitt, he wasn't going to have any interest in dating her when she had a screaming tot in tow. So—so she decided to do something about it."

"What are you saying exactly?" Beau asked. "That she had an *abortion*?"

"Yes," I said. "That she had an abortion."

Beau shook his head in near disbelief as he poured us each another glug of wine.

"So Devon Barr went through all the trouble of fertility treatments and then *ended* the pregnancy?" he said. "What kind of woman would do that?"

"A woman like Devon," I said ruefully. "You know, my mother said something to me yesterday on the phone about how after you've had a baby, your life is never the same, and it's been niggling at me ever since. Devon was totally narcissistic, someone who didn't give a damn about anything other than her immediate gratification. And while being pregnant worked for her one moment, it didn't the next. She was afraid that a baby would screw up the life she suddenly envisioned with Tommy."

"But how would that circle back to Whitney as a suspect?"

"I have no freaking clue," I said. "But if I'm right and Devon did have an abortion, maybe Whitney's suspicions were raised for some reason, and in digging deeper, she found out Cap was the father. Perhaps the whole fertility treatment thing was a lie—something Devon made up as a smokescreen to cover up the fact that Cap *was* the father. And of course, maybe Cap killed Devon when he learned she'd aborted his child. God, my head hurts just thinking about this stuff."

"And," I added, "there's a problem with the idea of Whitney as the killer. She seems really caught up in the lifestyle she has with Cap, and she would have known that in murdering Devon, she was slaughtering the golden goose. And yet—I don't know. I sense there's something there, but I don't know what yet."

"Tell me who else you loaned your phone to."

"Christian. I tossed it to him when the lights went out."

"But wouldn't he have been slaughtering the golden goose, too?"

"True, but Devon may have been holding something over him—something related to the modeling agency. Cap told me that Devon had a complaint she wanted him to share with the head of First Models, but he wouldn't say what it was about. Maybe it involved Christian, and he was wise to her."

"What could a model booker have done that would be so bad?"

"I'm not sure," I said, "but my guess is that it would involve money."

I was feeling a little anxious being on the current subject because the name Chris Wickersham seemed dangerously close to the surface. It wouldn't be hard for Beau to guess that this is why I'd met up with Chris. Time to move off the topic.

"Would you mind if we hit the sack now?" I asked. "Every muscle in my body aches. I guess my lack of training as a hay-bale tosser has caught up with me."

"Sure," Beau said. "And why don't I massage some of those achy muscles for you?" I accepted gratefully.

In the bedroom, Beau gently removed my clothes and lay me down on the bed for my massage. With his strong hands he started with my shoulders and back and eventually worked his way down my arms and legs.

I concentrated on the sheer pleasure of the experience. Though ten minutes earlier sex was the furthest thing from my mind, feeling Beau's hands on my naked body awoke something in me, and before long I felt a strong rush of desire. It was more than just physical. Mentally, I craved a kind of raw, intense connection with Beau. I eased onto my back and reached for him.

"You sure?" he asked in the darkness.

"Yes," I said. "It's almost a medical emergency."

I awoke the next day at eight thirty to clinking and clanging sounds emanating from my kitchen, and when I padded out there, I found Beau making scrambled eggs. Over breakfast he asked what my next move would be as far as the case was concerned. I had thought about that as I was falling asleep the night before, and I realized I was stalled for the time being. I was anxious to look into the abortion theory as best as I could, but I wouldn't be able to until Monday.

Beau suggested we spend a quiet day together. Still no follow-up on our "commitment" discussion, but I realized that because of what I'd been through, he wasn't putting any pressure on me. We read the paper, ordered in lunch, and then took a long walk around the Village and a windy Washington Square Park. Every few moments, I found myself glancing over my shoulder. Despite the weather, people sat crouched over some of the chess tables or perched on the edge of the fountain. The killer had come after me twice, and I couldn't help but worry there might be yet another attempt. After an early dinner on MacDougal Street, we headed back to my place, where Beau once again stayed the night.

We were both up early the next morning. Beau had meetings all day and said he might be hard to reach, but made me swear I'd leave messages letting him know whenever I went out. After he left, I cooled my heels for a while, and then, as soon as it was nine o'clock, I phoned the upstate coroner's office. A secretary or receptionist answered, with a level of excitement in her voice that made me suspect I'd caught her in the midst of tabbing file folders.

"Good morning," I said, "this is Belinda Hogan from the New York City Police press office. I'd like to talk to someone there about the Devon Barr autopsy. Who's the best person?"

"That would be Hank—Hank Cleary," the woman said. "But he's not—oh wait, he's back. I'll put you through."

"What can I do for you?" Cleary asked after I'd reintroduced myself. He was pleasant enough, but there was a hint of defensiveness in his tone.

"I wanted to pass along some information that I thought you should be aware of."

"*Okay*," he said, sounding wary now. "Shoot."

"As you might expect, we've received a ton of calls down here from press snooping around. Mostly they've been interested in the anorexia angle. But late on Friday a reporter called and inquired if it was true that Devon Bar had had an abortion. I was surprised somebody on the outside would know that."

That was a little trick I'd learned from an old reporter I'd once worked with. Sometimes statements worked better than questions when you were talking to people who were supposed to protect information.

"What are you suggesting exactly?" Cleary said.

"That you may have some loose lips up there. I'm not saying anyone leaked it to the press. Someone may have told a friend or family member, and then it got passed on from there. And it may have come from someplace else entirely—like her doctor's office. But I thought you should be aware."

"Well, I'm positive no one from this office blabbed it," he said defensively. "We may not be city folks, but we know enough to keep our mouths shut on a confidential matter like that."

Bingo. It sounded, at least, as if I'd been right—Devon had had an abortion. It fit with the spoiled, willful Devon I'd known briefly. She wanted what she wanted when she wanted it.

Next question to try to answer: Had Whitney learned of it somehow? I thought suddenly of something that Cap had said to me when I'd questioned him about his conversation in the woods with Devon. He'd told me he'd comforted Devon about losing the baby and mentioned to her that Whitney had spoken to the gynecologist. But still, this wasn't leading anyplace.

I took a shower next, hoping that the warm water would not only soothe my still-aching muscles but help clear my head. I sensed that there was a thought just out of reach, pestering me the way a pebble in your shoe does—at first not so much, but after a while, to greater and greater distraction. As I was toweling off, I heard my phone ring. To my relief, it turned out to be Collinson.

"I've spoken to the troopers in Pennsylvania," he said, "but I want to hear it from you."

"Of course," I said. "That's why I left you the message. Did you not get it?"

"Yes, yes," he said impatiently.

I told him the story but didn't whisper a word about the two suspects in my mind. It seemed unfair to throw them under the bus until I dug up more information.

"We're going to be working with several different law enforcement agencies and giving this our full attention," he said. "And I want you to butt out, Ms. Weggins. I appreciate your insights, but this is a police matter."

"I hear you," I said. That was my way of making it sound like I was taking his order while I really wasn't.

The phone rang again as soon as I had disconnected the call. Jeez, I thought, was he checking to make sure that his lecture had sunk in? But it wasn't Collinson. I froze as someone with a slight Texas twang said my name.

"Hello, Whitney," I said in reply.

"Have you got a moment to talk?" she asked. So much sweeter-sounding than the last time we'd spoken, but a warning siren was already going off in my brain.

"Sure," I said. "What can I do for you?"

"There's something I'd like to discuss with you."

"Oh, really?" I said. "The last time we met, you didn't seem to enjoy talking to me."

"I know I seemed impatient that day, but I hope you understood what an awkward position you'd put Cap and me in. However, there—there's something you need to know the truth about."

"About Cap?" I asked, more than curious where she was headed.

"No, not about Cap, for goodness sake. Why do you keep insisting that this is all about Cap? I need to talk to you about *Christian*."

Christian. Was there really something there? Or was she purposely leading me astray?

"Okay," I said. "Tell me about it."

"It needs to be discussed in private—I don't want to get into it on my cell phone. Can you come by my apartment again?"

The siren sound in my head was nearly deafening now. I wanted to hear what she had to say, but I couldn't take any chances.

"Uh—," I said, unsure of what to suggest. Should I invite her to my place? Or some kind of neutral ground—preferably with professional snipers posted nearby. "I have a pretty busy day ahead. Would it be possible for you to come downtown to my neck of the woods?"

"I wish I could," she said. "But I have two women here testing recipes all day for my cookbook. I don't want to leave them alone in the apartment."

Clearly, I told myself, if she *were* the killer, she wouldn't pull anything in front of two recipe testers. It was hard to imagine her chasing me around the kitchen with a butcher knife while her helpers whipped up a platter of pralines.

"All right," I told her. "When?"

She said in an hour. I used the time to think through the best strategy to use. Keep it neutral, I told myself. Listen, watch. Don't provoke. And make sure the minute I walk in that there are definitely others in the apartment.

I chose a cab over the subway to save time but ended up stalled in Christmas shopping gridlock by Macy's on Thirty-fourth Street. I felt flustered and anxious by the time I finally entered the Darby's huge apartment building. I gave my name, and the concierge called upstairs for clearance.

"Mrs. Darby says to go right up," the concierge announced, beaming. He'd obviously detected no homicidal tendencies with Whitney.

When she opened the door, Whitney had on the same kind of let's-do-brunch outfit she'd been wearing when I'd been at her apartment before—drapy beige slacks; soft cream-colored blouse; big gold earrings. It looked as if she'd just come in from running an errand because a short, fur-lined jacket lay on one of the straight-backed chairs in the hallway and a brown hobo-style bag was nestled on the table with all the silver-framed photos of her and Cap.

"Come in, Bailey," she said. She smiled, but it seemed about as real as her boobs, and there was something distant about her pale blue eyes. Am I an utter fool to be here? I wondered anxiously. But from far off in the apartment, the kitchen I guessed, I could hear the sound of people chatting and bustling about. The kitchen testers. There's no way, I reminded myself, that she would try anything nasty with them on the premises.

"I'm sure you're as busy as I am," she added. "But I did feel I should share what I know with you."

"I'm anxious to hear it," I said.

She lifted her hands, flipping over the palms slightly, and turned her head a quarter to the side, as if she was just now considering how we should proceed.

"Well, why don't you come on into the living room?" she said. As I followed her there, the chattering receded; the only sound in the living room was from wind whipping along the wraparound terrace. She gestured for me to take a seat on one of the plush, mint-colored sofas. I perched on the edge, and Whitney lowered herself gracefully into an armchair.

"How have you been, by the way?" she asked. "Cap and I went to the funeral, of course, on Saturday, and we're still decompressing from that. Were you out there, covering it? I didn't see you."

No, I was getting my ass baked in a local barn, I almost said, just to catch her expression. But I needed to stick to my game plan: stay neutral and not provoke.

"No, some other reporters were assigned to cover the funeral," I said.

She took a deep breath, raising her breasts up like an offering to the gods. "As I made clear before, I'm not in the habit of talking to the tabloid press," she said. "Cap may represent famous people, but we're very private ourselves. And I don't like gossip. It's evil. But I've been thinking about what you said—that Devon might have been murdered. And I don't want to stand in the way of the truth."

"I'm happy to hear that," I said. "You indicated on the phone that this has something to do with Christian."

She lowered her head and pursed her lips briefly.

"Yes, I'm afraid it does," she said, looking back at me. "Since you and I spoke, I've asked myself again and again if anyone had a motive to kill Devon. And I'm afraid Christian had one."

I waited, saying nothing. From far off I heard a muted burst of laughter in the kitchen.

"You may not have been aware of it," Whitney continued, "but Devon completely ignored Christian last weekend. She didn't say a *word* to the man."

"But according to Scott, she was the one who'd invited him there."

"Yes, that's true. But, you see, she did that to toy with him. Devon had discovered something Christian had done, something unethical at the agency, and she wanted Cap to tell his boss, Barbara Dern. But before she made certain he was exposed, it seemed she wanted to see Christian twist a little in the wind. Perhaps she was even hoping to use it to her advantage, that he'd become so worried that he'd work even harder for her."

"What had he done?"

"I'm not sure of the exact details—I'm getting this secondhand from Cap. But it has to do with clients from Asia that the agency does business with. The Asians, especially the Japanese, use a lot of Caucasian girls in their ads and magazines. Some models even move over there to kickstart their careers. It's very much a cash business—the Japanese arrive here with suitcases of money and turn it over to the modeling agencies. Apparently Christian has been negotiating certain rates with Asian clients, collecting the cash, but then indicating lower amounts on the books. He keeps the difference for himself."

She laid a hand on her chest and looked off, taking a breath.

"Forgive me," she said. "This is so upsetting for me—and it makes my asthma want to rear its head."

"How did Devon find out?"

"I'm not sure. She was always a snoop. She may have overheard something."

"And what would happen to Christian if the agency learned the truth?"

"Oh, more than a slap on the wrist—that's for sure. Barbara Dern takes no prisoners. She would have fired him, probably even had him arrested."

"Is that why Cap seemed to be dragging his heels? He didn't want to see Christian go to jail?"

"To be honest, he was thinking more of Devon. If Christian was arrested in the next few weeks and it came out that he was Devon's booker, it might reflect poorly on her album. And of course now I feel sick that he waited. Because it may have given Christian the opportunity to kill Devon."

"Possibly," I said, mulling it over. Was this legit, I wondered, or all some kind of setup? "I suggest you tell Detective Collinson this right away. Initially he seemed doubtful that Devon had been murdered, but some details have emerged to change his thinking. I'm sure he'll find what you told me interesting."

"*Interesting?*" Whitney said, sounding miffed. "That's all you have to say? Isn't it a motive for murder?"

"Sure, it could be," I said. "The police will look into it. But there are other details for them to consider as well."

"Oh, really?" she said, snidely. "You're not back to pointing the finger at me and Cap, are you?"

"I didn't say that. Just loose ends to tie up."

"Such as?"

"There's actually one matter I'd like to ask you about. Something regarding Devon's pregnancy."

Whitney's face froze. She lifted a hand upward and touched the corner of her mouth with one of her long slim fingers and then wiped at something that wasn't there.

"And what would that be?" she asked after a beat.

"Were you aware that Devon had an abortion?"

Even from where I was sitting, I could see the subtle but shocking changes in her face. Her nostrils flared, the rims of her eyes reddened. It was like a rage grenade had gone off inside her, but she was doing her best to contain the explosion. Instinctively I strained to hear the kitchen sounds. With relief I realized I could still detect faint voices in the distance.

"Who in the world told you that?" she said between clenched teeth.

"Someone who would definitely know," I replied. "I have to admit I was taken aback when I heard it. Here she'd gone to all that trouble to conceive, and then, poof, she decides to make it go away. Was it because of Tommy?"

Whitney snickered in disgust.

"But of course," she said, her voice tight with anger. "She was besotted by that pathetic man from the moment she met him."

"Did he say something to her about not wanting kids?" I asked.

"I assume so," Whitney replied. "He'd hardly want a groupie showing up backstage wearing a damn Snugli. Or maybe Devon just thought it would get in the way of all the hot sex they were going to have. God, the mere thought of sex with him is enough to make me gag."

"Did she tell you about the abortion?"

"What do *you* think?" Whitney snapped.

My mind was racing. I needed to get the answers right so she'd keep talking.

"I bet she didn't," I said after a moment. "Because you and Cap must have been there for her through the fertility treatments, right? Cap was always there for her. It would have troubled you to learn she'd just callously ended her pregnancy. And"—a thought suddenly snagged my brain—"you're a conservative Christian, right, and against abortion? You would have been very upset for that reason, too."

"Abortion is a *sin*," Whitney said fiercely, nearly spitting out the words. "The worst of all sins. The victims are the most innocent creatures in the world. It wasn't even *Devon's* baby. Not any part of it."

"Was the sperm from anyone she knew?" I asked, barely above a whisper. I was afraid of the testers overhearing us and of Whitney suddenly clamming up.

"Yes, an ex-boyfriend," she said. "I think he only agreed to donate his sperm because was he was too stupid to know it would actually produce a baby."

"But are you saying she used an egg donor, too?"

"Unfortunately Devon's eggs weren't nearly as pretty as her face. She was in the throes of early menopause."

"And the egg donor? Was that someone she knew as well?"

Staring at me, Whitney took a breath that made a slight wheezing sound and let it out very slowly. The rims of her eyes were even redder now, as if blood might start spurting from them any second.

And then the truth hit me hard—*she* was the donor. In some odd way the thought had been slowly forming in my mind all morning. I felt fear begin to slosh inside me, like water in the hull of a boat.

"The baby was yours, wasn't it?" I said. "Or at least the egg was."

Whitney squeezed her mouth shut tight, as if she were fighting to keep the rage inside her. Then a wicked little smile snuck onto her face.

"You'll never be able to prove it," she said. "It was all handled very hush-hush."

"But why?"

"*Why?*" she shrieked. "Because of Cap. He'd done everything for that selfish bitch. And he was always on call twenty-four/seven. It was almost over for her as a model, and as an actress she made Paris Hilton look like some Academy Award winner, but she'd run through tons of her money and she needed the work. So Cap launched her singing career. But despite all that, she was starting to make little noises of discontent. 'Cap, you need to do more for me.' 'Cap, I'm not happy.' When she said she wanted to get pregnant, it became *his* problem, of course."

"She must have been freaked when she heard about her medical issue."

"You got that right. It turned up when she first went in for artificial insemination. Silly me, I'd done a story on egg donors and actually encouraged the next step. But she didn't want *anybody's* eggs. She met a few donors and they made her think of her disgusting mother. So Cap begged me to do it. He knew I didn't want children myself. And that way Devon would owe him."

"How did you find out she hadn't miscarried?"

"Oh, I was very clever," Whitney said. "Almost as clever as Little Miss Bailey Weggins. I tricked one of the nurses at the OB's office into telling me. They'd learned of the abortion when the doctor who'd performed it had requested some records. I'd had my suspicions, though, right from the beginning. Devon had a hard time looking me in the eye after the so-called miscarriage. And then, when she didn't try to conceive again over the past year, I knew something was up."

I flashed again on what Cap had told me. He'd said he'd relayed to Devon that Whitney had been in touch with the OB, and Devon shouldn't have trouble conceiving again. But Devon had probably guessed that Whitney had been snooping and had learned about the abortion. That's why she'd seemed so scared when I saw her.

"It must have been awful to learn the truth."

"*Awful?*" Whitney said savagely. "If that's what you call it when you find that someone has taken a four-month-old fetus—with *your* blood—and destroyed it like a piece of garbage."

The wind tore across the terrace again. From where I sat I could see only the gray, smudged sky and the tips of a few high-rise apartment buildings. Thankfully, far off in the kitchen, the testers were still chatting and laughing.

"So you killed her," I said. I knew it was true. I knew just from looking at those red-rimmed eyes. The modeling agency story might be legit, but she'd offered it up just to throw me off her trail—because nothing else had worked so far.

Whitney flashed another one of her wicked smiles.

"Again, you'll never be able to prove it," she said smugly. "There's nothing linking anything to me."

"Devon fed nicely into your hands with her anorexia, didn't she?" I said. I knew I should get the hell out of the apartment, but I needed to know the truth.

"Yes," she said. "It was almost like a gift from God. At first I thought it had started again because she was so damn worried about her career, but I honestly think her conscience might have finally been catching up with her. She'd murdered her child so she could have Tommy, and then Tommy kicked her to the curb."

"Was her death this weekend just a coincidence? I mean, you couldn't really predict when the Lasix would do its magic."

"No, but I knew it might happen. You see, I'd already started the process at the spa. That's the reason I'd invited her away. And though I couldn't *bear* spending another weekend in that bitch's company, it gave me a wonderful opportunity to load up the Lasix every time she set her water bottle down. When I saw her stagger off to her room, Saturday night, I knew the end was near."

An answer started to form—to a question that had bugged me for days.

"Wait—did you call extension seven that night?"

"Oh, you're smart, aren't you, Bailey? You see, I started to worry it would seem odd that we hadn't checked on her, but then I changed my mind and hung up. Sometimes, the less done the better."

"Why did you take the ipecac from the bathroom, then? That could only arouse suspicions."

"I had no idea you'd seen it. I'd learned about ipecac when I was doing my news story and told Devon about it at the spa, knowing she'd be tempted to try it. But I couldn't be sure she hadn't told that idiot Tory that I'd talked about it. If the cops found the bottle, they might eventually connect it back to me. You really made me angry with all your poking around. If you'd just minded your own business."

"You snooped in my room, didn't you? You checked out my computer."

"You left me no choice, did you?"

"And as I started poking around even more, you came after me. You thought getting me suspended from *Buzz* might shut me down, but when that didn't work, you tried to kill me. Who was the man in the gypsy cab?"

"None of your business," Whitney said snidely. "And trust me, you'll never find him."

"How did you discover I was going to be downtown? Tommy told you, didn't he?"

"No comment," she said. "I can't let you know *all* my secrets."

"I bet you were talking to him about the funeral or something to do with Devon's death, and he mentioned he'd be seeing me."

"There's no proof of that or anything else."

"The police will call the doctor. They'll find out you knew about the abortion."

"That hardly proves I killed Devon," she said.

"They'll talk to Sherrie, they'll find out you told her to call my boss. And when they see you were trying to shut me up, they'll start trying to link you to the fire."

"Oh, please, Bailey, don't you *get* it?" She'd raised her voice again, the rage simmering just below the surface. Wasn't she worried about the testers hearing, I wondered. "Sherrie's on a six-month bender. No one's going to get anything out of her about me, and those local yokels in Pennsylvania aren't ever going to have a confab with the local-yokel cops in upstate New York. As far as the world is concerned, Devon Barr basically starved herself to death. And if anyone manages to feel bad about that, they can buy the fucking album."

She was probably right. Collinson seemed smart enough, but how would he tie it all together? Was Whitney going to get away with murder? I knew I had to do something.

"Maybe the cops won't figure out it was murder," I said. "But I bet if I tell Cap, he'll put the pieces together and realize I'm telling the truth."

She shot up from her chair then, making me jump in surprise. "Don't you *dare* bring Cap into this!"

I rose slowly from my own chair.

"Why not?" I said. "Because you know he'd leave you in a second if he found out? He might even be willing to try to point the cops to evidence."

Her whole body seemed to droop at that moment and she flung her head back and forth.

"You *can't* tell him!" she screamed. "I won't let you."

"But how much better for *you* to tell him than for him to find out from the cops," I said. "He must know how you feel about abortion. He'll understand."

"No, no, no," she yelled. And then suddenly she was taking off across the room toward the terrace door. She grabbed the handle and flung the door open. I could feel a rush of cold air even from where I was standing. Whitney stepped outside and, to my horror, flung herself against the outer wall of the terrace. My God, I thought, she's going to jump.

"I need some help," I yelled, into the bowels of the apartment. Then I rushed outside.

"Whitney," I said, coming up behind her. "Don't be crazy. You—"

Before I could say another word, she spun around and slugged me in the face with her fist.

I stumbled backward and simultaneously raised my arm to my face, anticipating another strike. She struck again, this time at my chest. Though the fabric of my coat absorbed the blow, the force of her punch made me stagger backward even more, until I backed into the outside wall of the terrace. I tried to right myself, ready to hit back somehow, but then she charged me, hurling her body into mine. Using the palm of my hand, I shoved hard into her shoulder, trying to push her away. As I raised my hand to strike her again, I felt her hand reach between my legs. I gasped in surprise and confusion. It took me a second to realize that she was trying to hoist me up. She was planning to throw me off the terrace.

22

Terrified, I yanked my left arm to my body, pointed the elbow toward Whitney, and with all my strength, drove the elbow into her face. She reeled back and doubled over. I braced myself for another charge, but when Whitney looked up, I saw that she was starting to wheeze. A second later she collapsed into a sitting position on the floor of the terrace

"Help me," she muttered. It didn't seem like she was faking it. "Please. My inhaler."

"Where is it?" I yelled.

"In my purse."

I charged back into the apartment, raced the length of the living room, and grabbed the brown hobo bag off the hall table. It would take extra seconds, but I needed to alert the women in the kitchen to call 911. I propelled myself down a hallway toward the still-constant sound of chatter until I found a huge, sprawling kitchen. But there was no one there. My eyes followed the sounds to a TV on the wall—it was playing a tape of some kind of cooking class. There had never been anyone in the kitchen at all.

I tore back out to the terrace. Whitney was wheezing heavily, searching desperately for air. I upended her purse, letting the contents splatter at my feet—keys, pens, a makeup bag, wallet. In the middle of the mess I spotted the inhaler. I snatched it and handed it to Whitney. Like a robot, she flipped off the top with her thumb. She pulled it to her mouth and pumped. Then pumped again. She continued to wheeze, harder, and her eyes grew wide with fright.

"It's empty," she said hoarsely. "Help me."

"Have you got another?" I yelled above the wind.

She flopped her head every which way, and it was impossible to tell if she meant yes or no, but then she flung her right arm toward the door.

"Where?" I was screaming now. "In the bathroom?"

No answer. Just desperate wheezing, her hands clutching her throat. I raced back into the apartment, toward where I assumed the master bedroom was. En route, I grabbed a phone and hit 911.

"There's a woman here having a bad asthma attack," I said. "You must send an ambulance right now." I rattled off the address.

"Does she have an inhaler?" the operator asked after I'd given the key information.

"Yes, but it's no good. I'm trying to find another."

"Try to keep the person calm. Tell her to inhale through her nose and exhale through her mouth."

The idea of me calming Whitney down seemed preposterous. I'd located the bathroom by now, and I pawed through the medicine cabinet, spilling cosmetics and prescription drugs onto the counter. No inhaler. I tried the bedside tables next, with no success. After that, with adrenaline coursing through me, I made a desperate stab at the kitchen, yanking open drawers and cupboards. Still no luck. Trying to calm Whitney seemed the only course of action.

I'd left the terrace door open, and the living room was now frigid, with wind whipping through it. When I stepped outside, I saw that Whitney was lying sprawled out on the cement floor, totally still. Bending down, I realized that she didn't seem to be breathing. I tried mouth-to-mouth resuscitation on her bluish lips, but there was no response. In desperation I picked up the inhaler. Was it really empty or just stuck? I turned it over. On the flat end was a small puncture hole, as if it had been stabbed with a sharp object.

I glanced back at Whitney, tears of anxiety welling in my eyes. It was pretty clear she was dead.

Five hours later, I was sitting in one of Landon's armchairs, bundled up in a thick sweater and sniffling and dabbing at my nose with a tissue. An hour earlier, a Godzilla-sized cold had suddenly invaded my system, in about the time it takes to say, "Please no, I so don't need this right now." My throat throbbed and my head ached. Landon had just served me a bowl of homemade lentil soup, but I was having a hard time even tasting it.

"I feel so guilty," Landon said. "I'm sure I'm the one who gave you this dreadful cold."

"Stop," I said. "I've been freezing my ass off in barns and on balconies for the last few days, and I probably have no one to blame but myself."

"And Whitney, of course."

"Yes," I murmured. "And Whitney."

The EMS team had arrived less than ten minutes after my futile attempts at mouth-to-mouth. Two patrol cops had followed practically on their heels. And not, it turned out, because of my 911 call. Someone from a nearby high-rise had seen the struggle on the terrace and alerted the police to it. Thankfully they had included the fact that a woman in a light-colored blouse was trying to give a woman in black the heave-ho over the edge. This provided me with a certain amount of credibility as I tried to explain my role in such a fucked-up mess to first the patrol cops, and then second, at greater length, to the two detectives who arrived at the scene about fifteen minutes later.

I was asked to accompany one of the detectives to the precinct, which was good because it spared me coming face-to-face with Cap—though I managed to catch a glimpse of him charging into the building just as I was being driven away in an unmarked police car. His face was drained of blood.

At the precinct I gave my statement in as much detail as possible, and when I was done, urged the detective to call Officer Collinson. They talked for at least fifteen minutes, with the detective standing far enough away from me that I couldn't hear what he was saying. He eyed me, though, through the entire conversation. I had a feeling Collinson was giving him an earful about what a bad girl I'd been. I knew I would have to call Collinson later and try to make peace with him.

"You can go now," the detective said, after snapping his phone shut. "But please be available tomorrow. We'll need to talk to you further as we pursue this matter."

On the cab ride home, I tried Beau but reached only his voice mail. As I disconnected I saw that I had a message. And lo and behold it turned out that my old friend at *Buzz*, Nash Nolan, had phoned. Automatically I started to dial in his number and then stopped.

I didn't have an ounce of desire to talk to the dude at the moment.

As soon as I reached my apartment, I did a quick search about asthma on the Internet and then staggered into a hot shower. It was while I was toweling off that the cold virus staged a sneak attack on my system, which sent me to Landon's for over-the-counter cold remedies and sustenance. He always seemed to have both.

"Does it bother you?' Landon asked me quietly. "That you couldn't save her?"

"Yes," I said, sniffling. "Though I probably shouldn't care—she thought nothing of turning me into a big, ugly splat on Amsterdam Avenue. You know, I just read on the Internet that cold air can trigger asthma. Whitney had obviously started to have an attack when we were in the apartment, but she was in such a rage about me threatening to tell Cap that she clearly wasn't thinking straight. She made her situation worse by luring me outside."

"Did her inhaler just malfunction?"

"The bottom was punctured, which must have caused all the medication inside to seep out. But I'm not sure how that could have happened. Some sharp object in her purse maybe—like a pen?"

"You don't think Cap did it, do you? That he got wind of what she was up to and decided to secretly off her?"

"No, that's not Cap's style. If he knew that Whitney had killed his star client, he would have just throttled her."

A few minutes later I nearly crawled back to my apartment. I threw myself onto the couch and pulled an old throw blanket up to my chin. As I was dozing off, Jessie called. I suspected by the silence behind her that she was probably safely sequestered in a conference room at *Buzz.*

"I can't believe you didn't call me," she said. "You've got to tell me everything."

"Oh God, sorry—I planned to call you. I've just got a bitch of a cold right now." I took her quickly through an abbreviated version of what had happened.

"Gosh, how weird and sad and everything else. I feel sorry for Cap, actually. He seemed like an okay guy."

"Yeah, I don't think he had any idea how unbalanced Whitney really was. She clearly loved the life she had with Cap. She'd said that they'd had a whirlwind courtship, and my guess is that she saw right away what the possibilities could be—a big fancy apartment, furs and jewelry, a ranch in Texas someday. And as long as everything was on an even keel, she probably seemed fairly normal. But then, to help preserve that lifestyle, she ended up giving Devon her eggs. And when she learned what Devon had done, she just snapped."

"If she hadn't gone off the deep end today, do you think she would have been arrested?"

"I honestly don't know. The fertility doctor Devon used might have confirmed that Whitney was the donor, and there would also be the confirmation of Whitney's call to the gyno. But unless they could have traced the Lasix to her, it would have been hard to prove she doctored the water."

I told her then that Nash had left me a few messages.

"I assume he's calling about Whitney's death," I said. "I'm sure it's eating him alive that I'm at the center of this whole thing but no longer on his payroll."

"You better believe it. Plus, one of the lawyers was down in his office earlier. I have a feeling they now realize that Whitney must have put Sherrie up to this."

"Whitney never came right out and said it, but it's clearly the case."

"So you're going to call Nash, right?"

"Sure. I want my name cleared."

"But what about the magazine? Are you going to write the story for *Buzz*?"

I hesitated. The answer was forming in my mind right then and there, and it caught me a little by surprise. I should have seen it coming, but I'd been so preoccupied, I hadn't.

"You know, I don't think so," I said. "I can't ever go back there after what Nash did to me."

"Oh, wow," Jessie said. "Though I can't blame you. Just promise me you won't make any rash decisions. Talk to Nash, see what he has to say. I don't think I can face this place every day without you."

"Thanks, Jess. Lets talk more tomorrow."

I had just laid my head back down on the pillow when Beau called. It felt so good to hear his voice. I gave him the same short version I'd offered Jessie because now my throat hurt so much I could barely talk. He said he wanted to come by, but I explained I was conked out, almost in a coma.

"I don't care, I want to see you," Beau said. "You shouldn't be alone at a time like this. Why don't I come over and let myself in, so that way I won't wake you. Later I can fix you something to eat."

It was a tough offer to refuse. After I hung up, I forced myself off the couch. Better to be in bed, I thought. As I staggered to my bedroom, I kept thinking about how much Beau had been there for me over the past few days. Not so elusive after all.

I fell into a deep sleep, waking only briefly when I thought I heard Beau come in the front door of the apartment. What seemed like hours later, I stirred again to find Beau sitting on the edge of my bed, dressed in jeans and a black pullover sweater.

"Don't get too close," I muttered. "This is brutal."

"How about something to eat? I could make you an omelet."

"Yeah, I am kind of hungry."

He returned a few minutes later with tea, toast, and a cheese omelet. I couldn't eat much of the omelet in the end, but the toast and tea definitely helped me to rally. I scooted up even higher in bed and mustered a smile at Beau. He was now sitting in the armchair at the foot of my bed.

"Thanks for the food," I told him. "I feel vaguely human now."

"The sleep probably helped, too. I checked a few online sites for you. This story has exploded. Lots and lots of speculation, of course, because most people don't have any clue what really happened. I bet a ton of outlets are trying to reach you to interview you."

"I should probably deal with that in a minute. There's just so much to think about right now."

"Do you still have unanswered questions about the case?" he asked.

"A few. I don't know who the guy in the gypsy cab was or how Whitney put him up to the job. But maybe the police can figure that out by going through her phone logs. One thing that *does* keep bugging me is the hole in the inhaler. Landon asked if Cap could have done it."

"Do you think so?"

"No, but it seems unlikely it could have happened accidentally. You would think those things were almost fail proof. If it wasn't an accident, then *someone* put the hole there."

"I think I'll hang around for a while, just to keep an eye on my patient. Do you need anything else right now?"

"Um, just my phone. It's in my bag, out in the living room."

"Sure," Beau said and started to rise from the chair.

"Wait, one second, though, would you?" I said. "There's something I want to say off the topic of murder and mayhem."

Beau came from around the bottom of the bed and sidled up next to me.

"What's up?" he asked.

"I know it seems crazy, but in the midst of all this nightmare stuff, I've had a chance to do some thinking. Remember what you said to me the other day about *me* being the one with the commitment issues? Well, you're not the first person to say that to me. You're not even the *second*. I'd like to have another chance with you. And now that I'm aware of what's going on with me, I think I can handle things differently."

"Great, Bailey. I'm happy to hear that." He laughed. "Besides, a friend of mine just invited us to his amazing ski house over Christmas, and I need to give him an answer by tonight."

God, this was getting better by the minute.

"That sounds like a lot of fun," I said.

Beau took three steps toward me and leaned down to kiss me.

"No," I said, throwing up my hand. "You'll catch this thing. It's mean as a pit bull."

"I'm sure I'm probably already infected," he said, laughing. "We did a lot of spit swapping this weekend."

He returned a few minutes later with my purse and set it down on the bed next to me. I reached toward it to retrieve my phone. I was anxious to see who might have called me for interviews. Maybe even a news outlet that I could form a partnership with, since I wouldn't be going back to *Buzz*. Gosh, I'd almost said it out loud: *I wasn't going back*. I'd never again have a first look at Suri's latest pair of kitten heels.

And then, just as I touched my purse, a thought jarred me, like a fellow subway passenger falling into me as the train rounded a curve. *Whitney's handbag*. The brown suede hobo bag. I'd seen it before. On Saturday afternoon I had followed Devon down the stairs at Scott's to talk to her, and I'd caught her putting something into her handbag. *A brown suede hobo bag*. But it hadn't been her bag, after all. It had been

Whitney's. It had happened, too, only a short time after Devon's discussion with Cap in the woods and her confession to me that she wasn't safe.

And at that moment, as the wind howled outside, I realized the final twist of the story: Devon had punctured the inhaler after she realized, from her conversation with Cap, that Whitney had probably learned about the abortion. She'd been terrified of Whitney's wrath and what she might do.

Whitney had killed Devon. But in the end, Devon had killed her back.

23

Beau asked if I wanted him to build a fire, and I told him yes. It had been a fairly mild January so far, but on that Friday, in the third week of the month, the night was suddenly crazy cold, and I craved extra warmth. There was a brief moment when I worried that seeing flames in his fireplace, the fireplace I'd never really noticed all fall, would trigger that old Why-is-Beau-such-a-freaking-mystery? feeling in me again, but as I watched him light the kindling and poke around with one of the irons, I could tell it wasn't going to happen.

First, he looked really good in the jeans he was wearing, and that was an excellent distraction. Plus, ever since I'd urged myself to (1) accept the fact that he was fully committed to me, and (2) stop going slightly psycho or pulling back, I'd been a pretty good girl. And even when I occasionally *did* feel a little weirded out, I would just recite a helpful mantra in my head, like "Bailey, don't be a total love *moron*," and "Bailey, just shut your freakin' brain down, okay?"

But something unexpected happened when flames finally started to dance and the smell of wood smoke filled the room. I was suddenly back in that barn fire in Pennsylvania, terrified that I would never find a way out and the smoke and the flames or both would be my undoing. Beau was in the kitchen at that point, carving up a rotisserie chicken he'd bought, and he didn't see the tears of phantom panic prick my eyes. Six weeks had passed since the barn incident, but I realized that it was still playing a bit of havoc with my psyche.

Of course it wasn't just the barn fire that still troubled me. It was everything else rolled up with that— being abducted in the gypsy cab and Whitney's death and discovering the awful things she and Devon had done to each other.

At least I hadn't landed in an iffy situation with the cops, which easily could have happened. Though a lot about the case was finally clear in my mind, I knew it must seem muddled and even far-fetched to the cops, especially without any solid evidence pointing to Whitney. Plus, I'd done enough crime pieces to know that the cops found me suspicious just from having been smack in the middle of it all. The day after Whitney's death, at the urging of Beau, Landon, and my mother, I hired a lawyer. I knew it would cost me big-time, but I needed the best advice possible.

Fortunately, a few things emerged fairly quickly that lent my story and theory credibility. The Upper West Side resident who had called 911 apparently confirmed that Whitney had been trying to push me off the terrace. She'd seen it with binoculars. (I said a silent prayer at the time to the patron saint of busybodies and voyeurs.) Also, Tommy admitted to me that he'd indeed talked to Whitney about the funeral from the Living Room, and told her I was dropping by. He shared this info with the police without even asking for any kinky favors in return.

And my attorney was able to suss out from a police contact that Whitney's father had a prescription to Lasix for high blood pressure and that she'd made an impromptu visit to see him right before she'd headed off for the spa trip with Devon. Though the cops never revealed this, I suspected that they were able to confirm that Whitney had made contact with someone in Devon's gyno's office during the fall. The cops stayed in touch with me for a while, asking for input, but that was it.

A week after Whitney's death, Detective Collinson called and thanked me for what I'd done. He revealed that with more specific questioning, Ralph, Scott's caretaker, recalled seeing Whitney take a bottle of Evian water out of her purse on Saturday and set it on the counter, though neither he, Sandy, nor Laura had ever seen her drinking bottled water that weekend. Collinson also shared a couple of details he'd picked up from the cops in New York. Whitney and Cap had taken separate cars to the funeral. Though the texts I'd received had been sent on a prepaid phone and there was no clue who had purchased it, the police found gasoline stains in the trunk of Whitney's car. He also told me that Cap didn't try to come to Whitney's defense in any way. I suspected Cap recognized the truth and was totally distressed and disgusted by it.

There was one other loose end I cleared up on my own—by calling Richard Parkin.

"Well, well," he said when he heard my voice. "Once again you've managed to dazzle us all with your Sherlockian skills. Bravo, Bailey."

Due to his tone, it didn't sound like much of a compliment, but I thanked him anyway.

"And are all these lurid details about a pregnancy and abortion true?" he asked.

"Tell you what," I said. "I'll share if you share."

"What do you mean?" he asked.

"Why did you visit Devon's mother the day of the funeral?"

"Oh, my. Was our fearless Bailey actually doing a stakeout in Pine Grove?"

"I don't have the time or energy to play cute with you, Richard. Just tell me."

"All right," he said, his voice suddenly stripped of either false jocularity or sarcasm. "I did go to see that pitiful wench. But it was out of nothing more than morbid curiosity. I wanted to see the place Devon was born. I wanted to see the house that could produce such a monster. I thought I might find some closure that way."

I didn't say anything for a moment. I just considered his grief and pain and wondered how much it had shaped his life.

"And did you?" I asked finally.

"No," he said. "I'm afraid not at all."

I signed off, feeling intensely sorry for the man.

There were other loose ends that, unfortunately I wasn't able to tie up. The odorous Zorro, for instance. I was still pretty sure Jane had wielded the branding iron that night at Scott's, but there just was no way to prove it. Then there was the gypsy cab driver. From what I'd learned, the police were searching Whitney's phone records to see if they could find a link, but as of this point, nothing seemed to have turned up. Not that the cops were going to call *me* with any news.

And lastly there was Sherrie. Jessie had heard she'd definitely gone on a major bender after Devon's death—maybe because most of Devon's money had been left to the Metropolitan Museum Costume Institute—and so the *Buzz* lawyers had no luck getting her to retract what she said about me. It didn't matter anymore, though. Nash told me that he and the lawyers were now certain that Whitney must have put Sherrie up to the whole thing.

Yeah, I finally talked to Nash. He kept calling, and I realized I was being childish not to return his calls. I was expecting the gruff-news-guy-with-a-heart-of-gold routine, with him doing a big mea culpa and begging me to come back, and I knew I'd have to fight hard not to be suckered in by it. Instead he offered this line of bullshit about how the lawyers had totally muzzled him during my suspension, but he'd been working doggedly the whole time to clear my name. Sure, right, I told myself—and Lindsay Lohan was about to be named the next UN Goodwill Ambassador. I knew I'd never ever be able to trust the guy. Which made it easier to tell him I was moving on.

"If you're holding out for more money," Nash replied, "I can probably do a little something."

"No," I told him, "it's not a money thing. But thank you. Best of luck."

I was surprised at how sad the decision to leave *Buzz* made me feel. I had arrived there knowing practically nada about celebs and caring even less—I mean, I would look at shots of people like Audrina Partridge and wonder how a woman whose only real accomplishment in life was sticking to a low-carb diet could be on the *cover* of *Buzz*—but it had been fun to be in that crazy, zany world for a while.

Despite all the turmoil of those December days, there was one definite upside. Once my lawyer felt the cops really accepted my version of events, I did a ton of press and my book took off, leaving *Napkin Folding for Beginners* in a cloud of dust. It even briefly made the *New York Times* best-seller list—okay, *extended* list, but still, it meant I was going to receive royalties. And several publishers approached my agent, inquiring about my doing another book, this one on the whole Devon mess. I'd pounded out a proposal during my ski trip with Beau over the holidays.

And there was news to share on the book front when I sat down to the roast chicken dinner at Beau's.

"So how did the meeting with your agent go?" Beau asked before I could even broach the subject.

"Great," I said. "She's tested the waters with my proposal, and she thinks we can actually sell the book in an auction, which means I might make some decent dough up front."

"That's fantastic, Bailey," he said.

"Yeah, I'm so relieved. I've got that small trust fund from my father, but it's just barely enough to live on. With the book advance, I should be fine this year. So I'm going to try the freelance route for a while. I'll work on the book and whatever assignments come up here and there."

"Will it be weird not to have an office to go into?"

"Yeah, I'm sure a little bit. Both *Buzz* and *Gloss* were only part-time, but it was still nice to hang around other people some days. And it's kind of scary to be totally on my own. But in the long run, I think it may be better for me. Bosses always seem to make me bristle. Now I don't have to be at the mercy of a Cat Jones or Nash Nolan or Mona Hodges. I like the idea of being a free agent."

"Should that alarm me?" he asked, locking his brown eyes with mine.

"I mean *professionally*," I said, smiling.

And I realized something at that moment. That part of why I felt comfortable becoming a free agent professionally and taking such a big risk was that I had Beau in my life. Not to bail me out financially. But because I was crazy about him and because I knew he had my back in so many ways. That at the end of a solitary day, we could share a good conversation, and later I'd be able to slip into bed beside him. No sooner had the thought formed, though, thant my heart fluttered a little with anxiety. Was I putting too much stock in a romantic relationship?

Quickly I recited one of my mantras—"Bailey, don't be a total love moron."

And next I reminded myself that Beau carved a chicken perfectly, and his ass looked great in jeans.

Acknowledgments

It was so wonderful to get back to Bailey Weggins, and I want to thank everyone who helped me with *So Pretty It Hurts*. In terms of research for the book, I'm indebted to Barbara Butcher, chief of staff, New York City Medical Examiner's office; Dr. Chet Lerner, chief, Section of Infectious Diseases, New York Downtown Hospital; Dr. Mark Howell, psychotherapist; Faith Kates-Kogan, president and founder of Next Models; Thomas Dolan, IAAI-CFI, patrol officer/crime scene investigator, Carlisle, Pennsylvania police department and fire analyst with NEFCO; and my husband, Brad Holbrook, who is so good with accents (among many other things!).

I also want to say a huge thank-you to my terrific new editor, Kathy Schneider, and to Maya Ziv, too, for all her awesome help. It's been fantastic working with both of them. Thank you, as well, to Rachel Elinsky, for her amazing efforts with PR. Others at Harper I'd love to give a big shout-out to are Jonathan Burnham, Leah Wasielewski, Katie O'Callaghan, Mark Ferguson, Tina Andreadis, and Leslie Cohen. And as always, thank you to my extraordinary agent, Sandra Dijkstra, whom I adore!

About the Author

Kate White, the editor-in-chief of *Cosmopolitan* magazine, is the *New York Times* bestselling author of the standalone novels, *The Sixes* and *Hush*, and the Bailey Weggins mystery series—*If Looks Could Kill*; *A Body to Die For*; *'Til Death Do Us Part*; *Over Her Dead Body*; and *Lethally Blond*. White is also the author of popular career books for women, including *Why Good Girls Don't Get Ahead but Gutsy Girls Do*. She lives in New York City.